until
LEAVES
fall in
PARIS

Books by Sarah Sundin

When Twilight Breaks

WINGS OF GLORY

A Distant Melody
A Memory Between Us
Blue Skies Tomorrow

WINGS OF THE NIGHTINGALE

With Every Letter
On Distant Shores
In Perfect Time

WAVES OF FREEDOM

Through Waters Deep
Anchor in the Storm
When Tides Turn

SUNRISE AT NORMANDY

The Sea Before Us
The Sky Above Us
The Land Beneath Us

until
LEAVES
fall in
PARIS

a novel

SARAH SUNDIN

Revell

a division of Baker Publishing Group
Grand Rapids, Michigan

Published by Revell
a division of Baker Publishing Group
PO Box 6287, Grand Rapids, MI 49516-6287
www.revellbooks.com

Printed in the United States of America

Library of Congress Cataloging-in-Publication Data
Names: Sundin, Sarah, author.
Title: Until leaves fall in Paris / Sarah Sundin.
Description: Grand Rapids, MI : Revell, a division of Baker Publishing Group,
  [2022]
Identifiers: LCCN 2021023642 | ISBN 9780800736378 | ISBN 9780800741051
  (casebound) | ISBN 9781493434152 (ebook)
Subjects: LCSH: World War, 1939-1945—Fiction. | Paris (France)—Fiction. |
  GSAFD: Christian fiction. | LCGFT: Christian fiction.
Classification: LCC PS3619.U5626 U58 2022 | DDC 813/.6—dc23
LC record available at https://lccn.loc.gov/2021023642

This is a work of historical reconstruction; the appearances of certain historical figures are therefore inevitable. All other characters, however, are products of the author's imagination, and any resemblance to actual persons, living or dead, is coincidental.

Published in association with Books & Such Literary Management, 52 Mission Circle, Suite 122, PMB 170, Santa Rosa, CA 95409-5370, www.booksandsuch.com

Baker Publishing Group publications use paper produced from sustainable forestry practices and post-consumer waste whenever possible.

21 22 23 24 25 26 27   7 6 5 4 3 2 1

In fond memory of Lucille McClure
and the Lucille McClure School of Ballet.
I still feel that invisible string.

1940

1

PARIS, FRANCE
WEDNESDAY, MAY 29, 1940

As long as she kept dancing, Lucille Girard could pretend the world wasn't falling apart.

In the practice room at the Palais Garnier, Lucie and the others in the *corps de ballet* curtsied to Serge Lifar, the ballet master, as the piano played the tune for the *grande révérance*.

Lifar dismissed the ballerinas, and they headed to the dressing room, their pointe shoes softly thudding on the wooden floor, but more softly than ever. Since Germany had invaded the Netherlands and Belgium and France earlier in the month, dancers were fleeing Paris.

"Mademoiselle Girard?" the ballet master called in Ukrainian-accented French.

Lucie's breath caught. He rarely singled her out. She turned back with a light smile full of expectation and a tight chest full of dread. "Oui, *maître?*"

Serge Lifar stood with the erect bearing of a dancer in his prime and the authority of the choreographer who had returned the Paris Opéra Ballet to glory. "I am surprised you are still in Paris. You are American. You should go home."

Lucie had read the notice from US Ambassador William Bullitt in *Le Matin* that morning. Yes, she could sail with the other expatriates on the SS *Washington* from Bordeaux on June 4, but she wouldn't. "This *is* my home. I won't let the Germans scare me."

He glanced away, and a muscle twitched in his sharp-angled cheek. "The French girls would gladly take your place."

"Thank you for your concern for my safety." Lucie dropped a small révérance and scurried off, across boards graced by ballerinas for over sixty years and immortalized in Edgar Degas's paintings.

In the dressing room for the *quadrille*, the fifth and lowest rank of dancers, she squeezed onto a crowded bench. After she untied the ribbons of her pointe shoes, she eased the shoes off, wound the ribbons around the insteps, and inspected the toes for spots that needed darning.

Somber faces filled the dressing room, so Lucie gave the girls reassuring words as she shimmied out of her skirted leotard and into her street dress.

Lucie blew the girls a kiss and stepped into the hallway to wait for her friends in the *coryphée* and the *sujet*, the fourth and third ranks.

She leaned against the wall as dancers breezed down the hall. After six years at the Paris Opéra Ballet School, Lucie had been admitted to the corps de ballet at the age of sixteen. For ten years since, she'd felt the sting of not advancing to the next rank, tempered by the joy of continuing to dance in one of the four best ballets in the world.

"Lucie!" Véronique Baudin and Marie-Claude Desjardins bussed her on the cheek, and the three roommates made their way out of the building made famous by the novel *The Phantom of the Opera*.

Out on avenue de l'Opéra, Lucie inserted herself between her friends to create a pleasing tableau of Véronique's golden tresses, Lucie's light brown waves, and Marie-Claude's raven curls.

Not that the refugees on the avenue would care about tableaux, and Lucie ached for their plight. A stoop-shouldered man in peasant's garb pulled a cart loaded with children, furniture, and baggage, and his wife trudged beside him, leading a dozen goats.

"What beasts the Germans are," Marie-Claude said. "Frightening these people out of their homes."

"Did you hear?" Véronique stepped around an abandoned crate on the sidewalk. "The Nazis cut off our boys in Belgium, and now they're driving north to finish them off."

Marie-Claude wrinkled her pretty little nose. "British beasts. Running away at Dunkirk and leaving us French to fend for ourselves."

"Let's go this way." Lucie turned down a less-crowded side street. "It's such a lovely spring day. Let's not talk of the war."

"What else can we talk about?" Véronique frowned up at the sky in the new Parisian mode, watching for Luftwaffe bombers.

At the intersection ahead, a blue-caped policeman carrying a rifle—still a jarring sight—checked a young man's identity card.

"I wonder if he's a German spy," Véronique whispered, her green eyes enormous. "I heard a parachutist landed in the Tuileries yesterday."

Lucie smiled at her friend. "If every report of a parachutist were true, the Germans would outnumber the French in Paris. We mustn't be disheartened by rumors."

In the next block, a middle-aged couple in expensive suits barked orders at servants who loaded a fancy automobile with boxes.

Marie-Claude brushed past, forcing the wife to step to the side. "Bourgeois beasts."

Lucie's mouth went tight. Typical businessman who lobbied for war to get rich and fled when war threatened those riches.

The ladies passed the Louvre, crossed the Seine, and entered the Latin Quarter on the Left Bank, home of artists and writers and others of like mind.

They turned down rue Casimir-Delavigne, and the cheery green façade of Green Leaf Books quickened Lucie's steps. She'd always thought a street named after a French poet was a lovely location for a bookstore.

"We'll see you upstairs." Véronique blew Lucie a kiss.

Lucie blew a kiss back and entered the English-language bookstore, a home for American and British and French literati since Hal and Erma Greenblatt founded it after the Great War. When Lucie's parents moved to Paris in 1923, they'd become fast friends with the Greenblatts.

Bernadette Martel, the store assistant, stood behind the cash register, and Lucie greeted her.

"Hello, Lucie." Hal peeked out of the back office. "Come join us."

"Okay." She flipped back to English. Why was he in the office? Hal liked to greet customers and help them choose books, while Erma did the bookkeeping and other tasks.

Lucie made her way through the store, past the delightfully jumbled bookshelves and the tables which fostered conversation about art and theater and the important things in life.

Boxes were piled outside the office door, and inside the office Hal and Erma stood in front of the desk, faces wan.

"What—what's wrong?" Lucie asked.

Hal set his hand on Lucie's shoulder, his brown eyes sad. "We're leaving tomorrow."

"Leaving? But you can't."

"We must." Erma lifted her thin shoulders as she did when her decisions were etched in stone. "In Germany, the Nazis don't allow Jews to run businesses. I doubt it'll be different here."

"They won't come to Paris." Lucie gestured to the north

where French soldiers lined the Somme and Aisne Rivers. "Besides, you're American citizens. They won't do anything to you. Our country is neutral."

"We can't take any chances," Erma said. "We're going to Bordeaux and sailing home. You should come too."

Lucie had already told them she'd never leave. But as a Christian, she could afford to remain in Paris, come what may. She could never forgive herself if she persuaded the Greenblatts to stay and they ended up impoverished—or worse.

An ache grew in her chest, but she gave them an understanding look. "You're taking the SS *Washington*."

Erma stepped behind the desk and opened a drawer. "If we can."

"Hush, Erma. Don't worry the girl."

"*If* you can?" Lucie glanced back and forth between the couple.

"We don't have money for the passage." Erma pulled out folders. "It's tied up in the store."

Lucie's hand rolled around the strap of her ballet bag. "You can sell the store, right?"

Hal chuckled and ran his hand through black hair threaded with silver. "Who would buy it? All the British and American expatriates are fleeing."

"What will you do?" Lucie's voice came out small.

"We have friends." Hal spread his hands wide as if to embrace all those he had welcomed. "Lots of friends."

Erma thumped a stack of folders on the desk. "I refuse to beg."

Hal dropped Lucie a wink. He'd beg his friends.

What if those friends didn't have the means or the heart to help? What if the Germans did conquer France, including Bordeaux?

A shiver ran through her. Lucie couldn't let anything happen

13

to them, not when she had both the means and the heart. "I'll give you the money."

"What?" Erma's gaze skewered her. "We can't take your money."

"Why not?" She entreated Hal with her eyes, as if she were thirteen again and asking him to dip into the allowance from her parents for new pointe shoes. "I'm practically family. I lived with you for three years. Because of you, I could stay in the ballet school when my parents returned to New York. You've always said I'm like the daughter you never had."

"You'll need your money to get home." Erma flipped through a folder. "When the bombs start falling, you'll change your mind about staying here. Look what Hitler did to Warsaw and Rotterdam."

It wouldn't happen to Paris. It couldn't. "I'll be fine. I want you to have my money."

Hal turned Lucie to the door. "Don't worry about us. Now, I know you're hungry after practice. Go. Eat. We'll talk to you tonight."

Out into the warmth of the store, her home, but it was all falling away, falling apart. The Greenblatts—leaving. The store—closing.

Green Leaf Books was their dream, their life, and they were giving it up.

Ballet was Lucie's dream. Her life. Could she give it up? If she did, what would she have? Who would she be?

She rose to demi-pointe and turned, taking in the shelves and tomes and the rich scent, and she knew what she'd have, who she'd be.

Lucie whirled back into the office. "I'll buy the store."

Erma looked up from the box she was packing. "Pardon?"

"I'll buy the store. Not a gift. A business transaction."

Hal's chin dropped. "Sweet Lucie. You are so kind. But you—you're a ballerina."

14

"Not anymore." Although she did stand in fifth position. She breathed a prayer for forgiveness for lying. "Lifar plans to cut me. I need a job. I'll run the bookstore."

After twenty-five years of marriage, Hal and Erma could speak volumes to each other with a glance. And they did. Then Erma sighed. "But Lucie, you're a *ballerina*."

Lucie's cheeks warmed. True, she wasn't terribly smart, especially with numbers, but at least she'd read all the books the Greenblatts had recommended. "I'm good with people, with customers—I can do Hal's job. And Madame Martel helps with the business end of things. She can do your job. She and I—we can run the store."

"Lucie . . ." Hal's voice roughened.

Her eyes stung. Her lashes felt heavy. "And when we kick the Germans back to where they belong, this store will be here waiting for you. I promise."

Erma stared at the folder in her hands, her chin wagging back and forth. Wavering.

"I want to do this." Lucie swiped moisture from her eyes. "I need to do this. Please. Please trust me with your store."

Erma set down the folder and came to Lucie, ever the stern one, the practical one, the one to say no. She gripped Lucie's shoulders and pressed her forehead to Lucie's. "It's yours. You dear, dear girl."

Lucie fumbled for Erma's beloved hands and tried to say thank you, but she could only nod. Then she broke away and ran out, ran upstairs to her apartment.

Now she couldn't change her mind about leaving Paris. Now she had to resign from the ballet.

And she had to figure out how to run a bookstore.

2

PARIS
MONDAY, JUNE 24, 1940

With every sense dull, every movement mired in liquid lead, Paul Aubrey led the German officer along the walkway overlooking his factory floor, all so he could negotiate another loss.

"This is a fine factory," Oberst Gerhard Schiller said in excellent English.

"Thank you." Never could Paul have imagined these circumstances. After the fall of Dunkirk, the German army had turned south and driven for Paris. On June 5. The day of Simone's accident.

Paul's eyelids succumbed to the molten lead, and he gripped the handrail.

"Given Aubrey Automobile's reputation for excellence," Schiller said, "I'm surprised to see assembly lines."

Fighting the heaviness, Paul lifted his gaze to his unwanted guest, one of the commissioners sent to each automaker. "My father used to handcraft each car, but it limits production. That's one reason I opened a subsidiary of his company here in Paris—so I'd be free to employ modern techniques. My suc-

16

cess convinced my father to follow suit at the main plant in Massachusetts."

The fine lines around Schiller's light blue eyes deepened. "For a son to change his father's mind is no small feat."

Paul tried to smile, but he didn't have it in him.

The colonel's mouth drew up apologetically. "Of course, you'll have to convert the factory to another use. Germany can't allocate resources for civilian autos."

"I'm not staying. I'm selling the factory."

Schiller tugged down the sleeve of his gray uniform jacket. "The Militärbefehlshaber in Frankreich isn't in the habit of buying factories."

Paul's mouth stiffened. "The military command would requisition my factory?"

"No, no." He waved his hand as if to wipe out Paul's words. "This is an American company. Your country is neutral. Germany is not America's enemy."

They weren't America's friend either. Paul turned back toward his office. "Whether I sell to a French company or German, I have no preference."

Either way, the factory he'd built would churn out German military equipment. But what choice did he have?

"Can we not convince you to stay? The armistice has been signed in Compiègne, and we have been in Paris over a week. Have we not behaved well?"

"You have." When the French government fled, they'd declared Paris an open city. The Germans had honored the French decision not to defend the capital and had entered without a shot fired.

"Please stay." Schiller opened his palms and raised a slight smile. "It would be good for relations between our nations."

"My company makes automobiles, the finest automobiles, the gold standard."

Schiller paused before Paul's office door, emblazoned with

the logo for Aubrey Automobiles, a golden "Au" on a black shield. "The chemical symbol for gold. A clever motto."

"It's more than a motto." Paul headed to the stairs. "It's how we conduct business at every level. If I can't make cars here, I'll go to the States and make them there, help my father expand."

Schiller bowed his blond head. "Very well, Mr. Aubrey. I'll help you find a buyer. But if you change your mind, please let me know." He handed Paul a business card with his office address at the Hôtel Majestic.

The German army had planned the occupation with precise detail, down to business cards for the hotels they'd requisition.

Paul tucked the card into the breast pocket of his suit jacket, led Schiller down to the main entrance, and saw him off.

Back inside, workers prepared the machinery to start the day's work.

Jacques Moreau leaned against the wall at the foot of the stairs. The general foreman was no taller than Paul's five feet ten but was twice as wide, with muscles earned by a lifetime of manual labor, a potbelly gained by sixty-odd years of French cooking, and oil-black eyes that registered only three emotions—indifference, disdain, and rage.

None was pleasant.

"Bonjour, Moreau." Paul eased past him and climbed the stairs.

"You are selling to the *boche*." Moreau's footsteps clumped behind him.

Paul's jaw clenched. None of Moreau's business. But in the past six years, Paul had learned Moreau knew everyone's business. One of the traits that made him an excellent foreman—and one of the reasons Paul had never fired him.

"I'll try to find a French buyer rather than a German," Paul said. "I do hate to put the workers in this bind."

Moreau let out a scoffing grunt.

"Pardon?" Paul faced him.

The foreman shook his swarthy, jowly head. "You bourgeoisie never understand. American, French, German—it matters not. You all treat labor like vermin."

Paul let his gaze burn into the older man's dark pits of eyes, then he marched upstairs. Same communist rhetoric, over and over. Aubrey Autos offered some of the best wages and conditions in France, and Paul listened to labor's concerns. Yet they were never satisfied.

Three years earlier, strikes and riots had swept France, and Moreau and his followers had occupied Paul's factory. To protect himself and his family, Paul had ended up carrying a pistol.

He opened the office door.

"Bonjour, Monsieur Aubrey." His secretary stood and smiled. "You have a visitor."

"Merci, Mademoiselle Thibodeaux." Paul entered his office.

Col. Jim Duffy sat in front of Paul's desk, and he rose. "Good morning, Paul."

"Good morning, Duff." Paul shook the American military attaché's hand. "I heard you were still in town."

"Yes. Roscoe Hillenkoetter, Robert Murphy, and I stayed behind with Ambassador Bullitt."

"Admirable," Paul said. Bill Bullitt had declared no American ambassador to France had ever left his post due to war. When the French government fled, Bullitt had become Paris's unofficial mayor and had helped negotiate the city's surrender.

Paul motioned for Duff to take his seat.

Duff rested his olive drab cap in his lap. More gray laced his dark hair since Paul had last seen him at an embassy party. "I was sorry to hear about Simone. Such a horrendous loss."

Halfway to his seat, and Paul had to grip the desk for balance.

Only one vision remained—Simone at the American Hospital in Paris, her beautiful legs encased in plaster, broken in a crash that should have caused nothing but bruises. She'd been having headaches, she admitted. Loss of balance. Pain in her limbs. She'd pooh-poohed the symptoms.

The doctors found tumors in her brain, her bones, everywhere. She'd wasted away in a matter of days, begging Paul to take little Josie to the States before the Nazis arrived.

How could he have abandoned his wife to die alone?

Paul sucked in a breath through his nostrils, nodded his thanks to Duff, and lowered himself into his leather chair. "Is this a social call or . . . ?"

"Business." Duff crossed his ankle over his knee. "I'll get to the point. We want you to stay in France and run this factory."

"Can't do that." Paul sipped lukewarm coffee. "The Germans won't let me build cars. I'd have to convert. But I can't build military equipment."

"Of course not. Forbidden under our Neutrality Acts. So convert to something else."

Paul leaned his forearms on the desk, straining the black armband ringing his biceps, and he gazed at his clenched hands. "My wife . . . died. A week ago today. I want to go home. Take my little girl and go home."

"I understand." Duff's voice softened. "But you could do your nation a great service by staying."

"How?" Paul sat back again and fixed a hard gaze on his friend. "By making—I don't even know what I could make."

"Trucks, vans, something of civilian use to the Germans. Something to keep you in contact with Colonel Schiller."

"You've met him."

His light eyes took on a mischievous look. "Went to Harvard a few years before you. A friendly sort. Talkative. Could be useful."

"Are you asking me to—"

"Listen attentively. Send me reports on things I might find interesting."

Paul gripped the armrests. "There's a name for that, Duff—espionage."

Duff's narrow face scrunched up. "You wouldn't seek information, only pass along what was freely given. And you're acquainted with men in companies like Renault, Citroën, others that'll produce military equipment. Schiller's job is to coordinate industry."

Paul's breath stilled. Conversions to new products, production figures, orders—he might indeed hear information that would be useful to Germany's enemies.

He rubbed his temple. "We're neutral. No one at home wants to get involved in this war."

"You haven't been home for a while. Opinions are shifting. With each new conquest, Hitler pushes the US closer to the Allied camp. It's only a matter of time."

A long breath rushed out, and Paul tapped his fingers on the armrests. Home. The only place he wanted to be now.

"We need to know what the Nazis are capable of," Duff said. "Every bit of information helps. You'd perform a great service to your country."

The photograph on his desk drew him—Simone holding Josie at Christmas. Although his wife's image was frozen, challenge shone in her dark eyes. Simone, the woman who'd chopped off her hair and dressed as a man so she could race cars. Simone would take the risk.

Or would she? Simone had given up racing when Josie came along.

"Josie," he murmured. "She's only three years old. If anything were to happen to me . . ."

Duff sighed deeply. "She's an American citizen. We'd take care of her, get her home to your family in the States."

Without a father. Orphaned.

Everything in him said go home, get out of danger, leave the pain behind, take the easy path.

But words niggled in his brain, his father's words. *"Nothing of any worth lies on the easy path."*

"As a citizen of a neutral nation, you can leave whenever you want." Duff gestured toward the door. "You could try this for a while. If it isn't helpful, or if you're in any danger, sell and go home."

Paul closed his eyes. Duff's voice. Simone's voice. His father's. He needed to seek a higher and wiser voice, and he needed time to make a decision. "I'll think it over and get back to you."

"Thank you." Duff stood, shook Paul's hand, and departed.

Paul shut the office door and leaned his forehead against it. Why did he have a funny feeling the Lord would guide him to the difficult path? He usually did.

1941

3

In the storage room upstairs from Green Leaf Books, Lucie rummaged among the books. Thank goodness Hal Greenblatt had built the false wall when the war began in 1939, a perfect place to hide titles on the German "Otto List" of books banned from sale in occupied France.

There was the book Alice Young requested—*Escape from Munich* by Evelyn Lang.

Lucie backed out, flipped off her flashlight to conserve the precious battery, and closed the door with its cunning hidden latches and hinges.

To camouflage the false wall, Hal had installed a barre where Lucie could practice each evening, and Lucie was painting a black-and-white mural. The doorway to the hiding place had become the side of an upright piano, with an elderly man at the keyboard. Today Lucie imagined he was playing "Spring" from Vivaldi's *The Four Seasons*.

Over time, the wall was filling with ballerinas practicing at the Palais Garnier.

"I shall finish you soon," she said to a sweet-faced young dancer whose body needed fleshing out over the pencil sketch.

Lucie fished in a case of German-English dictionaries, removed a dust jacket, and wrapped it around *Escape from Munich*. Then she tucked the dictionary into the wood box to serve as kindling.

She trotted downstairs to the store. Erma Greenblatt had warned that if the Germans occupied Paris, Lucie would no longer be able to order books from Britain. So Lucie had used the store's petty cash and her own to buy English-language books from fleeing Britons and Americans.

In the bleak days of the exodus, to stave off worries about the approaching German army, Lucie had hidden books by Jewish authors or books that criticized Hitler. After saving them from Nazi bonfires, she discreetly sold or lent them to her most trusted customers. Her tiny way to nourish an oasis in the cultural desert the Germans had created.

The store ran long and narrow with bookcases dividing the space into three bays, each with a table and chairs. In the nonfiction bay sat Lucie's friends, musician Charles Charbonnier and painter Jerzy Epstein, a refugee from Poland, along with two young men from the Sorbonne. Lucie greeted them warmly.

If it weren't for the students at the lycées and universities in the area, the store would have failed long ago. Only a few thousand Americans remained in Paris, and the Germans had placed the British civilians in internment camps.

The store assistant, Bernadette Martel, sat reading in her favorite armchair near the counter across from the nonfiction bay. The widow wore her gray-streaked dark hair in a loose bun barely clinging to the nape of her neck.

"Any new customers?" Lucie asked her.

Bernadette pointed to the front bay without raising her head from her book.

Alice Young, wife of a physician at the American Hospital in Paris, perused the fiction.

Lucie kissed her friend on the cheek. "Alice, darling."

"Sweet Lucie." In her forties, Alice wore a perfectly cut gray suit and a stylish hat angled over silver-and-gold hair. "How are you today?"

"Lovely now that you're here. I have the book you wanted." She held out the book cloaked in a dictionary's dust jacket.

Alice frowned. "That isn't—"

Lucie opened the book to the title page.

A smile bent Alice's red lips. "Clever. How much?"

"You're a paid subscriber. You can borrow it."

"I'll buy it. It's for Bentley's birthday."

After Alice paid at the cash register, Lucie saw her friend to the front door. "See you Sunday."

"Yes, Sunday." Although Dr. and Mrs. Young lived on Paris's bourgeois Right Bank of the Seine River, they had Left Bank sensibilities and attended the American Church in Paris rather than the more prestigious American Cathedral.

Alice raised her umbrella, stepped out into the light rain on rue Casimir-Delavigne, and passed a man in a field-gray German army overcoat.

Lucie sucked in her breath and ducked inside the store.

Too late. Lt. Emil Wattenberg grinned at her through the window. The man worked at the German Embassy in Paris, the institution responsible for promoting German culture in France, censoring French culture—and publishing the Otto List.

She turned to the bookshelf to . . . straighten books? Although jumbled shelves were part of the store's charm.

The door swung open. Bother. She hated having German soldiers in her store.

"Good morning, Miss Girard," he said in heavily accented English.

She took great pains not to learn German, and Wattenberg's

English was worse than his French, so she always spoke English with him. "Good morning, Lieutenant," she said with the elegant indifference Parisians affected with the city's occupiers.

Wattenberg removed his peaked cap and tucked it under his narrow arm. Dimples creased his not unhandsome face. "I would like a book. What do you recommend?"

"Pick what you'd like." She rounded the bookcase to the bay where her friends sat.

"I would like a book to . . . to build my English." The lieutenant followed.

Jerzy Epstein shot him a quick, dark look.

Lucie turned and gave the blond officer a sympathetic gaze. "What a shame that your trip to England has been delayed."

A snort of a laugh from Charles Charbonnier, but Lucie maintained her innocent expression.

Wattenberg smiled as if amused, but what German would be? After months of bombing London, they'd failed to break Britain's will.

"I'd rather be in Paris. This is the city of art and culture." Wattenberg's gray eyes shone.

With any other person, Lucie would have plunged into conversation. Instead, she entered the children's section.

Hobnailed footsteps followed. *"Ach! Die Brüder Grimm."* Wattenberg pulled a volume of Grimms' Fairy Tales off the shelf. "I know these stories. They will help me learn. I will buy it."

Lucie fought off a grimace. To refuse a sale was unwise, so she led the man to the cash register. Over the pale green bookplate that read "Borrowed from the subscription library of Green Leaf Books, Paris," she glued a new one that read "From the Library of . . ." with space for the owner to inscribe his or her name, and "Purchased at Green Leaf Books, Paris" at the bottom. A dark green vine edged the bookplate.

Lucie took Wattenberg's money, and he took his leave.

"You have an admirer, Lucie," Charles called in a teasing lilt.

Jerzy made an exaggerated frown. "The poor boy must be lonely so far from home."

"Good," Lucie said. "The lonelier they get, the sooner they'll go home."

The men laughed, but Bernadette met Lucie's eye and shook her head.

Bernadette was right. Although many of the French chafed under German rule, many welcomed the stability the Germans brought after the tumultuous 1930s. Even Lucie had to admit the soldiers were polite, with only a handful of ugly episodes, so polite they'd earned the tongue-in-cheek nickname of the "corrects."

The door opened. Monsieur Quinault shook out his umbrella and stepped inside.

"Bonjour, Monsieur Quinault." Lucie hurried forward to meet the printer. How unusual for him to visit the store. "Did you bring more bookplates?"

Monsieur Quinault did not return her smile. "Not until you pay for the previous order as well as this one. Since you no longer pay your bills, payment is now due upon order."

"Oh." Lucie eased back. "I'm sorry. Let me find out what happened. Madame Martel?"

After a pause, Bernadette raised dark eyes. "Oui?"

"Monsieur Quinault says he hasn't been paid."

Bernadette tipped her head toward the office. "The bill is on the desk."

The desk. Lucie shuddered and headed to the office. Erma had kept the desk clear with a tiny, neat stack of papers quickly whisked into the file cabinet. But Bernadette worked in a freer environment.

Lucie thumbed through the hill of papers on the desk, but she didn't know what she was looking for. She'd never had a head for such things. Bernadette did, but she preferred reading to paperwork, and the store did need her deep literary knowledge.

A bunch of papers cascaded off the desk, and Lucie knelt to pick them up.

"How much longer, mademoiselle?" Quinault's cigarette-roughened voice tightened. "I would like to be paid."

Lucie plopped the papers on the desk. "How much do I owe you?"

Quinault's craggy face froze. His eye twitched. "Two hundred francs."

He wasn't telling the truth, but without the bill, Lucie couldn't verify the amount. She'd write it down and ask Bernadette to reconcile it.

Besides, Monsieur Quinault was a widower, and the Germans held his only son as a prisoner of war, along with two million other French soldiers. Quinault might be having a difficult time making ends meet, and he deserved kindness. And having his bills paid.

Lucie opened the cash box and counted out the francs. The cash looked low, but it was the first of the month, right after the rent had been paid.

She wrote out a receipt. "I thank you for your patience and for your beautiful printing."

Quinault pointed the bills at her. "Next time, you will pay first."

"Yes, sir."

"Monsieur Greenblatt never should have left his store to a woman."

Somehow Lucie managed not to roll her eyes. *Madame* Greenblatt had been the one who paid the bills.

With a huff, Quinault departed, passing Véronique and Marie-Claude.

Lucie's roommates gaped after him, then entered the office.

"Oh, my pet, what are you doing in here?" Marie-Claude wrinkled her nose at the papers. "With . . . this?"

Véronique beckoned. "Come, come."

"You mustn't worry." Lucie waved her hands over the desk with a flourish. "I shall turn this all into papier-mâché and sculpt with it."

Véronique took Lucie's hand and drew her out from behind the desk. "We don't have practice at the ballet today. We're going to the cinema, where we'll flirt with the soldiers, then pretend not to understand a word they say."

"Thank you for the invitation, but I have to mind the store."

Marie-Claude gave Lucie a teasing look. "While you mind the store, mind you don't turn bourgeois."

"This is the only turning I do." Lucie sprang onto pointe in her brown oxfords, her feet tight together, then spun in a *soutenu* turn and blew a kiss to her friends.

No danger that she'd ever turn bourgeois.

4

SATURDAY, APRIL 5, 1941

Paul's pencil swooped over the paper. Only when designing cars at his mahogany desk at home did he feel like his real self.

Someday he would build this model he called the Autonomy, a nimble two-seater based on the Audacity race car. Since 1915, Dad's business had revolved around the stately Authority and the elegant Aurora. Although they'd been one of the few luxury carmakers to survive the Depression, Paul wanted to expand their line. Future success lay with serving bankers and physicians as well as business tycoons and movie stars.

Sure would beat his current work manufacturing delivery trucks. Since gasoline permits were only available to a privileged few, the trucks ran on wood gas. External wood-burning *gazogène* generators fed wood gas to modified engines. Paul privately called the model the Au-ful.

Saturday morning sunshine spilled over the desk as Paul sketched the Autonomy's engine compartment.

"Da-deeee." Josie's little voice rose before him with plaintiveness that said she'd already spoken his name several times.

He glanced across his desk to his four-year-old. "Hello, jelly bean."

She giggled, lighting up brown eyes the same shade as Paul's. Madame Coudray had pinned a yellow side bow in Josie's chin-length brown curls.

Paul wound one finger into a curl, the only feature she'd inherited from her mother. "What's up?"

"Want to see my Feenee story?" Josie plopped a lopsided booklet of crayon drawings onto Paul's desk.

His stomach soured. He ought to praise her work. That's what fathers did. But Josie's stories were odd. All about a strange creature she called Feenee.

Paul handed back the booklet. "Maybe tonight. Daddy's working."

"Oh." Light drained from her eyes.

His chest squeezed, but he needed to point the child to more acceptable pursuits.

In the doorway Madame Coudray gave Josie a gentle smile. "You did not finish your breakfast. We must not waste food."

"Yes, ma'am." Josie slipped away.

Paul raised one finger to bid the nanny to stay, then motioned for her to have a seat. "Have you noticed more of these Feenee stories? I'm concerned."

Well into her sixties, the nanny sat stiff and thin as a poker. She folded her hands in her lap and studied them. "May I speak plainly, Monsieur Aubrey?"

"Yes, please." Not only did the woman spend far more time with Josie than Paul did, but she'd raised Simone as well.

Madame Coudray raised her pale eyes. "Madame Aubrey has been gone almost a year."

Paul's breath snagged in his throat.

"You are at the factory more than ever." She frowned at his desk. "When you are home, still you work. Rarely do you go out. You do not have guests."

For reasons too complex and secret for her ears. "No, I don't."

She swept her hand toward the window. "Take your daughter

for a walk. Listen to her stories. They are mere childish fantasies and will soon be gone. You do not need to like her stories, but you need to listen to them."

Outside, past the vine-draped wrought iron fence, boulevard Suchet lay wide and empty. Paul and Simone used to go walking, driving, dancing. They'd gone to the races and the museums and the opera. They'd dined with friends. Always lots of friends.

So long ago.

He hauled in a breath. "You are a wise woman, Madame Coudray."

Paul strolled down a path in the Luxembourg Gardens between rows of chestnut trees grown together and pruned so they looked like giant hedges on stilts.

Josie chattered from her perch on Paul's shoulders. "Feenee stomped up to the big, ugly rock-monster. 'Get out of my house! You can't be here, Mr. Rock-Monster. It's *my* house.' Then the rock-monster ate Feenee's toes. Then it ate her feets. Then it ate her knees."

How macabre. Paul twisted his head to see his daughter. "What a sad story."

Her brown curls danced in the breeze. "No, Daddy. I'm not done."

"All right. Go on." The parallel paths and lawns and tree hedges opened up to a garden edged by statues.

"It's not sad. Feenee grew wings and flew away from the monster."

Paul tightened his grip on his daughter's ankles. "But she lost her legs."

"She had to," Josie said as if Paul were daft. "As long as she had legs, she couldn't have wings. She can't have *both*, Daddy."

Paul frowned, but three German soldiers neared, carrying

Der Deutsche Wegleiter für Paris guidebook. A frown could be interpreted as hostility, and he erased it.

"I want wings." Josie flapped her arms. "Wings are better than legs."

Childish fantasies that would soon be gone. Soon had better be before she started school. He could only imagine how teachers and children would react to Feenee.

"Down, please." Josie patted Paul's hat.

"Sure thing, gumdrop." Paul squatted, helped her to the ground, and pulled her dress and coat back down over her underpants.

Josie slipped her hand in his and skipped as they passed a lawn ringed by pink flowers. "I can skip now. See me skip?"

"I do. I've never seen such good skipping. Sometimes legs come in handy."

Josie looked up at him, and he winked. She grinned, flashing tiny white teeth.

A white board fence and armed guards blocked the pathway leading past the reflecting pool to the Luxembourg Palace, which was draped with red-and-black swastika flags. The German Luftwaffe used the former home of the French senate for their headquarters in France. Even after a year of occupation, the foreignness, the sense of violation remained. Like a panzer racing in the French Grand Prix. And winning.

Paul turned right to leave the gardens. He hadn't visited Paris's 6th arrondissement on the Left Bank of the Seine in ages, but the Odéon Métro station couldn't be far to the north. Certainly closer than the station south of the gardens where he and Josie had arrived.

Two familiar figures approached. Dr. and Mrs. Bentley Young, and Paul's chest tightened. "Good day, Mrs. Young, Dr. Young."

They didn't even meet his gaze.

How many lively evenings had the Youngs and the Aubreys spent together?

The tightness grew and darkened. In his first thirty years, Paul had never lacked for friends. In his thirty-first year, he'd lost them all. After a month or two comforting Paul after Simone's death, his friends had turned their backs on him for selling Auful trucks to the Germans.

Never mind that his trucks were for civilian use. Never mind that he sold just as many to the French. Never mind that those trucks helped deliver food to Paris. In his friends' eyes, he was a collaborator. And he had to remain a collaborator in their eyes so he could remain a collaborator in German eyes. That's why they trusted Paul with information. Information he fed to the US military.

Paul tromped north on the boulevard Saint-Michel.

The only American expatriates who would see him socially were an unpleasant assortment of opportunists, socialites, and fascists. Paul had even stopped attending church, tired of the whispers and glares.

The Odéon Théâter rose in the distance. The Métro station couldn't be far.

Josie's skipping turned to walking, and the stories stopped as she gawked at unfamiliar cafés and publishing houses. He'd never taken her to the Left Bank, home to the bohemian crowd—artists and writers and theater folk.

Paul passed the theater, built of creamy stone, and he paused. No sign of a subway station, and half a dozen streets ran off the plaza in spokes.

He flagged down a middle-aged woman and asked directions. She waved toward the spokes and went her way.

"Eeny, meeny, miny, moe." Paul headed down the closest street.

"Feenee?" Josie said.

Paul laughed. "No, it's an old rhyme." He recited it and told her how children used it to choose things.

"Like books?" Josie pointed to a store.

In the window display books with titles in English lay surrounded by spring leaves. By the door, a red US Embassy certificate labeled the store as owned by a neutral American, protecting it from German requisition. Overhead, the sign read Green Leaf Books.

"That's right," Paul said. A friend had once mentioned an English-language bookstore in the Latin Quarter. As a subscriber to the American Library in Paris, he'd never needed to go elsewhere.

"Can we go in, Daddy? Please?" Brown eyes melted him like chocolate on a warm day.

Madame Coudray had said Josie didn't have many books for a girl her age.

"Let's look inside," Paul said.

Josie hopped a few times, and Paul opened the door.

The store smelled of old books and woodsmoke. A counter stood on the wall to his left, flanked by bookshelves and magazine racks. Photographs hung over the counter—pictures of authors, it looked like. Bookcases jutted out from the wall to his right, and bookshelves covered every wall, even under the windows.

On the shelf before him, books ran in a proper row for half a shelf, then a stack of books on their sides. More books rested in front of the row, on top, wherever they fit. New books with crisp dust jackets stood beside older titles with spines shiny from wear.

More books covered a table by the window, circled by two mismatched wooden chairs and a stuffed armchair.

"I like it here," Josie said in a hushed voice.

"Bonjour, monsieur—ah!—et mademoiselle!" A petite young lady with light brown hair approached wearing a green suit. She clapped her hands together and beamed at Josie.

Josie shrank behind Paul's legs.

He removed his fedora. "Bonjour, madame."

"Miss Girard is my name. Is this your first time visiting my store?" she asked in flawless English. "I haven't seen you before."

"It is." Paul smiled. Pretty lady. And smart. She'd pegged Paul as an English speaker in two short words.

"Please make yourselves at home. Green Leaf Books has been a light in Paris for twenty years." Her hand fluttered toward the shelf, her fingers like feathers on a bird's wing. "May I help you find something?"

"Yes, for my daughter, Josephine—Josie for short. She's four."

Josie's head rubbed against Paul's trouser leg as she nodded.

Miss Girard gave him an amused smile, her eyes bright and expressive. Light brown, maybe hazel. "Four is a nice age for girls. The nicest, I think. Does she—she looks like the sort of little girl who likes kitty-cats."

A tiny gasp behind Paul's knee. "I am!"

"Please come with me. I'd like you to meet someone special."

Paul followed the woman deeper into the store with Josie in tow.

"You saw the fiction section. Here's nonfiction." Miss Girard's arm drew figures in the air, and she walked quick and light, her toes turned out, her full skirt swinging around her knees. She rounded the last bookshelf and stopped, pointing her foot and circling it behind the other, like a dancer at the ballet. "Voilà! The children's section."

The same jumble of books but more colorful and with a low green table in the middle.

"Very nice," Paul said. "Josie, would you like to look at the books?"

She clung to his leg.

Miss Girard pressed up to the tips of her toes—just like at the ballet—and rummaged through a box on the shelf. Then she spun back and effortlessly dropped to her knees before Paul.

She held one hand across her chest, topped by a papier-mâché puppet. "Josie, this is my friend Monsieur Meow. He is very shy." The puppet quivered against her shoulder, and the young woman patted its back. "There, there, Monsieur Meow. This is Josie, and she's a nice little girl."

Paul stared down at the bookseller, her hair pinned up in front and tumbling in waves to her narrow shoulders. He'd never met anyone like her, so . . . ethereal. He'd never used that word in a sentence, but no other word fit.

Josie peeked from behind Paul's leg.

Miss Girard kept stroking the puppet's back. "Perhaps, Josie, if you pet him like this, he won't be so shy."

Josie eased out and rubbed the puppet's gray-and-white striped head. "There, there, Monsieur Meow. I think you're a pretty cat."

The puppet lifted its head, turned to Josie with outstretched paws, then turned to Miss Girard's ear.

"Is that so?" Miss Girard gave Josie a nod. "He thinks you're pretty too."

Josie giggled.

"Hi, Josie. I'm glad you came to my store," Miss Girard said in a funny voice. "What stories do you like?"

"Everything." Josie talked straight to the puppet. "My daddy reads to me every night."

Miss Girard flicked a smile up to Paul, then addressed Josie. "I'm sure your mommy reads to you during the day."

A slash of pain, and Paul braced himself against it.

Josie shook her head. "My nanny does."

"My wife . . ." Paul cleared his raspy throat. "Her mother died almost a year ago."

"Oh, I'm so sorry." Miss Girard looked up to him, her gaze penetrating, understanding, feeling his grief, his loneliness. For one moment she seemed to bear the burden of his pain on her slight shoulders.

For one moment Paul breathed more easily. "Thank you."

Miss Girard returned her attention to Josie. Her smile wavered. "Monsieur Meow would like to pick books for you to look at. Would you like to sit at the table?"

Josie climbed into a little chair and stroked the table as if it were an enormous emerald. "It's so green."

Miss Girard darted around, collecting books. "That's because my store is called Green Leaf Books. See?" She flapped a book open and pointed to a bookplate. "Each has a green leaf inside."

"Pretty," Josie said.

Miss Girard left a stack of books for her, and Josie opened the top volume.

Paul didn't want the bookseller to return to selling books yet. "Which came first? The store's name or the bookplates?"

She stood before him, assessing him. "The original owners were my dear friends, Hal and Erma Greenblatt, and Greenblatt means *green leaf*. Also, Hal is fond of John Greenleaf Whittier's poetry. Do you like poetry, Mr. . . . "

Ah, now he was making progress. "Aubrey. Paul Aubrey."

"Oh, that's a fine name. Paul Aubrey." She pronounced it slowly as if tasting each syllable. "That has a nice sound."

"My parents say thank you."

She tipped her head. "Do you like poetry, Mr. Aubrey?"

"I read as little poetry as possible to get through college and none since. Do you think less of me?" He gave her half a grin.

"Not at all. You look like the sort . . . I can see you reading history, biography."

Paul chuckled. "You're in the right business. When I have time, that's what I read."

Miss Girard waved to the nonfiction section. "I hope you find something that interests you."

He had, but not on a shelf. "What would you recommend?"

"Come with me. What eras are you interested in? Countries?"

Paul followed her. He hadn't planned to buy a book for himself, but now he wanted several. "Do you have any on French history? As long as I've lived here, I don't know much about this country."

"Would you please hold him?" Miss Girard whispered. She removed the puppet and handed it to Paul. "Put him on, so he won't look lifeless if your daughter comes over."

"All right." Paul slipped his hand into the cloth glove and studied the whiskered face. He hadn't worn a puppet since grade school.

"How long have you lived in Paris?" Miss Girard's fingers ran along book spines.

"Eight years. And you? Are you French?" Although she sounded American, she didn't seem either American or French.

"I'm an American citizen, but I've lived here since I was nine. Paris is my true home."

"It grows on you, even in today's . . . difficulties."

Again she assessed him as if she saw each one of Paul's difficulties. "You were brave to stay."

"So were you." Even more so for a single woman running a store for English speakers when English speakers fled in droves. A store far too empty for a Saturday.

He'd buy every book she showed him. "What do you recommend?" He gestured to the shelf. He still had the puppet on his hand, and he laughed.

She did too, lilting and lovely, and he wanted to hear more. He held up the puppet so it faced him. "My apologies, Monsieur Meow."

"He forgives you because you brought him a new little friend. He's thankful."

"As am I." If only he could talk with her all day, but she had a store to run. If only . . . no, he should get to know her better. And it was too soon, not even a year since Simone passed away.

Yet hadn't Simone pleaded with him to remarry and quickly,

for Josie's sake? For his own? He wasn't ready for marriage yet, but he craved conversation and companionship. And this woman intrigued him.

Miss Girard pulled volumes off the shelf.

Paul stared at the puppet's painted eyes and stripes. An idea formed. The wild, artistic Left Bank had to be infecting him. "What did you say, Monsieur Meow?" He put the puppet to his ear and wiggled it, as Miss Girard had done.

She turned back with a quizzical look.

Paul frowned at the puppet. "Oh no, I couldn't. I just met her. She barely knows me." He put the puppet back to his ear, and he stared into the distance, shaking his head. "No. I'm not that sort of man. No, Monsieur Meow. I'm a gentleman. I don't want her to think I'm forward."

Miss Girard's mouth bent—in anticipation or suspicion?

Paul heaved a sigh. "Monsieur Meow told me to ask you out to dinner. I told him it was far too early, but he won't listen to reason. You know what cats are like."

"May I talk to him?" She held out her hand.

Paul passed her the puppet. The cat had better not rat on him.

Miss Girard wiggled her hand into the puppet. "Monsieur Meow, that isn't like you, meddling in other people's business. What got into you?" She put the puppet to her ear. "Oh, Mr. *Aubrey* got into you."

Paul had to smile. Guilty as charged.

"It's out of the question," she said. "I know nothing about him. Oh . . . yes, that's true. I could get to know him over dinner."

"You could." Paul stood up a bit straighter.

"Yes, I'm tired of rutabaga soup." Miss Girard lifted those pretty eyes to Paul. "Does the restaurant serve rutabaga soup?"

"Never." He ran through restaurants in the neighborhood that he remembered.

"That's a good idea, Monsieur Meow." She nodded to her friend, who was rapidly becoming Paul's friend. "He says I could meet you at the restaurant."

"Wise cat. Are you free tonight?"

"Yes. The store closes at eighteen hours."

He needed to give her time to close up shop and change clothes. "Would you like to meet me at Lapérouse on quai des Grand Augustins at seven o'clock? Or nineteen hours, if you're in the Army, the Navy, or France."

She studied him again as if gauging his character. "I'd like that."

"Daddy!" Josie ran over with a pile of books. "Can I? Can I?"

Ordinarily he'd have her choose one, but not today. He took the books and turned to Miss Girard. "What do you have for me?"

She gave him a playful look as if she knew she could coax him into buying half the store. She set one book on the stack. "Let's start with this."

A woman who didn't take advantage of a man's weakness. He approved.

After he paid for the books, plus a year's subscription to the store's lending library, he led Josie outside.

"I like that lady." Josie waved her arms as Miss Girard had done. "She has legs *and* wings."

Paul chuckled. She did indeed.

5

L ucie stepped over the elegant threshold of Lapérouse.
What had Monsieur Meow gotten her into?

She usually dated rumple-haired painters or writers in
ill-fitting suits or musicians in wild-colored neckties, meeting
at cafés and parks.

Not this. Not one of Paris's finest restaurants in her best
shoes and hat and her dress of rose gold silk. It was all so conventional.

She fought back a frown as she checked in her coat. The
maître d'hôtel led her upstairs into a small room ornate with
gilt mirrors and wood paneling and antique paintings.

Paul Aubrey stood to greet her, so conventional with his
groomed brown hair and tailored black suit.

But then he smiled, and her breath caught. He appealed to
her for a reason she couldn't name, which was why she'd come.
To name it.

"Good evening, Miss Girard. You look lovely."

"Thank you, Mr. Aubrey." She settled onto the red brocade
divan at the corner table.

He took a seat along the other wall to her right. "Please call
me Paul."

"Thank you. My name's Lucille—Lucie."

Paul rested one elbow on the table, revealing a gold wristwatch. "With an American *y* or a French *ie*?"

She smoothed her skirt. "Y for the first nine years, *ie* ever since."

He chuckled, a tone as round and manly as his first name.

The maître d' handed Lucie a menu. It listed actual meats and cream sauces and cheeses, and her stomach gurgled. Not only was rationing strict and food pricey, but running the store made it difficult to track down scarce items and stand in long lines. Véronique and Marie-Claude did what they could between practices, but she hadn't had a full belly in months.

At the other table in the room, two well-dressed Frenchwomen dined with German officers—to get a good meal, maybe more. Lucie would rather starve.

After they both ordered the chateaubriand, Paul gave her a stiff smile.

She knew little about him, but she'd sensed something deeply good in him. Behind the pain and loneliness and good humor, she'd sensed strength and integrity, and she wanted to put him at ease. "I hoped you'd bring Josie. She's darling."

"I don't think she's ready for this place," he said with a grin. "How about you? Did you bring Monsieur Meow?"

Lucie heaved a dramatic sigh. "He is definitely not ready for this place. He acts shy, but he's a troublemaker."

"So I've seen."

Then silence pressed between them, pushing them apart.

"Where do you—" Their words collided, and they laughed.

"Ladies first." Candlelight reflected in Paul's dark eyes. "Where do you come from, Lucie? What brought you to Paris?"

"I'm from New York. We came here in 1923 for my father's work—he's an architect. The rest of the family went back when I was thirteen, but I stayed."

His eyebrows rose. "At thirteen?"

"It isn't as scandalous as it sounds." She gave him a teasing look. "I stayed with the Greenblatts, the bookstore owners."

"All right. That makes sense for a girl who wants to run a bookstore."

Lucie had to laugh. He wasn't telling her story correctly. "I wanted to dance. I was studying at the Paris Opéra Ballet School. I'd worked hard to be accepted, and there isn't a school anything like it in America."

"Ballet." Paul gave a knowing kind of nod. "Yes. I see it."

She lifted one shoulder. Ballet training never left one's muscles. "Thanks to the Greenblatts, I was able to stay here. After I finished school, I danced with the corps for several years."

"At the Opéra Ballet? We saw *Giselle* there, *Coppélia*, *Oriane et la prince d'amour*."

"Then you saw me perform. I played villagers in *Giselle* and *Coppélia*. I was good at standing and watching the principal dancers." She struck her watching pose, one finger to her chin.

"I'm sure you were charming. And what an honor to dance for such a prestigious ballet."

"It was."

Paul leaned a bit closer. "Then the bookstore? How did that come to be?"

"The Greenblatts left last May." She glanced at the gray uniforms at the other table and lowered her voice. "They're Jewish. I quit the ballet and bought the store so they could sail to New York."

Paul regarded her with a soft look. "What an admirable thing to do."

She shrugged and inclined her head toward the boches. "If the tourists ever go home, I want the store to be waiting for my friends."

An appreciative smile joined Paul's regard.

But Lucie hadn't done anything noble enough to deserve admiration. "Where are you from?"

"Outside Boston. I'm sure you can tell by my accent." He tapped his throat above the knot of his tie.

"Honestly, no. I haven't spent enough time in the States to develop that ear."

A waiter brought over steaming bowls of consommé. Lucie relished the beefy smell and picked up her spoon. "What brought you to Paris?"

"Work. I'm an engineer. I came to France to work on my company's race car."

"Race cars? How exciting." She sipped a spoonful of soup. Oh, the heavenly taste of beef. She'd almost forgotten.

"That's why I came. I stayed because of Simone." A twitch around his eye hinted at grief.

"Your wife?" Lucie asked gently.

"Yes." He stirred his soup.

"Does it hurt to talk about her?"

Paul lifted his gaze. "It does. But in a good way. I don't know how to describe it."

"Because it keeps her alive in your mind."

His spoon stilled. "Yes. I have . . . no friends who remember her."

Maybe the only purpose in this evening was to help a widower remember his wife. And what an excellent purpose.

Lucie leaned in. "What was she like?"

"I'll tell you how we met." He ducked his head, and a grin broke out. "We hired a driver to test our cars. Great driver. Won lots of races. Cool headed, quick thinking, savvy. Told me everything I needed to know—adjustments to make in the engine, the gears, what worked, what didn't. But an odd sort. Barely looked you in the eye, barely spoke."

Lucie swallowed some soup. "Many people who are good with their hands aren't good with words."

Paul's mouth wiggled as if suppressing a laugh. "One evening I attended a dinner party. A young lady intrigued me—tall, elegant, wore a turban, very sure of herself. I kept trying to speak with her, and she kept slipping away, which only intrigued me more, of course."

"Of course." She smiled with him.

Paul paused to sip his consommé. "I finally cornered her. In a few minutes I realized she was my race car driver."

"She was?"

"She wore her hair short and dressed like a man so she'd be taken seriously."

"How fascinating. I wish I could have met her."

"She was an incredible woman." He smiled into his bowl as if seeing her face. "I fell hard. Took a long time to convince her to go out with me. I had to promise not to expose her. She didn't want to lose her position."

"I don't blame her." Lucie studied the contentment flooding his face. "You must have been very happy together."

His gaze rose back to hers, to the present. "We were."

"Is Josie more like you or her?"

"Neither, really." One side of his mouth pulled in.

"Well, she's a doll. She was shy at first—common at that age—but she warmed up."

"I was glad to see that. We don't get out much, and people find her . . . odd."

"Odd? Oh, I hope so. She's four." Lucie let delicious memories of being four wash over her. "Isn't it a delightful age? Society will mold her into an acceptable shape, but now—now she's the most purely Josie she'll ever be, the Josie God created. What were you like at four, Paul?"

"Me? I don't remember being four." He sat back and squinted at the ceiling. "But at five and six, I was traipsing through the woods with my brother and our friends, building forts and tree-houses."

"You're still building."

"I am." He lifted a broad hand. "But without mud under my fingernails."

Over dinner, Lucie coaxed more stories out of him, of growing up near Boston, acting out Revolutionary War battles, losing his older brother to the Spanish Flu, and turning his love of building into an engineering degree from Harvard.

She talked about dancing and about the interesting people she'd met through the ballet and the bookstore.

The more they talked, the more Paul relaxed. With a serious expression, he was a good-looking man with average features. But his smile was extraordinary, communicating both confidence and humility, a touch of mischief, and a genuine interest in others. In her.

The waiter came to their table. "It is one hour before the curfew."

"It is?" Paul looked at his watch. "I can't believe it. Time has flown."

After Paul paid the bill, he walked Lucie to the entrance and helped her with her coat. "May I walk you home? It's after dark."

"That would be nice. I live above the bookstore." Outside, she took his arm, and they strolled down the street in the crisp cold.

His coat had a nice cut. Engineers made more money than artistic sorts, but at least they weren't part of the snooty *beau monde* set.

Paul lifted his chin to the night, the stars snuffed by clouds, the lights snuffed by war. "It seems strange to end an evening in Paris without music and dancing and talking into the night."

"Oh, this isn't really Paris. It's only a dim shadow."

"True." His voice sank low.

She was supposed to be cheering him up. "On the bright side, a curfew makes it easier to wake up in time for church."

Paul chuckled. "It does. Where do you attend?"

"The American Church."

"Hmm. Simone and I used to attend there."

She didn't remember seeing him there, but attendance had been high before the war and people did gravitate to their customary seats.

But why did he no longer attend? Did he blame God for his wife's death? Or had he stopped attending when the pastor returned to America? "Mr. Pendleton insists he doesn't actually give sermons, but his 'talks' are very good. And his organ-playing is divine."

"I agree. I went for a while after . . . but it was difficult."

She watched his shifting emotions in the dim light. "It must be difficult to have everyone feel sorry for you all the time."

Paul turned to her, his eyes full of gratitude, sadness, and something almost sardonic. "It is."

"Here's my building." She released his arm. "Thank you for a wonderful evening."

"Thank you for the wonderful company. Will I see you tomorrow in church?"

Yet another purpose to the evening, and her smile grew. "You will."

Sunday, April 6, 1941

Edmund Pendleton, the organist and director of the church, said the benediction, and Lucie peeked over the dark wood pews. Far to the front, Paul Aubrey sat with Josie.

He'd kept his word, and her heart warmed. Perhaps they could spend the afternoon together, strolling along the Seine or in the Tuileries, where Josie could play.

Mr. Pendleton dismissed the dwindling congregation of American expatriates. From Lucie's place on the aisle, she could casually wait for Paul to come her way.

"Hello, Lucie." Alice Young kissed her on the cheek, took her arm, and swept her down the aisle. "Wasn't that a wonderful talk?"

"It was." Lucie glanced over her shoulder.

His face in profile to her, Paul talked to Mr. Pendleton and accompanied him down the aisle.

"So what do you say?" Alice asked.

"Pardon?"

Alice laughed. "I asked if you'd like to come to our house for dinner. Cook managed to get a fine chicken." She finished in a whisper. One didn't ask *how* someone obtained food nowadays.

As much as Lucie would have enjoyed meat two days in a row, she didn't want to limit her options. "Thank you, but I have plans."

The ladies stepped outside into the courtyard, and Lucie frowned. Dark clouds threatened those plans.

"Where did Bentley go? He must be chatting. You know how men are." Alice winked.

Lucie laughed, and the ladies crossed the tiled courtyard to a spot near the red-brick parish house.

"There he is," Alice said. "With the Hartmans."

Dr. Young came out of the sanctuary, talking to a couple with two young redheaded girls.

Soon Paul appeared with Mr. Pendleton. Josie pulled on Paul's hand, said something to him, and he nodded. She ran toward the Hartman girls.

But Mr. Hartman pulled his children away and left Josie standing by herself. Bereft.

What on earth? Lucie sucked in a breath.

Paul stood alone with Mr. Pendleton, unusual since people swamped the director after a service. Then Paul caught sight of his daughter, and his face fell as low as hers.

Lucie had to find out what was happening. "Excuse me, Al—"

"I can't believe he's here. The nerve of him," Alice said in a stern tone that defied her sweet nature.

Lucie tore her gaze from her new friend to her old. "Who? What do you mean?"

"Paul Aubrey." Alice said his name as if it tasted of rotten fish.

"Paul Aubrey?" Lucie whispered, his name sweet on her own tongue.

Alice took Lucie's arm and turned away from Paul. "You've heard of him, haven't you? Aubrey Automobiles?"

Aubrey . . . Automobiles? He'd said he was an engineer. When he'd said "my company," she'd assumed he worked for it, not that he owned it. "He—he makes cars?"

"Before the war he did. Now he makes trucks, tanks, and airplane engines for the Nazis."

Lucie's eyes hurt, her stomach, but she'd known Alice for years, trusted her. "He's a collaborator?"

"And he has the nerve to show his face at church. His former wife would be appalled at what he's become. They were good friends of ours."

The pain in her stomach grew, and Lucie glanced across the courtyard. Paul held Josie and patted her back. Josie was snubbed because her father was snubbed. And he deserved snubbing.

"I—it's time for me to go," Lucie choked out.

"Ah yes. Those plans of yours. I'll see you next week."

Lucie managed a smile, and she ducked through the gate to the quai d'Orsay. She hurried along under the chestnut trees, her hand pressed to her stomach.

If she hadn't already digested the meal Paul Aubrey had bought her—with German Army money!—she would have heaved it into the Seine. She'd let a plate of beef and a charming smile entice her. How was she different from those fur-draped women consorting with German officers in the restaurant?

Anyone who saw her there—with a known *collaborateur*—would have thought she was just like those women.

"Oh, Lord." She raised her face to the overcast sky. "Please forgive me, but I liked him."

A heartless, moneygrubbing, collaborating business tycoon, and she'd liked him.

6

MONDAY, APRIL 7, 1941

Outside his office, Paul stood at the balcony overlooking the bustle of activity on the factory floor. Not as bustling as the Germans wanted.

To Paul's right, Col. Gerhard Schiller clasped his hands together, one finger tapping away. "We're disappointed that you only partially fulfilled our order this month."

"I apologize," Paul said, "but it required a significant increase in production. We tried, but the order will be delayed."

To his left, Jacques Moreau rested heavy fists on the railing.

Ordinarily Paul would have asked Moreau to explain the fall in production—because it was indeed a fall. Paul suspected the workers had deliberately slowed their pace, but he'd never tell Schiller that.

The main assembly line ran left to right below them, lit by daylight streaming through sawtooth skylights. On the far side of the factory, a craneway ran the length of the building, bringing materials from the railroad. From the craneway, a dozen tributary lines assembled parts and fed them to the main line, from axles to engines to seat cushions.

Schiller frowned. "Your production figures are far lower than for factories in Germany."

Paul adjusted the sleeves of his dark gray suit, which didn't fit as well as it used to. "Tell me, Colonel. How many calories a day do German workers receive?"

"Calories?"

"In their diet. How many calories?"

"I—don't know." Schiller narrowed pale blue eyes in thought. "We have little rationing."

Of course not. Plunder from occupied countries fattened Germany. "That isn't the case here. The average adult receives thirteen hundred calories a day. For a man like me, it's enough to live, although with constant hunger. Laborers receive a higher ration but not enough. The men are slow because they're hungry."

Surprise flickered over Schiller's face. Regret, even. "I see."

"Also, this past winter was one of the coldest in memory, and no one received coal for heating. Cold steals the strength of the heartiest of men. Even a German worker wouldn't be productive in such conditions."

Schiller extended his hand. "I shall see if I can help."

Paul accepted the handshake. "Thank you. We'll do our best to meet your order."

After the colonel left, Moreau turned to Paul, his face no longer as jowly but as indifferent as ever. No, not indifferent. His eyebrows drew together, his mouth pulled into a thoughtful frown.

"Yes, Moreau?"

"Do you want me to speak to the men about the fall in productivity?"

"Not necessary. Tell them I know they're trying."

"Yes, sir." He gave Paul a strange look and thumped down the stairs.

Paul glanced at his watch. Just enough time to drop his

report at the US Embassy and get to Green Leaf Books before it closed.

In his office he checked his attaché case. Deep in a pocket in the lid, a sealed envelope held his typed report. At the embassy he'd address it to Jim Duffy and have them send it in a diplomatic pouch. Duff now served at the US Embassy in Vichy, across the demarcation line in the unoccupied zone of France.

Paul snapped the case shut, donned his coat and hat, said goodbye to his secretary, and trotted downstairs.

Duff would find much of interest in Paul's report for March. The Germans had placed increased orders for February, March, and April. Last night on the radio, Paul had learned why.

The Germans had invaded Yugoslavia and Greece. It sickened him.

Hitler kept saying he didn't want more territory. He'd said it after he annexed Austria. Then after he took over Czechoslovakia's Sudetenland. Then the rest of Czechoslovakia. Then Poland. Then his rash of conquests in 1940. Now he'd struck south.

Paul passed the sales and administrative offices, tipping his fedora to accountants and secretaries.

Under contract, the Germans were forbidden from converting Paul's trucks for military use. But the Nazis had proven faithless in honoring treaties. Why would they honor a contract?

His stomach twisted, but he wouldn't change his decision. Duff said Paul's information was helpful, not just from Aubrey Automobiles but from Paul's conversations with others in industry.

Besides, his factory was running. If this madness ever ended, he could build cars again.

At the Odéon Métro station, Paul stepped out of the second of five cars in the train. He avoided first-class seating in the middle car, favored by German soldiers, who rode for free.

He weaved through the crowd on the platform, his step light in anticipation of seeing Lucie and relieved of the burden of his report.

Despite what Duff said, it was espionage. Paul passed on industrial and military information, and for the twelve hours each month between when he typed his report at home and when he delivered it, the weight pressed hard.

Paul had given Madame Coudray instructions that in case of his arrest or disappearance, she would take Josie immediately to the embassy. A plan he'd rather not activate.

He climbed the stairs with men and women returning home from work. With all taxis and buses requisitioned by the Germans, Parisians relied on bicycles and the Métro.

The Germans had also requisitioned all late-model cars, including Paul's 1939 Aubrey Aurora, but had left his 1935 Authority, although it was useless without a gasoline permit.

Outside in the chilly air, Paul headed south. Narrow cobblestone streets bent and divided. Gray stone buildings rose on each side with businesses on the ground floor and apartments above, many with wrought iron balconies and window boxes.

An elderly man in a purple cape pedaled past. Only on the Left Bank.

Was Lucie as flighty as the rest of these characters? He hadn't seen her at church, and she'd promised to attend.

Paul took a road jogging to the left, and he groaned. He could have used an ally at church. If people wanted to reject him, fine. But to break the heart of a little girl? Josie just wanted to play.

She'd cried all the way home.

Edmund Pendleton had encouraged Paul to return to church,

to please return, to not let people come between him and the Lord.

True, singing hymns and hearing the message had brought peace and joy. But could he endure weekly public humiliation from those he'd once called friends?

"I don't know, Lord," he whispered. "I love you, but I'm not so sure about your people."

There—rue Casimir-Delavigne. Paul's pace picked up.

On the surface, Simone and Lucie were nothing alike, but they shared a directness of speech and a core of strength. Lucie had given up her ballet career and stayed in Paris when panzers approached and everyone assumed bombers would raze the city—for her friends.

A smile rose. For courage and compassion like that, Paul would gladly endure some artistic flightiness.

The dark green façade neared. After Paul coached his expression down a few notches from infatuated schoolboy, he opened the door.

Lucie stood with her back to him, shelving books in the nonfiction section. She wore a muted green sweater over a skirt of the same color, sprinkled with pink and yellow flowers, like spring itself.

A young couple sat nearby, so he addressed her formally. "Good evening, Miss Girard."

Her head popped up, and she turned to him. Not spring. The coldest of winters.

She knew.

His mouth filled with that cold.

Lucie jutted out her chin. "I'm sorry, but I'll have to ask you to leave. Your money isn't welcome here."

"I beg your pardon," he said calmly, even as the chill spread.

She swept past him toward the door. "Dr. and Mrs. Young are my friends. Mrs. Young told me you lied to me."

Paul marched close so he could keep his voice low, ice in his vocal cords. "I never lied to you."

Lucie drew back, and her eyes widened as if shocked that he'd returned ice with ice. "You said you were an engineer."

"I am."

"You own a . . . business." She spat out the last word. "I saw your entry in the 1940 *Americans in France* directory. You own Aubrey Automobiles. You belong to the American Chamber of Commerce."

"Yes. Nothing wrong with that." Had she forgotten she owned a business as well?

"It's wrong if you're a collaborator." The strength he'd admired turned on him. "It's wrong if you sell trucks and tanks and airplane engines to the Germans."

"Tanks? What? No. I only sell trucks. Delivery trucks for civilian use. I also sell to the French."

"And the Germans."

It was over before it had begun. "Yes."

Her cheeks reddened, and her mouth curled. "How could you?"

Part of him wanted to tell the truth and have one other person know him for who he was. But to continue his work, he had to be seen as a collaborator. That overrode his desire for romance, for companionship, even for respect.

So he set his jaw and let the ice show. "If I closed, hundreds of men would lose good-paying jobs. Do you want that?"

One nostril flared, and she scanned him from head to foot. "It doesn't hurt that you make a profit so you can buy fancy clothes and eat fancy dinners and live in the 16th arrondissement with fancy collaborating friends."

She saw him as a coldhearted opportunist. Fine. He could play that role. He took a step closer. "Isn't that why you own this store? To make a profit?"

Lucie flung open the door. "I care nothing about money. The purpose of this store is to enlighten minds."

Paul strode through the door. "I wish you all the best, Miss Girard, with your . . . business." He tipped his hat to her. He'd never even had time to remove it.

His shoes pounded on the cobblestones. A single set of footsteps. That was how it had to be.

7

WEDNESDAY, APRIL 9, 1941

Through the bookstore window, Lucie waved to her friends Jerzy Epstein and Charles Charbonnier. They were over an hour late, the darlings. She mouthed, "I'll be right out."

Lucie scurried to the office, past the American journalist choosing a novel, the French university student thumbing through the philosophy section, and Bernadette helping a French writer select a literary journal.

In the office Lucie put on her overcoat and a knit cap. The receipt from Monsieur Quinault lay where she'd set it over a week before. Bernadette hadn't reconciled it with the bill, wherever that was.

Lucie pushed her bicycle out of the office and caught her assistant's eye. "Thank you for minding the store this morning, Madame Martel."

Bernadette looked over the writer's shoulder. "I am happy to do so."

Lucie's hands rolled over the handlebars. "Perhaps it would be a good day to do the books."

Bernadette's round face took on the same "the child isn't terribly bright" expression Lucie's schoolteachers had given when they'd found her daydreaming instead of doing her times tables. "My dear Miss Girard, if I were to do the books, how would I mind the store?"

"Oh. Yes. Another day then." Lucie continued on her way.

The university student slipped a piece of paper inside a book and placed it on the shelf. He strode away, spotted Lucie, and stopped.

One of her regular customers. A black curl dangled between intense dark eyes in an angular face.

"Bonjour," Lucie said.

None of his features moved. Then he blinked, returned her greeting, and left the store.

Perhaps "regular customer" wasn't the proper term, since he'd never made a purchase. Why had he acted as if she'd caught him stealing? In fact, he'd left something behind.

What was it? A school assignment? A love note?

Lucie couldn't resist. She leaned the bike against the counter and opened the book. A slip of paper read "Thuillier" and then a strange symbol—a letter *L* with an arrow coming out from the corner, down and at an angle.

Cryptic and unromantic.

She put the note and the book back where she'd found them.

Out on rue Casimir-Delavigne, she greeted Jerzy and Charles. "You're over an hour late," she said in a teasing voice.

Charles sat on his bicycle seat, his long legs braced wide. His oversized checkered suit shouted that he was a nonconformist "*zazou*"—and concealed the clubfoot that had kept him out of the French army. "Shame on you for noticing we were late."

"There's no shame in noticing, only in caring." Lucie straddled her bike. "I'll only care if the eggs are gone. A *crémerie* on rue Mouffetard has them."

"Eggs?" Jerzy scrambled onto his bike so quickly he almost tipped over. He scrunched his hat down over his black curls.

"If you'd mentioned eggs, I would have dragged myself out of bed an hour earlier."

Unlikely, given the hours the painter kept, but Lucie smiled and motioned him onward.

They pedaled past the Odéon Thèâtre and Le Jardin du Luxembourg. Lucie's muscles protested from the previous evening's ballet practice in her storeroom, with only her mural ballerinas for company.

With Marie-Claude and Véronique deep in rehearsals for *Giselle*, they had no time to practice with Lucie and little time for shopping. If Lucie hadn't been able to leave the store, they would have all gone hungry tonight.

"Pedal faster, Lucie," Charles called from behind. "Maybe the wind will catch your skirt. I miss seeing those legs on stage."

Lucie glanced over her shoulder, lifting one eyebrow and one corner of her mouth.

Charles was harmless if she kept a distance from his hands, as quick and dexterous with a woman as they were on the piano keyboard.

"How's life at the club, Charles?" she called.

"I find the *haricots verts* endlessly amusing."

"Green beans" referred to the German soldiers in their greenish-gray uniforms. "Amusing?"

Charles's long zazou-style haircut fluttered in the breeze. "In Germany jazz is banned as degenerate, but in Paris all the haricots on leave come to my Montmartre club and try to snap their fingers to the beat."

In front of Lucie, Jerzy leaned back his head and sighed. "I wish they tolerated my art as well as they do your music. Eggs will be some small consolation in the pitiful desolation of life."

Poor Jerzy. Encouraging the artist had always been a full-time job, but now even more so. Although Lucie had never understood his surrealist paintings, she'd never dream of banning them. And the antisemitic laws limited the jobs available to him. "At least you can still paint."

"Only with a fake name." Jerzy led them through a round-about and down rue Gay-Lussac. "Only pretty little paintings of the Tour Eiffel and Notre-Dame and Pont Neuf. Pretty little paintings for our finger-snapping visitors to take home to their hausfraus after cheating on them in Paris's brothels. But—I take my revenge in each painting."

Lucie held her breath. "You do? How?"

"I work the letter *V* into every design." Jerzy jerked his chin toward a German propaganda poster, marked up with a giant chalk *V*.

"Clever." After a BBC broadcast to France in January, the "V for Victory" had spread throughout Paris, and throughout France and Belgium and Holland, if the rumors were true.

They crossed a street, where the plaque on the wall read "Rue Louis-Thuillier."

Thuillier? Like the note in the book. Did the note refer to the street? Was that where the student planned to meet his lover? Or was it for a resistance meeting?

Since the Germans arrived, resistance had been sporadic and limited. Vandalism. Graffiti. Slashing tires on German vehicles.

On Christmas Eve, a young man had been executed, accused of punching a German soldier in a brawl. Then in February and March, scholars at the Musée de l'Homme had been arrested for publishing an underground newspaper.

Even defacing a poster carried a fine of ten thousand francs.

Lucie turned onto rue Claude-Bernard. If the student was a *résistant*, his life was in danger. But oh, what courage!

What if her imagination was running wild? It often did. Maybe her friends could puzzle out the message.

However, Jerzy was as reckless with his words as Charles was with his passions. Too many people would gladly sell information spoken in a reckless or passionate moment.

Some secrets were too dangerous even among friends.

Long lines wound in front of the markets on rue Mouffetard. Lucie and her friends divided among lines, exchanging ration tickets.

Lucie pushed her bike to the end of the line at the crémerie. "Pardon?" she asked the elderly lady in front of her. "Do you know if they still have eggs?"

"Oui, but how many I cannot say."

"Merci." Lucie hadn't had eggs in ages. Or meat.

The decadent dinner with Mr. Aubrey didn't count. She refused to think of him as Paul. Paul had sad eyes and an engaging smile and kind ways. Mr. Aubrey cared about money above all else. Mr. Aubrey erased Paul.

Lucie sighed and pushed her bike forward in line. She usually perceived a person's true nature. How could she have failed? And why had she continued to find him attractive even as she denounced him to his face, even as he hardened before her eyes?

"Integrity. Something deeply good," she murmured. That's what she thought she'd seen in him.

Her brain felt topsy-turvy the last few days. If she couldn't trust her intuition, what would she do?

Ahead of her in line, a small girl plopped to her bottom. Children often waited alone as mothers planted them in several lines in front of the baker, the butcher, and the greengrocer.

The girl's brother tugged on her hand, and she shook her head of brown curls and cried.

The poor child looked like Josie, and Lucie's heart wrenched. Not only was sweet Josie punished for her father's sins, but she had to be raised by such a man.

"Lord," she whispered. "Protect her from his hard-hearted ways."

8

TUESDAY, APRIL 15, 1941

Paul rubbed his forehead, but no amount of rubbing could make the numbers align.

From outside his office door, factory machinery rumbled and clanked in its steady pace, a pace Paul couldn't increase enough to fill Colonel Schiller's new order plus the earlier contracts with French firms. With so many French men in German prisoner of war camps, new hires were scarce.

Schiller had been clear—German orders came first. Every truck made by Aubrey Autos in May would go to Germany.

Paul shoved away the paperwork, but he couldn't shove away the fact that he was losing control of the factory he'd built.

If it weren't for his reports to Duffy, he'd chuck the whole thing.

Paul rolled his stiff shoulders. He'd given up so much for those reports.

Stung by Lucie's rejection, on the night she'd kicked him out of her store, he'd retrieved invitations from his wastepaper basket and accepted them all. An American society widow who kept house with a high-ranking German officer. A French banker who knew everyone's business and told it under the influence of champagne. A French businessman whose company made airplane engines for the Luftwaffe, as Lucie had accused Paul of doing.

If Paul had to embrace the role of collaborator to conduct espionage, he might as well give it all he had.

A loud whine pierced his office door, then an ominous thunk.

Paul bolted out of his office and to the balcony overlooking the factory floor.

White smoke plumed above the steel presses.

"Oh no." Paul ran down the stairs and jogged across the floor to the most expensive equipment in his factory, the machines that pressed steel into fenders and hoods.

Jacques Moreau was already there, overseeing an argument among half a dozen men. French words flew so quickly, Paul caught only a fraction of them.

"What happened?" he asked.

"I saw him." One man pointed at another. "Foulon threw a wrench into the press."

Foulon flapped a broad hand at his accuser. "You lie, Lafarge. A belt broke. It happens."

Lafarge thrust his sharp nose in Foulon's face. "It happens when you throw a wrench in."

Paul held up both hands. "Enough. Moreau, what happened?"

Moreau and Foulon exchanged a glance, then Moreau turned his insolent gaze to Paul. "A belt broke."

Lafarge's face grew as red as the scarf around his neck. "You weren't here. You saw nothing."

Paul saw clearly. Foulon had committed sabotage, and Moreau was covering for him.

He swept a hard gaze over the men. "Did anyone else see anything?"

Murmurs of "non" circled.

Lafarge shoved another man. "You! You saw him."

"I saw nothing."

Foulon stared at his scuffed shoes, his cheeks pitting. Guilty.

No anger surged in Paul's chest. Only . . . admiration. Envy. "I won't fire a man based on a single witness." Much less a witness like Lafarge, whose name frequently surfaced in Moreau's reports as a whiner and brawler.

"Start the repairs," Paul said. Then he beckoned to Moreau and Foulon, led them to a private spot near the wall, and looked Foulon full in his close-set eyes. "Don't do that again."

"I didn't—"

"Don't do it again," Paul said slowly, firmly.

Foulon's scruffy jaw shifted forward.

Paul crossed his arms. "The Germans have stiff penalties for sabotage, and I don't want any extra attention from the occupation authorities. Understood?"

Foulon's jaw remained set, but the fire in his eyes dimmed. "Yes, sir."

"Good. Back to work."

The man shuffled toward the assembly line.

Moreau remained, staring at him. "That's all?"

Before the Nazis came, if a worker had deliberately damaged equipment, Paul would have fired him, had him arrested. Paul drew in a long breath. "That's all. Excuse me."

He crossed the factory floor, climbed the stairs, and leaned on the balcony railing.

Sabotage.

A roiling sensation built up, and Paul wanted to rip off his shoe and throw it into a machine. *His* machine.

How could he fault Foulon for doing what Paul wished he could do? And how could he crack down on saboteurs? That would make him even more of a collaborator.

Maybe he could find some way to stop sending trucks to Germany.

No. Even if he could bring himself to damage his own property, Duffy had forbidden it. Sabotage would erode German trust and cut off the flow of information America needed.

Paul pushed away from the railing. As he'd told Foulon, the penalties were severe. He needed to protect his family and his employees.

He opened the office door marked with the golden "Au" logo. The Gold Standard.

Quality. Dad prized it. Paul prized it. The company instilled quality into every element, from design to materials to business practices. Sabotage would violate his most cherished value.

Paul nodded to Mademoiselle Thibodeaux, entered his private office, and shut the door.

Too restless to sit, he studied the stylized sketches of Aubrey models on the walls. He stopped in front of his favorite—the Audacity race car.

If only he could build something that aided his country.

Now that President Franklin Roosevelt had been elected to a third term, he seemed determined to steer America to the Allied side. If German-American relations disintegrated, Paul would need to go home and his work for Duffy would end.

And relations were strained. In March, Congress had approved Roosevelt's Lend-Lease plan to send matériel to besieged Britain.

Not the action of a neutral nation. Hitler was livid. Paul was relieved.

Earlier that day over lunch at Maxim's, Paul had conversed with a former officer in a German panzer unit, wounded and assigned to a desk job in Paris. Quite drunk, the officer had detailed the strengths and weaknesses of his own tanks and of the French tanks he'd battled.

Paul still had the plans for the Char B1 bis tanks that a French general had begged him to build in the desperate days of the invasion. The general had died in battle, and in the chaos of the occupation and Simone's hospitalization, Paul had filed the plans and forgotten them.

With a rush of energy, Paul unlocked his file cabinet and pulled out the plans. At his desk he wrote down all he could remember from the panzer officer's conversation. Comparisons of guns, armor, power, maneuverability, reliability, speed.

Paul could combine the best of each. Add Aubrey quality and dependability. Ask military men what they needed. Build it for the US Army.

The project lit up his nerves in a way he hadn't felt in years.

He tapped his pencil on his notes. It would be wise to work on this at home and lock the plans in his safe.

The Germans might control what he did in his factory, but not in his home.

Paul slipped the plans and notes into his attaché case, and he added extra paper. Lately Josie had been snitching paper from his study at home.

Every day she asked to return to Green Leaf Books. Every day Paul told her he didn't plan to return. And every day Josie did something naughty.

It wasn't like her.

How could he explain to a four-year-old that he'd been banned from the store?

Paul's head felt heavy, and he shook it hard. He couldn't even explain it to himself.

The market for English-language books had to be small. How could she turn away every customer who worked with the Germans? How could she run a business not caring about profit?

He sighed and locked his attaché case. That wasn't the source of his frustration. Lucie's rejection was.

For one brilliant day, he'd basked in the hope of having someone in his life again who would know him and like him.

The Lord did. Only the Lord.

9

MONDAY, APRIL 21, 1941

Madame Villeneuve stormed out of the office, and Lucie laid her head on the paper-strewn desk, her mind reeling.

If she'd known Bernadette hadn't paid April's rent, she never would have purchased more stock. But how could she resist a print run of Shakespeare plays and sonnets?

Since it was Bernadette's day off, Lucie couldn't even ask why the rent hadn't been paid.

The concierge had accepted partial payment—every centime in the cash box—but she'd threatened eviction. Apparently this was a continuing problem. And Lucie hadn't known.

"You're a ballerina," Erma Greenblatt had said and not unkindly.

"Good thing she's pretty," Lucie's third-grade teacher had said and quite unkindly.

Lucie burrowed her head into her crossed forearms. Numbers didn't sing as words did. They didn't dance like leaves and music. Numbers stood silent and rigid. Horrible, inscrutable things.

Now they mocked her. Because she hated them, they'd kill her dream, the Greenblatts' dream. "I'm sorry, Hal. Sorry, Erma."

"Hallo?" a man called from the store.

Lucie put on her performance face and left the hideous desk behind. "Oui? Bonjour."

Lt. Emil Wattenberg stood with hat in hand. "Good day, Miss Girard."

Her performance face kept steady. "Good day, Lieutenant."

He gestured to the door with a concerned look. "Your concierge asked me to talk to you."

"Is that so?" At the counter Lucie picked up a stack of her beautiful new books to shelve. Since the publisher had made the print run just for her, he'd never buy them back.

Wattenberg groaned. "She told me to make you pay, but I am only an office man."

Now she knew where Madame Villeneuve's sentiments lay—with the Germans and the Vichy and the collaborateurs. Lucie found space for the new books.

Heavy boots followed her. "She said you have not paid the . . ."

"Rent. The word you want is rent." She gave him a pointed look.

Compassion bent his lips. "May I help? My family is rich."

Lucie swept past him to retrieve more books. "That is not necessary." The thought of a German paying her rent nauseated her, but she sent him a quick smile for his generosity.

"Then I will buy a book."

Lucie nodded toward the shelves. "I can't stop you."

He sent her a curious look, then entered the fiction section.

Indeed, she couldn't refuse service to anyone.

Except Paul Aubrey.

Her stomach twisted, and she pulled out a box of bookplates. She'd shown Paul the door because he took German money. And here she was, about to take German money.

Except she didn't have a choice.

Maybe . . . what if he didn't have a choice either?

Nonsense. She licked a bookplate and stuck it inside *Hamlet*.

There was a world of difference between selling a book and selling hundreds of vehicles. He did it for money. She did it because refusing a sale would mean . . . what? They wouldn't arrest her. But they could shut down her store.

The door opened, and a young man entered, the one who kept leaving notes inside books. He returned Lucie's greeting, passed Wattenberg without flinching, pulled a book from the nonfiction section, and settled into a chair.

Lucie stuck a bookplate inside *Othello*, flicking glances at the two men. Wattenberg, skimming a novel. Mystery Man, absorbed in his book.

She'd sneaked a look at his notes—although it wasn't sneaking if he left them in *her* books. Other young people fetched the notes, sometimes buying the book and sometimes slipping out the note and leaving.

Always, Lucie pretended to be oblivious.

But she wasn't. They were part of the resistance, and ideas spun in Lucie's head.

Wattenberg came to the cash register. "Have you books from Ernest Hemingway?"

"Hemingway?" She had a dozen of his books in her hideaway behind the mural.

"Ja. Years ago I read *The Sun Also Rises*. It was . . ." He pressed a fist to his chest and got a faraway look. "Good. The language was straight. I understood the English."

Straight. Not the most poetic way she'd heard Hemingway's prose described, yet it fit.

"It is why I come to the Latin Quarter. I feel him here." Wattenberg's eyes shone silver.

An impulse burned inside her to return his kindness. To tell him she'd met the author many times in this very store. To free a novel from banishment to give to a man who talked of arts and literature, never of ideology or conquest.

Intuition overrode impulse. She only sold those books to

trusted customers. What if Wattenberg meant to trap her into committing a crime?

Lucie affixed a bookplate into a volume of sonnets. "Your nation has banned the sale of Hemingway's books."

Wattenberg's face scrunched up. "Hemingway also?"

"Hemingway also." Along with a thousand books on the Otto List published by the German Embassy where Wattenberg worked.

"May I be honest?" The officer leaned closer, his elbows on the counter.

Lucie drew back. "Of course."

"I was in Berlin that night—big fire, books burned. I cried like a child."

Yet he still put on the Wehrmacht uniform.

Wattenberg straightened up. "I will buy this instead."

An Ellery Queen book, *The Greek Coffin Mystery*. Sadly appropriate as his fellow German soldiers trampled Greek soil.

At last he left.

From a table in the fiction section, Lucie picked up books discarded by three gangly boys from the Lycée Louis-le-Grand. She left some behind to keep the homey atmosphere.

Then she rounded the bookcase to nonfiction.

Mystery Man slipped a book onto the shelf and left the store.

Lucie straightened chairs until he closed the door. Then she snatched up the book. Another note. The word *Placide* faced page 13. Then a letter *J* with an arrow pointing down.

Impulse and intuition danced in harmony, with conviction thumping in rhythm.

Lucie slapped the book shut and returned it.

Only half an hour until closing time, and the store was empty. With her identity card and store key in her skirt pocket, she flipped the store sign from *ouvert* to *fermé* and locked the door.

Mystery Man was almost down to the place de l'Odéon.

Lucie followed, noting pedestrians to slip behind, doorways to duck into. But he never looked behind him.

In market lines and in her store, Lucie had heard more whisperings of resistance. More than once she'd reminded students that if she could hear them, others could too.

After a few minutes, the man turned in to the Jardin du Luxembourg. Lucie quickened her pace, her steps silent. Her plan had been germinating, and now it could see the sun.

Lucie spun as if relishing the spring air under the spreading trees. Not a soul in earshot, and she fell in beside the young man. "Bonjour, monsieur."

He glanced at her, and dark eyebrows rose. "Mademoiselle?"

"Oui. Mademoiselle Girard from the bookstore. I'd like to discuss something with you."

He sighed, his face young and unlined. "I know. I do not buy books, but—"

"No, I want to discuss your notes."

"Notes?"

"In the books. Your code is clever, but I figured it out."

His pointy jaw shifted, and he turned down a narrow, curving path. "I do not know what you are talking about."

Lucie kept pace. "The word is a street name. Placide for rue Saint-Placide. And the page number is the address. I noticed sometimes the notes face left and sometimes right, facing the street number. Then the symbol. The letter is the day of the week—*J* for *jeudi*—and the arrow is the time, like a clock's hand."

He lifted his palms. "Mademoiselle, I do not know—"

"My point is, if I—and I didn't attend a lycée, much less a university—if even I can figure it out, so could the police or the Germans."

The young man's step hitched.

Lucie gave him a reassuring smile. "I'd like to help."

His upper lip curled. "You think I am—"

75

"Standing up to the Germans, yes, and I want to help. I have an idea."

"You are American. Your country refuses to help. This is not your fight." He marched down another shaded lane.

"I am a Parisienne, so it is my fight. It's the fight of all who love freedom."

"Mademoiselle—"

"Please listen. I can prevent your notes from falling into the wrong hands. You leave them on the bookshelf where anyone can find them. As you saw, I can't bar Germans from my store."

His arms swung hard. "Get to the point. I would like my dinner."

A thrill ran through her. He'd admitted his involvement. "The solution is simple. Bring the book to me. You could ask me to put it on hold—you forgot your wallet and will pay later. Or you could bring two books—buy one and decide not to buy the other."

The man's pace didn't slow, but the swinging of arms lessened.

An elderly couple approached, and Lucie kept silent until they'd passed. "I'll keep the books behind the cash register. Your friends would ask me for the title—they already know which books to look for. They could say they'd called earlier, or they'd brought their wallet, or a friend put it on hold for them. Then I'd pass it on."

One masculine hand rose to block her words. "If I were involved in such things, why on earth would I trust someone so indiscreet?"

Inside, Lucie bristled, but she didn't let it show. "On the contrary. I have not asked your name. You never knew I'd been reading your notes. You didn't notice me following you, and I waited until we entered the gardens to talk to you. Also, I danced with the Paris Opéra Ballet."

He gave her a befuddled look.

She crossed her hands over her chest in a classic pose. "A ballerina is trained never to show her emotions. We dance with blistered and bleeding feet, with pulled muscles and broken hearts. Once I danced with a broken toe. And all the audience sees is the character's emotion. Never, ever my own."

He raked back his black curls. "I fail to see how that would help."

"Haven't you noticed? This whole conversation I've kept my expression light and pleased as if enjoying a stroll with a friend."

"Yes, but—"

"But you don't know if I can be trusted? I could have taken your notes to the police. I could have let that German officer find them. I didn't. I came to you with an offer to help, to protect you and your friends."

The résistant faced her, his expression fierce. "That is all. I must ask you never to speak to me again. Au revoir."

Lucie's performance face didn't crack, but her heart did. "Au revoir."

She went down a separate path, and her sigh rose to the leafy branches overhead. What had gone wrong? Her idea had seemed as smart as the codes.

Who was she fooling? Her friends used many sweet words to describe her, but *smart* was never one of them.

10

MONDAY, APRIL 28, 1941

The factory grumbled awake from its Sunday slumber, and Paul strode down the factory floor past the tributary lines feeding parts to the main assembly line. This week more trucks would drive off his assembly line and straight to Germany.

His breakfast porridge felt slimy in his stomach. On Saturday, he'd taken Josie to see the children's movie *Le Roman de Renard*. Newsreels had shown smiling German soldiers in truck convoys. They'd rolled through Yugoslavia and Greece in less than a month, and they were rolling through Libya toward Egypt. If they took the Suez Canal, they'd cut off oil to Britain. Churchill would have to sue for peace. The war would be over.

America would remain neutral, but Germany showed no respect for neutrality.

Paul frowned at the belt conveying wood-burning gazogène generators from the craneway to the main assembly line. The modified engines relegated his trucks to civilian use, but Paul's production of trucks freed German factories to produce military equipment.

Sickening.

With a slap to the conveyor belt, Paul resumed his march. He ought to pull up stakes and go home. Nothing left for him in Paris. No wife. No friends. He couldn't build cars. And everyone thought he was a collaborator.

Maybe he was.

He'd taken some comfort at church the day before. He'd decided not to let Lucie Girard and the Youngs and Hartmans and other gossipers keep him away.

Paul and Josie had arrived early, left late, and sat in the front row. Up front, he couldn't see the scowls and glares, and he could focus on the music and preaching.

On his way out, he'd seen Lucie from a distance, but she never glanced his way. Fine. He didn't attend church to see her.

Paul passed men checking the radiators on their rack. If he returned to Massachusetts, he'd have friends again. And if Josie made friends, it would help her through this Feenee phase. He could attend church. He could date. And he could build the Autonomy instead of the Au-ful.

To his left, two workers shared a laugh as they prepared their tools.

When Renault or Citroën bought his factory, the Germans would control it completely.

Lately Paul had let sluggish work and reports of sabotage pass without comment. The Germans wouldn't ignore such things. Production would kick into high gear.

Paul groaned. If he remained, he could at least allow his workers to decrease production. If only he could reduce it even more, maybe reduce quality.

His insides churned, turning over and over, thumping and thumping.

Duffy forbade sabotage. Paul's conscience forbade it. The Gold Standard forbade it, and the Gold Standard was the highest standard.

Or was it?

The churning slowed. Stilled. Stopped. There was a far higher standard than quality.

Do good. Resist evil.

By working slowly, the laborers resisted. By throwing a wrench into the steel press, Foulon had resisted. What could Paul do?

He stared up at the motor running the overhead conveyor belt for the main assembly line, purring perfectly. If it were to stop, the whole line would shut down.

A mechanic climbed down a ladder by the motor, and Moreau approached Paul with a clipboard for his morning report.

Paul knew what he had to do. He gestured with his thumb to the motor. "Does that sound right to you?"

Moreau frowned. "Pardon?"

"I don't like the sound it's making."

The mechanic cocked his head. "But that is the sound it is supposed to make."

Paul shook his head. "Something's wrong."

"But monsieur, I just—"

"I don't like the sound." Paul fixed his gaze on the older man. "Shut it down, take it apart, and find out what's wrong."

Moreau gaped at the mechanic, then at Paul. "That would shut down the line for hours."

"Days maybe," Paul said. "Shut it down. Take it apart. Fix it."

The two seasoned workers stared at each other a long moment. A slight nod from Moreau, and the mechanic turned to Paul. "Oui, monsieur."

Paul marched up to his office as the machinery whined to a stop.

From now on he'd embrace the Silver Standard.

Golden evening light filled the garden behind Paul's home, and Josie's voice darted around, a mix of French and English as she sang to the flowers and talked to the bugs.

In Josie's story tonight, this Feenee sang out of a horn on its head and used the horn to poke its enemies.

In his garden chair, Paul turned a page in his book on French history. For the past few weeks, he'd set it aside as a painful reminder of Lucille Girard, but tonight he'd picked it up. She could ban him from her store but not from the book he'd bought with his own money.

After Paul finished his chapter, he glanced at his watch. On Madame Coudray's evening off, he made sure to follow his daughter's routine. "Josie, time to go inside."

"Okay, Daddy." Little feet ran up to him.

Paul brushed dirt off her knees. "Okay, my little nougat, you have an hour before bedtime. Would you like me to read to you or—"

"I want to color."

Paul now stored blank paper on a high shelf. "You know there's a paper shortage. We need to save it for important things."

"This is 'portant." She slipped her hand into Paul's. "I have a new story about Feenee and Monsieur Meow. I want to give it to the book lady. When can we go back?"

Paul opened the door from the garden to the sitting room, and light from the setting sun bounced off the panes. How could he explain to a little girl that she wasn't welcome because of her father's business? And why did *he* have to do the explaining?

"Daddy?"

"Hmm?"

His daughter's plump lips bent in confusion. Paul stood with one foot inside, one foot outside. He'd been standing there a while, hadn't he?

He headed to his study for paper. "Tell you what, cocoa bean.

You write that story for Miss Girard, and I'll take you to the bookstore this weekend."

"Hooray!"

How could even the high-minded Miss Girard say no to his little scoop of sugar?

11

Saturday, May 3, 1941

Iron. Although the concierge stood several inches shorter than Lucie, Madame Villeneuve had iron at her core, flowing out in her iron-gray hair, molten in her iron-gray eyes. All that iron forged into a dagger of a gaze. "This is unacceptable, Mademoiselle Girard."

"I'm sorry, madame." Lucie turned to the bookstore's office. "Madame Martel? Madame Villeneuve hasn't received the rent yet."

From behind the desk, Bernadette set down a book and came to the office door. "I will pay soon."

"Soon?" The concierge brandished a tiny bludgeon of a fist. "May's rent is three days late, and you never paid the rest of April's rent."

"Soon, madame." Bernadette stepped back inside the office and closed the door.

Madame Villeneuve's ire swung back to Lucie. "Every month you pay late. How long must I tolerate this? I should find a new tenant."

Lucie's mouth went dry. If she lost the store, Hal and Erma's dream would die, and Paris would lose one more bit of culture.

Lucie would have to go home to New York. But what could she do there? "I—I'll take care of it, madame. I'll get the rent to you."

"See that you do." With a huff, she stomped out of the store.

A customer stared at the concierge's turbulent wake, a dark-haired man in a gray suit, holding the hand of a little girl—who beamed at Lucie.

Josie Aubrey. And her father.

Mr. Aubrey faced her, his eyebrows raised under the brim of his fedora.

How dare he come? How dare he use his little girl to prevent Lucie from enforcing her ban? And why did he have to come when she was rattled?

But a ballerina never let it show when she was rattled, so she squatted down and gave the child a genuine smile. "Hello, Josie."

"Hello, Miss Gee-jard. I brought you something." Josie wore a dark blue coat and a matching hat, and she clutched a booklet to her chest.

"How sweet of you. Why don't you sit at my little green table? I'll be with you in a minute."

"Okay." She ran off to the children's section.

Lucie straightened to standing.

Mr. Aubrey held up one hand. "Please let me explain. You banished me, not Josie. And she's been begging me every day for weeks. I put her off as long as I could."

Lucie glanced back to where Josie sat, grinning expectantly, papers in hand. Oh, her heart. The poor little thing shouldn't suffer because her father was a heel.

"To respect your wishes," the heel said, "I'll wait outside."

Lucie's eyes slipped shut. How ridiculous her ban sounded. She didn't screen customers at the door. For heaven's sake, she sold to enemy soldiers. A sigh leeched out. "You may stay."

"Thank you." Why did his voice have to sound so rich and

resonant? "You said your store was in the business of enlightening minds. Obviously my mind needs enlightening."

She faced him and allowed the slightest smile. "I can't disagree."

Mr. Aubrey broke into a grin. In her mind she'd painted his eyes a menacing shade of red, but they were the warmest brown. An illusion.

He gestured past her. "If you wait much longer, Josie will bounce right out of her seat."

Indeed, she would. Lucie joined her and perched on a tiny chair. "What do you have, Miss Josephine?"

"I wrote you a story." She handed it to Lucie.

Colorful drawings and a few scrawled letters covered the pages. "Oh my! Look at the lovely colors."

"Grandma Aubrey sends me crayons from Am—am—"

"America?"

"Yes." Josie wiggled one finger like a worm. "Sometimes they're melty and bendy, but I like them that way."

"I would too." Lucie turned the pages. Such craftsmanship for such a young child. The story featured a fantastical girl with wings and a horn like a unicorn, and with curly hair that changed color on each page. There was also a black-and-white-striped cat. Lucie gasped. "Is that Monsieur Meow?"

"It is!" Josie's smile opened wide.

Should she pull out the puppet? No, Lucie didn't want to detract from Josie's artwork. "Monsieur Meow is taking a nap, but he'll be so excited. He's never been in a storybook. Would you read the story to me, please?"

Out of the corner of her eye, Lucie saw Josie's father lean against the wall beside the table, a column of gray wool, his hat in hand, his ankles crossed.

Josie scowled. "The rock-monsters stole all Monsieur Meow's food, and he was so hungry."

Lucie pressed her fingers to her mouth. "Poor Monsieur Meow. He loves his tuna fish."

"Feenee was very angry." Josie pointed at the winged girl. "She said, 'You rock-monsters are mean. You can't take all the food.'"

"No. That isn't nice at all." Lucie turned the page.

Josie put her hand to her forehead like a unicorn's horn. "So Feenee poked her horn in the rock-monsters' house, and she flapped her wings very hard, and the walls fell down, and Feenee gave all the food to Monsieur Meow and the other kitty-cats."

"Feenee is very brave." Lucie flipped pages as she followed Josie's narration. "And kind."

"She is. She's in all my stories. She's never scared."

Lucie traced the purple hair on the Feenee on the last page. "Is Feenee short for Josephine as Josie is?"

"Uh-huh. She's my friend."

Her father sucked in a loud breath, and Lucie looked up to him. To the surprise in his expression. The embarrassment. He hadn't known where the name Feenee came from, had he?

Josie twirled a curl around a finger. "No one plays with me, but I have Feenee."

No one? Impossible for a child so cute and imaginative. "Oh, I'm sure you have lots of friends."

A shadow fell over Josie's brown eyes. "I have Feenee."

Mr. Aubrey gave Lucie a brisk shake of his head, his lips folded in. Hadn't Lucie seen the parents pulling their children away from Josie at church? And Josie's tears?

Those tears soaked Lucie's heart, and in that dampened soil a flower bloomed, then another and another, and Lucie gathered them into a bouquet of an idea.

She sprang to the box of puppets. "Monsieur Meow is your friend too. He told me an idea the other day. Let me wake him up. Monsieur Meow? Josie's here to see you."

After she wiggled into the puppet, Lucie put on her kitty

voice and spread the puppet's paws wide in delight. "Josie! Hooray!"

"Hi, Monsieur Meow." Josie bolted to her feet and hopped. "I missed you."

Lucie had the puppet hug Josie, then she put him to her own ear. "Yes, I'll tell her your idea."

"What idea?"

Lucie settled into her chair, cradling the puppet like a baby. "You were so kind to share your friend Feenee with Monsieur Meow, and he wants to share his friends with you."

Josie stared at the puppet box in awe. "There are more?"

"The children who come to this store. Starting next Saturday, I'll have a Children's Hour each week. We'll read stories and have a puppet show and play games. Doesn't that sound fun?"

But Josie lowered her chin. "Children don't like me."

Lucie's chest ached, and she had the puppet dance back and forth. "These children will, because you'll be Monsieur Meow's special helper. The children love Monsieur Meow."

"Miss Girard?" Mr. Aubrey beckoned. "May I please speak with you?"

Lucie wasn't in the habit of obeying officious businessmen, but he'd asked politely. She set a picture book before the girl. "Excuse me, Josie. I'll be right back."

Mr. Aubrey led her to the cash register—how fitting. "I appreciate what you're trying to do, but it won't work. She's correct about the children."

"I know. I saw what happens at church. She's rejected because of you."

He winced and turned his head as if her words had slapped him. A muscle in his neck worked, below the faint darkness on his jawline.

Lucie felt no guilt. He deserved to know how his greed affected his daughter.

His mouth agitated. "I see no need to compound her pain."

"Good. Bring her to Children's Hour. It's for children only. The parents may read or run errands. But no child will be unwelcome. I won't have it."

He stared at the author photos over the cash register, that neck muscle still working.

Lucie gentled her voice. "If she's my special helper and the puppets love her, the children will warm to her. She's cute and sweet. How could they not like her?"

"She needs friends." His voice sounded hoarse, and he rubbed his fist over his mouth. "She . . . thank you."

"Very well. Next Saturday at fourteen hours." She spun to return to Josie.

"Wait," Mr. Aubrey said.

"Yes?" She turned back. He'd better not ask her out again.

"I apologize for eavesdropping, but I heard your conversation with your concierge." He flicked his chin toward the office. "If you need help with the business, with the money end of things, I'd be happy to help."

Why did the most horrible men who entered her store have to be the most generous? "That won't be necessary."

His lips smiled, but his eyes looked as sad as Josie's. "That's right. The store's sole purpose is to enlighten minds."

"Yes." She returned the smile, because kindness deserved some reward in a cruel world. "To enlighten minds."

12

MONDAY, MAY 5, 1941

Paul checked the envelope in his attaché case. Signing off on
repairs had kept him at the factory late, so his trip to the embassy would have to wait until the next day.

Duff would like this report.

Over the past few weeks, Paul had attended several dinner
parties. At one, the manager of a tire factory had been quite free
about the numbers and types of tires the Germans were buying.

Since the German army had conquered Yugoslavia and
Greece and had crossed the Egyptian border, why did they
need so many tires?

Also, older soldiers were arriving in France, sending the
younger soldiers back to Germany. As if the plan to invade
England were abandoned. As if Hitler planned to attack to
the east.

What lay to the east? Hungary, Romania, Bulgaria, and the
Soviet Union—all allied with Germany. Hitler had violated
many a nation's neutrality, but to strike an ally would be the
height of treachery.

Paul left his quiet office.

Down on the factory floor, the mechanics had finished

repairing the overhead conveyor belt, and the assembly line would start up again in the morning.

A full week behind schedule. That would keep a lot of trucks out of German hands. The thought lightened his step as he descended the stairs in his factory.

At church yesterday, Mr. Pendleton had discussed steward-ship, not just giving to the church but about the concept of ownership.

Every resource, every gift, and even the power to gain wealth came from above. Hadn't God placed Paul in his father's house-hold and given him a mind that grasped both engineering and business?

Paul passed machines made with metal God had created, lubricated with oils God created, run by hands God created, housed by stone from God's hills and glass from God's sand.

"My factory. My company." Paul let out a wry chuckle. He didn't own it. He was a steward, placed in charge by the true owner.

He'd have to puzzle out how that might change his business practices.

Paul passed the sales and administrative offices and said good night to the last workers filing out.

Going to church again felt right. In all honesty, spiting the gossips gave him a pleasurable rush of defiance.

Yesterday he'd been rewarded. After church, Josie had rushed to Lucie while she chatted with the Youngs. Lucie had greeted Josie warmly and Paul stiffly.

The Youngs had looked uncomfortable and remained close as if to protect Lucie from Paul's evil influence.

Paul couldn't care less about the opinion of the Youngs and their like. He wanted for Josie what he couldn't have for himself—friendship.

Outside, the sun hung low as Paul headed to the Métro.

If only Lucie would let him help the failing store. He'd done the single most effective thing to secretly shore up the bookstore, but far better if it didn't need shoring up.

"Monsieur Aubrey?" Jacques Moreau called from behind.

"Yes, Moreau?"

The general foreman caught up to Paul and gestured to the driveway beside the main building. "Come with me."

"What's this about?" Paul followed the man in his thick overcoat and misshapen hat.

"When we get there."

Paul pressed his lips tight. For years, he'd put up with surliness because Moreau had a way with the men, like a father with a passel of boys. His affection for the workers was obvious, his instructions clear, his guidance firm, and his discipline terrifying.

Moreau passed the employee parking lot, empty since the occupation. Then he passed the parking lot for finished Auful trucks and zigzagged between outbuildings. He rounded a corner and stopped.

In the shadows Henri Silvestre and Jean-Pierre Dimont leaned against a shed, arms crossed.

Paul stopped short, and a tendril of fear wound into his gut. These three men had instigated the strike in '37. The occupation of the factory.

And almost two years ago, Paul had given away his pistol.

"Good evening." He retained an ounce of suspicion in his voice to let them know he was on guard.

"Bonsoir, Monsieur Aubrey," Silvestre said, and Dimont echoed. They didn't sound hostile.

Paul turned to Moreau and raised his eyebrows.

Moreau jammed his hands into his coat pockets. "Boucheron said nothing was wrong with the motor for the conveyor belt."

"I know." Why had Moreau led him across the property to tell him what the mechanic had already reported?

"He heard no strange sounds."

"I did. I don't want to take any chances."

"When Foulon damaged the steel press, you only told him not to do it again."

Paul's gloved fingers tingled around the handle of his attaché case. "You said a belt broke. I took your word for it."

"You told me not to talk to the men about the work slow-down."

Paul's breath came fast and shallow, and he eyed the inscrutable faces of his most seasoned workers. Communists all. Did they plan to turn him in to the German authorities?

He couldn't overcome them, but he could outrun them, and he firmed his jaw. "What's this about?"

Dimont passed him a newspaper clipping. A photo showed grinning German troops climbing out of a truck. "That's an Aubrey. They cut it down to an open truck, converted to a petrol engine, and removed the logo. But it's an Aubrey."

The lines of the truck—Paul knew them as well as his own hand, because that hand had drawn those lines. Now that hand clenched and shook. "They can't do this. It's in the contract."

Silvestre tapped his cigarette with his finger, and glowing ashes tumbled to the gravel. "We can't stop them."

Paul's teeth gritted. He'd always known it was possible, but now he knew it for a fact. They had no right. No right at all.

Moreau dragged the toe of his work boot through the gravel, drawing a line. "We can't stop them from converting our trucks, but we can decrease how many trucks they receive."

Paul stared at that line in the gravel and tracked Moreau's line of thought.

"We have ideas," Silvestre said in his raspy voice. "A plan."

His gaze snapped up to his stock foreman. "Do you expect me to turn a blind eye while you do what? Commit sabotage?"

Moreau swiped away the line. "We expect you to help."

"Help?" The cold cut through his overcoat. Was this a trap to get him arrested? Executed?

Dimont nudged Silvestre with a scrawny elbow. "He does not trust us."

"Why would I?" Paul gestured to the main building. "Four years ago, you occupied my factory. You're communists, *n'est ce pas*? The USSR is Germany's ally, and Moscow has instructed the French communists to cooperate. And you expect me to believe you?"

"That pact." Moreau spat on the ground. "We are French first, French always, and the boches are bad for France."

"They plunder our land," Silvestre said. "They keep our sons as prisoners of war."

Dimont's large eyes turned pleading. "We want the Germans to fail, to leave France. Is that not what you want?"

It was.

In those faces he'd often hated, he detected sincerity. Solidarity. A path to do good and resist evil. For some reason he did believe them. He did trust them.

Paul ran his tongue along the back of his teeth. "I refuse to endanger this company or the lives of the workers."

Silvestre puffed out a cloud of cigarette smoke. "We too prefer to avoid the firing squad."

"I'm glad we agree." Words stuck in his throat, but he shoved them out. "What do you propose?"

Moreau held up a stubby finger. "First, slow production."

"Work slowdowns, machinery repairs." Dimont pressed a hand to his flat belly. "An epidemic of dysentery."

"Second, slow conversion." Another stubby finger pointed at Paul. "Can you modify the gazogène installation to make it difficult to convert to petrol?"

Paul mentally flipped through designs. "Yes, I can. I will."

"Third, cause parts to wear out more quickly."

"Yes." The idea lit up in Paul's mind. "Our machine tools come from America, so we can't import parts or replacements. German parts don't fit. They need retooling."

"Each replacement part drains materials from the Reich," Silvestre said around the nub of his cigarette.

Dimont shrugged. "Many parts will wear down. Sad, but unavoidable."

"Parts in our trucks too," Moreau said. "So the Germans have to repair them more often."

"Hold on." Paul held up one hand. "We need to be careful. We need to coordinate these incidents, spread them out, implement them randomly, create good explanations for Colonel Schiller."

Moreau nodded his heavy head. "Every act must be approved by you and by me. Silvestre will coordinate efforts in his division, Dimont in his. Only a few of our most trusted men will be involved."

A long breath poured out, twisting white in the air before him. Everything about this plan ran counter to his values. Yet it aligned perfectly with those values.

Paul extended his hand to the man he'd once pointed a gun at. "Let's do it."

13

THURSDAY, MAY 8, 1941

When would spring weather arrive? A chilly breeze penetrated Lucie's burgundy suit as she sipped ersatz coffee outside Café de Flore with Marie-Claude and Véronique.

Two German officers passed along boulevard Saint-Germain. Lucie ignored them, but Marie-Claude lifted a wiggling little wave. "Bonjour, Klaus."

His handsome face split in a rakish grin. "Bonjour, Mademoiselle Desjardins."

Marie-Claude faced Lucie, turning her back on Klaus. "This weather—is it not horrible?"

"Yes." After the soldiers passed, Lucie gaped at her friend. "You know him?"

With a sly smile, Marie-Claude adjusted her Breton hat adorned with a spray of red flowers. "The more the soldiers like us, the more they come to the ballet. Lifar believes we can be ambassadors of dance to the Germans."

"Don't look at her like that, Lucie," Véronique said with a laugh. "It isn't collaboration. It's *le système D.*"

Le système de débrouillage—getting by, coping. It meant drinking coffee made of chicory, doing without eggs and milk, and buying wooden-soled shoes since leather was unavailable.

Lucie relaxed her features. She might not be friendly with German soldiers, but she sold them books.

Véronique fingered a blonde curl. "Did we tell you? Serge Lifar is preparing two new ballets to premiere in July—*La Princesse au Jardin* and *Le Chevalier et la Damoiselle.*"

"With my last name, I should be the princess," Marie-Claude said. "It's time I became a star."

"I hope so. You're so talented." Lucie patted her arm. But with ballerinas like Yvette Chauviré and Solange Schwarz and Lycette Darsonval, Lifar didn't have to look far to cast starring roles.

"Tell us how your own star is coming." Véronique lifted her coffee cup to Lucie.

Her newest puppet was indeed a star, Josie Aubrey's Feenee brought to papier-mâché life. Lucie scooted her chair on the sidewalk to allow a couple to pass. "I finished the wig. I cut colorful strips from our fabric scrap bag and soaked them in starch to make little curls."

"It is kind of you to help this little girl who has no mother, no friends." Véronique waved to a group of artists passing by with their portfolios.

Marie-Claude narrowed one hazel eye. "Wasn't the *collabo* who took you to dinner a widower with a little girl?"

Lucie stiffened. "This is his daughter."

Both ladies gasped.

Lucie stirred her coffee, although she could only dream of sugar and cream. "It isn't the child's fault her father is a collaborator."

"A factory owner who lives in the 16th arrondissement." Marie-Claude shuddered. "No feeling, no heart, no soul."

Only partly true, and Lucie sipped her coffee. She'd seen pain in his eyes. And his offer to help with her store showed heart. Perhaps she shouldn't have turned him down.

She opened her mouth to ask her friends' opinion, but they'd only tease her about wanting business help and imply she'd lose her standing in the artistic community.

Stores lined the boulevard—publishers and art supply shops and costume designers. The artistic community needed businesses to support it, businesses like hers, a place to find books, a place to read and discuss. It was one of the reasons she'd bought the store, one of the reasons she couldn't let it fail.

At the table to Lucie's left, a woman stood and departed, and a paper fluttered on the chair. Bold letters across the top proclaimed *Liberté*. A resistance newspaper!

Lucie averted her gaze, restrained her itching fingers, and plotted a way to sneak it into her purse when she left. Oh, the brave souls who wrote and printed and distributed the papers.

"Excuse me, Mademoiselle Girard?" The mystery man stood before her table, the résistant who'd told her never to talk to him again. Talking to her.

Lucie pulled herself together. "Bonjour, monsieur."

He tipped his shabby hat. "My apologies, mademoiselle. I come often to your beautiful bookstore, but I have never made a purchase. I am but a poor university student."

Lucie let a smile rise. "You are always welcome, no purchase required."

"I am grateful. To thank you, I want to give you a book. You may read it or sell it. It is for you, dear lady." With a slight bow, he held out a volume of Tennyson's poetry, the same volume she'd sold on Monday with a note tucked inside.

"How kind of you." Lucie held the book to her heart. "Tennyson is a favorite of mine. Merci beaucoup."

"*De rien*." He dipped his head to the ladies. "Au revoir, mesdemoiselles."

Véronique leaned closer. "What a sweet gift."

"It is." But Lucie had a hunch the sweetest part of the gift lay pressed between the leaves of the book. A gift she'd wait to discover until she was alone.

Everything about the evening was a test, even the time. Lucie scurried over the cobblestones on rue Royer-Collard.

The note in the book had read "Collard 5-A" with the writing facing page 22. And the letter *J* for jeudi with an arrow pointing to ten o'clock. She would arrive home after the curfew at twenty-three hours, which was a test. Would she risk arrest and a night in jail for this meeting?

She would.

At number 22 she entered. The door to the concierge's apartment was shut, so Lucie tiptoed upstairs to apartment 5-A.

Now came the tricky part. Under the street name had been a string of symbols—dash-dot-dot-dash-dot. Thinking it might be Morse code, she'd looked it up in a book in her store. It could be DN or NR, neither of which held a clue.

Or was it unrelated to Morse code?

The rhythm called to her, and she knocked once with her fist, rapped twice with her knuckles, fist, knuckles.

"Who is it?" a male voice asked.

"I come from the bookstore."

And the door opened.

The résistant shut the door behind her, then headed into the kitchen.

Lucie held her breath. The radio in the living room played Radio-Paris, the collabo announcer praising the Vichy government's agreement to allow German troops to cross French territory in Syria to reach Iraq, where they were fighting the British—and how in response, Germany had graciously lowered the tribute France paid to cover the cost of her own occupation.

The man peered out of the kitchen and gave her a quizzical look. "Come. Sit."

As soon as she'd approached him in the park, she'd committed herself, so she joined him in the kitchen.

He leaned against the wall and took a puff from a cigarette. "Do you still want to aid us?"

Us? So it was a group. Lucie lowered herself into a rickety wooden chair and gripped her purse in her lap. "Yes, I do."

"If you must call me something, call me Renard."

Renard—the fox. "Oui, monsieur."

Renard wore a black pullover sweater and gray trousers, and he regarded her with sharp, dark eyes. "Your store is a letter box, a place to pass messages. From now on, we will work with you, but only you. Tell Madame Martel nothing."

"I understand." Why did it feel more dangerous knowing she'd work alone?

"We will bring books to you for various reasons, as you said in the park." He motioned to her with his cigarette. "You will place the books behind your desk. You will never read the notes again. Do you understand?"

Her breath hitched, but she nodded. "Yes, sir."

"When our friends come to retrieve the messages, they must ask for the title and they must indicate they know it's behind the desk—a friend put it on hold, they called for it, now they have their wallet. This is vital."

"That makes sense." They had to keep the notes out of the wrong hands. "How do they know which book to ask for?"

"You do not need to know." He raked back the black curl on his forehead. "When they ask for a title, you must ask, 'Have you read this author before?' They must answer in these exact words—'No, but I am determined to better myself.' In English."

"All right."

"I am the customer." The cigarette dangled between Renard's long fingers. "I say to you, 'My friend recommended I read *Moby-Dick*, and he placed a copy on hold for me.' And you say . . . ?"

Lucie smiled as if behind the desk of her store. "Let me check. Have you read Melville before?"

"And the customer must say . . . ?"

"No, but I am determined to better myself."

"Good. If they don't answer correctly, you must not give them the book."

Lucie pressed her hand to her chest. "I'm sorry, monsieur. I sold the last copy."

Two streams of silver smoke blew from his nostrils. "If we must change the code phrase or if we must communicate with you, we will bring you a journal, not a book. We will ask the price, declare it too expensive, and leave. The message will be inside. You must read it privately, then burn it."

"All right." Lucie imprinted the information into her brain—lives might depend on her memory. "If I need to communicate with you—"

"You will not."

"But what if—"

"If you sense danger or believe messages should not be exchanged, move the potted plant from the mantel to the window. Remove it when it is safe. If you must cease operations permanently, place the pot on the sidewalk by the door."

Lucie breathed slowly, deliberately. She prayed she'd never have to do such a thing.

"In that situation," Renard said, "you will burn any remaining messages. Do you understand?"

"Yes." Her voice wavered.

"If you see me, you may greet me as you would any customer. That is all. Do you have any questions? This is your last opportunity to ask."

A smarter woman would have questions. But the only questions flying through her head had to do with safety, danger, consequences. And none of those mattered when she had the opportunity to do something of value.

"No, monsieur. No questions. No regrets."

14

SATURDAY, MAY 10, 1941

Josie tugged on Paul's hand. "Are we there yet?"

She'd run and skipped all the way from the Odéon Métro, and he put on the brakes and opened the door. "You almost missed it."

With a squeal, she ran into Green Leaf Books.

Lucie Girard floated over like a wisp of cotton candy. She wore a pink knee-length skirt, a pink sweater that crossed in front and tied at the waist . . . and toe shoes.

Paul flipped up a smile. "Going to dance class?"

"I'm performing a puppet show. I need to move." She leaned down to Josie. "Hello, Josie. I'm glad you're here."

Paul unbuttoned Josie's coat and slipped it off. "Toe shoes?"

"They're called pointe shoes. What a pretty dress. Like sunshine." Lucie fingered the yellow ribbon in Josie's hair. "You're my helper, so find a seat close to the front."

Josie ran to the children's section.

Lucie straightened up. A pink band held light brown waves off her face. And that face—her forehead puckered and her lips tucked in.

Paul wasn't welcome. "You said parents could run errands. I'll go to a café."

"I owe you an apology." She fiddled with the sweater's ribbon hanging over her hip. "I don't approve of your actions, but you didn't actually lie to me. I was rude. Please forgive me."

"All forgiven." She'd made it clear where he stood, but it was just as well. With the increasing secrets and danger in his life, a new relationship wouldn't be wise.

The puckering and lip rolling hadn't stopped. "You'll think I apologized because—oh, I might as well get on with it. I shouldn't have refused your offer to help with the store. I can't lose it. I can't. Could you stay? I could really use your help."

She looked so tiny, and the urge to help swelled inside. "I'd be honored. What do you need help with?"

"I don't know."

"You don't know?"

Her nose wrinkled. "The Greenblatts—Hal ran the front of the store and Erma the back. I do Hal's job, and Madame Martel is supposed to do Erma's—money and papers and all." Her voice drifted low.

Paul lowered his too. "Supposed to? Ah, the rent going unpaid."

"The office—I can't make head or tails of it. Could you look at it?"

"Yes." Paul spotted Madame Martel in an armchair on the far side of the counter. "Please introduce me to your assistant."

Lucie's cheeks grew pinker than her outfit. "She wouldn't like that."

Puzzle pieces shuffled into place, and he gestured toward the armchair. "Please introduce me and inform her of what I'm doing."

After Lucie drew in a long breath, she led Paul to the woman, who sat curled up with a book. "Excuse me, Madame Martel. I'd like you to meet Mr. Aubrey. He's a businessman."

The assistant rose and shook his hand. Almost as tall as Paul and big boned, she had a forceful look, but not unfriendly. Lucie offered no further information.

Paul took over. "Please excuse me, madame, but I couldn't help but overhear the conversation with the concierge the other day. I've offered business help to Miss Girard."

Madame Martel shot a withering glance at Lucie, and Lucie . . . withered.

Steel entered Paul's smile. "She accepted out of concern for the store, for her livelihood, and for yours. While Miss Girard conducts the Children's Hour, I'll look at the files and books." He gave her an unbending gaze but bowed his head in respect.

Her face darkened. "You will find no irregularities. If you think—"

"Ah no, madame. I'm only looking for ways to economize or increase efficiency."

Madame Martel harrumphed, plopped into her chair, and raised her book. "Don't make a mess."

Lucie led him into the office.

Papers covered most of the desk, and Paul let out a low whistle. How could he make it messier?

Lucie eased a leather ledger from the edge of the pile. "I think this is what you want. And Erma's files are here." She opened a cabinet, showing off neat lines of folders.

"Thanks. I'll look around."

Lucie stepped out of the office, then glanced back. "By the way, I know how much is in the cashbox."

Paul grinned. "I assure you, I have no need for cash."

"That's never stopped a rich person from stealing before." She swept away to the children's section, where several families gathered.

Paul chuckled. If Lucie could direct that sass to Madame Martel, the store might stand a chance.

After he hung up his and Josie's coats on hooks, he thumbed

through the files and took notes. From the 1920s to May 1940, the files were in perfect order. Of course, records were sparse from May to July of 1940, when over two-thirds of Paris's population had fled. Records were filed regularly in the autumn, then slumped off in the winter.

Paul scooted a pile on the desk to clear space, and he opened the ledger. He angled his chair so he could see out the office doorway to where Josie and five other children sat on a mat.

Lucie closed a storybook. "Who would like a puppet show?"

Six small hands shot up.

"Oh, good." Lucie stood and set her chair aside. "Today's story is special because the author is here. Josie, would you please stand?"

With his hand on the open ledger, Paul gasped. Josie's story? The previous Saturday, Josie had told Lucie her Feenee stories for half an hour.

Josie sprang to her feet. "My story?"

"Yes." Lucie patted her shoulder. "I know the children will enjoy it as much as I did."

No, they wouldn't, and Paul groaned. Whatever prestige Josie had gained by being Miss Girard's helper would evaporate when the children heard the strange story. *Lord, don't let them laugh.*

Lucie rummaged in a box, then spun to the children with her hands behind her back. "Once there was a little girl named Feenee. She thought of herself as an ordinary little girl, but she was anything but ordinary."

With a flourish, Lucie whipped out one hand with a puppet—curls of every color sprang from its papier-mâché head. "Sometimes Feenee's hair was purple, sometimes yellow, and sometimes as green as the table beside you."

"That's Feenee!" Josie cried.

Paul cringed.

"She's so pretty," a little girl said.

104

"I think so too." Lucie made Feenee dance back and forth, cloth legs swinging under the puppet's dress. "Some children laughed at her, but Feenee was brave and made friends with the nice children instead. Then one day, a horrible thing happened."

"What?" a boy cried.

"The rock-monsters came to town." Lucie thrust out her other hand, covered with a gray sock with a scowling face. "They came clomp, clomp, clomping into town."

Paul's hand curled around the ledger, but the children weren't snickering. They were engaged.

Lucie rose to her tiptoes and darted like a leaf in the wind. "The children were afraid and hid. But Feenee was brave. She marched right up to the rock-monsters."

A big step forward, and Lucie raised both puppets. "'You rock-monsters don't belong here. You need to leave.' Oh, the rock-monsters were angry. They jumped on Feenee."

The bookseller jumped and spun, her feet and skirt in a blur. "They ate Feenee's toes! They ate Feenee's knees! They ate Feenee's legs!"

Paul couldn't stop watching, even with rows of numbers before him.

Lucie came to a stop. While spinning and jumping, she'd detached the puppet's legs. "Oh no! Poor Feenee."

"Poor Feenee," the children said.

"All seemed lost." Lucie sank to her knees. "But then a funny thing happened. She felt a tickle in the middle of her back. Suddenly wings sprang out!" Lucie attached wings to the puppet.

"Feenee flapped her wings once, and she rose from the ground." So did Lucie, revealing the rock puppet under her knees. "She flapped twice and rose above the rock-monsters. Then over and over, creating a wind." Lucie waved her arms like wings and twirled around.

Paul couldn't keep his eyes off her. She didn't dance to call attention to herself but to the puppets and the story, to move the children's hearts.

"She flapped and flapped, and she blew those big, clomping rock-monsters out of town." Lucie swung her leg practically to the ceiling, and the rock puppet sailed over the children's heads.

They cheered and clapped.

Lucie dropped to her knees again. "So, my dear boys and girls, never be sad that you're different. Be glad. And be brave. And if you're sad because you've lost something . . ." She fingered the puppet where the legs had hung. "Remember sometimes we have to lose what we most love before we can find what we most need." And she stroked the puppet's wings.

Paul's throat clogged. He'd lost so much. Maybe that wasn't the end of his story. Maybe it was only the beginning.

Lucie leaned toward the children. "Make sure you come back next week. I have another story for you about Feenee and Monsieur Meow. Josie wrote it for me."

The children looked at Josie with admiration. At his little girl.

That was her story.

Paul thumped back in the chair, his mind spinning. Lucie had fleshed out the story and animated it. But Josie had created it. Even the moral. Hadn't Josie said Feenee couldn't possibly have both legs and wings? That had come from the mind of a four-year-old child. His child. His child whom he'd thought odd.

That four-year-old leaned around the other children, seeking his gaze and his approval.

"All right, boys and girls." Lucie pulled over a box. "Would you like to play? I have blocks and wooden animals waiting for you and your imagination."

Josie ran to the office, and Paul met her in the doorway. "Daddy, did you see? Did you see my Feenee story?" Her smile beamed, but her eyebrows drew together in apprehension.

106

Paul scooped her into a giant hug. "I saw. That was good. Such a good story."

More words filled his throat, but she needed to see his face when he said them. Paul eased down to one knee, set his daughter's feet on the ground, and grasped her by the shoulders. "I am so proud of you, lemon drop. You're a very clever girl."

The wonder of a father's approval sank in, relaxed her countenance, and shone back at him threefold.

An older girl ran over. "Josie, come play with us."

"Can I, Daddy?" She hopped, making the yellow bow on her head bounce.

"Yes, you may."

She ran off with her new friend.

Lucie's ribbon-wrapped ankles stood before him. Shapely ankles. "How bad is it?"

Bad? Nothing bad about the story, the puppet show, or those ankles. He lifted his gaze to her face, where it belonged. She frowned into the office.

Ah yes, the office.

Paul stood and joined her frowning. "I need another hour to go through the ledger, another for that pile. Then I'll need about an hour to sit down with you and give my analysis."

"That won't work." Lucie glanced past him. "It's Madame Martel's day off. She only came in to help during Children's Hour. Now I need to mind the store."

Indeed, parents roamed with books that needed to be rung up. "Are you open tomorrow?"

"On Sunday? No."

"Perfect. Could I come by after church—with Josie?"

Lucie stared at the desk, her mouth tight. "Only if you bring Josie."

His tiny chaperone. "Thank you for what you did for her today."

"It was a pleasure. She has a gift."

"A gift." Paul rubbed the back of his neck and chuckled. "Too bad it won't be useful when she grows up."

"Useful?" Fire burned in her hazel eyes, but Paul preferred it to ice somehow. "Isn't that typical of you bourgeoisie? A gift is only good if it makes money."

He grinned. "Isn't that typical of you artistes? No gift that actually makes money is good."

"Say what you want." She matched his smile. "I have the Lord on my side."

This could be interesting. He leaned against the wall and crossed his arms. "Please elaborate."

She matched his posture, leaning against the wall on the far side of the doorway. "Not everything God created is useful, but it's all good. He didn't have to create beauty, but he did. He didn't have to create color, but he did. He didn't have to create music, but he did. None of it useful. Then he created us in his creative image with the ability to make beauty and color and music. It might not be useful, but it's good."

"Good . . ." he whispered. On the floor, his little girl sat surrounded by blocks and children. Children who accepted her.

Maybe her gift was useful after all.

15

SUNDAY, MAY 11, 1941

Seated at her little green table, Lucie chewed the last bite of the ham sandwich Paul Aubrey had brought. He might not be fat, as so many collabos were, but he certainly ate well.

She sneaked a glance to her office, where Paul rustled papers. His cook's elderly mother lived in the country, where food was more plentiful, and the cook stocked the Aubrey pantry so Josie had enough cheese and meat to grow.

On the floor, Josie lined up the wooden animals by color, her Feenee stories exhausted over lunch.

Did that cook's mother know she was paid with German money?

Lucie forced the morsel down her throat. This morning at church, Alice Young told Lucie she'd seen Paul coming out of Maxim's restaurant with two German officers. Paul didn't just sell to them because he had to—he sought out their business and dined with them.

Was Lucie a hypocrite for accepting his help? For eating his sandwich? Maybe, but keeping the store open kept resistance messages flowing.

She grinned and wiped her mouth. What would Herr Aubrey say to that?

A chair scuffed, then Mr. Collaborator leaned against the doorjamb in his white shirt, silk tie, and dark gray trousers and suit vest. "I've gone through what I can. Ready for a business lesson?"

Lucie groaned. Why couldn't he wave a magic business wand and make it go away? "I suppose so."

Paul glanced past her to Josie. "All right, jujube. You have plenty of toys and books."

The little girl nodded and made two monkeys talk to each other.

Lucie straightened the jacket of her golden-brown suit and joined Paul in the office.

He pulled a chair to the end of the desk for her, sat behind the desk, and tapped his pen on a notepad. "In a nutshell, your store is wounded, but not mortally."

"That's good." She crossed her ankles.

"As in any struggling business, you need to cut expenses and increase income." He tipped his head toward Bernadette's hill of papers, revealing the perfect side part in his smooth brown hair. "In addition, organization."

Lucie shuddered. "I don't even know where to start."

"You just need to go through systematically. The bills and receipts checked against the ledger, then—"

Lucie plopped her hand on the pile and fixed her gaze on Paul. "You don't understand. I don't know how, and it's no use teaching me. I didn't go to university. I didn't go to a lycée. I have what you in the States call an eighth-grade education. Maybe seventh."

Brown eyes widened. "Your father's an architect. Why'd he let you drop out of school?"

"I didn't drop out." She folded her hands in her lap. "I went to ballet school. At that time in France, school was only required until the age of twelve."

"Twelve? But you're so well-read."

"The Greenblatts gave me a reading list. That was much better than school. I was never good at learning, especially numbers. It's no use teaching me."

Paul crossed arms encased in crisp white sleeves. "I find that hard to believe, but that isn't the point. You don't need to learn bookkeeping—you just need to learn how to manage."

"Manage?"

"Manage." He leveled an authoritative gaze, but not patronizing. "I don't do every job in my factory, nor do I know how. My job is to manage my employees, to provide the tools and time they need, to lay out expectations, and to make sure they fulfill them. Your job is the same. Now, how long has Madame Martel been with you?"

Lucie shifted in her seat. "She's been with the store since I came to Paris."

Paul's lips curved up. "When you were a little girl. Ah yes. Everything's becoming clear. And you've owned the store a year now?"

"A year in June."

"From what I see, Madame Martel has adequate bookkeeping skills." He flipped a page in the notepad. "Everything was done properly for about four months after you took over. Then she slacked off, getting worse each month. She needs management."

Lucie sat up taller. "I refuse to boss her around."

"Good. That rarely works." He patted the ledger. "She just needs schedules and deadlines, and you need to follow through."

Everything squirmed inside her. "That wouldn't work."

Paul rested his elbows on the armrests and shot her an understanding smile. "Because she's older, she's worked here longer, she treats you like a child, and she intimidates you."

"Intimi . . ." Lucie's jaw dropped. "I wouldn't say that."

"I've seen it. But"—he pointed his pen at her—"it isn't for a general lack of courage on your part. Many of my employees find me intimidating, but you had no trouble telling me what to do." Amusement danced in his eyes.

She smiled a little. "That was easy."

"You have a backbone. Use it with her." He waved a hand over the mountain of paper. "First, give her a week to clear this desk. Tell her you'll mind the store so she has time."

Bernadette wouldn't like that. And Lucie couldn't even picture herself "managing" her.

Paul scooted his chair closer. "Listen. You're the owner. You pay her to do a job. You have the right to tell her to do that job. Even you artistic sorts only get paid if you work, right?"

Lucie groaned, but he was right. A ballerina who read books during practices would be cut from the corps. "I guess I can do that."

"I know you can." He turned the notepad to her. "From the files and ledger, I made a list of regular tasks—paying bills, ordering books, etc. Look it over. Add to it. Decide which are her tasks and which are yours. Assign deadlines. Remind her of her tasks and make sure they're completed."

"Regimentation. Discipline." Lucie screwed up her mouth. "I'm not good at that."

Paul drew back and hiked up his eyebrows. "You tell yourself a lot of lies."

"I beg your pardon!"

He flipped his hands open. "I don't know much about ballet, but on stage I saw you work together in precision—regimented. And didn't you have regular practices? That requires discipline."

"Yes, but that was for art."

"The point is, you can be regimented and disciplined. Apply it in a new field."

She wrinkled her nose at all the nasty papers.

Paul crossed his ankle over his knee. "If I may quote a certain ballerina bookseller—I have the Lord on my side."

A laugh escaped. "Oh, do you?"

"I do." Crinkles formed around his eyes. "I agree with what you said yesterday, but only to a point. Yes, the Lord creates, but always for a purpose. Even color and music and beauty serve a purpose—to inspire awe and turn our eyes to the Lord. And creation operates according to laws—most of them mathematical, by the way. So embracing discipline is a way of embracing God."

His vision of God—of life—was so different. Did that make him wrong?

She gave her head a little shake. Why would she take theology lessons from a man who earned profits by exploiting workers, who did business with evil men?

Paul opened the ledger. "After Madame Martel finishes her reconciliations, I'd like another look at this so I can assess current expenses. But nothing strikes me as unnecessary. That's good."

"All right." Lucie swallowed to moisten her mouth. She might not need his theology lesson, but she did need his business lesson.

"Income is your main problem." He shifted his mouth to one side. "The British are in internment camps, most Americans have fled, wages are stagnant, and prices have risen. These all undermine your sales."

A sigh flowed out. "I know."

"Let's look for creative ways to increase business. How much did the Children's Hour increase sales yesterday?"

"I have no idea."

"You use a sales ledger by the cash register. May I see it?"

"Sure." Erma had taught her to immediately log each sale.

Lucie led Paul out of the office. Josie lay on a blanket Paul had brought, fast asleep, with wooden animals around her.

Lucie turned to Paul, pressed one finger to her lips, and quietly made her way behind the cash register. From the open shelving under the desk, she pulled out the sales log.

"What are these? Returns?" Paul scrutinized the half-dozen books waiting for résistants. He picked one up.

"No." She snatched it from his hand. "They're—they're holds, not returns."

"All right." A question turned up his voice.

Lucie cringed and returned the book and its precious message. She'd reacted too abruptly, calling attention to her resistance work. "I'm sorry, but my friend has waited ages for this book. She'd be heartbroken if someone else bought it. Now, the ledger. What would you like to see?"

She set it on the desk and opened it.

Paul ran his finger down the page. "Date, title, price—nice. See, you can follow routines."

His grin was so close, so personal, and so very warm. It would be easy to forget who he was. She feigned interest in the log. "It's for a good cause."

"It's all for a good cause, so stop telling yourself you can't do it. Now, let me see . . ." He muttered numbers as his finger moved down the page. He turned backward in the log, more muttering, backward again.

"Good." He faced her and set his elbow on the desk. "Yesterday's sales were three times higher than the previous Saturday, four times higher than the Saturday before that."

"That's nice."

"Nice?" He laughed. "It's excellent. The store is inviting. When people come inside, they buy. You just need to bring them through your doors. The Children's Hour was excellent. Keep that going. Set up other events. Tell your customers, encourage them to invite friends, spread the word in American institutions in town."

His enthusiasm was contagious, and yet the whole thing left a sour taste in her mouth.

Paul cocked his head to one side. "Don't look at me like that."

"Like what?"

"Like I'm asking you to sell your grandmother. Business isn't inherently evil. You provide goods that people want and need. In exchange, they pay you money so you can buy what you want and need."

He made it sound innocent and simple. And maybe it was. "I see. I do."

His smile grew, not gloating but rejoicing with her.

Why did agreeing with Paul Aubrey feel more dangerous than aiding the resistance?

16

SATURDAY, JUNE 14, 1941

Nothing lonelier than a crowd like this.

With a drink in hand, Paul studied the "notables" sauntering through the ornate reception room in the German Institute in the Hôtel de Monaco, formerly the Polish Embassy.

In his years at Harvard, he'd perfected the appearance of imbibing without actually doing so. In a room swirling with German officers and administrators, French collaborators, and American opportunists, he needed his wits about him.

He passed a French soprano warbling a tune by the grand piano and a group praising German advances in Crete and Egypt. He gave the men a nod and passed by. Nothing that Jim Duffy didn't already know.

Ladies in colorful gowns and men in tuxedos and uniforms filled the room decorated with painted ceilings and priceless artwork.

At society events Paul missed Simone more than ever. At even the dullest function, she'd be at his side, sparkling one moment, droll the next.

Today marked the first anniversary of the occupation of Paris. Tuesday would be the anniversary of Simone's death.

Heaviness shoved his heart hard against his lungs, hindering his breathing.

He stepped to the window to collect himself. Books lay on a small carved table, and he picked one up—a volume of German poetry. Of course. The German Institute had been founded by Otto Abetz, the German ambassador to occupied France, to promote German culture in France. And to censor French culture.

Poetry. He set down the book and swirled his tumbler of amber liquid. At that moment, Lucie Girard was hosting a poetry reading. Even though Paul didn't care for poetry, he'd still rather be at Green Leaf Books.

Paul gazed at the heavy blackout curtains as if he could see past them to the manicured gardens. In the past month he'd been helping with the bookstore, Lucie didn't like him any better, but at least she accepted his business advice.

The office desk was now clean. Madame Martel gave him stony glares when he brought Josie to Children's Hour, but he didn't care.

"Paul darling!" Mary de la Chapelle swept up in a long silvery gown, and she offered him a cheek to kiss.

Paul complied, his nose filling with her sophisticated perfume. "Comtesse de la Chapelle, you look luminous."

Well into her fifties, the blonde beauty, a former Philadelphia socialite, had married into French nobility after the last war. One sculpted eyebrow lifted, and she looked Paul up and down. "So debonair. If I were still in my prime . . ."

Paul laid his hand over his heart. "My dear lady, your prime lies in your future."

The countess gave him an arch look, which if rumors were true, had lured many lovers into her snare. "Don't let the count hear you talk like that."

He took a mock sip of his beverage. "Any news from the States?"

117

She sniffed. "Those blasted British keep seizing our mail when it passes through Bermuda—off our very own ships. Still treating us Americans like wayward children. Have they forgotten we won our independence?"

"I wonder."

"One good piece of news." Full red lips curved up on one side. "Charles Lindbergh is speaking at rallies for America First."

"I heard." After the famed aviator visited Germany in the late 1930s, he'd become enthralled with Hitler's policies. Now he'd joined the isolationist group determined to keep America out of the war.

The countess pressed red-tipped fingernails to her chin. "Maybe people will listen to him and stop Roosevelt's warmongering. The man believes all Churchill's propaganda."

"He certainly does." The president kept pushing Congress to aid beleaguered Britain.

A spark flashed in blue eyes. "Doesn't the president consider how war would affect the American Colony in Paris? Why, we'd end up interned like the British, our property and assets seized."

"We mustn't let that happen," Paul said with a frown. Although war would have far graver consequences than disrupting the lives of a few thousand Americans in Paris, Paul took it into consideration. He wanted to leave France before war was declared, but predicting when that would happen was like predicting the stock market.

Today's paper announced the sinking of an American cargo ship. The German-controlled French newspapers declared the British sank the *Robin Moor* to entice America into the war, but the US government blamed a German U-boat.

"Aubrey!" a man called from halfway across the room— André Rousselot, a member of the *comité d'organisation* for the automobile industry and an excellent source of information.

Paul gave the Comtesse de la Chapelle a slight bow. "Please excuse me, dear lady."

"I'll still be here." She sashayed away.

Paul sent Rousselot a lift of his chin to signal he was on his way, and he worked his way through the crowd.

When had Rousselot decided to call him Aubrey? At Harvard he'd gone by his last name because his fraternity president was also a Paul.

He missed his fraternity brothers. Peter Lang was teaching German in the States, and Henning—more properly, Baron Henrik Ahlefeldt—Paul hadn't heard a word from the Dane since the Germans occupied Copenhagen.

Although Rousselot had to be in his sixties, no gray flecked his thatch of black hair. "How goes it at Aubrey Automobiles?"

"The orders come in faster than we can fill them."

About six feet behind Rousselot, Col. Gerhard Schiller conversed with a French couple. Paul sent him a smile and a lift of his tumbler, and Schiller returned the gesture.

Rousselot took a long swig from his glass. "Good days for our industry, *n'est ce pas?*"

Paul gave him a mischievous smile. "I'd rather build race cars."

Rousselot chuckled and rested his tumbler on his protruding belly. "Wouldn't we all? At least we're building for a good cause."

"Good? I make ugly delivery trucks."

A waiter passed with a tray, and Rousselot exchanged his empty glass for a full one. "Most of us aren't burdened by your Neutrality Acts. We're able to do more."

The opening Paul desired. He angled himself so he could see Schiller and shrugged as if he didn't believe Rousselot. "What can we do? We make bicycles and delivery trucks and civilian aircraft. How does that help France?"

Rousselot's dark eyes had a bleary look, and he stepped closer, his liquored breath assaulting Paul. "My company built 1074 aircraft engines in May. They are for German transport planes. But they also fit bombers. What our friends do with them—what is that to me?"

Paul faked a smile and a sip, and he eased back to draw Rousselot farther from Schiller. "You're doing a great service. France is unarmed, and I don't trust the Soviets. Only Germany can protect us. I hope your company is not alone."

"Not at all. I am on the organization committee, you know." His chest puffed out.

"I know." Paul gave him an admiring look. As a lady passed, he used the opportunity to back up more.

Rousselot brushed droplets off his bushy mustache and stepped closer. "You will be pleased with what we do to protect our nation."

He listed companies, products, numbers. Paul listened intently, itching for pen and paper, committing numbers to memory, senses tingling with excitement and danger.

This would be his most detailed report for Duffy ever. With the US Embassy on the place de la Concorde officially closed, Paul now took his reports to the few remaining embassy officials in their rooms in the Hôtel Bristol. The US military would be thrilled with this list of war matériel being produced in France for the Germans.

Rousselot hailed a waiter and exchanged glasses. "Now our work can aid France directly."

"The Paris Protocols, oui?"

Pride flashed in his eyes. "A brilliant piece of diplomacy. Now the Germans respect us. They allow us to defend our empire abroad from the British and the so-called Free French under that traitor Charles de Gaulle."

Paul made a scoffing noise. "Nothing but a brand-new brigadier general, and he calls himself the leader of France."

"As if anyone could replace Marshal Pétain, the true leader of France."

"Indeed." On his second day as prime minister, Pétain had

led France into an undignified surrender, and now he led a government in Vichy that danced to Germany's tune.

Rousselot swallowed a significant portion of his drink. "The nerve of de Gaulle, sending troops to help the British invade Syria. That's French territory!"

From what Paul could sift from the censored newspapers, the Allies only invaded Syria because Pétain allowed the Luftwaffe to use Syrian airfields to bomb British bases in Iraq. One mess after another. "Never mind, Rousselot. The true France will prevail."

"Yes, she shall. And you"—Rousselot clinked his glass to Paul's—"you tell your Roosevelt to stay out of Europe's business."

Paul steadied the man's wobbling shoulder. "You overestimate my influence, my friend."

With a laugh, Rousselot left, and he hailed another waiter.

Paul joined Schiller and the couple—the owner of a fascist newspaper and his wife—and he dove into the conversation about music.

Let Schiller see Paul as congenial. Then when Schiller heard engine parts in Aubrey trucks wore out quickly—due to a corrosive agent added to the lubricant—Schiller wouldn't suspect a thing.

Paul laughed at Schiller's joke. The commissioner didn't seem wise to the German army's conversion and use of Paul's trucks. Last week Paul had told Schiller he'd received complaints about the gazogène generators bouncing loose, so Paul had the generators welded firmly to the body of the truck.

Schiller had been pleased. He wouldn't be when the Wehrmacht realized removing the generators would cause major structural damage.

So Paul laughed at jokes and praised Schiller's taste in music and made references to Harvard to recall their shared alma mater.

As if they were friends. Allies.

When they were anything but.

17

SATURDAY, JUNE 14, 1941

Saint-Yves clasped Lucie's hand. "Merci, mademoiselle. It was a beautiful evening."

She smiled at the poet who refused to use either a first name or punctuation. "Thank you for making it so."

Several of his fans bustled him away to pepper him with questions.

Green Leaf Books glowed in electric light and buzzed with conversation after Saint-Yves's reading of Walt Whitman's poetry.

In the corner, Lt. Emil Wattenberg browsed books. He wore a civilian suit and hadn't spoken, thank goodness. A single one of his accented words would ruin the evening.

Why had he come? Because he loved poetry? Or to spy on the clientele?

In the past week, several resistance messages had been exchanged each day, one right under Wattenberg's nose, which had been thrilling. Renard changed the code phrases the next day.

Marie-Claude and Véronique came over and kissed Lucie's cheeks.

"A rousing success, *ma chére*," Véronique said. "Saint-Yves's reading was inspired."

Marie-Claude adjusted her enormous hat over her black curls and wrinkled her nose. "I still can't believe you charged admission. You're turning into a typical bourgeois American."

Lucie bristled inside but gave her an innocent smile. "So the next time I go to the ballet, it'll be free?"

Her roommate blinked. "Well, no."

"Ballerinas like to eat, no? So do poets. But Saint-Yves's books are banned, and he cannot be published. At least I can pay him a pittance to read someone else's poems."

Véronique nudged her fellow dancer. "Lucie had to rent chairs too."

"I did." And yes, the store would keep part of the proceeds. Lucie had resisted Paul's suggestion to charge admission, but she didn't regret doing so. The fee was a trifle, and Bernadette was busy ringing up purchases.

Edward and Betty Hartman caught Lucie's eye over Marie-Claude's shoulder.

Lucie excused herself and joined the American lawyer and his pretty redheaded wife. "Thank you for coming, Mr. and Mrs. Hartman."

Edward's smile bent his sandy mustache. "We're glad you sent the reminder card. We'd forgotten we had a store subscription. If I hadn't come in to renew, I wouldn't have heard about the poetry reading."

Betty leaned on her husband's arm. "And I never would have known about the Children's Hour. Margie and Annie had a wonderful time today."

"They're a delight." Over a dozen children had attended this afternoon.

Betty laughed, low and musical. "The reminder card was darling. 'Don't let your green leaf fall,' and that darling cartoon leaf and the darling expression on his face as he fell."

Madame Martel would have made a snippy comment about Betty's need for a thesaurus, but Lucie thanked her. Lucie had designed those cards years ago for Hal and Erma, but she'd forgotten about them. Only when Paul discovered how many subscriptions had lapsed did she remember them.

Lucie's tongue tickled, eager to tell the Hartmans that the idea to mail the cards and the idea for the poetry reading had come from a man they snubbed every Sunday.

But Paul wouldn't want that. Once he'd stated, with a pained expression, that he didn't want his reputation to harm the store.

Betty went on and on about how her daughters had gone on and on about Children's Hour, and Lucie smiled on and on.

When Paul had dropped off Josie that afternoon, Lucie commented how happy the girl was to see the other children.

Paul had looked surprised. "She's happy to see you. You read her like a book. I—I can't even crack the cover."

Such sadness, such regret in those handsome brown eyes, so Lucie kept her tone soft. "Her gifts come from the Lord as surely as yours do. When you truly accept that . . ."

"I'm trying," he'd said.

She knew he was. Oh, why did he have to be so appealing? How could he be kind and honorable in some ways and despicable in others?

After Children's Hour, she'd reminded him he was welcome at the poetry reading, but he'd said he had another engagement. In a tight voice.

Lucie's mind conjured up the worst names—Otto von Stülpnagel and Otto Abetz and Pierre Laval. "I don't want to know about it, do I?" she'd asked.

"No," Paul had said. "You do not."

Laughter arose behind her, and Charles Charbonnier and Geneviève Plessis grabbed Lucie's arms and pulled her away from the Hartmans.

"Excuse me," Lucie called back to the couple, and they smiled and waved her away.

Charles and Geneviève released her by the front window.

"What are you doing?" Lucie said with a teasing smile.

Geneviève pressed the back of her hand to her forehead and heaved a sigh straight from one of her theatrical performances at the Comédie Française. "Rescuing you from pretentious Americans."

Lucie gave the brunette a mock glare and set her hands on her hips. "Have you forgotten I'm American?"

"Oh, but you do not have a pretentious bone in your body."

"And a fine body it is." Charles leered at her legs.

Lucie pointedly took a step backward.

Charles laughed, his dark hair brushing the shoulders of his oversized suit. "Thank you for giving Saint-Yves a gig. Now he can afford wine to cry into."

Lucie gazed toward the poet, clad in a red velvet jacket and entertaining starry-eyed students from the Sorbonne. "Maybe he should write about happier subjects than existential angst."

"Ah, but existential angst makes him happy," Geneviève said.

"True." Lucie stepped aside to let a couple pass. "Speaking of angst, how's Jerzy? I haven't seen him lately. I didn't expect him tonight, but . . ."

Charles and Geneviève gaped at each other.

"Have you not heard?" Geneviève said, her voice low and her forehead creased. "He was arrested in the *rafle*."

"No." The word plummeted from Lucie's mouth. A month earlier, over three thousand Jewish men, mostly from Poland, had been rounded up and sent to camps in northern France. It was all she could do not to march up to Wattenberg and pitch him out of her store. "The Germans arrested him?"

"The Germans?" Charles crossed his arms. "They ordered the arrests, but the French police carried them out."

Lucie knew that. But now it gnawed at her fresh. Dear angsty Jerzy. He'd never hurt a soul. And now he was locked away.

Geneviève clucked her tongue. "I'm sorry, Lucie. We ruined your glorious evening."

"We'll cheer you up at La Méditerranée," Charles said. "It's time to send people to the restaurant anyway."

"It is." With her performance face concealing her heartbreak, Lucie thanked those who were departing, reminded friends to join the party at La Méditerranée, then relieved Bernadette at the cash register so the assistant could escort Saint-Yves to the restaurant.

After the last guest left, Lucie locked the cash register and the front door. Tomorrow after church, she'd count the cash, clean the store, and return the rental chairs.

Night sounds drifted to her as she made her way to the place de l'Odéon in the deep darkness. A violin played. Families laughed, argued. Music from Radio-Paris floated down. Although everyone listened to the BBC, no one would allow it to be heard on the street.

"Excuse me, Miss Girard." A man's voice came from behind her.

She whirled around, her hand pressed to her chest.

Emil Wattenberg stepped up, his hat low over his darkened face. "Pardon me. I did not mean to frighten you."

"I'm not frightened. Just startled." But her heart thudded against her fingers.

Wattenberg motioned down the street. "I do not want to stop you, only to talk to you."

"Oh?" She resumed walking, cringing inside. Had he discovered a resistance note? Would he ask to help with the rent again? Or for a date?

"I did not want to talk to you with your friends. They will not welcome me as you have."

Welcome? She'd ignored him all evening. Lucie murmured

to encourage him to continue. She didn't want to be seen with a German officer, even one in civilian clothes.

"You know I work for the German Embassy," Wattenberg said. "You are familiar with the Otto List."

"The list of over one thousand books the Germans have banned from sale in France? Yes, I'm familiar with it." Sarcasm crept into her voice.

"On July 1, the list will have more titles."

Lucie's steps dragged, her shoes shuffling on the pavement. More books for the Germans or their lackeys, the French police, to confiscate. "How many more?"

"You will not like it. The list will include all books by English or American authors published after 1870."

"Americans?" Lucie sucked in a sharp breath. "But we're neutral."

"It is—what is the word?—the influence of Jews and Negroes, of communists, of modernism." His voice warped with disapproval—disapproval of censorship or of those influences?

"All books . . . 1870 . . ." So many books. So many wonderful and lovely books.

"I wanted to warn you," Wattenberg said in his harsh German accent.

She huffed. "So I can prepare to turn over half my stock to be burned."

"I am afraid so." At least he had the good grace to sound sad. "I will leave now. Good night, Miss Girard."

"Good night, Lieutenant."

The street opened up to the place de l'Odéon, facing the dark and brooding theater. The smell of seafood wafted over from La Méditerranée, its blue awnings blackened by night. But the rich scent passed right through her.

"What now?" she whispered to the moonless sky.

Just when she'd found ways to increase sales. Just when

Bernadette had cleaned the desk, although with much dilly-dallying. Just when Lucie was getting used to her schedule of tasks.

Now she'd lose half her stock. Half her sales.

All her hard work in vain.

18

SUNDAY, JUNE 15, 1941

Organ music flowed over Paul, washing away the tension of spying at the German Institute. Of lying.

> Abide with me—fast falls the eventide,
> The darkness deepens—Lord, with me abide;
> When other helpers fail and comforts flee,
> Help of the helpless, O abide with me!
>
> Hold Thou Thy word before my closing eyes,
> Shine thru the gloom and point me to the skies;
> Heav'n's morning breaks and earth's vain shadows
>   flee—
> In life, in death, O Lord, abide with me!

Standing on the pew, Josie swayed in rhythm and studied the hymnal, her bell-like voice chiming in on a few phrases. Paul moved his finger under the lyrics to help her learn to read.

Edmund Pendleton played the final chord, the music reverberating to the neogothic ceiling. Then he said the benediction and dismissed the congregation.

Paul took his time returning the hymnal and tying on Josie's hat. He'd be the last to leave.

"Mr. Aubrey, may I ask a favor?" Mr. Pendleton stood before him in a dark suit. "Would you please meet with me in the pastor's apartment? It's on the fourth floor of the church house. Perhaps in twenty minutes?"

Paul tried to interpret the church director's strained expression. "Yes. I'd be honored."

"Thank you. I'll see you then," Mr. Pendleton said in his Midwestern accent, and he headed down the aisle.

"Josie!" Two girls in red pigtails ran over and hugged Paul's daughter.

The Hartman girls, and Paul tensed.

The younger girl played with the ribbon of Josie's hat. "You look so cute. Would you like to play with us?"

Josie beamed up at Paul. "Please, Daddy?"

His mouth hung open. He longed to let her play, but even more he longed to shield her from rejection.

"Come along, girls." Betty Hartman came up behind her daughters. "It's time to leave."

The older girl hugged Josie's shoulders. "This is Josie. She was at Children's Hour. Remember the puppet show? *She* wrote the story."

Betty speared Paul with an accusing, indignant glare, as if the Feenee story were Paul's nefarious plot to lure children into evil.

It was so ludicrous, he almost laughed. Instead he gave his former friend a slight smile and shrug. Could he help it if his daughter was adorable?

"Come along, girls." Her tone cut off discussion.

The girls whined, hugged Josie, and followed their mother.

Josie grinned at Paul. "They're my friends."

Not for long, but Paul returned her smile.

Holding Josie's hand, Paul ambled down the aisle, well behind the other worshipers.

Lucie Girard stood a few rows back wearing an olive green suit. She beckoned to him.

He must have been mistaken. "Me?" he mouthed.

She nodded, beckoned again, and frowned. Not an angry frown, but fretful. Had the poetry reading gone poorly? Or was it something he'd said?

Paul turned down her row, and Josie flung herself at Lucie's legs. "Miss Gee-jard!"

"Hello, Josie." But Lucie glued her gaze on Paul. "May I ask your advice?"

"Of course." Tension flowed from his shoulders. At least he hadn't done something to endanger Josie's one true friendship. "The poetry reading?"

"It went well." She sat on the pew and pulled Josie onto her lap, but her forehead furrowed.

Paul set his Bible and hat in his lap. "I'm glad."

Her hazel eyes swam with worry. "I found out the Germans are adding to the Otto List."

"The Otto List?"

"The list of books banned for sale in France. It's named after Otto Abetz, the German ambassador to Paris."

Paul murmured his understanding. He didn't dare mention he'd attended Abetz's party the night before, even conversed with the man.

Lucie drew in a shaky breath. "On July 1, they're adding all books by British or American authors published after 1870."

Paul's mouth fell open. "After 1870? That has to be—"

"A quarter, maybe half my stock. I haven't had time to check."

"I like your flower." Josie touched a golden brooch pinned to Lucie's shoulder.

Lucie held up one hand, a gentle reminder to the child not to interrupt. "I don't know what to do. In two weeks, they'll confiscate the books. I can't afford that." Her voice trembled, and her gaze stretched down into his heart.

If only he could take her in his arms and tell her he'd never let the store close. But that fact needed to remain secret.

He kept both hands clamped on his hat and Bible. "Does the ban apply to private ownership of the books?"

"No. Only to selling them."

Paul kept his voice soothing. "Hold a sale. Mark those titles down 50 percent. You won't make as much money as if you sold them full price, but you'll make something. Notify your subscribers. You can sell lots of books in two weeks."

"All right. But the rest. I can't bear the thought of them being burned."

"Can you store them in your apartment?"

Lucie's gaze darted above Paul's head. "I have room for one hundred, maybe two. Nowhere near all of them."

"I have plenty of room at my house. I'll store them."

"You?" Her eyebrows rose to meet the brim of her hat. "You'd store banned books?"

Paul's mouth tightened. Although he had to play a collaborator, there were limits to what he'd allow others to believe. "I may be an opportunist, Miss Girard, but I am not a fascist. I'm opposed to censorship. I'm opposed to restricting civil rights. And I'm vehemently opposed to antisemitism. Please do not equate my desire to make a profit with approval of oppression."

Her eyes widened, and then her eyelids slipped shut. "I—I'm sorry. Please forgive me."

"All forgiven." He sighed. "On June 30, bring the books to my house. I'll inventory them and give you a receipt. Then if the situation changes, we'll restock your store."

She opened pretty, shimmering eyes. "Thank you. You're so kind to me. I've been nothing but mean to you, and you—"

"As I said, all forgiven." He dropped her a wink. "Now if you'll excuse me, I have an appointment with Mr. Pendleton."

"Oh?"

"You know as much as I do. Come on, butterscotch." He

scooped Josie into his arms and smiled at Lucie. "Everything will be all right."

"Thank you. I'll go straight home and prepare for the sale."

Paul resisted the urge to tell her he'd come and help. For the sake of her reputation, he needed to limit his time with her.

After he left the sanctuary, he crossed the courtyard to the church house and climbed to the fourth floor.

The housekeeper answered the door, gushed over Josie, and spirited her away to the kitchen, barely taking time to show Paul to the study.

Bookshelves lined the study walls, full of theological tomes abandoned when the pastor left Paris a year earlier.

Mr. Pendleton entered, a fair-haired man in his forties, and the men sat on opposite sides of the desk. After a few pleasantries, the church director's face grew grim. "I find myself in a bind. I'm a musician, not a pastor, and situations like this . . ."

Dread settled heavy in Paul's chest. "Is there some way I can help?"

The director leaned his forearms on the desk and frowned at his clasped hands. "Several members are opposed to your presence at church."

"Opposed." The word came out clipped.

"They say you sell military equipment to the Germans."

"Trucks. I sell civilian trucks."

Mr. Pendleton massaged his hands with his thumbs. "Your return has caused upheaval. Perhaps if you were repentant . . ."

Paul ran his fingers through his hair. "Repentant? Of selling a civilian product? Of employing eight hundred men? Is that a sin?"

Pained eyes lifted. "You collaborate with the enemy of God's chosen people."

"I don't—" His eyes slammed shut. He couldn't say more without endangering his missions. "Please, sir. I've lost so much. My wife, my friends. And this place . . ." His throat clogged, and he pressed his hand to his forehead, shielding his eyes. "I need this. So does Josie."

"I'm sorry, Mr. Aubrey."

"It isn't what you think, what any of them think." He rubbed his forehead. How could he lose this new source of peace in his life? He couldn't lose it. He couldn't.

Paul slapped his hand to his thigh and leveled his gaze at Mr. Pendleton. "I know you're not ordained, but do you follow the same rules of confidentiality as a pastor?"

The director blinked and sat back in his red leather chair. "I do."

"This room. Is it secure? Any chance for the Germans to install listening devices?"

"Listening—of course not. What is this about?"

Paul shoved up out of the chair and paced the office, rubbing his mouth. He trusted Mr. Pendleton, but he had to be careful, not just for his own sake, but for his employees, and even for the safety of Mr. Pendleton.

"You seem agitated." The director slid a silver cigarette case across the desk. "Would you care for a smoke?"

Paul planted both hands on the desk and leaned close to Mr. Pendleton. "I can't tell you all that I'm doing. Too much is at stake. And you mustn't breathe one word of it to anyone. Do you understand? Do you promise?"

Deep-set eyes widened. "I promise."

Paul sorted his words. "The United States military asked me to remain in France and keep my factory running. It's for the good of our country. That's all I'll say on that matter."

"That . . . seems wise."

"And in my factory, I do what I can to hinder the Germans."

"Are you—you're in the resistance?" Mr. Pendleton whispered.

"The resistance?" Paul rubbed his thumbs on the polished desktop. "Nothing official. No connection to any group. I just— I do what I can."

Mr. Pendleton assessed him for a weighty moment. "I'm glad to hear. This is the Paul Aubrey I remember."

Paul collapsed into his chair, his arms limp on the armrests. "I shouldn't have said that much."

"You're playing a dangerous game."

He was. "Please? If anything happens to me, Josie's nanny has instructions to take her to the US Embassy in Vichy. I have friends there. They'll get her home. But she'll need permission to cross the demarcation line into Vichy France. I think they'd let her across for a reason like that, but could you assist if she needs help? Please?"

Mr. Pendleton leaned forward. "You have my word, Paul."

The use of his given name somehow sealed it, and the director's respect seeped into the raw void of Paul's heart.

"As for church," the director said, "I'll see what I can do."

"You can't tell anyone. I have to be seen as a collaborator."

"As a sinner, yes." Mr. Pendleton lifted a bit of a smile. "I'll explain this simple truth. If I were to ban sinners from this church, the pews would be empty. So would the pulpit."

Paul chuckled. A simple truth, easily forgotten.

19

MONDAY, JUNE 30, 1941

At the cash register Lucie opened the notebook she called her perpetual calendar. She'd numbered the pages one through thirty and listed daily tasks, spreading out the unpleasantness.

Page thirty read "Make sure rent is paid," and she groaned. Paying the rent might be Bernadette's job, but it was Lucie's responsibility.

With her nose in a book, Bernadette swished a feather duster over the shelves in the children's section.

Maybe Lucie could ask after lunch. No. In ballet she had to work through routine barre exercises before dancing. In the store she had routine work too.

She straightened her shoulders and approached the older woman. "Madame Martel? I was wondering if you'd paid July's rent yet."

Bernadette didn't look up from her book. "It's still June."

"It's June 30. We agreed the rent would be paid by the end of the month."

"It's due tomorrow. I'll pay it then."

Lucie gripped her hands together. She'd have to remind her again tomorrow. On page one of her notebook, capital letters declared, "RENT MUST BE PAID!" But what if Lucie forgot to open her calendar? On July 2, Madame Villeneuve would storm in, threatening eviction.

"All right, then," Lucie said. "I'll pay it myself."

Bernadette murmured and rounded the bookcase into non-fiction.

With her lips pressed tight, Lucie marched into the office. She followed Paul's advice—she stated expectations, provided time, and checked up. Still, Bernadette only completed half her tasks.

Lucie opened the cashbox, pulled out the rent money, and stuffed the francs in her skirt pocket. With the store empty, now was a good time to leave.

She harrumphed and strode outside. Now would have been a good time for Bernadette to have left too.

Lucie stepped through the *porte cochère* into the courtyard. Madame Villeneuve swept the steps in front of her apartment.

"Bonjour, madame. I am here to pay the rent."

The tiny concierge stopped sweeping and raised her iron-gray head with a confused expression. "It has already been paid."

Bernadette forgot she'd paid? But if she'd paid, why was the rent money still in the cashbox? "Madame Martel paid?"

"No. The same man who paid in May and June."

"Man?" Lucie gasped. "What man?"

"He wishes to remain anonymous." The concierge brushed dust from her gray apron. "That is fine with me. The rent is paid."

A man? Last month Bernadette had said the rent was taken care of—was this what she'd meant? Lucie refused to have some man pay her rent and expect who-knew-what from her. "Who is he? I must know."

"I will not tell you." She thrust up her narrow chin. "I will not let you tell him to stop."

"Then you must tell him to stop. I won't have it. I have the money."

Madame Villeneuve's chin lowered. A sly smile rose, and she resumed sweeping. "Very well. Next month I will tell him, and you may pay."

Why, that little cheat. She planned to say nothing to the man and collect double rent.

"Never mind." Lucie hurried back to the store. It had to be Wattenberg. He'd offered, and his interest in her was clear, if undeclared. She absolutely could not allow a German to pay her rent.

Paul? Lucie paused outside her store and stroked the deep green paint. Paul knew her financial situation, but he also knew it was improving. Besides, he was a pull-yourself-up-by-your-bootstraps man. An opportunist, not a philanthropist.

It had to be Wattenberg.

Inside the store, Bernadette's feather duster hovered in the vicinity of a shelf as the store assistant turned pages in her book.

Lucie pulled herself taller, although she could never approach Bernadette's height. "Madame Villeneuve said an anonymous man paid our rent. He also paid in May and June."

"Yes, she told me," Bernadette said in a nonchalant tone.

"You didn't tell me."

"Why would I?" Another page flipped. "It has to do with money. The rent was paid. That's all that matters."

No, that wasn't all that mattered, but how could Lucie word it?

"Excuse me, Mademoiselle Girard?" A young woman approached wearing a turban in an abstract print in reds and purples and golds. "A friend recommended I read an English version of *Les Misérables* to improve my English. He asked you to set aside a copy for me."

"Ah yes." A message, and Lucie slipped behind the counter and into her resistance persona. Every word had to be exact. "Victor Hugo is one of my favorites."

"My father read everything he wrote." The résistante spoke slowly, her English stiff. But the message was perfect.

Lucie handed the volume to the girl, who couldn't be older than twenty.

"Merci. I will buy it."

As Lucie made the transaction, she smiled at the young lady who risked her life for the cause of freedom, far more than Lucie did. The process was designed so Lucie looked oblivious.

The résistante put the book in her bag, adjusted her turban, and said goodbye.

Although turbans were fashionable, they seemed even more popular among résistantes. It made sense. If followed, the girl could duck into an alley or store, whip off her turban, and be transformed.

"So many books on hold." Bernadette leaned out the door and shook out her feather duster. "Hal never put books on hold. You should put them on the shelves where people can find them."

Lucie stiffened, and she entered the sale in the ledger. "People like the new service."

Bernadette grunted and shut the door.

The number of holds had doubled in the past week—after Germany invaded the USSR. The Soviet order for the French communists to cooperate with the Nazis had always fit them like an itchy sweater. Now they'd thrown off that sweater and flung themselves into resistance activities.

"Are you taking the books away today?" Bernadette tipped her head toward the books stacked by the door. "Didn't you say nine thirty?"

"Yes." Any minute now.

Although the sale had been successful, she still had hundreds of books on the upcoming version of the Otto List. In her upstairs hideaway behind the mural, she'd stored the books most likely to be sold undercover.

But her hideaway was full, and her apartment was stuffed with three women and their belongings.

139

Today Paul was paying for a horse-drawn carriage to take the remaining books to his house. Carrying them in a suitcase on the Métro would have taken dozens of trips, and although Paul owned a car, he didn't have a gasoline permit—even as a collabo.

A boy of about fifteen entered, short but sturdy. "Bonjour. I am Albert. I am to take you and your books to the house of Monsieur Aubrey."

"Thank you." Lucie picked up an armful of books. Paul had suggested she accompany the books to ensure they weren't stolen to be burned for fuel.

Albert gathered a stack, and even Bernadette helped. Soon all were loaded in the back of the open black carriage, probably hauled out from decades in storage.

Albert helped Lucie inside.

How exciting. She always traveled by foot or bike, with an occasional Métro ride, but never by carriage or *vélo-taxi*, the bicycle-driven rickshaws common on Parisian streets nowadays.

Albert clucked his tongue, and the two brown horses trotted down the road. The carriage wheels bumped over the cobblestones, and Lucie gripped the edge of the seat and laughed.

She'd just read Jane Austen's *Pride and Prejudice*, a title she was still allowed to sell. She felt like Elizabeth Bennet riding in an open carriage to Pemberley. Fitting. Like Lizzy, Lucie also counted on the owner of the manor not being at home. Thank goodness, Paul was at his factory.

The carriage clattered past shops and apartments with intricate wrought iron balconies. Then it turned left along the Seine.

Even as the glorious buildings of the Louvre shone in the morning light, Lucie frowned. Elizabeth Bennet thought Mr. Darcy hard-hearted and cold, but he'd been the best sort of hero, a man of quiet honor and integrity.

Paul Aubrey, on the other hand, was an enigma. He sold to

the Germans, loved making a profit, called himself an opportunist, and associated with the worst sorts.

Yet he gave freely of his time and expertise, and he was tender with his daughter, calling her all sorts of candy nicknames. And she'd seen his face in profile in church, glowing during the hymns and Scripture reading.

Only during Mr. Pendleton's announcement yesterday did Paul's head droop.

She could still hear the director's ringing words. "It has come to my attention that we have collaborators in our congregation. It has also come to my attention that we have gossips. We have those who covet and those who bear false witness, those who commit evil for the Germans and those who commit evil against the Germans. We have sinners in our midst, my friends! Sinners!"

Holding her breath, Lucie had glanced around at all the stunned faces.

"Hallelujah!" Mr. Pendleton had cried. "What better place for sinners than where they can hear the Word of God. So welcome to all of you, my fellow sinners, my friends."

Guilty looks had passed between some members, huffy looks between others, but Paul hadn't even raised his head.

Indignation pulsed in Lucie's veins as the carriage passed the Gare d'Orsay. Someone must have asked Mr. Pendleton to kick Paul out of the church. How dare they? Why, that seemed a greater sin than what Paul was doing.

The carriage rolled around the bend in the Seine past elegant bridges and trees in full leaf and public buildings hung with garish swastika flags. The Eiffel Tower poked its spindly head above the buildings and soon dominated the view, seeming to arch over the road. Lucie held on to her hat and craned her neck to enjoy the sight.

Then the carriage turned onto the Pont d'Iéna and crossed to the Right Bank, another world, where those who called

themselves "respectable" lived—professionals and businessmen and government ministers.

Lucie had only been in the wealthy 16th arrondissement a
handful of times, always on her way to the wooded paths of
the Bois de Boulogne.

The streets in the district were broader with more trees and
deeper sidewalks, lined with hotels and embassies and high-
class stores, with cars parked outside. Only Germans, physicians, and the most outrageous collaborators were allowed to
drive.

Lucie sat back in her seat, glad she'd worn her smart taupe
suit—not so she'd fit in, but so she wouldn't draw attention.

They turned down a broad boulevard, and the homes grew
grander, with wrought iron fences and gardens in front.

In a few minutes, Albert drew up the reins. "We are here,
mademoiselle."

Lucie did her best not to gawk. A four-story home, surrounded on all sides by gardens and fencing, decorated with
ornate balconies and arched windows. Did Paul own the whole
house or only the swanky ground-floor *rez-de-chaussée* apartment?

After Albert gave her a hand down, Lucie adjusted her hat
and passed through the gate to the front door.

A middle-aged woman in a black dress and white apron
opened the door.

"Bonjour," Lucie said. "I am Mademoiselle Girard of Green
Leaf Books."

A smile brightened the woman's plain face. "Please come in.
I am Claudette, the housekeeper."

Lucie stepped inside, greeted by an expanse of glistening
marble, a chandelier, an elegant curving staircase, and large
rooms to each side.

Paul lived there, and Lucie felt small and out of place.

"Is—is Josie here?" she asked.

"The nanny of *le petit* took her for a walk so she would not be underfoot." Claudette leaned out the door and hailed Albert. "Young man, please bring in the books."

Lucie turned to help Albert.

But Claudette motioned Lucie deeper inside the house. "Monsieur Aubrey said the books were precious to you and you might want to see their new home."

Apprehension battled with curiosity, and curiosity won. "Thank you. I would."

Claudette led her into the room to the right, a sitting room or parlor or whatever rich people called it. Chairs and couches in deep red upholstery and rich dark wood sat on a parquet floor. Gold drapes framed the arched windows.

Lucie found herself tiptoeing, as if she were breaking in.

Over the fireplace hung two portraits, and Lucie stopped.

Wedding portraits faced each other in profile, one of the bride and one of the groom. Paul in white tie, his dark hair slick, his face smooth and free of pain and sadness. And Simone with a lacy veil over her dark hair, her jaw square and features strong.

Claudette turned back and joined her. "They were a happy couple."

"I can see. Have you worked here long?"

"Oui. I was a maid for Madame Aubrey's family—this was one of their homes. Then I became madame's lady's maid. After the war began, many of the staff joined the army or left in the exodus. Now we are but three—the cook, the nanny, and me."

Albert entered with an armload of books.

Claudette motioned to the next room. "In the study, please."

Lucie should help, but the portraits enchanted her. Like Lizzy Bennet with the miniature of Darcy, Lucie couldn't resist the glimpse into the soul of a baffling man. "Is he—is Monsieur Aubrey a good employer?"

"Good?" Claudette laughed. "He doesn't know how to treat staff."

143

Lucie ripped her gaze from Paul's face to Claudette's, her heart in her throat. "What do you mean?"

"I do not mean he is lax." The housekeeper flapped her hand. "But he's American and comes from new wealth, not old. He forgets we are staff, not family. Sometimes he asks us to dine with him. Of course, we decline."

Lucie studied the portrait again, the easy grin and warm dark eyes. "He is kind? Fair?"

"But of course. Come along. I will show you where the books will be."

In the study stood a large mahogany desk, leather chairs, and bookcases along the walls. Several shelves were empty.

Albert entered with another stack of books.

"Set them here." Claudette pointed to a spot on the floor, then to cardboard boxes beside the desk. "On your way out, load these."

Was Albert running an errand for Paul when driving Lucie home?

Claudette looked at Lucie and tipped her head. "Did Monsieur Aubrey not tell you? You sell used books, right?"

"Yes . . ."

"These are books he no longer wants, books you can sell, in exchange for those you are loaning him."

Lucie's throat swelled shut, and she pressed her hand to her mouth. The books would fill several newly bared shelves in her store. "That is . . ." Her voice warbled, and she swallowed hard. "That is a generous gift. Please thank him for me."

"I will."

Lucie blinked until her vision cleared. All her life she'd been able to read people and discern character. But Paul Aubrey became a greater puzzle every day.

20

THURSDAY, JULY 10, 1941

Josie stood on the scale in the hall in her underwear, and the nurse lowered the bar to the top of her head. "Ninety-two centimeters, fourteen point six kilograms. Come this way, Mr. Aubrey."

Paul scooped up his barefoot daughter and followed the white-uniformed nurse through the halls of the American Hospital in Paris. If only Madame Coudray could have brought Josie to her doctor's appointment as usual.

But Dr. Bentley Young's office had called, insisting Paul needed to bring Josie—and to Bentley's hospital office rather than the office in his home.

Not only would Paul have to endure his former friend's scorn, but the antiseptic smell took him back to Simone's bedside as she took her last labored breaths.

The nurse, an American woman in her sixties, glanced over her shoulder at Paul. "How unusual for a father to bring a child. Is her mother not available today?"

Why not just kick him in the gut? "Her mother passed away." Just over a year ago. In this very building.

"I'm sorry." The nurse pinched Josie's cheek. "Never you

mind, dear. Someday your father will remarry and you'll have a new mommy."

Paul held back a groan. *Lord, save us from busybodies.*

The nurse opened the door to the examination room. "Dr. Young will be with you shortly."

"Thank you." Paul set Josie on the exam table.

Josie fiddled with her white undershirt. "When can I have a new mommy?"

"Not for a long time." Paul straightened the blue hair bow that flopped onto Josie's forehead.

Her big brown eyes glowed. "Where can I get one?"

"It doesn't work that way. Daddy would have to meet a woman—a woman who doesn't have a husband—and we would have to fall in love."

Josie swung her legs. "She should be pretty and nice, and she should read me stories."

"I'll keep that in mind." He gave her a little smile.

"Like Miss Gee-jard!"

With effort, Paul suppressed his groan and grimace, and he refolded Josie's blue dress lying on top of her slip and shoes. "Miss Girard is not an option."

Josie's face scrunched up. "Op-shun?"

How much explanation was needed to help her understand? "I like Miss Girard as a friend, but we don't love each other like a husband and wife."

Josie's mouth slipped into a pout. "But I like her."

"That's why I take you to Children's Hour."

Her face reddened, and she kicked the exam table. "I want her to live in our house. She can sleep in my room."

It definitely didn't work that way. Paul grabbed one flailing foot. "No kicking."

"But she came to our house." Her voice rose in a whine. "I wanted to show her my room, but Madame Coudray took me away. It isn't fair."

He grasped the other foot. "Don't argue with Madame Cou-dray. She knows best."

"But I want Miss Gee-jard to live in our house. She likes my stories. You don't!" She glared at him.

Paul planted his hands on the exam table on either side of his daughter and pinned her with his gaze. "Josephine Simone Aubrey, that is enough."

Josie's eyes widened and flooded. Her chin quivered.

His chest collapsed in on itself, and he pulled her into his arms and patted her back as she sobbed into his shoulder. Big, heavy sobs of a child who needed a story-loving mommy in-stead of a number-loving daddy. "I'm sorry, marshmallow. I know more about cars than about stories. But I do like your stories. I do. More importantly, I love you."

The door opened, and Dr. Bentley Young entered with his white coat matching his wreath of white-blond hair. "There now, Miss Josephine. I promise. No needles or shots today."

Without looking at his former friend, Paul set his sniffling girl on the table and dried her face with his handkerchief.

"I see Josephine is four years and four months. How is her health?"

Paul settled into a chair in the corner. "Fine. A few colds. The usual bumps and bruises."

"Good." Bentley smiled at Josie. "Bumps and bruises mean you're playing outside in the fresh air. Now, this is my special light. I'll use it to look in your ears and eyes and mouth."

After Bentley showed Josie how his light worked, he con-ducted his exam with a soothing, cheerful manner. He listened to her heart and lungs, tickled her belly and made her giggle, and checked her reflexes and made her giggle even more.

Then Bentley leaned against the table and looked Paul in the eye for the first time. "How is her diet, Mr. Aubrey?"

"She gets her full ration, plus my cook brings cheese and meat from the country."

The doctor scanned his clipboard. "She's small for her age, but nothing to be concerned about. And she shows no signs of deficiencies. She's in better health than most children in France these days."

"Good." Did Bentley expect Paul to be ashamed he provided better than most? Because he wasn't.

Bentley made notes on his clipboard. "Have you considered taking her home to America?"

Where she'd never want for food. "Not yet, but if international relations continue to deteriorate . . ." He chose words lofty enough to soar above Josie's head.

"Iceland. Quite interesting."

"Indeed." A year ago, the British had occupied Iceland to protect their transatlantic shipping routes. But just yesterday President Roosevelt had announced the US Marines had landed in Iceland to relieve the British, which infuriated the Germans.

Over the rims of his glasses, Bentley looked Paul hard in the eye.

Paul didn't flinch. Refused to.

Bentley cleared his throat. "I'd like to talk to you privately in my office. My nurse will dress Josephine and give her a puzzle to play with while we talk."

No . . .

Paul's heart, his lungs, his thoughts screeched and crashed like Simone's car. The last time a doctor had spoken to him privately . . . *Not Josie too. Not . . . Josie.*

Somehow he steadied himself and followed Bentley down the hall and into his office.

Until the door closed. "Please, Dr. Young. Not Josie. Please. She's healthy. She's fine, isn't she?"

Bentley spun to him, his pale eyebrows high. "Oh my. I didn't mean to alarm you. Josie's fine. In excellent health. Please have a seat."

His breath still chuffing, Paul lowered himself into a chair and closed his eyes.

"I apologize," Dr. Young said. "I didn't stop to think how that would sound." A chair creaked on the far side of the desk. "I wanted to talk to you about something unrelated to your darling and very healthy daughter."

Paul released a tense breath and opened his eyes. Bentley's face was kind and open, almost friendly. But most likely this man had called for his ouster from church, and he braced himself. "Proceed."

Bentley lowered his chin and sighed. "First, I apologize for how I've treated you this past year."

"Why?" Paul let his voice harden. "I'm a ruthless, conniving collaborator who makes tanks for the Nazis. Isn't that what the rumors say?"

Bentley's head swung back and forth slowly. "I know that isn't true. I know you only build trucks. I'm telling people."

"How kind of you." He didn't even try to tone down the sarcasm.

Bentley rolled a pen on the blotter on his desk, his expression pensive. "I understand why you allow everyone to think the worst of you. It's an excellent cover."

"Cover?" For the second time that hour, his heart failed. What did Bentley know?

"I talked to Mr. Pendleton yesterday. Your name came up. He didn't tell me what you're doing, but he assured me we're on the same side."

What on earth had Pendleton done? Paul had spoken to him in confidence. If the Germans or the police heard, Paul could be shot.

"Don't be angry with Mr. Pendleton." Bentley eyed Paul over his glasses. "He knows what I'm doing. He only gave me your name because I asked for help. I'm desperate."

Paul fought to still his expression, his breathing. "I don't know what you're talking about. I'm a carmaker, making trucks, trying not to go bankrupt."

"Yes, and you have the courage to do something dangerous, something good. That sounds like my friend Paul."

His life depended on not reacting. His workers' lives. Duffy's work. "Thank you for the apology, Dr. Young. Misinformed, but appreciated. I'm leaving now." He moved to stand.

"Please, Paul. We've been hiding British airmen in the hospital since the armistice, helping them escape. We're out of room. I need help." Light blue eyes reached to Paul. Begged.

That was dangerous information. Deadly. Information you only shared with someone you trusted.

Paul settled back into his seat and ran his tongue inside his dry mouth. "The RAF?"

"They get shot down over France and the Low Countries." Bentley leaned over the desk, his voice low. "Britain is in bad straits, and they need all the trained pilots they can get. The hospital is an important stop on the escape line, because the Germans don't come in here. They leave us alone. But we're out of room. I have a few airmen in my home, but we need more safe houses. Mr. Pendleton suggested your name."

"My house," Paul whispered. He had room, and he trusted his staff. But . . . Josie. What if she said something in public? What if the police followed airmen to his house?

"Josie," he said. "What I'm doing now—she's already at risk of losing her father. But this would bring the danger right to her."

Bentley waved his hand before his chest, erasing his request. "That's all right. If my children were still at home, I'd feel the same."

Paul racked his brain. Who could he ask? He'd lost the confidence of all who might be inclined to help.

Besides, he was doing enough already. This past week they'd sent out a shipment of trucks with sabotaged tires. The men had filed grooves in the tread so they'd wear out quickly, putting the trucks out of commission and depleting Germany's stock of scarce rubber.

In the next shipment the dipsticks would be recalibrated so the drivers wouldn't know the oil was low until it was too late.

His factory. His mind flew over the schematics.

"Thank you anyway," Bentley said. "And once again—"

"Aubrey Automobiles."

"Pardon?"

"My factory. I have storage rooms, sheds. Only certain people have the keys. Hundreds of workers come and go each day. It's perfect."

"For—"

"The airmen."

Bentley's eyebrows lowered. "Are you sure?"

Paul held his breath. This concerned more than him. "I'll discuss it with my foreman. He's on our side."

Bentley pulled out a notepad. "My nurse will schedule an appointment for you next week. That ulcer you're developing—we need to discuss treatment."

Paul cracked a smile and rubbed his belly. "Thanks, doc."

After he finished his note, Bentley stood and extended his hand to Paul. "Thank you."

"Thank you. For trusting me." His voice thickened, and he coughed to cover it.

"You realize, in public I'll have to pretend not to trust you." Bentley frowned.

"I know." He kept shaking hands. "You can't see me socially. You'll shun me at church."

"I can't tell anyone. Even Alice."

"I understand." For once, he didn't mind. And he gripped Bentley's hand hard.

21

SATURDAY, JULY 26, 1941

"Simon says, 'Flap your arms like a chicken.'" Lucie flapped her arms, and a dozen children in Green Leaf Books did likewise, giggling.

"Peck like a chicken." She pecked at imaginary corn.

Half the children pecked, and the others squealed, "She didn't say 'Simon says!'"

Groans and whines, and the pecking children plopped to the floor, including Josie Aubrey.

"Simon says, 'Flap your arms and peck and strut like a chicken.'"

Along the wall, parents waited to collect their chicks. And Lt. Emil Wattenberg watched with an amused smile, although the parents kept a wide berth from the uniformed figure.

Only Paul Aubrey hadn't arrived. To avoid the other adults, he brought Josie early and picked her up late. And at church when Josie ran to Lucie, he hung back in the distance, alone.

He might be a rogue, but he had nobility that touched her almost as much as his pain and loneliness. If only that nobility ran all the way through.

The children stared at her expectantly. Oh yes. The game.

"Simon says, 'Spin and spin, but don't fall down.'" She sprang to pointe and spun in *chaîné* turns down an imaginary line, her heels close together, spotting the plant on the mantel with each turn so she wouldn't get dizzy.

A tall young man in a brown cap walked to the mantel, met Lucie's twirling gaze, held up a book, and set it on the mantel. A résistant with a message.

They were supposed to hand the books to her and never leave them lying around. Lucie hopped out of the turn and gave the man a quick glare, but he ignored her and left the store.

Childish shrieks grabbed her attention. Only Margie Hartman remained standing and spinning. The others lay tumbled on the floor.

Lucie clapped her hands. "Very good, Margie. You're the winner."

Everyone applauded, and Margie blushed.

"That's all for today, boys and girls," Lucie said. "I'll see you next week."

The children ran to her for hugs and thank-yous, and Lucie responded to each while edging toward the fireplace.

"We won't be here next week." Margie's hazel eyes brimmed with tears. "Or—or ever again."

Betty Hartman rested her hands on her daughters' shoulders. "We're going home to Chicago. The food situation is horrible. It isn't healthy for children. And it isn't safe." She tipped her head toward Wattenberg.

Wattenberg, who stood by the mantel, who reached for the book.

Every impulse screamed to leap in a *grand jeté* and spirit the book away, but that would only call more attention to it.

Lucie properly tuned herself to the Hartmans, and she hugged the two little redheads to her side. "I'll miss you."

Wattenberg read the front cover, flipped to the back cover.

"Also," Betty said, "with so many Americans leaving, my

husband's law practice is suffering. I'm sure you have the same problems."

"I do." But falling sales would be the least of her problems if the German officer discovered the note. Although he appreciated the arts and had alerted her to the changes in the Otto List, she didn't trust him.

"Let's go, girls. You'll see Miss Girard one last time tomorrow in church."

After the Hartmans left, two mothers remained chatting, and Josie Aubrey played with the other children.

Wattenberg read the inside flap.

Lucie donned a polite expression and joined the lieutenant. "Oh dear. Customers can be so careless, leaving books lying around. I'll put that away." She held out her hand.

He studied the cover. "Charles Dickens. I have not heard of this book—*Barnaby Rudge*. Is it good?"

She had to get the book. "It isn't one of his best. Have you read Dickens?"

"I have not."

"You should start with something better. Let me see what I have." She dashed to the fiction section, praying she had lots of Dickens titles.

She did, and she slid one off the shelf. "*A Tale of Two Cities*—it's set in Paris and one of his best works. I also have *Great Expectations*, *Oliver Twist*, several others you'd enjoy more than *Barnaby Rudge*." She held out *Two Cities* in one hand and extended the other for *Barnaby*.

Instead, Wattenberg stacked *Two Cities* on top of *Barnaby*. "I will buy both."

Inside, she groaned. What could she say that wouldn't sound suspicious? Nothing. She headed for the cash register. She couldn't retrieve the book, but maybe she could retrieve the message. But how?

Behind the counter, she took the books from him. She bobbled them, let them slide through her fingers and thump to the floor. "Oh dear! How clumsy of me. I'm sorry."

She dropped to her knees, leaned over the books, thumbed through for the note—found it, facing page twenty. Twenty, twenty, she pounded into her memory. She set the note on the shelf.

Clucking her tongue, she made a show of dusting off the books as she stood. "I apologize, Lieutenant."

Paul Aubrey stood behind the Nazi, his fedora and his smile tilted at the same rakish angle. "Good day, Miss Girard. I'll go find Josie. I see you're busy with a customer." His eyes sparkled as he said the last word.

Oh, she'd hear it later for selling to a German. And she'd deserve it. "Thank you, sir." She poured syrup into her voice.

Wattenberg glanced after Paul. "Who is that?" he said in a tight voice.

Oh my. He was jealous. It wouldn't be wise to reveal anything about Paul to a man who might consider him a rival. She rang up the books and assumed a casual tone. "The father of one of the children."

Wattenberg frowned. "Does his wife know how friendly he is with pretty young women?"

If he knew Paul was a widower, things would be even worse. "You think he's flirting?" Lucie said with a chuckle. "No, he's just an American. It's how we are. That'll be twelve francs."

After the German paid and departed, Lucie sank behind the desk and pinned the loose note between books. The résistant who picked it up would be perplexed, and Lucie wouldn't be able to explain.

Maybe she should risk sending another message to Renard to tell him of his colleague's behavior. When the Otto List had changed, she'd tucked a note to him inside a journal. He'd looked furious when she'd handed him the journal, but she had to tell him many of the titles they used would disappear.

Lucie headed toward the children's section and passed Bernadette, who had actually risen from her armchair to straighten the rack of literary journals by the fireplace.

At the little green table, Paul sat in a too-small chair while Josie pretended to read to him.

So precious, and her heart squeezed, trying to squeeze out all she knew about Paul, leaving only what she felt.

He glanced up to her with a laughing grin.

She understood why one couldn't always refuse to sell to the Germans, but she wouldn't admit it. "Don't say anything."

"I wouldn't dream of it . . . Fräulein."

She gave him her most withering glare, but he just kept grinning.

Josie stood and tugged on Lucie's pink practice skirt. "Miss Gee-jard? Why don't you love my daddy?"

"Pardon?" Lucie spluttered out while Paul gasped, "Josie!"

"Why not?" Little pink lips twisted. "He's smart and he's nice and he's handsome. Don't you think?"

She did think, but she couldn't let Josie—or Paul—know.

Paul stood and took Josie's hand with a new shade of pink in his cheeks. "I apologize, Miss Girard. Someone told her recently about remarriage, and she's been—"

"That's all right." Lucie knelt in front of the little girl. "Sweet Josie. I'm honored you'd want me as your mother. But if I were, who would run Green Leaf Books?"

"Oh." Josie's big brown eyes gazed around the store. "You can't do both?"

Not in Paul Aubrey's world. In that world, wives joined the American Women's Club and the Chamber of Commerce auxiliary. They attended luncheons and auctions and fashion shows. They didn't run Left Bank bookstores.

"No, sweetie," Lucie said. Even if Paul weren't a collaborator, they wouldn't belong together, and something ached inside.

"How are things at the store this week?" Paul shifted his feet and the topic, tilting his head toward Bernadette.

Lucie stood and met his brown-eyed gaze, a manly version of his daughter's. "The same." Her assistant accomplished only a fraction of her work. The only tasks she completed without prompting were helping customers and manning the cash register. Even then, she wasn't exactly approachable with a book in her face.

"It's time," Paul said, his voice somber.

The previous Saturday, he'd told her to fire Bernadette—or threaten to. She hated the idea, but he was right. A ballerina who didn't dance would be cut from the ballet.

"You're a strong woman. I know you can do it."

Lucie glanced at Bernadette—decades older, better read—and completely disrespectful. Yes, it was time.

Bernadette inspected the leaves of the potted plant on the mantel, then whisked the pot away and set it in the window.

The signal to the resistance that it wasn't safe to exchange messages!

"Excuse me." Lucie held up a hand to Paul, accidentally brushing his arm, and she rushed to the window. "Why did you put the plant in the window?"

"It's pale. It needs sunlight."

"Not there." She waved her hand over her artful display. "I—I arranged the window just so. The books, the summer leaves—"

Bernadette snatched up the plant, shoved open the door, and set the pot on the sidewalk.

The signal for the resistance to cease operations at the store permanently!

Lucie gathered the pot in her arms and fought to control her voice. "Someone could trip. I—I'll put it in my apartment window for a few days."

A dark glare, and Bernadette flounced back to her armchair. But she hadn't entered the week's sales and expenses into the ledger, a task she was supposed to have completed the day before and the sole reason Lucie was paying her to stay after Children's Hour.

Her indignation rose above her insecurities, and she set the plant back on the mantel. "Excuse me, Madame Martel. I need to speak with you in the office."

Halfway into her seat, Bernadette sighed and rose.

Ignoring Paul at the table with Josie, Lucie entered the office. She stood beside the desk, blocked Bernadette's path to Erma's chair, and motioned to the chair in front.

Bernadette paused, then took her seat. "What is this about?"

After closing the door, Lucie claimed the seat and tone of authority. "When the Greenblatts left, you promised to keep the books and pay the bills. Since you don't do these tasks, I need to let you go and hire someone who will."

Bernadette's mouth flopped open. "You—you want to fire me?"

"No. I want someone to do this job."

"I—I've been with this store since the beginning, over twenty years. Why, you were but a child." That look in her dark eyes was meant to intimidate. It always worked.

Not today. Lucie held up her chin. "It's clear you're no longer interested in working here. I'm sure you'll be happier elsewhere."

Bernadette's chest heaved under her shapeless gray dress. "But—but you need me. I know more about modern literature than you do, about the journals, the writers."

Lucie's queasiness about her lack of education swirled up and threatened to drown her authority, but she forced it down. "The modern authors are banned. I need someone to do the books and bills."

Bernadette's eyebrows bunched together, and she shook her head, making her loose bun wobble. "I—I won't be able to get another job. Not at my age."

"I'm sorry, but I need someone—"

"I'm a widow. I need the job. I'll do the work. I promise, I will. Only please, please don't fire me."

Lucie released a long sigh. "I know you're capable, but—"

Bernadette's breath puffed like a locomotive, and her eyes went wild. "I'll do it. Everything you need. And then some. Only please. I can't lose this job. I can't."

For a long while, Lucie assessed the panic on the older woman's face, the sincerity. Bernadette had grown lazy, but with good management—and a healthy dose of fear—the diligent worker might return.

Lucie sighed. "All right. If you promise."

"I promise." She sprang to her feet. "I'll do the books this minute. And every day from now on. You'll never have to ask me twice."

"Thank you." Lucie didn't offer a smile, only a look that said she'd be watching.

Then she left the office and shut the door so Bernadette could do her job for once.

Paul got up from his tiny chair and stepped close. "Well?"

Lucie's hands shook, and she clamped them together. "It was awful."

"But how did it go?" He stood closer than ever, close enough to show flecks of gold and green in his eyes.

"I threatened to fire her," she whispered. "She promised to do her job. She's doing the books right now."

A proud smile transformed his face—not the patronizing pride of a teacher, but the congenial pride of a friend. "I knew you could do it."

Lucie shuddered. "I never want to do it again."

"But now you know you can."

She did, and she had him to thank, this puzzling contradiction of a man, a man who saw more in her than she saw in herself. "Thank you," she breathed out.

He chuckled. "Ah, you know me. It was a simple mercenary act. I like this store, and I want it to remain open. Come on, lollypop. Ready to go?"

Josie whined, but she took Paul's hand.

Lucie studied him with a strange rush of fondness. Mercenary, maybe. But there was nothing simple about him.

22

FRIDAY, AUGUST 8, 1941

In the boiler house behind the assembly building, Maurice Boucheron shined his flashlight inside the boiler circulating pump. "As you can see, messieurs, the rotary blades are worn down."

Paul translated to Colonel Schiller, but he didn't relay the truth—the part was worn down because Boucheron had been throwing in sand.

"The pump came from America," Paul said. "Of course, we can't receive shipments from the US, so we ordered a new pump from Germany. Over a month ago."

Schiller clasped his hands behind his back and frowned. "It was shipped last week, but terrorists derailed the train. The boxcar fell down an embankment into a river. Everything was lost or ruined."

Recently the papers had reported sabotage of rail lines and locomotives. Paul huffed as if the *cheminot* resistance disgusted him rather than delighted him.

Then he crossed his arms. "Boucheron is not just my maintenance and repair foreman—he's my best mechanic. He says the boiler has to be shut down. That'll leave only one boiler, half the steam we need to run the factory."

"No need to tell me this month's shipment will be delayed," Schiller said. "It cannot be helped."

"No, it can't." And fewer Aubrey trucks would carry German troops through the Ukraine.

Paul led Schiller back inside the assembly building and toward the employee entrance, which led to the parking lot.

"Have you heard—" A hiss of compressed gas interrupted the German commissioner. "Have you heard the Berlin Philharmonic will be in town next month?"

"I've heard." Paul nodded to three workers stoking the fires in the enamel drying oven. "I hope to attend."

"I'll get tickets for you. Shall I get two? Any beautiful ladies in your life?"

"I'm afraid the only lady in my life is four years old. But if I do say so myself, she is quite beautiful."

Schiller chuckled. "A proud father."

"Indeed." He passed men tacking upholstery to seat cushions. He'd been listening to Josie's stories with greater deliberation. He didn't understand the fantastical elements, but he recognized the creativity. More importantly, he saw themes of courage in the face of adversity, helping the downtrodden, and standing up to evildoers. And of that he was immensely proud.

Schiller turned his broad smile to Paul. "Perhaps I can introduce you to a woman in my office. A nice German woman to help relations between our countries. The situation is getting worse."

"It is." The US had frozen German assets, and Germany had retaliated. Then America had increased naval patrols to prevent German U-boats from attacking shipping in the western Atlantic. The United States might not have declared war, but she'd chosen a side.

"My colleague is intelligent and cultured and quite pretty," Schiller said. "You'd like her."

Paul rounded the end of the assembly line. "Thank you, but the timing is wrong."

"I understand."

The timing was very wrong. Paul was falling hard for a woman he had no chance with. His business help had softened her opinion of him but hadn't changed it—nor was that the reason he helped. Besides, in the intimacy of a romantic relationship, secrets had a way of rising to the surface. And Paul's secrets could get people killed.

At the employee entrance, a rack of time cards hung by the time clock. Three workers loafed by the clock—two hours after the factory opened.

"You're late for your shift," Paul said.

The men startled at the sight of the company owner and a German officer. Two of them ducked their heads. The third blanched, his eyes wide. "Oui, monsieur. Pardon."

A British accent.

Paul's heart seized. Downed RAF flyers were supposed to enter with the morning rush and be met at the time clock by Silvestre, who would escort them to the safe room.

Paul shot up a quick prayer that Schiller hadn't recognized the accent and that he'd overlook the porcelain complexion of the redheaded airman.

He turned his back to Schiller, faced the airmen, and put on his sternest voice. "Stay here. I'll speak to you later." He held one hand in front of his stomach and flashed a V for Victory.

The French speaker's eyebrows rose slightly, and he hunched his shoulders as if a chastened employee. "Oui, monsieur."

Paul shepherded the German commissioner to the door. "I suppose you do not have problems with tardiness in Germany."

Schiller gave him a rueful smile. "Our workers are motivated."

Motivated to help the fatherland? Or to avoid brutal punishment?

Outside, Paul shook Schiller's hand and said goodbye. After Schiller's requisitioned 1938 Aubrey Authority pulled away, Paul returned to the factory and beckoned to the three alarmed Englishmen in French laborers' clothing.

Paul led them into the warren of offices. Down an out-of-the-way hall, he unlocked a storage room. Only he, Moreau, and Silvestre had the key.

Inside, crates were stacked high to create a wall. On the far side, Paul showed the airmen their temporary home—cots, chairs, a jug, a plate of sandwiches, and a stack of English-language books from Lucie's banned titles. "Make yourselves at home, gentlemen."

The redhead stared at him. "You're American."

"A fact you will promptly forget." Paul leaned back against the wall. "You're late."

"We do apologize." The French speaker sat on a cot. "We were to meet our contact at a church, but she was delayed. A frightful nuisance."

"I'm sure it was. Let me brief you fellows. Factory hours are eight to six. During those hours, the door will be locked. Lights off, no talking, no smoking. In the morning and evening, we'll feed you and let you out to use the restroom. Use the bucket in the corner during the day. Please clean it out at night."

"Smashing accommodations," the redhead said with a smirk.

His buddy poked him with an elbow. "Better than a German prison camp."

"Don't forget that," Paul said. "My men are sacrificing their meager rations and risking their lives. You will treat them as fellow fighters for the Allied cause. In fact, you'll treat them as if they outranked you. Last week one of your comrades acted like an officious, condescending prig. I will have none of that, understood?"

"Yes, sir," they said in unison with matching salutes.

"Good." Paul allowed a smile. "I don't know how long you'll be here. When it's time to leave, we'll give you further instructions. We have sandwiches for you and a jug of ersatz coffee. No tea—don't even ask."

"We—we do appreciate this." The French speaker's close-set eyes shone with gratitude.

"Thank you," Paul said. "You may leave the light on to eat. But the sooner you turn it off, the better. Not everyone who works here can be trusted. And as you saw, we get visitors."

The redhead stood and swept a courtly bow. "We shall comport ourselves like gentlemen to the utmost of our ability."

"Glad to hear it." Paul grinned, left the room, and locked it.

Back on the factory floor, he scanned for Moreau. There he was, near the end of the assembly line, where a crew installed windshields.

Paul stood in Moreau's line of sight, and the foreman soon excused himself and joined him.

"Walk with me." Paul led him along the far side of the assembly line, mindful of the workers they passed and thankful for the factory noise. "Our delivery arrived, but late—and right under Schiller's nose. Three packages are in storage."

Moreau blew out a harsh breath. "I'll inform Silvestre. How was your meeting?"

"Schiller believed Boucheron. Once the pump arrives, we'll need to meet the timeline we gave him. In fact, I'd like to come in early."

Light glimmered in Moreau's onyx eyes. "Make us look eager to please."

"Exactly."

"Dimont had an idea." Moreau glanced back to the windshield installers. "Next time we receive a shipment of windshields, drop them, break them, maybe make it look as if they broke in transit."

Paul pondered. "That's good. After we get the boiler running again, I'd like a week or two of smooth—if slow—operations. The windshield idea will need to wait."

"I agree. Dimont can use the next few weeks to plan."

Only twelve men were involved in the resistance work, each man screened by Paul, Moreau, Dimont, and Silvestre for capability and discretion. Each man brought different gifts, a factory within the factory, all parts working together for a common cause.

At the stairway, Paul paused. "I have an appointment with the accountants in a few minutes. Anything else?"

"No, monsieur. Everything goes well."

Paul regarded this man, long his nemesis, but also long his most valuable employee. "Thanks, Moreau. I couldn't do this without you."

Moreau raised one heavy black eyebrow. "You never could."

Paul chuckled. "No, I couldn't. You know these men, their strengths and weaknesses. You know every working of our factory."

With a grunt, Moreau glanced down and scratched at his jaw as if embarrassed. As if pleased.

Realization and conviction flooded Paul's mind. Just as he craved respect, so did Moreau. So did all these men. And they deserved it.

Moreau hitched up one thick shoulder. "Hate to say it, but we couldn't do it without you either. Your designs, your organization, your business sense."

Dare he say it? "My capital?"

The capitalist-hater glared at Paul. "Even that."

"Don't worry. I won't tell anyone. I'll talk to you later." He mounted the staircase.

"Monsieur Aubrey? You said 'our factory.' Not 'my factory' but 'our.'"

"Did I?"

"You did." Then Moreau smiled. The first smile Paul had ever seen from the man.

It was brilliant.

23

SUNDAY, AUGUST 24, 1941

In the church courtyard, Lucie hugged little Bobby Bishop to her side. "I'll miss you. Children's Hour won't be the same without your jokes."

Bobby hugged her back. "Bye, Miss Girard."

The Bishops were leaving for the USA. The expatriate community in Paris grew smaller each week, and each loss ate away at Lucie.

After Bobby scampered away, Josie Aubrey tugged on the skirt of Lucie's favorite summer dress. "I'm not leaving."

Lucie leaned down to the child's level. "I'm glad you're here."

The courtyard was almost deserted. Paul leaned against the brick wall of the church house in a navy suit, his fedora shadowing one eye, the other eye fixed on her.

Lucie's breath caught. She'd never been attracted to men in conventional suits, but Paul wore them well.

He gazed around the courtyard, then approached.

Lucie smoothed the skirt of her light green dress sprigged with blossoms of blue and yellow. She loved the sweetheart neckline and how the gathered skirt swished as she walked.

"Before you refuse my offer," Paul said, "hear me out."

"Offer?" Her voice came out squeakier than she liked.

"Tensions have been high." He dipped his chin toward his daughter as if reminding Lucie of listening ears. "I'd like to walk you home."

"That isn't—"

"I won't rest until I know you're safely home. Josie and I will follow you anyway."

Josie's expectant smile tugged at her, and Lucie squeezed the girl's hand. "All right."

Paul motioned to the gate, and Lucie led Josie out and onto the tree-lined quai d'Orsay along the Seine. Any apprehension she felt about spending time with Paul seemed trifling compared to the terror gripping Paris the past few days.

"It feels like an ordinary summer day." Paul gazed up through the trees.

"It does." A breeze blew, and puffy clouds dotted the blue sky. But nothing was ordinary.

On Tuesday, two men had been executed for participating in a communist demonstration. On Wednesday, four thousand Jewish men had been rounded up in the 11th arrondissement and locked away, joining Jerzy Epstein and the others arrested in May's rafle.

Then on Thursday, a résistant had shot and killed a German naval cadet as the cadet boarded a Métro train.

Paul watched a black car pass dozens of bicyclists on the street. "We'll have to be careful to stay on the right side of the law. Even keeping curfew."

"I know." On Friday, Gen. Otto von Stülpnagel, the German military commander in Paris, had decreed that for every act of violence against a German, hostages would be pulled from prisons and shot—even if imprisoned for minor offenses like breaking curfew.

Lucie paused while Josie examined a rock under a tree. Following the rules might come easily to Paul, but Lucie was deliberately breaking the law.

Her insides twisted. Not because she could be executed—although the thought terrified—but because her work might lead to violence.

Passing messages had seemed romantic as she imagined resistance members holding clandestine meetings and publishing underground newspapers. But to gun down a young man, a complete stranger, in cold blood?

Across the Seine rose the ornate glass roof of the Grand Palais, now home of "La France européene" exhibition promoting France's place in a German-dominated Europe. For the first year of the occupation, many Parisians had embraced that vision, especially when German behavior was "correct." That was no longer the case.

"The American Colony gets smaller each day," Paul said. "Do you ever consider going home?"

Lucie stopped at the base of the Pont des Invalides and waited to cross the street. "Paris is my home, and I promised the Greenblatts I'd keep the store waiting for them. But I don't see how they could ever return." The Germans conquered every country they invaded, and no one had the strength and will to drive the Nazis out of France.

A blue-caped gendarme waved them across the street.

"Daddy, my feets are tired," Josie said.

"Would you please hold this?" Paul handed his Bible to Lucie, then hoisted his daughter up to sit on his shoulders.

She giggled. "See me?"

Lucie held on to her hat and peered up. "Barely. You're so high."

Paul's hat tipped over both eyes.

Lucie laughed and plucked it off his head. "I'll carry this too."

"Thank you."

Lucie studied him as they passed the little green *bouquiniste* bookstalls along the quay. Was profit enough of a reason for

Paul to stay in France even with all the difficulties? "Do you ever consider going home?"

Paul gripped Josie's legs in their ankle socks. "Every day. But if I leave, the factory will be requisitioned. Conditions will become more difficult for my workers. I want to delay that as long as possible."

With both Bibles in the crook of her arm, Lucie inspected the fedora crafted of fine wool. Once before he'd mentioned his workers as a reason to stay and to sell to the Germans. Maybe collaboration wasn't as black-and-white as she'd thought.

"It's a gamble," he said. "Leave now, and we'll sacrifice something dear. But if we wait too long, we'll be interned like the British. I don't want to waste time idling in an internment camp."

The British men were interned in a camp in Saint-Denis, and the women and families in a hotel in Vittel. Paul and Josie would be together, but in captivity.

"Let's talk about something lighter." Paul cast a glance to the little girl on his shoulders, quiet but listening. "I have a burning question, Miss Girard."

"You do?" She smiled at the humor in his voice, but—attractive as he was—she had to resist the impulse to flirt.

"You're wearing green again. Is it a subtle advertisement for the store?"

"I never would have thought of that." She laughed. "No, it's my favorite color."

"Mine too. We found something we agree on."

Lucie smiled up at the linden trees rustling in the breeze. "Nothing more beautiful than the light green of a new spring leaf in the sunshine."

"I like forest green. It has weight to it."

Of all the shades of green, he'd picked the dullest. "Oh no. That weight—it's why the color can't dance."

Paul's lips curved, then he stopped and gazed up into the

branches of a linden. "Say, Josie? Can you pull down one of those branches?"

"I can! I'm so tall." Josie brought a branch down in front of Paul's face.

"Look up, Lucie," he said. "The underside of the leaves. One leaf, two sides, two colors."

Not really. It was an illusion played by shadow and light. And yet . . . the dark sides of the leaves provided contrast that allowed the light sides to shine all the more. She let deep green fill her eyes. "It's as if the weight of this color allows the color on the other side to dance."

He chuckled. "That's a clever way to see it. And the top side—that's where photosynthesis takes place. Your dancing side nourishes the whole tree."

Lucie met his gaze through the leaves between them, the light and dark flashing and mingling.

"Like Josie," he said in that resonant voice. "Like you."

"Me?"

Gold shone in the warm brown of his eyes. "Stories, dancing, music—they nourish. They make us think and feel. They distract us from the hardness of life. That's a gift from God."

Lucie stroked the ribs under a leaf, the structure that held it together. "And math and science and business—they make things run. They're necessary. Weighty. Gifts from God."

Why had she never realized before?

The branch sprang out of Josie's hand, high into the air.

Lucie laughed and raised her hand to that branch, to the truth.

"Hold that." Paul brought his hand under her wrist, his gaze intense. "That line."

"Line?" She could barely speak. His touch—so warm.

"The line of your arm." With one finger, he brushed under her bare arm from wrist to elbow.

Shivering, awakening delight.

"That line." He wasn't looking at her, only her arm, not flirting, oblivious to the reaction he'd stirred.

Lucie fought for control of her breath, her senses, even as one strong finger traced back to her wrist and came to a rest under the heel of her hand.

"It's ballet, isn't it? Does it have a name?"

"A . . . name?" At that moment she didn't even know her own.

"Your arm. What you're doing with it." His gaze slid along her arm as his finger had.

"It's a wing, Daddy."

Josie—sitting on Paul's shoulders. Flapping her arms.

Paul locked his hand onto Josie's leg and his gaze on Lucie. He blinked a few times as if he too needed to come to his senses.

Her lips were parted, soft, ready, and she closed them and let her arm drift down.

With a sheepish smile, he headed back down the walk. "I'm sorry. That was strange. I—well, your arm looked like the perfect hood of a car."

"A car?" The tension of attraction broke into bubbles of laughter.

"Yes. That curve. Aerodynamic, sleek, and graceful. Does it have a name?"

Lucie let her right arm float up, but her left arm held Bibles and fedora. "If I used both arms, it'd be an arabesque."

"Arabesque." His face took on that intent look again. "Spelled A-R-A, right?"

"Right." She sent him a quizzical look, but it bounced off that intensity, focused in the distance.

"Arabesque," he said. "AH-rabesque."

"Paul?"

He looked at her, laughed, and tilted back his head. "What do you know, Josie? It's been under my nose all this time."

Josie folded her arms on top of his head. "What's under your nose, Daddy?"

"I've done it all my life, and I never realized it. Function and design go together. They always have. The other side of green."

"You're funny." Josie giggled as if she understood what he was saying.

But Lucie understood—the joy of comprehension, of expanding one's views, of appreciating more about the world.

Then Paul turned that joy to Lucie, and his smile deepened.

Lucie lowered her performance face and let her own comprehending, expanding, appreciating joy shine freely.

24

MONDAY, SEPTEMBER 1, 1941

Attaché case in hand, Paul walked up rue Saint-Charles as if on his way home from work. At every intersection he checked for traffic.

Mostly he checked to make sure the two British airmen followed half a block behind him on the other side of the street.

He and Moreau and Silvestre took turns escorting their guests to meet their next contacts. The meeting places ranged from parks to cafés to churches. Today Bentley had called to thank Paul for finding the pen he'd lost in church—after a child threw it like a javelin.

Paul hadn't found a pen, but "church" and "javelin" told him to make the exchange at Église Saint-Christophe de Javel on his route home.

Two German soldiers wandered toward him, arguing over a map.

Paul's chest clenched. The Germans didn't faze him, but the RAF men might spook or hide or draw attention to themselves. And neither spoke French.

One of the soldiers hailed Paul and frowned at a booklet. *"Où—est—la Tour Eiffel?"*

Even as the Eiffel Tower rose behind that soldier like the infamous German helmet spikes from the previous war. Paul pointed to their objective. *"C'est là-bas."*

They turned and exclaimed in German, then headed for the tower without thanking Paul, arguing again, probably blaming each other for getting lost.

Paul slowed his pace to widen the distance from the soldiers. A vélo-taxi pedaled by, and Paul followed it with his gaze until he spotted the airmen. Still there, thank goodness.

He turned left on rue Sébastien-Mercier.

With gendarmes swarming the factory, today was a lousy day to bring out the airmen. But he had no means of communicating with the next contact in the escape line.

On Sunday night, résistants had sneaked onto the factory grounds and stolen two completed Au-ful trucks—Moreau's idea, approved by Paul.

This morning Paul had reported the theft to the police, full of outrage at those who stole from the hardworking men of Aubrey Automobiles. A fine speech to deflect attention from the sabotage committed by those hardworking men.

One block ahead, a young woman approached in a golden-brown suit and with a familiar walk, light and airy.

Lucie? His chest clenched harder than at the sight of the German soldiers. What was she doing in the 15th arrondissement?

She inclined her head, smiled, and waved to him.

Not now. The timing at the church was critical. He couldn't spare more than a minute.

He raised his hand in greeting, and her smile glowed.

The last two weeks at Children's Hour and walking her home from church, he'd noticed a sweet and soft connection. She was beginning to fall for him.

Part of him was elated. He was falling in love with her, no doubt about it. Of course he wanted her to return his feelings.

Yet he didn't. How could this darling, principled woman fall

175

for a man she knew as a collaborator? She couldn't. It would taint her.

And what life did he have to share? A life of secrets and danger.

One street lay between them. Down that street, the church's modern red brick façade rose. The airmen's fate depended on him entering and leaving that church on schedule.

With each step he took across the street, Lucie's smile grew more beautiful.

The solution to his dilemma slashed through his soul. He had to be a collabo she could never love.

His soul ached. But he stepped up onto the curb and tipped his hat to her. "Hello, Lucie. What are you doing in this neighborhood?"

"I have a dentist appointment." Her smile revealed pretty teeth any dentist would love. "My family lived in the 15th arrondissement when I was a girl. I've seen the same dentist all these years. He even schedules evening appointments."

"I hope you aren't in pain."

"No, just a checkup." In the early evening sun, the color of her suit brought out gold in her hair and eyes.

He wanted to keep her there and watch the light play as the sun set. But he couldn't.

"On your way home?" she asked.

He hated to drive a wedge between them again, but he had to for her sake and the sake of his resistance work. And the perfect wedge lay in his toolbox, written on his calendar.

Paul set his chin, clamped his heart shut, and hammered that wedge into place. "I'm afraid I'm in a hurry. I'm expected this evening at the German Embassy."

The light drained from her face. "The German Embassy?"

"You've heard of Otto Abetz?"

Lucie's lips pinched. "I have."

"He's holding a reception for visiting German industrialists." Paul grinned. "It's excellent for business."

He braced himself for searing fire, for shuddering ice. Instead her eyes saddened and her lower lip poked up. She was disappointed in him. He hadn't braced for that.

He tipped his hat again. "I'll see you Saturday."

"Yes. Saturday." She brushed past him and crossed the street.

Paul turned down rue du Capitaine Ménard, his gut churning with shame at knowing Abetz, frustration at not being able to show his true self, and pain—such pain—at disappointing her.

In front of the church, he paused to make sure Lucie was out of sight and the airmen were in sight. He pulled himself together. Distraction was a luxury he couldn't afford. Too many lives were at stake along the escape line that ran to Gibraltar.

On the pediment above the door stood a statue of St. Christopher, the patron saint of travelers. Appropriate for these RAF men.

He stepped through the wooden doors and removed his hat. As a Protestant, he'd needed coaching on how to act in a Catholic church, coaching he passed on to the airmen.

At the font, Paul dipped his hand in the holy water and made the sign of the cross. Quietly he entered the sanctuary, which smelled of candle wax and incense. A rounded ceiling rose high, and light streamed through stained glass windows in sunbeam designs.

A handful of people occupied the sanctuary, mostly elderly men and women. Anyone could be an informant though, so Paul needed to follow protocol and stay alert.

Five rows from the front, he went down on one knee, then entered the row of chairs to his right, knelt, and made the sign of the cross. The airmen had been instructed to take seats two rows behind him and to the left.

Paul folded his hands on top of the chair before him. His watch read 6:43. At 6:50 he was to leave the church while the airmen remained. Ten minutes later, their contact would take Paul's seat. After a few minutes, the contact would ask the men

177

if they'd light a candle for a dying mother. The men would respond in a phrase they'd memorized.

What better way to spend seven minutes in church than to pray? With his eyes open and his ears tuned, Paul prayed hard. He prayed for the airmen's safety, so they could return to England to fly again. He prayed for the helpers in the escape line, who could be executed if caught.

And he prayed for the ache inside. Now he had men who respected him—Bentley and Pendleton and even Moreau. He grew closer to Josie each day. To want Lucie's love on top of that felt selfish.

To protect his work and all the people he aided, he had to push her away. He had to.

When the seven minutes passed, he made his way down the aisle. The airmen knelt two rows back, heads bowed. He didn't look their way.

One more prayer for their safety, and Paul departed for home, to dress for the hateful reception at the German Embassy. But it was for a higher good.

TUESDAY, SEPTEMBER 2, 1941

The poster offended Lucie to the core. A grotesque caricature of a Jewish man hovered with greedy fingers digging into a globe. The poster advertised "Le Juif et la France," a new exhibit at the Palais Berlitz run by an antisemitic French organization with German funding.

If there hadn't been so many people passing over the Petit Pont, Lucie would have ripped down the poster, wadded it up, and thrown it in the Seine. The Greenblatts, Jerzy, all her other Jewish friends—nothing greedy about them—unlike the Nazis, who stole and plundered.

Lucie marched over the bridge to the Île de la Cité. The hideous exhibit blamed everything wrong in France on the Jews rather than the Germans or the French. And people went to the exhibit. They paid three francs and went, thousands of them, even Véronique Baudin.

Just curious, Lucie's roommate had said. Just something to do with her friends, she said. It made her think, she said.

Thinking of it made Lucie feel ill.

Thank goodness she saw her roommates less and less each week. Last night Marie-Claude and Véronique had grumbled about résistants destroying the peace in Paris.

Was that how Paul felt too? Was that how he talked to his collaborating friends at his fancy soirees?

To her right, Notre-Dame de Paris rose in the partly cloudy sky, graceful and majestic.

On the plaza in front of the cathedral, Lucie sank onto a bench and set her lunch basket beside her. She'd come here to eat lunch away from roommates and customers and résistants.

Not much of a lunch, but she didn't have much of an appetite. She shoved aside her cloth napkin and pulled out a little jam sandwich.

A pigeon waddled over. For hundreds of years, people had sat on these benches and fed pigeons. The bird cocked its iridescent head at her and cooed.

"I only get 250 grams of bread a day," Lucie told him. "I'm not sharing. Be glad worms aren't rationed."

"Lucille Girard?" An elderly woman in lavender stood before her, the Marquise de Fontainebleu, formerly Ethel Marshall of Manhattan.

Lucie rose and greeted the woman, who attended the American Church in Paris.

"May I join you?" The marquise pointed to the bench.

"Please do. I was about to eat my lunch."

"I brought mine too." She sat and gazed at the cathedral.

179

"Our Lady and I have weekly lunch dates. She's remarkably accepting of this old Protestant."

Lucie mustered a smile and studied the edifice. The twelve apostles flanked the central door, including the Apostle Paul.

Paul. Her heart sank.

"Please pardon my prying, but I noticed your face was downcast." The marquise's blue eyes homed in on Lucie. "It isn't like you."

Lucie picked at her sandwich. "Oh, you know. The résistants and the Germans keep killing each other. It's escalating, and it's horrible."

"It is. I guess I was wrong." The marquise tipped her tiny chin. "I thought it was about a man. You had that look."

There was a specific look?

The marquise studied her with a knowing twist of her lips.

Lucie sighed. "It shows?"

"Paris is the city of love, my dear, so it is also a city of heartbreak. I have seen much in my many years here. And on Sunday, I saw you and a handsome widower trying not to eye each other."

A groan filled her throat. The last few weeks, she'd come close to forgetting who Paul Aubrey was. Yesterday he'd reminded her, inflicting more pain than her dentist had.

"Would you care for a listening ear?" Silver hair swept back from her kindly face to a chignon below her hat.

Lucie took a bite of her sandwich. She did want a listening ear. Talking to her parents or the Greenblatts was impossible. Her artistic friends wouldn't listen to one word about an industrialist, and her church friends had made their opinions of Paul clear.

The marquise had a reputation for fair-mindedness, and Lucie had never heard her gossip.

Lucie swallowed her sandwich and her pride. "Do you know him? Mr. Aubrey?"

"We're fairly well acquainted. Is he courting you?"

Courting—such a sweet, old-fashioned word. "No. He brings his daughter to my bookstore. We've become friends."

"And you're smitten with each other."

"I wouldn't say that."

The marquise clucked her tongue. "Friendship doesn't produce such disconsolate looks."

Above the cathedral's main doorway, Jesus sat on his throne, separating the righteous from the unrighteous. "Do you know he sells trucks to the Germans? He's a collaborator."

"Ah, but he is wealthy. Money has a way of covering faults."

Lucie managed a smile. "Is that what happened to you?"

"Ah no. My Pierre had not a penny. I fell in love with his title and château. He fell in love with my inheritance." She winked.

A common occurrence in France during La Belle Époque, and Lucie smiled.

"But we were happy. So happy. If he had lived longer, I might not remember him so fondly." Another wink.

Lucie tried to laugh.

The marquise patted Lucie's arm with elegant fingers. "You are not the first woman to fall for a wealthy man."

"Oh no, that's not it. He and his money represent everything bourgeois I dislike."

"Good little Left Bank bohemian, you are. And yet this wealthy collaborator has gotten under your skin."

Lucie shook her head, not in disagreement, but in befuddlement. Yes, he had.

The marquise brushed a loose silver hair off her high cheekbone. "There's something about the rogue that appeals, isn't there?"

"That's what I don't understand." Lucie hauled in a lungful of air. "I'm not attracted to his roguishness, but his goodness. I don't understand why. He sells to the Germans and goes to receptions at the German Embassy and socializes with German officers. He isn't even ashamed of it."

The marquise murmured compassionately.

Lucie threw up her hands, almost losing her sandwich. "I don't know what to think. My eyes and ears say he's no good. But my heart says he's good. I've always been able to read people. But this time I can't. I can't."

"So your eyes say one thing, and your heart says another. Ah, Miss Lucille, you're listening to the wrong voices." A gentle smile rose. "What does the Lord say?"

"The Lord . . ." Her heart sank even lower, because how could the Lord want her to be involved with a collaborator? And a growing part of her did want to be involved.

"Pray, Lucille. Pray, and God will guide you. Pray, and God will change your heart in one direction or the other. And I will pray for you too, dear."

"Thank you." Lucie's eyes swept up the cathedral's intricate design and solid structure. *Lord, guide me.*

25

Paul hung up the phone. Bentley Young's nurse had called to set an appointment to discuss treatment of Paul's fictitious ulcer. That meant Bentley had to communicate a change of procedure.

Thank goodness for the French tradition of two-hour lunch breaks that gave Paul time to go to the American Hospital in Neuilly on the outskirts of Paris.

Miss Thibodeaux leaned into his office. "Excuse me, Mr. Aubrey. Colonel Schiller is here to see you."

"Thank you. Please send him in." Paul did a quick survey. He'd tucked away his notes on this morning's inspiration for his tank design, his report to Duffy had already been delivered to the embassy officials, and he never committed his work in sabotage and aiding the RAF to writing. All was fine.

Colonel Schiller entered in his gray uniform.

After the men shook hands, the colonel sat across from Paul. "I wish I came under happier circumstances. I'm afraid one of your employees was arrested yesterday."

"Arrested?" A chill raced up his arms. No one had escorted airmen away from the factory yesterday, but someone had been caught doing something—that pointed to Aubrey Automobiles. "Who was it?"

"Gilbert Foulon." The faint lines in the colonel's face grew starker. "He was working with a prostitute in the Pigalle district. She lured a German soldier to her room, and Foulon stole his pistol and money."

Paul accentuated his frown even as relief surged. Foulon knew nothing of the resistance work in the factory. Moreau had vetoed his involvement because Foulon was reckless. "I'm surprised. Foulon is a good worker."

"Is he?" Schiller pulled a notepad from his pocket. "We received a letter of denunciation from an employee—René Lafarge. He witnessed Foulon throwing a wrench into a machine."

Paul let out a dry chuckle. "Lafarge is the troublemaker, not Foulon. If I didn't have a shortage of skilled laborers, I would have fired Lafarge long ago. He's always getting in fights and lodging complaints over trivial matters."

Schiller's square jaw shifted to the side. "Sabotage is hardly trivial."

"There was no sabotage. I'll have my secretary find the paperwork." Paul stood and went to his office door. "My best mechanic investigated. He didn't find a wrench, only a broken belt."

"I'd like to see that paperwork."

Paul leaned out the door. "Miss Thibodeaux, would you pull the files on employees René Lafarge and Gilbert Foulon?"

"Yes, sir." She wrote down their names.

Paul returned to his seat, eyeing the colonel. "Not that I'm unhappy to see you, but may I ask why you're here? Isn't this a police matter?"

"Ordinarily, yes." Schiller's gaze followed Paul's every step. "But as you know, terrorist acts like this have been spreading. The terrorists usually meet through school or work. We need to know who Foulon's friends are."

Paul lowered himself into his chair. "Once again a matter for the police, not an industrial commissioner."

Schiller spread his hands wide and raised an eyebrow. "You must admit you've had problems here recently. A series of problems, all seemingly unrelated and all readily explained."

"And yet . . ." Paul kept his hands relaxed on his armrests although every muscle tensed.

"Because of Foulon, I can't help but wonder if terrorists are here. My commission knows how factories run, so we'll work with the police."

"You're investigating my factory." His voice came out clipped.

"It'll only be a few days. We'll try not to interfere with operations."

"Good." He sharpened his voice. "If one of these men betrayed my trust, damaged my property, smeared the name of Aubrey Automobiles—well, you'd better catch him."

"I wouldn't worry. This investigation is a formality. I'm sure we won't find anything."

"I certainly hope not." He especially hoped they wouldn't find the five British flyboys in the storage room.

Schiller stood and sighed. "I'm afraid my commanding officer no longer sees your nation's status as an advantage but a liability. Did you see the newspaper article this morning about Roosevelt's Fireside Chat?"

"I did." Paul spoke in a grim voice and stood to walk the colonel to the door. After German U-boats had sunk three American merchant ships and had tangled with a US destroyer, the president had ordered the Navy to shoot on sight any German ships in American waters or attacking American ships. He also announced the Navy would escort Allied convoys to Iceland.

The Parisian papers only printed what the Germans allowed—and they called the president's order an act of war.

Schiller's mouth buckled on one side. "I have fond memories

of my time at Harvard and of my American friends—including you. I hope our nations never go to war."

"As do I."

Schiller tucked his cap under his arm. "Honestly, the German Military Command doesn't know which side the Americans in Paris are on."

"I don't know about the rest of my countrymen, but I'm on the side of making money."

Schiller laughed. "Good. Then we shall remain friends."

After the colonel collected the personnel files from Miss Thibodeaux, Paul returned to his office.

He sank into his chair, his heart thumping. German officials and French police would swarm the factory, and Paul had no control over what they would find.

Weak sunlight shone through the overcast onto the gardens of the American Hospital as Paul walked with Bentley.

He'd been tempted to skip the appointment and stand guard at the factory as if his presence could protect those under his care. Instead he'd decided that keeping the appointment would make him look unworried.

A nurse in a white cap and dress pushed an elderly woman in a wheelchair. Bentley greeted them, and Paul tipped his hat.

Bentley clasped his hands behind his back. "The procedures for delivering your packages are changing."

"All right." Paul gazed at the stately hospital building of red brick and white stone.

"They'll arrive as before, unannounced in the morning. But I'll no longer communicate with you unless something needs to be said in person."

Paul brushed his toe over a pebble on the walk. "How will I find out how to deliver the packages?"

"You'll use what we call a letter box, a location where we pass messages. Twice weekly you'll visit and pick up your messages. You'll read them at home, then burn them," Bentley said in a low voice. He pulled an envelope from the pocket of his lab coat. "This has two pieces of paper inside. One lists the codes used in the messages, plus code phrases you'll use to pick up the messages. Read it here, memorize it, then burn it in my office."

"All right." Paul slid his finger under the envelope's seal.

"The second is a list of books. In my office you'll transcribe it into your own handwriting. Take the copy and burn the original."

Paul looked up. "Books?"

Two nurses approached, chatting and laughing.

Bentley made small talk about the cloudy weather until the ladies passed. "Your messages will be tucked inside books. You'll ask the bookseller for each title in the sequence on your list. When you reach the end, you'll find a new list inside that book."

"Bookseller?" He could only picture one, but he couldn't picture her involved in work like this. "The letter box—is it a bookstall on the quai d'Orsay?"

Bentley gazed around, the breeze ruffling his white-blond hair. "It's Green Leaf Books."

"Green—what? No. I—I know the owner."

"That's why they chose this letter box. Since you're a regular customer, it won't require a change in routine that might draw attention."

"No." Paul shook his head, not caring if he no longer looked casual. "I refuse to draw *any* attention to that store, to Lucie."

Bentley stopped and faced him. "Lucie is the one you'll work with. Only Lucie. Never her assistant."

Glowering, Paul shoved the envelope at his friend's chest. "I refuse to get her involved in this. It's too dangerous."

"Paul." Bentley crossed his arms. "Think about it."

He *was* thinking about it. He was imagining that skinny German officer watching while Paul said the code phrase and Lucie . . .

No . . .

The only way she could know the proper response . . .

Paul's breath froze. Lucie was already involved.

26

Voilà!" At the cash register Bernadette opened the box from Monsieur Quinault.

Lucie pulled out a postcard announcing a reading by Saint-Yves of John Greenleaf Whittier's *Snow-Bound* in early October. "They turned out beautifully. Now we need to mail them to our subscribers."

"I will do that, and—see!—we can also hand them to our customers." She set a stack on the desk. "Now, come look. I have entered this week's expenses and income into the books."

Three young ladies entered the store, and Lucie greeted them. Then she faced Bernadette. "After they leave."

"Very good. See? We need each other, like Hal and Erma." Bernadette bustled toward the office.

Lucie smiled as she pulled out paper to plan the book reading. In the month and a half since Lucie had threatened to fire her, Bernadette had been the model of efficiency and diligence. Bills paid, papers filed, books tidy.

Yes, they did need each other.

Lucie nibbled on the end of her pen. On Sunday, Edmund Pendleton had read Scripture about how the church needed all the different gifts working together. Her gaze had flown to the dark-haired man in the front row with his very different gifts.

She'd been praying to find out what God said about Paul. Maybe Mr. Pendleton's message was the answer.

Or was it? Lucie frowned around the end of her pen. She could make peace with Paul being a wealthy businessman, but not with how readily he associated with the Germans. "It's excellent for business," he'd said. Cool and brusque.

"Hello, Lucie." Paul Aubrey stood in front of her.

Her pen clattered to the desk, and she scrambled to grab it. "Hello. It—it's Friday."

"Yes, it is."

It had made sense in her head. "You come on Saturdays."

"I—I'm looking for a book." He gazed around, his eyebrows pinched together.

What book couldn't wait until tomorrow? And why did he look nervous? Her heart tugged toward him, but she had to remember who he was at the core.

Paul glanced over his shoulder to the young ladies, who chatted at a table by the window. Then he leaned closer to Lucie, his expression grave, questioning . . . hopeful? "I'm looking for *The Decline and Fall of the Roman Empire*, the first volume. It's on hold."

On hold? The only books on hold were for résistants. And *Decline and Fall* was one of them. A coincidence. A strange coincidence. She couldn't give the book—and its message—to Paul.

"Let's see if I have a copy." She headed out from behind the desk.

Paul laid his hand on her arm. "No. It's on hold. I called for it this morning."

He'd done no such thing, and she stared at him.

His gaze intensified, with a lift of his eyebrows for emphasis, and he squeezed her arm.

He was a collaborator. Not a résistant. The message wasn't for him.

"It's—on—hold," he said, low and firm.

Her breath jolted in her lungs, and she stepped back, breaking his grip and his gaze. This was why they had code phrases.

On went her performance face, and she scanned the titles under the desk. "I love Edward Gibbon's writing."

"I do too. His use of language is sublime."

The most recent code, and she locked her gaze on him. "Sublime?"

Paul gave her a slow nod. "Sublime."

Lucie's head swam, and she fumbled for the desktop to brace herself. He was a résistant? How could that be?

His gaze continued in unflinching strength—and those eyebrows pinched again, pleading for her trust.

He was a résistant. Paul Aubrey was a résistant.

Her voice—where was it? "You—you don't seem like the sort of man to read Gibbon."

At the junction of his lip and his cheek, a smile flickered. "Perhaps you don't know me as well as you thought."

Her own lips twitched with a smile desperate for release. That sense of goodness and integrity—she'd been correct all along.

"May I?" He slid a masculine hand across the desk. "May I have the book, please?"

Her eyes, her ears, her heart, her soul—all sang in harmony. She retrieved the book and set it before him. "For you."

"Thank you." He paid her.

She could barely see to ring up the purchase and make change. Paul Aubrey—résistant. She didn't know him at all. And yet she'd known him well from the very start.

Paul held the book. There was a lightness and clarity about him, as if a veil had lifted that had weighed him down, that had concealed him from view.

"The store closes at seven, right?" he said. "Are you free tonight? Will you meet me—"

She was already nodding. "When? Where?"

He smiled, quick and gone. "I'd like to take you out, but a restaurant won't do."

"No." They needed to speak in private.

"Pont Royal at seven thirty? We won't have time to eat dinner beforehand, but we need to get home before curfew."

"I'll eat afterward." How could she eat anyway?

Paul slipped on his hat and bowed his head with delicious intensity in his eyes. "Until then."

She could only nod. After he left, she sank back against the wall, making the frames of the author photographs rattle. "Until then."

At 19:25 she crossed Pont Royal from the Left Bank of the Seine, her step light and eager. The sun hovered above the horizon, casting golden light on the river.

As she neared the center of the bridge, Paul came toward her from the Right Bank with a glow of anticipation.

They met in the middle. "Hello." It was all she could say.

"Hello." He stood close, filling her view, not moving for the longest moment.

All she wanted was to throw her arms around his neck and kiss him. She no longer needed words to know the truth about this man. And yet words seemed wise.

"Shall we walk?" He gestured north toward the Louvre and the Tuileries.

She fell in step beside him. "I have so much I want to ask you, so much to tell you, but I don't know where to start."

Paul glanced at the passersby, the men in business suits and ladies in colorful dresses. "Right now we shouldn't say anything."

"No." She stepped closer to him to let a bicycle pass. Her shoulder brushed his arm, and warmth surged through her.

Paul's hat shadowed his eyes, but his mouth bent in an appealing smile. He'd felt it too.

Lucie dipped her chin to conceal the admiration flooding her face. She needed answers first. Just a few.

"It's almost sunset," he said. "The Tuileries will be quiet after dark."

"Good." Then they could speak more openly. And with the curfew extended to twenty-three hours, they had time.

Paul passed the elegant buildings of the Louvre, open to the public only a few days a week—but the paintings had been carted into storage anyway.

Although they couldn't talk freely yet, she wanted to hear his voice. "How's Josie?"

He chuckled. "I told her I had a meeting. If she knew I was here without her, she'd be vexed."

"I'm so fond of her." She watched the toes of her gray lace-up pumps in step with his polished black oxfords.

"You're good for her." His voice rasped. "And for me."

Lucie didn't dare look up, but she let her shoulder rest against his. "You're good for me too."

The backs of his fingers brushed the back of her hand, and her breath caught. Oh, goodness. What would she do if he embraced her? Kissed her? She just might fall to pieces.

He turned in to the Tuileries, down a broad walk edged with marble statues and topiaries in want of pruning, a casualty of the occupation. Only a few people roamed since most were eating dinner or on their way home.

"I gather I'm not your only . . . customer." His voice barely rose above the sound of their footsteps on the gravel.

"No, you are not."

"I won't ask any more."

"Thank you." She studied his profile in the twilight. "What can you—can you tell me anything?"

He stopped at a round reflecting pool. A couple of sparrows bathed, their wings rippling the water, and Paul watched them, his jaw working.

Then he circled the pool. "I can't say why I'm visiting the store. Not that I don't trust you. I do."

"It's all right. I understand." The primary rule in the resistance was to only discuss operations with people vital to those operations. Even the strongest men and women caved under torture, and the fewer names known, the fewer revealed.

Paul cleared his throat. "Our long-term visitors would not approve of what I do."

"The rock-monsters."

He stopped and faced her, his jaw dangling. "Rock . . . ? Is that what Josie means?"

"I'm pretty sure. Their helmets, clomping around, stealing food."

"I didn't . . . she's very clever."

"Very."

Yet he frowned as he continued down the path, which headed between perfectly spaced rows of trees. "This isn't a good place for little girls."

No, it wasn't, but he needed reassurance. "Thousands of little girls live in this city."

"They don't have an opportunity to leave. Mine does."

"But you care about your workers." How could she have seen him as a heartless oppressor? He was anything but.

Paul slipped his hands in his trouser pockets. "I also care about the factory. To be honest, I've invested a lot of time and money and heart into this venture, and I can't bear to lose it."

Lucie nudged him with her shoulder. "That's why you stayed."

He shook his head. "Simone and I planned to leave last year

in the exodus. She wanted one last drive at Montlhéry—the racetrack. But she crashed. Not a bad crash, but she had so many broken bones. They found cancer in her bones, throughout her body. She was dying. She begged me to take Josie to the States. But how could I leave her to die alone?"

The poor man. Lucie slipped her hand into the crook of his arm. "Of course, you stayed. You loved her very much. You did the right thing."

He was silent for a bit. "After the Germans came, I had another chance to leave." His voice sounded faraway, drawn-out, pondering.

Lucie squeezed his arm and sighed in the graying light. Grief didn't end on an ordained schedule. Maybe Paul wasn't ready for a new romance yet—not truly. But for a man like this, she'd wait.

Paul peered between the trees, then tugged her arm and led her off the path. They passed through rows of trees and into a small meadow.

He led her around the edge of the meadow, glancing out between the trees. "In your store do you talk to your customers?"

An odd thing to ask. "Of course."

"I talk to mine too, even the rocky ones."

The Germans. "I'm sure you do."

"Sometimes they tell me interesting things. So do their friends, the ones I meet at dinner parties and receptions."

"Oh." The collaborators. The German officers. Paul was telling her something clandestine, so she joined in his scan of the area, her breath high in her lungs.

At the corner of the meadow, he turned. "It gives me interesting things to tell my friend from home, my friend in uniform."

Lucie strained to hear his voice. Was he—he was spying?

"That's the real reason I stayed." He gave his head a sharp shake. "I shouldn't have said that much, but I'm only endangering myself. Your store isn't involved in this."

"It's safe with me." Not only was he spying, but he was also doing something for the resistance that required passing messages. Her opinions and knowledge of Paul Aubrey rearranged in her head, dizzying her, and she clutched his arm for support. "Oh, Paul. Everyone thinks the worst of you. I thought the worst. I'm sorry. I said such horrible—"

"Don't be hard on yourself." Paul made another turn and checked through the trees. "You believed what I wanted you to believe, what you needed to believe. If I hadn't been ordered to use your store today, you'd still believe it."

"But I was wrong about you."

"No, you weren't." He sent her a little frown. "I sell to the rock-monsters. I make a profit. And I like making money."

Yet he'd stayed in Paris when going home would have been safer, more comfortable, and possibly more profitable. He stayed for the good of his workers and for the good of his country. As for that profit, surely he used that for good too.

In the dying light outside and the growing light inside, her eyes opened wide. "Paul? For the last few months, someone has been paying my rent anonymously."

They completed their circuit of the meadow, and Paul checked in all directions. Then he led her into the middle of the meadow, his shoes swishing in the unkempt grass. "One benefit of having money is being able to support noble causes—like the enlightening of minds."

A few weeks earlier, she would have been furious. Not now. He'd helped her back when she was barely civil to him. He'd helped her anonymously with no thought of impressing her or winning her heart.

In so doing, he'd accomplished both.

With her heart full and warm, she laid her head on his shoulder. "Thank you for doing that."

"Thank *you* for doing *that*." He folded her in his arms and rested his cheek against her temple.

Her arms encircled his waist, and her heart and mind danced a pas de deux, all she'd sensed about him now confirmed by knowledge. And their breath rose and fell in unison.

"Oh, Lucie." His voice puffed by her ear. "You have captured me completely."

Many writers had tried to woo her with flowery words, but none had touched her as deeply as those words from a man of numbers.

She lifted her face and pressed a kiss to his jaw, warm and solid and manly.

His chest rumbled, reverberating in hers, and he nuzzled her cheek.

They met in the middle, lips and hearts and breath joined. And he—he captured her completely.

This man who sacrificed his reputation and friendships, who risked his life for the sake of freedom.

Her throat clamped shut. She broke off the kiss and pressed her forehead to his shoulder, dislodging her hat a bit. "Oh, Paul. What you're doing—it's dangerous."

He sighed and rubbed her back. "I know. From the start, I've made provisions for Josie. Now I need to consider you too."

In the purple night, she raised her face to look him in the eye. "I would never ask you to stop. I wouldn't."

Paul kissed her nose. "Nor I you. And you're in danger too."

"Barely. It's all designed so I look innocent. Even ignorant."

He groaned, long and deep, and he clutched her tight. "Oh no."

"What?" Her voice muffled in his suit jacket, and her hat tumbled down her back.

"We can't do this again."

"What? What do you mean?"

"We can't date. We can't take romantic walks, can't even sneak away to meet each other."

She squirmed in his embrace, not understanding, not wanting to. "I don't see why not."

Paul pressed both hands to her cheeks. "Think about it. To do what I do, who do the rocks have to think I am? A collaborator. An industrialist who only cares about making a buck."

Lucie shook her head in his grip, glaring into his intense eyes.

"And to do what you do?" His voice gentled. "Who do you have to be? A darling, ethereal soul who cares only for art."

She kept shaking against the pressure of his hands. Of his words. But those words sank in regardless, sank into a dark void. "No . . ."

"That's what we have to be to each other." His thumbs massaged her cheekbones. "Oil and water. If I get caught, nothing must point to you. Nothing."

Her heart sank into that void too. "And vice versa."

Paul squeezed his eyes shut and nodded. "We can't be seen together except at the store and at church. Polite but cool. Nothing more."

Lucie clutched at the fine wool of his jacket, grasping for some other way, finding none. "I—I hate this."

"I do too." He straightened up and gazed around the meadow. "But no one's around."

"Hmm?"

"Right now the wise choice would be to walk you home and say good night at arm's length." He pressed his forehead to hers, his voice throaty, and his hands burrowed back into her hair. "Or the foolish choice."

The foolish choice—to make the most of the moment, knowing it might be the only moment they'd ever have.

Lucie chose the pain and kissed him, full of longing and dread, with all the wonder of their first kiss and all the poignancy of their last.

27

MONDAY, SEPTEMBER 15, 1941

On the factory floor below Paul, the workers went through their Monday morning routine, nervously glancing at blue-uniformed French policemen and gray-uniformed members of the German industrial commission.

Gerhard Schiller looked up to Paul on the balcony. In greeting, Paul raised a hand but not a smile.

Moreau told him the saboteurs had erased all signs of clandestine activity. Paul prayed they'd been thorough.

From what he could tell, the investigators had found nothing, but ironically they'd slowed production.

Since Saturday had been the first day of the investigation, Paul had come to the factory and sent Josie with Madame Coudray to Children's Hour. Paul blamed Schiller for stealing a precious hour with the woman he loved.

Seeing Lucie from a distance at church pained him now that he knew the feel of her lithe form in his arms and the taste of her lips and the sound of adoring words in her voice. For now, knowing she cared for him had to suffice, knowing she knew of his involvement with the resistance even though he couldn't reveal the details.

Footsteps thudded on the staircase to his left. René Lafarge ascended wearing a self-important smile, and Jacques Moreau followed, his face grim.

Paul eased back from the railing. What was going on?

"Monsieur Aubrey?" Moreau said. "We need to speak in private."

Paul glanced between the two men, one looking as if he'd lost a fortune and the other as if he'd found it. "Come into my office."

He opened the door and addressed Miss Thibodeaux at her desk. "I mustn't be disturbed."

"Yes, sir."

As Paul held open the door to his private office, Lafarge sauntered in. Paul shot Moreau a questioning look.

Moreau shook his head, his eyes pinched as if in pain.

Paul raised a mental shield and a mental sword, and he shut the door. "What is this about?"

Lafarge strolled around the office and ran his hand over unruly gray hair. "Nice place. Bigger than my apartment. Fancy rug, fancy desk, fancy chair." He trailed his fingers along polished mahogany and plopped into Paul's chair. "How much money do you make each week, Aubrey?"

Heat puffed out Paul's chest and burned up his throat. "I beg your pardon."

Lafarge stroked the leather armrest. "Do you prefer Paul?"

"I prefer 'Monsieur Aubrey,' and I prefer you get out of my chair."

"You do not dictate terms to me, Paul."

"What is going on here?" Paul snapped his gaze to Moreau.

The foreman stared at his scuffed shoes, his jaw jutted forward and his fists clenched behind his back.

Leaning back in the chair, Lafarge lifted his sharp nose high. "I dictate the terms. Unless you want me to talk to those German soldiers."

A fist clamped around Paul's heart and shut off blood flow, but he kept his face still. "I expect all my employees to cooperate with the investigation."

Lafarge laughed and wagged a finger at him. "You do not want me to tell them what I saw."

What had he seen? Sabotage? The airmen? The kisses in the Tuileries?

Paul knew better than to react or reveal. He strode in front of his own chair, crossed his arms, and looked down his nose at Lafarge. "What did you see?"

Too-full lips spread in a smile. "Sabotage."

"If so, I want to know. And I want you to tell the investigators."

Lafarge chuckled. "No, you don't. They'll arrest your workers and execute them. They'll turn this factory inside out. Why, they'll probably arrest you."

Paul glanced at Morcau. "What does he think he saw?"

The foreman shrugged. "He says he saw someone hiding evidence."

"I did see it." The chair creaked as Lafarge rocked forward. "On Friday afternoon, I saw Boucheron with a big bag of sand. I followed him outside, and he locked it in a shed. He looked like he was up to no good, so I broke in. I found acids and tools and sandbags—locked away from the Germans. Then I remembered parts wearing down after Boucheron fixed them. Crates falling apart, breaking all those windshields. The nails were corroded—by acid, I'll bet. Then I remembered a strange smell in the lubricant."

Paul thrust his chin at Lafarge. "If you're convinced this is happening, tell the police."

Lafarge spun the chair in a lazy circle. "If I tell the police, you'll be ruined. But what do I gain? A pat on the back? A citation? What good is that?"

Moreau shook his head, slow and ponderous.

Heaviness pressed on Paul's gut. He was about to get black-mailed.

Lafarge folded his hands on his belly. "By telling you, we both gain. You stay out of prison, and I—how much money do you make, Paul?"

Paul set one hand on his hip, slapped the other on his desk, and leaned into Lafarge's face. "You think you can blackmail me? Think again."

Lafarge laughed sour breath into Paul's face. "Think of it as an investment, keeping this factory open . . ." He picked up a framed photo of Josie. "Making sure this little thing doesn't become an orphan."

Paul snatched the frame out of Lafarge's greasy hand. "Get out of my office."

"Monsieur Aubrey," Moreau said in a heavy voice, "you must listen to him."

Chest heaving, Paul stared down his foreman. Moreau's gaze leveled at him—sad, determined, almost fatherly.

If Lafarge reported to the police, the saboteurs would be arrested, the factory scoured. They'd find the airmen, maybe trace the escape line. How many men in the factory and the resistance would be arrested? Executed? Maybe even men who weren't involved. The Germans weren't known for finesse.

How could Paul let good men die?

"These are my terms." Lafarge patted the armrest. "You will double my wages."

Paul clutched the brass picture frame and gave a sharp nod.

"Also, the sabotage must stop. The German army is the only thing protecting us from the Russian hordes. We need to get as many trucks to them as possible."

A low growl rose from Moreau.

Lafarge pointed a spindly finger at Moreau. "Tell your friends to stop. For each new act of sabotage, my price doubles. Or you all die."

"No one will die," Paul said between gritted teeth. "You win. Now get out."

Lafarge stood and bowed. "A pleasure doing business with you, Paul."

"Out. Now."

After Lafarge ambled out of the office, Paul shoved the door shut and motioned Moreau to the window, far from the door.

Moreau stood close, his thick eyebrows bunched together. "You can't fire him."

"No." If he did, he'd be pointing those German rifles at his own head and the heads of a dozen men or more.

"I don't think he suspects you," Moreau said in a low voice. "He only wanted to scare you."

Paul pressed Josie's photo to his stomach. It had worked better than it should have. "Does he know about our guests?" If Lafarge discovered the flyboys, Paul was doomed. The Germans offered a ten-thousand-franc reward for each airman, a price he couldn't match.

"No," Moreau said. "We can keep our hotel open, but we'll need to scale back everything else."

Paul blew out a hot breath. "Everything's on hold during the investigation anyway. We'll need to consider how we can proceed."

"*If* we can proceed."

Denial squirmed inside, but what choice did they have? It was one thing to risk your life, another to commit suicide. "Very well. Every Friday, I'll give you Lafarge's cash from my funds. It can't go through payroll."

"You did well. Very well." Moreau thumped him on the arm and left the office.

Paul sank into his chair and set Josie's photo where it belonged. Taken the Christmas before Simone died, the photo showed the two-and-a-half-year-old perched on a stool holding her stuffed cat, with a halo of curls around her laughing baby face.

If anything happened to Paul, Edmund Pendleton and Bentley Young would help Madame Coudray take Josie to Vichy, where Jim Duffy would get her home.

But he'd rather live. He'd rather live and watch Josie grow up. Preferably with Lucie by his side.

28

MONDAY, SEPTEMBER 15, 1941

At noon, Lucie stepped out of the bank after depositing checks for the store. She didn't mind running to the bank as long as Bernadette did the math beforehand.

Only pedestrians remained on the Champs-Élysées, which was cleared for the Nazi soldiers' daily parade, an event Lucie would rather miss. Too bad the Marbeuf Métro station was closed today and she had to go to the Champs-Élysées-Clemenceau station.

Yellowing leaves of plane trees whispered above her in the cool air, the skirt of her taupe suit brushed her knees, and her wooden-soled shoes clopped, as if saying, "Champs, champs, champs."

Lucie tilted her head and frowned. On Saturday at the store, a book had been turned in with a message sticking out. When she'd slid the note in, she'd glimpsed the message—"Champs" with symbols she'd never seen before.

A woman strolled toward her clad in a designer dress of deep plum and an outrageous hat. She even had a poodle on a leash.

Lucie didn't belong on the Champs-Élysées.

But Paul did.

Her stomach twisted, and not just from hunger. As much as she adored him, what sort of future did they have?

If the US and Germany went to war, the men would be interned almost immediately, assuming the Germans followed the same policy they had with British civilians. British women hadn't been interned until December 1940, several months after the men. Lucie might remain free—but separated from Paul.

If they went to America, then what?

Paul belonged in New England high society. Could Lucie become a bourgeois wife who hired help and attended luncheons? Paul might find her charming now, but what if she broke into a pirouette at a dinner party in front of some stuffed shirt?

The door to a milliner's store opened, and Alice Young stepped out wearing a burgundy suit. Lucie waved.

"Lucie, darling!" Alice kissed Lucie's cheek, then lifted a hatbox. "My latest purchase. What would we do without hats?"

"I can't imagine." Lucie tapped the green bow on her taupe pompadour beret. With clothing scarce and strictly rationed, Parisiennes kept up their morale and their love of fashion through *chapeaux*. "How have you been, Alice?"

She sighed. "Not as busy as I'd like. The membership of the American Women's Club and the hospital auxiliary is falling rapidly. I'm not sure how long we'll keep meeting."

Lucie murmured in sympathy. "Will the hospital close?"

"Not if we can help it. This spring we named a French director and placed the hospital under the Red Cross so it couldn't be requisitioned even if the . . . inevitable happens."

War, and Lucie nodded.

"Bentley will stay as long as he can, but he wants to send me home." A frown bent Alice's burgundy lips. "He thinks the Germans will let him remain free as a physician but might intern me."

Lucie patted her friend's arm. "I'd miss you, but I'd understand."

"How are you? I worry about your store."

"I'm making do." Through Paul's generosity, and her heart warmed.

"Still holding your Children's Hour?"

"I am." Although only four children had attended the previous Saturday, and Josie had been accompanied by her nanny, not Paul.

"Is Paul Aubrey still coming?"

Lucie stiffened. "Josie is one of my regulars. She's a delight."

"She is." Alice clucked her tongue. "Paul might not be as nefarious as I thought—did I tell you he doesn't make guns or tanks? Only trucks?"

"You did." Lucie respected her for admitting she was wrong and for diligently retracting the gossip she'd helped spread.

"Still he let his head be turned by money."

Everything in Lucie wanted to defend him, to tell Alice he was noble, not nefarious. But she clamped her impulsive tongue between her molars and shook her head. "I'll never understand people like that."

"Of course, you won't, you darling girl." Alice's blue eyes glowed. Then she gasped. "You poor thing. You're on your lunch break, and here I am chattering away. Why don't we continue this chat over lunch? My treat."

"Any place as long as it isn't on the Champs-Élysées. The daily parade starts soon." Then the beat of drums pressed on her chest. "Too late. There they are."

"Never mind them." Alice strode down the street. "Horrid brutes, but they won't bother us."

Hobnailed boots pounded toward them, but the French studiously ignored the soldiers in their gray-green uniforms and stony helmets.

Lucie found herself mesmerized by the synchronization of the goosestep, each leg rising to the same height, each boot clomping at the same time.

But the thud of German boots on France's most elegant boulevard shuddered through her, and she snapped her gaze away.

Half a block ahead of Lucie, three men walked close together. Oddly close. All wore poorly tailored business suits.

The man on the left made a knifing motion and held up one finger, two fingers, three.

Lucie's heart slowed. Her pace slowed. She grasped Alice's arm.

The men stopped and stood in a triangle. The man facing the street raised his arm, his hand hidden between the forms of the two others.

Sunlight glinted off steel.

Lucie slammed to a stop.

Three shots rang out. Alice screamed. So many screams.

Two soldiers fell in the street. Red stained gray.

Running, shouting, soldiers leveling guns.

The three résistants ran away from Lucie and scattered into buildings.

Alice hunkered by a tree, covering her ears, screaming.

"Run, Alice!" Lucie half-dragged her back the way they'd come. "Run!"

More shots rang out, but farther behind. Alice ran with Lucie, hatbox abandoned.

Lucie ducked into a boutique that smelled of silk and perfume and fear.

Two shopgirls stood at the plate glass and turned to Lucie, their eyes wide. "What happened?"

"Someone shot at the soldiers," Lucie said.

One of the girls rapped a slender fist on the glass. "Those résistants! They do not care about us. Now the Germans will kill—how many? How many must die so these cowards can feel brave?"

Alice moaned. "Are they—are they dead?"

Lucie put her arm around her friend's shaking shoulders. "I—I don't know."

"I've never seen—never seen—" Alice pressed her hands over her eyes.

"Me neither." After things quieted down, Lucie would see Alice home.

"What are they thinking?" The shopgirl folded her arms across her stylish white silk blouse. "In broad daylight."

The attack was planned. Choreographed. A chill shimmied up Lucie's arms. The note—the one that read "Champs"—was it for this?

A cry strangled in her throat. The note, the signal for the attack—*she'd* passed it along. She'd played a role in this shooting. This violence.

How many times had people reminded her she was too impulsive, not bright enough? Whatever made her think she could be levelheaded and clever?

Two men lay bleeding, maybe dying. In reprisal, other men would be shot.

And Lucie—Lucie had played a role.

Saturday, September 20, 1941

Sometimes Paul wished he spoke German. At a café on boulevard Saint-Michel, he read a book while two German soldiers sat at the sidewalk table to his right.

When Josie was at Children's Hour, he always chose a table close to the rock-monsters. Sometimes they sat with French people and spoke French, and Paul eavesdropped. Rarely did they discuss anything but home and women and movies.

An elderly man in a black coat sat on the far side of the Germans and leaned toward them. "Excuse me? May I ask a favor?"

A dark-haired soldier set down his cup. "You ask a favor of us?"

"I read in the paper—in *Je suis partout*—that in Germany you make the Jews wear stars so you can tell them apart. When can we have that here? I would like that. I don't want their kind in my store."

The soldier smiled. "It is a good idea, ja? Maybe someday here too."

Paul's stomach warped. He slapped down his payment and left. It was time to pick up Josie anyway.

How could people be so cruel? And if Nazi racial theory enabled them to pick out Jews by the shape of their heads and noses as they claimed, why did they need to label them?

"What have we come to?" he muttered.

He marched down the narrow street. A bilious yellow poster rimmed in black fluttered on a wall, partly torn. *"Avis"* it proclaimed, listing three men executed for espionage by the Germans. Someone had painted a bright red *V* over the poster, and dried-out bouquets lay on the sidewalk, defying the law against memorializing résistants.

Paul averted his eyes. Twice this past week, résistants had shot Germans—and in turn, ten hostages had been hauled out of prison and shot.

Restlessness hustled his step. He ought to return to Massachusetts. He really ought to. That could have been his name on that poster.

But how could he leave yet? He and Lucie and Josie needed papers, including passes to cross the demarcation line between occupied and unoccupied France, which could take weeks to obtain. As soon as Paul applied, Schiller would move to requisition the factory. Which meant all resistance work would have to be shut down beforehand.

They'd have to stop using the factory as a safe house, and right now seven airmen were crammed in that room.

Paul blew out a sharp breath.

At least Schiller's investigation had found nothing. And although Lafarge's blackmail put a damper on sabotage, Paul's men were plotting subtler methods. If Paul left, even subtle sabotage would have to end.

At the place de l'Odéon, he turned onto Lucie's street and tried to calm down for Josie's sake and Lucie's.

Something was wrong with Lucie, which had made it even harder to leave during Children's Hour. Not only did he want to watch Lucie spin stories and spin on her toes, but he also wanted to find out what had stolen the sparkle from her eyes.

Paul entered the bookstore. Lucie stood by her office in her pink skirt and sweater. She chatted with a young mother while two children played on the floor with Josie.

Josie had insisted on wearing pink today with her hair ribbon tied around her head like Lucie's rather than in a bow above her ear. She'd been trying to stand on her toes too. His daughter could do far worse than to emulate Lucille Girard.

Lucie's posture was stiff, her face tense, even as she smiled at something the other woman said.

Then she glanced his way, and everything softened—her shoulders, her smile. His heart.

He gave her a nod as if any other father picking up a child, but his gaze lingered longer than was wise.

"Hi, Daddy!" Josie ran to him.

He swung her up to his hip. "Hello, bubble gum. Did you have fun?"

"Uh-huh." She played with his necktie. "Monsieur Meow per-tended to be a lion so he could live in the zoo, and he met a real lion, and he learned to roar, and we learned too. Want to hear?"

"Why don't you show me outside so you don't scare anyone?"

The mother said goodbye to Lucie, gathered her children, and left. But a trio of young men sat in the nonfiction section

211

talking with Bernadette. Not private enough. Never private enough.

He turned to Lucie. "Hello there."

"Hello." Her eyelashes fluttered as if she were trying not to cry.

Paul stepped as close as he dared. "Are you all right?"

"Yes." She spun away and picked up blocks.

She was definitely not all right, but he couldn't take her in his arms or talk with her plainly. His desire to help banged against the walls of his chest.

He was trapped in small talk. Code phrases. He cleared his throat. "Do you have the book I ordered—*The Count of Monte Cristo?*"

Kneeling by the box of blocks, Lucie shook her head.

Paul mashed his lips together. More bad news. How much longer until those airmen could leave? Did the resistance know his storeroom was full and not to send any more guests?

Lucie gazed at a wooden giraffe in her hand. "Would you like me to call when it comes in?"

"Yes, I would. Do you have my phone number?"

"Let me check your subscriber card."

Paul shifted Josie higher on his hip and followed Lucie to the cash register, savoring how her skirt swirled around her pretty legs.

At the desk Lucie opened a wooden box and pulled out a card. "No phone number."

Paul set Josie on the floor. "Why don't you help Miss Girard and make sure all the blocks are put away?"

"Okay!" She ran to the children's area.

Paul pulled out his pen and wrote down his home and work phone numbers. "Call any time," he said in a low voice. "Day or night."

She nodded, her head still lowered.

They couldn't even talk freely on the phone. The lines could be tapped, and Paul gritted his teeth.

Lucie rubbed her thumbs over the card. "Would Josie like a ballet lesson?"

"A ballet lesson?"

"I have a barre in my storeroom upstairs." Her voice barely reached his ears. "My roommates and I practice there. I could give her a lesson. Maybe tomorrow after church?"

Paul stared at her bowed head, the light brown hair curling about her cheeks. "Just Josie?"

"You could stay." She raised her eyes, and devastation washed through the hazel depths—then washed away.

In her storeroom. They'd have a little chaperone, but they could speak.

"Would she like that?" Lucie asked.

"Yes, I would—*she* would."

"All right." She tucked Paul's card back in the box.

He tapped his finger on the box to get her attention, then flashed a smile. "Miss Girard, you are brilliant."

She winced and turned her head as if he'd had onion soup at the café instead of ersatz coffee. "I'll see you tomorrow."

"Tomorrow." Paul stared after her as she flitted to the back office. How could he wait that long to find out what was wrong?

29

SUNDAY, SEPTEMBER 21, 1941

No one but Paul and Josie stood outside Green Leaf Books, but Lucie peered out the window one last time. As requested, the Aubreys arrived half an hour after Lucie, so she had time to change into leotard, tights, and a wraparound skirt.

She ushered them in and led them through the empty store. "Shh. We mustn't wake Monsieur Meow. He naps all Sunday afternoon, the lazy cat."

Josie giggled, then clapped her hand over her mouth.

The back door opened to the stairwell, where another door led out to the courtyard. Coming through the store, they'd avoided the nosy concierge.

Lucie climbed the stairs and entered the storeroom. Sunlight poured over the wooden floor. Boxes were piled against two walls, leaving the floor and the barre clear for dancing.

Paul closed the door. "This is where you ladies practice?"

Lucie sat on a crate and exchanged her pumps for ballet slippers. "I practice here every evening after the store closes. Marie-Claude and Véronique used to join me, but not anymore." Without the ballet to bind them together, the friendship was fraying, and Lucie frowned.

Paul removed his hat and stepped up to the mural. "Did this come with the place?"

"Oh no." The mural was almost what she'd imagined. Perhaps two more dancers. "I've been painting it bit by bit."

Paul turned to her, eyebrows high, smile wide. "You never fail to amaze me."

Her throat threatened to close, and she focused on her slippers so she wouldn't dissolve. Although she wanted to unburden herself to him, Josie deserved her full attention.

Josie swung her arms back and forth. "When can I dance on my toes?"

"Not for a long time, little one. I didn't get my first pointe shoes until I was ten. All ballerinas learn to dance in soft ballet slippers like I'm wearing." She lifted a pair, the dusky rose leather scuffed and cracked. "This is my first pair. They're a little big for you, but we'll make do. Sit down, and I'll help you."

Eyes huge, Josie plopped to the floor and stuck out her legs from under her brown plaid dress.

Lucie took off Josie's Mary Janes and slid on the slippers. She pulled the strings tight, tied a bow, and tucked it inside the slipper.

"Let's start with first position." Lucie stood and removed the knee-length wraparound skirt from over her skirted black leotard. "Stand with your heels together—"

Scraping and thumping sounds. Paul sat lopsided on a crate, his feet scrabbling under him. He averted his eyes, his color high. "I—uh, missed."

Because he'd never seen her in a leotard before? Lucie almost laughed for the first time in days.

But she didn't want to embarrass the man, so she stood in first position with her heels together. "Only turn out your feet as far as is comfortable."

Josie wobbled, her legs bent.

"Good. Even more important than turnout is posture. A

ballerina stands tall and straight. Shoulders over hips, hips over knees, knees over toes. Now imagine a string coming out of the top of your head." Lucie tapped the crown of her head and pulled the imaginary string. "Imagine someone pulling up that string at all times—when you stand, walk, bend, kick, or jump."

Josie lifted her chin, hunched her shoulders, and stretched tall, her eyes shining.

Lucie tapped Josie's curly head and lifted the string. Then she guided Josie's chin level, her shoulders down, her hips forward, her knees straight, and her arms gently rounded. "Do you feel that string?"

"I do!"

"I can tell. You already look like a ballerina. So graceful."

"I do?"

"You do. Let's come to the barre. Mine is too tall, so you'll use this chair." She led her to a wooden armchair, then Lucie laid her hand on the barre. "First position. Now we'll learn to *plié*, to bend. Keep your heels glued to the floor and bend your knees. Keep your back straight—remember that string."

Lucie demonstrated, and Josie copied. After a series of pliés, Lucie showed her how to rise to the balls of her feet in a *relevé*, then to point her toe in a *battement tendu*.

Watching Josie learn the moves warmed Lucie's heart. She used to love helping *les petit rats* in the Paris Opéra Ballet School, and she'd hoped to teach at the school after she retired from the stage. But since she'd retired at only twenty-six and from the lowest rank, she'd never have a teaching position there.

Sitting on his crate, Paul smiled at Lucie, no veil concealing his affection. Now that warmth touched every corner of her heart. If only they could stay in this room forever, where they could be open with each other.

Even now she couldn't be completely open, not with young ears in the room.

Paul tilted his head and gave her a concerned frown.

Lucie blinked and spun to the phonograph. "You're doing well, Josie. Now you may dance." Her own teachers would have fainted. They believed in developing a dancer's training in a proper sequence. But Josie was younger than most girls when they started, too young for rigidity.

She pulled a record from a sleeve and placed it on the turntable—the waltz from Tchaikovsky's *La Belle au bois dormant*, or as it was known in English, *Sleeping Beauty*. "All right, Josie. I'm going to talk to your father. Go ahead and spin and jump, but I also want to see pliés and relevés and tendus."

After she lowered the arm to the record, majestic music swelled. Josie swayed, raised her arms, and turned, all very charming.

Paul stood, and Lucie joined him by the wall, facing Josie.

"What's wrong?" he said in his low, rumbling voice.

Despite her turmoil, Lucie smiled for the child's sake. "Did you hear what happened Monday on the Champs-Élysées?"

"I did." The wool of his jacket sleeve brushed her bare arm.

"I was coming out of the bank and ran into Alice Young. We—we saw it."

"Oh no. But you—"

"We're all right. We ran."

"I'm sorry you had to see that."

That wasn't what kept her gut churning. "One of the notes that came through my store read 'Champs.' One of the men—I realize I've seen him before. I think . . ." Her throat closed off.

Paul rubbed her back and murmured to her.

Out on the floor, Josie had stopped spinning and was doing pliés.

Lucie swallowed hard. "Then on Thursday, a man handed me a book. It was far too heavy. After the store closed, I opened it. Someone had hollowed out the pages. There was a—a revolver inside."

"Oh no."

"I won't have it." She shook her head rapidly. "I told my contact I won't be a part of shootings and if I find another weapon, I'll shut down operations immediately."

"That was wise. If you get caught with weapons . . ."

She'd be shot, and she shuddered.

Josie found the full-length mirror in the far corner, and she did pliés, watching herself.

Lucie leaned against Paul's side. "I won't ask you to tell me what you do for the resistance, but does it—does it take lives?"

"Saves them, I hope." He brushed one finger along the side of her hand.

"I'm glad."

The record ended, and Lucie dashed over to flip it. "Those are beautiful pliés, Josie. I love how you keep your heels glued to the floor."

"I'm trying."

Across the room, Paul leaned against the wall, strong and compassionate.

She hurried back to his side. "What have I done? I thought the whole thing was clever and romantic and exciting, but I can't control the messages that come through. I was stupid."

"Stupid?"

Lucie twisted her hands together. "I've always been stupid. Why did I think—"

"Hey, now." Paul grasped her arm above the elbow. "You're not stupid, not in the slightest. Don't confuse education with intelligence."

"Oh, I know you can be smart without going far in school, but I didn't go far in school *because* I'm not smart."

"Don't talk like that." Paul touched her cheek and turned her face to him.

Footsteps pattered across the room, and Lucie whipped her gaze away to find Josie. The girl ran to the mural and mimicked a painted ballerina's arabesque.

"Lucie." Paul stepped in front of her, his gaze piercing. "Do you think I'm smart?"

What a silly question. "Of course."

"All right, then. I, as an intelligent person, consider you my equal. You're well-spoken and well informed. Never once have I thought you weren't bright."

Lucie scrunched up her face. He hadn't seen her stumble through math homework or daydream during history.

Paul gathered her hands in his. "Your intelligence shows in so many ways—how you understand people, your knowledge of books, your creative solutions, like this ballet lesson."

Lucie edged over so she could eye the petite ballerina, now copying a painted curtsy.

"If that doesn't convince you . . ." He squeezed her hands. "Do you honestly think I would have revealed my secret to a stupid woman?"

Her gaze flew back to him. He had a point.

Paul glanced back to his daughter, then at Lucie. He pressed a kiss to her lips. Too short. Too sweet. "I never want to hear you talk that way again about the woman I love."

Her knees went limp. "Love?"

Paul blinked, then his eyes stretched wide. "Didn't I say that the other day? In the Tuileries?"

He'd said many fine things, and his lips had communicated many more fine things. "I—I would have remembered."

His Adam's apple slid to the knot of his tie and back up. "Do you mind?"

Where was her voice? She struggled to find it. "Why would I mind hearing that from the man I'm falling in love with?"

Paul's voice rumbled in his chest, and he rested his forehead against hers and sought her lips.

"Daddy! Did you see?"

He whirled away from Lucie and slapped his hand to the back of his neck. "See?"

"Look!" Josie poked one arm before her, one behind her, kicked her leg back—and fell over.

Lucie smiled, rushed to the child, and helped her up.

With a pout, Josie pointed to the mural. "Why can't I do that?"

"An arabesque? That takes time."

Paul took Josie's hand. "An arabesque, you say? Why don't you show us?" He winked at Lucie.

She remembered his touch under her arm on the quai d'Orsay. Longed for it. But his words and gazes had to do for now. She raised her arms and leg in first arabesque.

Paul sat cross-legged on the floor, leaned against the wall, and pulled his daughter onto his lap. "Show us more."

For the first time in her life, she hesitated to dance in front of an audience, but Paul and Josie's expectant grins tore down her reservations.

After Lucie put on her pointe shoes, she started the "Sleeping Beauty Waltz" again. The familiar strains of the garland dance flowed through her, and she performed the beloved *balancés* and *pirouettes* and *assemblés*.

Never before had she performed for such an appreciative audience. Never before with such pure joy.

30

Angry shouts and stamping feet reverberated through the factory, and Paul marched across the floor, fists clenched, glaring at his workers.

"Aubrey injuste," they chanted, shaking fists in the air.

Memories crashed around in his head of the strikes and riots and the occupation of his factory in 1937. Except this time, he didn't have a pistol in his jacket for protection.

This time he didn't need it.

Because this time he'd planned it.

Jean-Pierre Dimont stepped in front of Paul, his tiny eyes on fire. "No more oppression! Forty hours!"

"Out of my way." Paul elbowed past him.

For the past two weeks, Dimont, Moreau, and Silvestre had agitated about factory hours, demanding a forty-hour week, a luxury enjoyed by no other industrial workers in Europe. After the Germans tolerated massive strikes in Belgium and the Pas de Calais region of France with only minimal arrests, Moreau had hatched the plan.

"Forty hours!" the men chanted.

Paul scowled at them and marched toward his office.

The ringleaders had done a magnificent job stirring up anger and slowing production, while avoiding violence that would bring in the police.

And René Lafarge's filthy blackmailing hands were tied. If the workers had demanded higher wages, Lafarge would have insisted Paul comply to get the men back to work. But a shorter workweek would decrease production of trucks that could carry the Wehrmacht to Moscow as Lafarge wished. So Lafarge had to take Paul's side in the labor dispute.

Moreau was brilliant.

The general foreman stood at the foot of the stairs, his burly arms crossed.

Paul pointed at him. "You! In my office—now. This must stop immediately."

Moreau thrust out his chest. "It'll stop when we have a forty-hour week. You demand too much of us on short rations."

As he stomped upstairs, Paul kept his voice raised. "I can't meet our production quotas with a forty-eight-hour week. How on earth could I do so with forty? It's absurd!"

"That's not my concern. The men are my concern. Forty hours!"

"If you didn't get it in '37, what makes you think you can get it in '41?"

"Hire more men!"

At the top of the stairs, Paul threw up his hands. "Who? You tell me—who?"

He flung open his office door and barged in.

Miss Thibodeaux looked up, her eyes huge.

"Pardon me, Miss Thibodeaux," Paul said. "Why don't you take your lunch? Then you won't have to listen to this yelling boor of a man."

"Boor?" Moreau bellowed. "Better than a pompous bourgeois pig!"

Miss Thibodeaux scurried out.

222

Paul entered his private office with Moreau on his tail, and he slammed the door for good effect.

Then he grinned at Moreau. "Pompous bourgeois pig? Nice touch."

Moreau thumped his fist over his chest. "It comes from the heart."

Paul laughed and pulled a chair to his side of the desk so they could review plans, then he opened his lunch tin. "My cook packed two lunches. This pig is providing ham."

But Moreau studied the drawings on Paul's desk. "I don't recognize this design."

Paul traced one finger along the lines. "I call it the Aura-besque, inspired by a ballerina's arabesque." Someday he'd build the elegant sedan that would carry a family but make drivers feel as if they were in the Monaco Grand Prix.

"It's good." Moreau tapped the drawing. "Your best yet."

"Thanks. I think so too." He could already see the ad campaign—Lucie in a golden tutu, lit to bring out the gold in her hair, photographed in arabesques paralleling the car's lines—a full color spread in the major magazines.

Alone at night, Paul could only think of Lucie—dancing, saying she was falling in love with him, glowing with trust. If only they could meet more often in her little ballet studio.

But they hadn't done so once in the past month. Lucie insisted they could only meet when they absolutely needed to speak in private. Paul had joked that Josie needed a lesson every day, but he'd received only a watery smile in response.

Lucie was right. They had to follow the original plan to see each other only at church, Children's Hour, and his midweek visit to check for messages. All at a polite distance. Anything more would risk unraveling the webs they'd spun.

Seated at the desk, Moreau unwrapped his sandwich. "That went well on the factory floor. You reminded me why I used to hate you."

Paul laughed and placed his drawings in his attaché case. "Same here. Everyone believes it, including Lafarge."

"Lafarge." Moreau spat out the name with a few bread crumbs. "Always snitching, making up sabotage that doesn't exist, opposing our strike."

"He'll make no friends that way." Paul sat and unwrapped his sandwich. "What's next?"

"The men are worked up enough. On Monday, we'll start our sit-down strike."

"Good." Paul chewed his ham sandwich. They'd chosen a sit-down strike so the workers would come in and out of the factory as usual—but without working. That would allow them to continue to move British airmen.

"How long do you think we can strike?" Moreau wiped his mouth with the back of his hand.

"I don't know. As long as the men are peaceable, I can hold off the police. I'll have to notify Schiller—and sound irritated. We'll have at least one day, plus the slowdown this week due to the agitation. Every day we can stretch it out will help."

Moreau swallowed a bite. "We're running out of time. America is sure to enter the war, and the Germans will take over the factory."

"I know. We're making plans for our guests." Yesterday he'd met with Bentley for a supposed ulcer flare-up. They'd discussed when and how to shut down the safe house and to get Paul, Josie, and Lucie out of France. Paul hadn't mentioned his relationship with Lucie, but he'd insisted on including her.

If the Germans found evidence that Green Leaf Books was a letter box, Lucie would be shot or sent to a work camp in Germany. And if they discovered any of Paul's activity, he'd be tortured and shot. Neither of them could risk internment.

But timing their departure was tricky. Before they left, either legally or via the escape lines, all resistance activities had to stop. With the strike on the horizon, Paul wanted to delay his departure as long as possible.

Moreau gathered the last crumbs, squished them together, and popped them in his mouth. "If things happen fast, Silvestre and I will take the guests home. We won't let them get caught."

"Thanks. I hope it doesn't come to that. You two would be in great danger."

Moreau gave Paul a sidelong glance. "A few years ago, you wanted me dead."

Paul cracked a smile. "I never wanted you dead. I just wanted you to behave."

"You shoved a gun in my face."

"Self-defense."

Moreau narrowed midnight-black eyes at Paul. "I never understood—why didn't you fire me?"

Paul returned the napkins to the lunch tin. "You're a good foreman—the best. And the men like you and respect you, but they also obey you."

"You could have found someone just as good, someone who didn't fight you."

With a shrug, Paul latched the lunch tin. "If he got along well with me, the workers would have hated him, would have seen him as the boss's lackey."

"Well . . . yes."

"The men would have turned their anger from me to the new general foreman. I didn't want that. I'll take the anger myself and let the foreman have a strong relationship with the men."

Moreau grunted, his mouth bent down. "That—that was good of you."

Paul rested back in his chair. "You and I—we've always gotten things done while meeting the men's needs. We're a good team."

"I know. I—I've always known."

"You have?" Paul's eyebrows rose.

"You're a fair employer. You treat us well. Doesn't mean I'll stop pushing you." He gave Paul's shoulder a light shove.

"You'd better. It's your job. And it's my job to push back." Paul returned the gesture.

Moreau chuckled. "Pig."

"Boor." Paul grinned at him. "So how's your wife? Your daughters?"

Moreau talked away, mostly about his little grandsons, his pride.

In about half an hour, Moreau would storm out of the office with Paul on his heels, yelling insults at each other for anyone in earshot.

For now they could talk as colleagues. Friends.

31

WEDNESDAY, OCTOBER 29, 1941

Hunkered in her overcoat at a café table on place de la Sorbonne, Lucie smoothed Paul's letter with her gloved hand.

She should have burned it, but how could she?

Heart-shaped yellow linden leaves swooped down in the chilly breeze, and she brushed one off Paul's letter. In his neat, bold handwriting, he'd addressed her as "my beloved" and signed it, "he who loves you." Lucie would trim and save those bits before burning the rest.

Last night when he'd picked up *The House of the Seven Gables*, he'd slipped the letter to her between franc notes.

"It's time for a lesson," he'd written. Apparently he had important information to relay. And she craved his presence, even if chaperoned by a tiny ballerina.

Lucie's breath whirled silver, joining the breeze among the drifting yellow leaves, the spindly black trees, and the men and women in winter coats. At the end of the place de la Sorbonne, the Sorbonne Chapel lifted its ornate golden seventeenth-century façade to the gray sky.

Her lunch break over, Lucie tucked Paul's note into her purse and left payment for her meager fare. Strolling down the cobble-

227

stone plaza, Lucie picked up a dozen of the prettiest linden leaves for her store display.

As she approached the boulevard Saint-Michel, Lucie stayed to the left side of the plaza. The Librarie Rive Gauche stood on the right corner. Opened in April, the largest bookstore in Paris specialized in Nazi and collaborationist literature, and she'd only ever seen German soldiers enter.

The store window displayed memorabilia and writings from fascist French writer Henry de Montherlant. His new book, *Le solstice de Juin*, celebrated the German conquest of France as the inevitable triumph of paganism over Christianity.

Lucie wanted to spit in that direction, but she wasn't the spitting sort.

She crossed Boul' Mich' and headed down the narrow rue de Vaugirard toward home.

It wouldn't be home for long. For the first time ever, she was anxious to leave Paris.

In early October, French fascists had set off bombs in six synagogues in Paris. And in the past week, résistants had assassinated German officers in Bordeaux and Nantes, leading to the execution of almost 150 men—and a seventeen-year-old boy. From London, Gen. Charles de Gaulle pleaded with the resistance to stop such killings to avoid further reprisals.

After the attack on the Champs-Élysées, Lucie had pinned down Renard in a private conversation in the bookstore. She'd made him promise no weapons would pass through her store, nor any messages about shootings or bombings. To keep him honest, she'd told him she'd no longer follow his order not to read the notes.

At the next intersection Lucie waited for a bicycle to pass, then she trotted across, the freezing wind pushing her from behind.

Leaving for the States seemed wise.

Lucie passed the Odéon Théâtre. Leaving required reams

of paperwork—an "Ausweis" exit permit from the Germans to cross the demarcation line, an exit visa from Vichy France, and transit visas for Spain and Portugal. A time-consuming process that might turn dangerous German attention to her store and Paul's factory.

Leaving would also deprive the resistance of an important letter box, where dozens of messages passed each week.

And leaving would mean abandoning Green Leaf Books. Who would buy an English-language bookstore, stripped of stock and devoid of customers? She could sign the deed to Bernadette, but without Paul's financial support, the store would fold.

Usually the thought of losing the store prompted a crush of guilt, but now only a soft, sad wave. Yes, Hal and Erma's dream would die, but Lucie had done her best.

Today she needed to inform Bernadette so she could search for a new job.

At the place de la Odéon, Lucie turned up her street to the beloved green façade. The store windows displayed bright and appealing books, surrounded by fall leaves.

The back office was dark, but Bernadette wouldn't return from lunch for at least an hour.

Lucie placed her purse and hat in the office but kept on her coat and gloves to ward off the chill. The Germans gave out no coal for heating, and Lucie wanted to save her firewood for winter.

With the store empty, Lucie arranged the yellow linden leaves among the orange plane leaves and the chestnut leaves, her favorite. Each of the seven rounded lobules changed from green in the center to yellow to orange to brown on the serrated edges.

Soon all the leaves would be brown, but that would be attractive too.

A young man in a gray coat entered, a man who'd frequented the store the last few weeks. He had a memorable face with a long jaw that reminded Lucie of a spade. And he always bought books, although he spoke no English.

Lucie addressed him in French. "Bonjour, monsieur. May I help you find a book?"

He stood by the cash register. "My wife put a book on hold and asked me to pick it up."

A new résistant. The harsher the Germans became, the faster the resistance grew.

After she laid down the last linden leaf, Lucie went behind the desk, where half a dozen books waited. "What is the title?"

"I do not know. My wife told me to pick it up."

Lucie's mouth opened, ready to recite the titles on hold, but a dark sensation niggled inside and pressed her tongue to the roof of her mouth. The title was the opening step in the choreographed dance of code phrases.

She gave him a patient smile and turned the phone to him. "Why don't you ask your wife the title?" Although few Parisians had phones at home.

That long jaw edged from side to side. "We don't have a phone. Tell me the titles you have. I'll recognize it."

Prickles raced up her arms. What if he wasn't a résistant but an informant? What if he'd been watching the store and had seen the exchange of books?

She refused to get ruffled, so she kept her patient smile in place. "Why don't you ask her at home and return later? You don't want to buy the wrong book."

Annoyance flickered in his dark eyes. "Read the titles. I'll know it."

The worst thing she could do was tell him the titles. He could choose any one and intercept a message.

She slid the telephone back in place, her heart thumping. She absolutely could not give him any of the books. Each was reserved for a specific person.

Lucie shot him a smile. "What's your name, sir?"

"My name?"

"Yes, sir. Each is labeled with a name." A lie, but if he was genuine, he could find out the title at home and return.

The man's gaze skittered about. "Jean. My name is Jean."

The most common men's name in France. She murmured and shook her head. "I don't have a book for a Jean."

That jaw thrust out. "Read the titles."

"Your wife's name? Your surname?" She batted her eyelashes, as innocent as could be.

His chest heaved.

She kept smiling.

"Stupid woman." With a loud grunt, he marched to the door. "See if I ever shop here again."

As soon as he disappeared from sight, she sagged against the desk and her breath poured out. No, he'd never return. But someone else might.

Time to end this forever. She rushed to the mantel, grabbed the plant, and flung open the front door.

Across the street strolled the young résistante in her bright, abstract-print turban. She met Lucie's gaze, and her eyes widened.

Was Lucie being hasty? Impulsive? Cowardly in the face of danger that others endured without flinching?

Before she did anything permanent, she needed another talk with Renard. With shaky steps, she backed up.

For at least another day, she'd keep the plant inside.

32

Paul leaned against the wall outside Lucie's office. Since none of the families attending Children's Hour today knew him, he felt no need to banish himself.

Standing before the children in her pink skirt and a thick gray sweater, Lucie held up the Feenee puppet. "Feenee loves spaghetti. One day she ate so much spaghetti that it made her hair grow and grow. So she cut her hair and wound it into balls and gave them to the kitty-cats to play with. Which color do you think Monsieur Meow chose?"

"*Vert!*" a little blond boy called, one of only four children present. "Green."

"Right." Lucie fingered a green curl on Feenee's head. "Some were pink and some purple and some yellow. Only the brightest colors. Nothing dull like brown or gray or . . ." She sent Paul a mischievous smile.

He wiggled the knot of his forest-green tie and mirrored her smile.

"Or beige," Lucie said. "Only happy colors."

Her happiness flowed to the children, and Josie bounced in

her seat as her stories came to life. Paul could watch the two of them all day, every day, forever.

"One day those mean rock-monsters came back to town—with fishing poles." Lucie held up a pencil with a string dangling from it. "'You beat us last time, Feenee,' the rock-monsters cried, 'but this time you can't stop us. We'll fish all the tuna out of your river so your kitty-cat friends can't have any.'"

"Oh no!" The towhead popped up from his chair.

"Oh no, indeed." Lucie motioned the child back to his seat. "Monsieur Meow loves his tuna fish."

Paul didn't have the heart to mention tuna swam in oceans, not rivers.

"Feenee was scared." Lucie sprang to her toes and zigzagged backward with tiny steps, making her skirt swing around her knees. "But she was also brave. She couldn't let the rock-monsters steal the tuna fish. So she went to her friend Monsieur Meow."

Lucie twirled to a bookshelf, and when she twirled back, Monsieur Meow covered her other hand. "Monsieur Meow had an idea, and he ran off to gather the kitty-cats. Then Feenee went to the top of the hill. A road ran down the hill to the river, where those mean rock-monsters sat with their fishing poles. Then Feenee blew the horn on her head—Toot-toodle-oo! Can you say that, children? Toot-toodle-oo!"

The children called out, "Toot-toodle-oo!"

Josie grinned back at Paul, so he said it too—and his daughter giggled.

Lucie held up a bowl. "Then all the kitty-cats came out of the houses on that road, and each had a ball of colorful Feenee spaghetti hair."

Monsieur Meow reached into the bowl and pulled out a bright green ball.

"What do you think the kitty-cats did? They did what kitty-cats do best—they batted those balls. And the balls rolled down the hill." Lucie poured out the bowl, and colorful balls rolled around.

The children squealed and grabbed at them.

Lucie swept her hand in front of her. "The balls smacked into the rock-monsters, knocked them into the river, and they were washed away. Hooray!"

Paul chuckled. Parisian color sweeping away Nazi gray.

If only Paris had a kitty-cat army.

Then again, who could command cats?

"Remember, boys and girls," Lucie said. "Always help your friends. And look for bits of color. You never know when they'll come in handy. Now, you may each take a ball home. I'm afraid they don't bounce—just papier-mâché wrapped with fabric, but they're colorful. And make sure you come back next week."

The children picked out colors and ran to their parents. How many would be here next week?

The American flight from Paris continued, and last week Bentley Young had sent Alice to Lisbon to sail home.

"Isn't it pretty, Daddy?" Josie cradled a walnut-sized ball of bright pink satin.

"Not as pretty as you." He tweaked her chin. "Why don't you pick up the extra balls and put them in the bowl for Miss Girard?"

"Okay. Can you hold this?"

"Sure." Paul stared at the brilliant pink. Had he ever in his life touched anything that color?

After the families left, Lucie sent Bernadette home. Only two young women remained in the store, seated by the window.

Lucie came to Paul and motioned to a rack near the office. "Josie's occupied with the balls. Stand here, where you can see Josie and I can see the door. Pretend you're interested in the literary journals."

Pretending would be required. He picked up a copy of *Comœdia*. "Do you recommend this?"

234

She shrugged. "It's moderate for a journal allowed by the government. We don't carry most of them—horrid, fascist, antisemitic rags."

"You don't sell . . . the underground press?" he asked in a voice as low as hers.

"They don't distribute in stores."

Paul didn't want to waste their few minutes in semiprivate talking about journals. "How are you?"

"Missing you."

They were isolated enough. Paul could embrace her, steal a kiss. But Lucie held herself stiff, and her gaze darted between journal and door. An embrace would be dangerously distracting.

He leaned closer until his arm met hers. "I miss you too."

She turned her head enough to reveal a whisper of a smile. "Any news on our plans?"

"My contact is setting up a rendezvous in Orléans." Bentley was his contact, a man Lucie knew—all the more reason not to reveal his name.

Lucie nodded, her attention on the door.

"Josie's grandparents live in Orléans. I told Colonel Schiller I didn't want Josie in an internment camp with me but living free with her grandparents. He granted me permission to take her to them if an internment order goes out."

But Simone's parents were the last people he'd want raising Josie. They'd been indifferent to Simone and had shown no interest in Josie the few times they'd seen her. Simone had weathered their neglect, but she was strong-willed and brash. Josie was sensitive and gentle, and she'd wither.

Lucie squinted out the window at a couple on the street, but they passed by. "I'm ready to leave. My bag is in the office. Monsieur Meow and Feenee live there when they aren't performing."

Paul resisted the urge to press a kiss to Lucie's temple. How considerate of her. Josie would have been heartbroken if the puppets were abandoned.

Josie sat on the floor in her blue coat, lining up balls by color, and Paul nudged Lucie. "I love watching you with the children."

Her face softened. "I do love them."

She would be an incredible mother someday, and Paul prayed he could be the father.

The door opened, and Lucie eased away from Paul. An elderly couple entered.

"Bonjour," she said. "May I help you?"

"Oui," the gentleman said. "Do you have a French-English dictionary? My grandson is learning English."

"Excuse me, sir," Lucie said to Paul, then she glided off to a bookshelf near the cash register. She pressed up to her toes to reach the top shelf, one leg lifting to a thirty-degree angle behind her.

The lady raised her eyebrows in a curious way. How many booksellers danced on their toes?

"Voilà!" Lucie settled down to earth and described the dictionary to the couple.

Paul thumbed through the journal. At Green Leaf Books, he could almost forget the chaos in the world. On October 31, a German U-boat had sunk the destroyer USS *Reuben James*, killing over one hundred American sailors. Even though the incident had led to nothing but diplomatic noise, Paul had come close to grabbing his daughter and Lucie and trekking off on his own.

But trying to cross the demarcation line without either official passes or resistance help would get all three of them shot. He had to wait and do it right.

At least the strike at Aubrey Automobiles had gone well. After a week of loud but toothless striking, Schiller had promised increased rations at the factory canteen. Moreau had faked reluctant concession, and the strike ended.

Not only had they deprived the Germans of a week's worth of trucks, but Schiller saw Paul as an ally who stood up to labor's demands. Surely he'd never think Paul would engage in resistance activities with those same laborers.

After the couple left with the dictionary, Lucie chatted with the young ladies at the table by the window, then returned to Paul with her mesmerizing step.

He welcomed her back behind the journal. "I haven't told you, but you inspired a new car design."

"Me?"

"I call it the Aurabesque. All our car models start with *Au*."

"After the arabesque." The shape of her lips as she smiled inspired other thoughts as well.

Paul turned his attention to the safety of the journal. "I've always considered form the least important part of car design. Sure, the body should be attractive, but it mainly serves to contain the engine and passengers. However, with this model the form came first. Now I'm designing a car to fit it. Form and function go together. They always have. I can use this concept to build better cars."

Her face took on a dreamy look. "Art and engineering working together."

"Because of you." His voice rasped. "I love you so much."

The two young ladies entered the nonfiction area, only fifteen feet away, and they perused a bookshelf.

Lucie edged away and studied the journal. "You mustn't talk that way."

The truth strangled his heart. No, he mustn't talk that way, not in a world where they couldn't be seen together outside this store, where every sentence needed to be in code, where either one of them could be arrested and shot.

"No," he said in his lowest voice. "That kind of talk is for another world. Not ours."

Lucie sighed and watched her customers browse. "You can imagine such a world, can't you?"

"I can."

She raised eyes brimming with idealistic determination. "If you can imagine it, you can work for it. And if you work for it, someday you might be able to achieve it."

Paul lost himself in her enthusiasm. If you couldn't imagine it, sketch it, plan it, it would never come to pass. Wasn't that what the resistance was doing? Daring to imagine a world without rock-monsters? Daring to roll colorful balls downhill? Even if they failed, at least they'd dared.

The two women selected a book and returned to their table.

"Paul? What do you imagine when you return to Massachusetts?" Her voice sounded thin. She wasn't asking about building cars.

It was too early, far too early, but vulnerability in her eyes broke down his inhibitions. "I imagine us. As a family."

She squeezed her eyes shut. "Do you? Can you imagine me in your world?"

Paul's stomach muscles tightened. "I can't imagine it without you."

"Can you see me as a bourgeois wife, going to luncheons and sitting on committees and whatever else women do in your world? I don't fit there."

"I hope not."

She gaped at him.

Paul tipped up half a smile. "Simone was a race car driver. She didn't sit on committees, although she was always busy. I don't know what I'd do with what you call a bourgeois wife."

"But you have . . . functions. Didn't Simone have to attend with you?"

"She survived. You would too. You're friendly and charming and knowledgeable about the arts." Paul lowered his voice to a murmur. "Who wouldn't love you?"

"Excuse me, Miss Girard." A male voice with a thick German accent.

Paul schooled himself not to startle and look guilty, and he looked up as if unperturbed.

That skinny German officer stood before them in his gray overcoat. Frowning.

"Good day, Lieutenant," Lucie said in a lukewarm tone Paul knew well. "May I help you?"

"You are"—he narrowed his eyes at Paul—"occupied."

"Please." Paul smiled at Lucie and motioned to the officer. "Thank you for recommending this journal, Miss Girard. I'll see how many books my daughter has picked out."

He joined Josie at the little green table. "What are you reading, candy corn?"

Josie giggled. "What's candy . . . corn?"

Poor little thing had never tasted any of the candy he used for nicknames. Paul described candy corn with his ears tuned to that German accent. He had no intention of leaving until after that man did. That jealous man.

Paul felt no jealousy in return. He'd never been the jealous sort anyway. And if Lucie had rebuffed Paul as a collaborator, a Nazi stood no chance at all. Most importantly, Lucie loved Paul and cared whether she fit in his future.

Josie giggled at the idea of candy crafted to look like a vegetable.

Paul intended to handcraft his future around the two ladies he loved.

33

Friday, November 21, 1941

Lucie had to be dreaming. How else could she smell the buttery scent of pastry?

Lying in bed, she opened her eyes. Golden light came from the kitchen, along with Marie-Claude and Véronique's soft voices.

Lucie inhaled. Patisseries were forbidden to sell pastries to anyone but Germans. The French were allowed nothing but plain bread.

But the smell persisted. Penetrated. Tantalized.

Lucie pulled on her robe in the frosty apartment, stuffed her toes into her slippers, and padded into the kitchen. "What smells so good?"

Véronique sat at the table in her bathrobe. "Good morning. Would you like a croissant?"

"Croissant?"

Marie-Claude sat at the table in her stunning silver evening gown—from last night. She smirked and pointed to a pink pasteboard box. "Courtesy of Klaus von Behren."

"Klaus?"

"Aren't we glad he's madly in love with Marie-Claude?" Véronique giggled and stroked a bowl full of at least a dozen eggs. "We can have omelettes for dinner."

Eggs? Eggs were rationed, only two per month—if you could find them.

Numb, Lucie lowered herself into a chair. "When—when did this happen? With Klaus?"

Marie-Claude raised one artful eyebrow under disheveled black curls. "I talk about him all—oh, you are never here."

Lucie squeezed her eyes shut and opened them, but her roommate still wore a smug smile and an evening gown at half past six in the morning. She'd just gotten home from a date with a German, and she didn't look one mite guilty.

Véronique slipped a croissant onto a plate, golden and flaky. "How many times did he propose last night?"

"Every time he came up for air."

Lucie clutched the knot of her bathrobe. "You're marrying—"

"Heavens, no. He insists he'll leave his wife for me, but I'm not foolish enough to fall for that lie. Besides, why would I leave the ballet to become a German hausfrau?"

"At least he takes you out and gives you food." Véronique turned the box toward Lucie. "Croissant?"

The smell no longer tantalized. "No, thank you," she said softly.

"No?" her roommates said together.

"I don't want one." She was hungry. Very hungry. But not for that, and she pushed back her chair. "Excuse me. I need to get dressed for work."

Véronique stared at her. "You just asked what smelled so good."

Marie-Claude twisted a pastry apart. "You forget, my dear Véronique. Little Lucie has these silly American notions of love. She's shocked at my wanton behavior." She popped a bite in her mouth, eyebrows high in amused defiance.

Lucie stood. "You used to call the Germans beasts. Now you eat their food."

241

"This is French food." Marie-Claude gestured to the spread.

Lucie headed into the bedroom. "I'll eat my ration."

"No need to be a martyr," Véronique called after her. "Enjoy it."

Lucie pulled out a skirt, a blouse, and a sweater. "No, thank you."

Marie-Claude flounced into the room. "She isn't a martyr. She's a hypocrite."

"A hypocrite?" Lucie whirled around.

Her roommate glared at her. "Eat your ration? You shouldn't have a ration in the first place. You don't belong here. If you went home, there would be more food for the rest of us."

Lucie gasped. "Paris *is* my home."

Marie-Claude's nostrils flared. "You're no more French than Klaus is."

"I—but I've lived here—"

"You sell your American books." Marie-Claude slashed one hand through the air. "You speak your American language and go to your American church for—what did you call it?—the giving of the thanks?"

"Thanksgiving." Just yesterday at the church Thanksgiving service, she'd enjoyed a concert by the Paris Philharmonic Choir with Edmund Pendleton on the organ. And she'd exchanged sweet small talk with Paul.

Marie-Claude slacked her hip. "You talk about the turkey and the corn—of all things! Only pigs eat corn. No Parisienne would ever eat pig food."

Véronique gave a long-suffering smile. "We're your friends, Lucie. But even if you never speak English again, you'll never be a true Parisienne."

Eyes burning, Lucie dressed. She'd lived in Paris since she was nine, stayed when leaving would have been safer, and dedicated herself to the city's welfare by aiding the resistance. Yet her roommates would never see her as one of them.

"Come, Véronique," Marie-Claude said. "More food for you and me."

Two sets of footsteps receded. "Don't mind her, Marie-Claude. We're just getting by."

After Lucie finished dressing, she slipped on her coat, hat, and gloves so she could find bread for breakfast before the bookstore opened at eight. Then she grabbed her flashlight, the lens covered with blue tissue to meet blackout regulations.

The Germans had placed Paris on Berlin Time, so the sun wouldn't rise until nine, but at least curfew ended at five in the morning.

Lucie headed down to the courtyard. Madame Villeneuve's head was silhouetted in the window of her apartment, and Lucie gave the concierge a nod and swept through the porte cochère to the darkened street.

The blackout persisted even though the RAF had never bombed Paris. They bombed French ports where the German navy had bases, and they passed over France to bomb Germany. But only the Germans had bombed Paris, and only once, during the terrifying days of the invasion.

Her wooden soles clopped on the damp sidewalk, following the pale blue cone of light. She was registered at the bakery on the place de la Sorbonne to buy rationed bread.

With her hand pressed to her empty stomach, she turned a corner. Dinner had been the usual stew of beans and carrots.

"Just getting by," Véronique had declared.

Getting by meant standing in long lines and finding out which stores had food. Getting by meant occasionally buying on the black market or accepting food from friends in the country. Getting by meant defying silly German laws and growing vegetables or raising guinea pigs and rabbits.

But sleeping with German soldiers to receive food was far more than getting by.

Lucie turned down a narrow lane, praying the bakery had

bread. She needed nourishment to sustain her at work. Any day now, Bernadette would find a new job and Lucie would run the busy store by herself. Although book sales dwindled, resistance messages continued.

After the imposter had tried to intercept a message, she'd met privately with Renard again. For over a week, he'd paused operations and posted lookouts. When he became convinced the imposter was a solitary opportunist, Renard resumed operations but with stronger security. Code phrases changed almost daily, and résistants conducted exchanges only when the store was empty. Renard was also looking for a new letter box, no easy task.

Since then, Lucie hadn't noticed any more suspicious behavior.

Thank goodness, because important information flowed through her store. She'd seen transcriptions of BBC broadcasts to be printed in the underground press and news of executions and resistance activities to be transmitted to de Gaulle's Free French in London. Messages also went to Paul to aid his work, whatever it was.

She hadn't seen any notes concerning violence, from what she could discern in the codes and symbols. After October's horrific executions, the resistance had conducted no further assassinations.

When she reached Boul' Mich', her shoes squished in leaves soggy from the previous night's rain. Bicycles pedaled past, wheels spraying up a fine mist. Across the boulevard in the place de la Sorbonne, the Sorbonne Chapel rose black. To her right, faint light glowed from the bakery's open door, illuminating a long line. To her left stood the Librarie Rive Gauche, its windows as dark as the fascist publications the store sold.

Men ran across the place de la Sorbonne, steps whishing through damp leaves, voices low but strident.

Lucie stood still, frowning. What was going on?

244

The men stopped in front of the collabo bookstore. Arms swung overhead.

Glass shattered, tinkled down on the pavement.

Lucie gasped, stepped back into the lane, and flicked off her flashlight.

A boom. An eruption of sound and light and fire. Flames flickered orange inside the store. Men cheered.

A bomb. Lucie took one step back. Another. Turned. Ran.

Police whistles screeched.

No! Her feet slipped on wet leaves. She stumbled, braced herself on a wall, and ran.

She couldn't get caught in a roundup. She couldn't. Not with all the reprisal killings. Innocent or guilty, anyone held in prison could be shot as a hostage.

The whistles and shouts and crackling fire and thumping feet faded behind her.

Lucie ducked down a side street and slowed to a walk so she'd look innocent.

Her breath heaved. Her face tingled with ice.

She pressed her gloved hand to her cheek, and it slipped away. She was . . . crying.

Her beloved Paris seemed determined to evict her.

34

TUESDAY, DECEMBER 2, 1941

Fog hung low in the dark courtyard of the Hôtel Beauharnais, the German Embassy in Paris.

Paul climbed the steps of the Egyptian-styled portico and entered the embassy. Warm air and golden light enveloped him, along with laughing voices and piano music.

Col. Gerhard Schiller greeted him with a handshake. "I'm glad you came, Paul."

"Thank you, Gerhard. How could I pass up an opportunity to meet Hermann Göring?" Paul checked in his coat, hat, and scarf, and he tucked his invitation into the pocket of his tuxedo.

Wearing his best uniform pinned with medals, Schiller led Paul out of the foyer. "Abetz's guest list is quite impressive—all the notables in French society and the German Military Command. I made sure my favorite industrialists were invited, especially you. It's vital to put a friendly face on America. Göring has much sway with the Führer."

Paul stifled his smile as they climbed a grand marble staircase with wrought iron balustrades. As if one minor automaker could avert war.

America's entry into the war seemed not only inevitable, but also Europe's last chance for liberation. Britain had defended her island and her empire, but with the United States in alliance, perhaps an offensive war could begin.

Schiller led Paul into the Salon of the Four Seasons.

It glittered. The walls, ceiling, chairs, drapes, chandeliers, wall sconces—all shone white with lavish amounts of gilding. Four floor-to-ceiling murals portrayed women representing the seasons.

About a hundred ladies in couture gowns and men in uniforms and tuxedos filled the salon. All had come to greet Göring. The head of the Luftwaffe was on his way to Vichy to meet with Marshal Philippe Pétain, head of the French State.

Tonight, Paul hoped to smooth tensions, deflect suspicions of sabotage, and douse rumors.

Schiller nabbed two glasses of champagne from a passing waiter and handed one to Paul. "Having a friend with me also keeps away the pretty little ingenues."

Paul smiled and lifted his glass to Schiller. He did admire how the colonel stayed faithful to his wife in Germany.

"Quite a collection of ingenues and notables," Paul said as they made their way deeper in. French movie star Arletty held court in the center of the room, hanging on the arm of an officer in Luftwaffe blue. Not far from her stood blonde beauty Danielle Darrieux with a crowd of movie fans.

Laughter rose from near the mural of summer, centered on actor and playwright Sacha Guitry.

Two men in tuxedos passed, and Schiller nodded to them. "Two of France's most famous writers, Robert Brasillach and Pierre Drieu la Rochelle."

Infamous was more like it. Brasillach was the editor of the fascist paper *Je suis partout*, and Drieu la Rochelle had turned the esteemed literary magazine *Nouvelle Revue Française* into a fascist rag Lucie would never carry in Green Leaf Books.

A soiree like this made it look as if every notable in France supported Germany, but Paul knew a great number opposed them. Only no one knew their names. No one threw them a party.

A dark-haired man in his thirties approached, a man with an intense and sculpted face, and he greeted Schiller with an accent Paul couldn't place.

Schiller turned to Paul. "Maître Lifar, I'd like to introduce Paul Aubrey, owner of Aubrey Automobiles. Monsieur Aubrey, this is Serge Lifar, director of the Paris Opéra Ballet."

Serge Lifar also had the imaginary string stretching his posture, and Lucie's name tipped Paul's tongue. However, although mutual acquaintances aided conversation, mentioning her name here would be dangerous.

Paul bowed his head. "Bonsoir, maître. It's a pleasure to meet you. My former wife and I enjoyed many of your performances— *Giselle, Coppélia, Oriane et la prince d'amour.*"

Lifar smiled. "I enjoy meeting a champion of the dance. But have you not attended recently?"

"I regret not. My wife passed away a year and a half ago. I've only recently returned to society."

"You must attend." Lifar reached inside his tuxedo jacket. "If you are free tomorrow, I have tickets for *Le Lac des cygnes*. I insist you have one, Monsieur Aubrey, and you, Colonel Schiller."

Swan Lake. Turning him down would be rude, so Paul accepted. "Will the ticket serve as a pass to be out after curfew, like the reception invitation tonight?"

"But of course."

Schiller nodded. "The police won't bother people in autos or carriages. The curfew is meant to keep the rabble off the streets."

"Indeed." Paul tucked the ticket into his pocket. A rash of resistance bombings and attacks in the past few weeks had led the Germans to change the curfew to six o'clock in the evening. This forced Paul to close the factory at five so his workers could

248

get home safely. Ironically, by shortening factory hours, the Germans aided Paul's sabotage.

A plump German officer in his sixties approached. "Pardon me, Herr Lifar, but my friend is eager to meet you."

The men said goodbye, and Lifar departed.

"Would you like my ticket?" Schiller asked in a low voice. "I do not understand the French fascination with ballet."

Paul hesitated, then wrapped his fingers around the ticket. "I have an acquaintance who might be interested."

Dare he? Dare he meet Lucie in public? If he could find a way to protect her and still spend time with her . . . His blood warmed and raced at the idea.

Schiller's light blue eyes took in the scenery, and he sipped champagne. "Roosevelt seems determined to go to war with Japan."

"Or vice versa." Paul raised half a smile. "Roosevelt offered Japan a reasonable proposal."

Schiller drew back his square jaw. "Reasonable? Japan offered to withdraw from Indochina, but the president insists they withdraw from China too. Let them be."

"China might object to that." He gave a friendly smirk and took a fake sip. "Tell me, if the US and Japan go to war, will Germany declare war as well? You are bound by the Tripartite Pact."

Schiller grumbled. "I hope not."

A finger tapped on Paul's shoulder from behind. "Excuse me."

Paul turned.

A tall, skinny German officer frowned at him. "Are you called Monsieur Aubrey?" he asked in accented English.

The man from Green Leaf Books, but Paul tilted his head. "Yes. Have we met?"

"I have seen you at the bookstore. I am called Lt. Emil Wattenberg. I must talk to you."

"Excuse me, Lieutenant," Schiller said. "You interrupted our conversation."

Paul waved his hand. "If you'll excuse me, Colonel, I'll give the young man one minute. I'll be right back."

"Very well."

His heart rate rising, Paul led Wattenberg across the room to the painting of autumn. Did Wattenberg know about the messages at the store? Or was he just a jealous suitor?

Paul faced the lieutenant. "You wished to speak with me? About books, I presume."

From the fire smoldering in Wattenberg's grayish eyes, books were the last thing on his mind. "Does your wife know you flirt with Miss Girard?"

At least he hadn't challenged Paul to a duel. "My wife, Lieutenant, passed away in June of 1940."

The fire died, and his eyes widened. "I—I'm sorry, sir."

Although he enjoyed his little victory, he needed to conceal his romance with Lucie. "I'm afraid you're also mistaken about my relationship with Miss Girard. My daughter is fond of her and her . . . puppet shows." He let a tinge of disdain enter his voice.

Wattenberg's expression hardened a bit.

Paul let out a wry chuckle. The snobbier he sounded, the better. "She's too eccentric for my tastes. Can you see her at a soiree like this?"

That fire threatened to spark to life again.

So Paul gave him a genuine smile. "However, she is a good woman, and I'm glad she has a friend and protector in you."

Wattenberg's scrawny chest inflated, and he made a sharp little bow. "Thank you, sir."

"Now, if her honor and mine have been restored, may I return to my friend, the colonel?"

"Yes, sir." His face blanched, and he glanced back to Schiller, who outranked him by far.

As Paul weaved through the maze of black tuxedos, gray uniforms, and shimmering gowns, something twinged inside. Lucie had voiced concerns about functions like this. He did have a hard time picturing her in this crowd—but mostly because they were Nazis, collaborators, and those who accommodated the invader rather freely.

In any other crowd, she would enchant.

Schiller beckoned to Paul from by the painting of winter, a woman in white against a frosty blue background.

Nearby, German Ambassador Otto Abetz, a tall blond man in his late thirties, stood with Reichsmarschall Hermann Göring. Time for Paul to meet one of the highest-ranking men in Germany, yet Paul didn't feel honored in the slightest.

Paul joined Schiller and gave a dismissive chuckle. "The lieutenant saw me talking to his girlfriend in a bookstore, but I was only asking her opinion about a journal."

Amusement danced in Schiller's eyes. "Ah yes. The American habit of excessive smiling could get a man in trouble in Europe."

"I'll try harder to look stern."

The couple speaking to Göring stepped away, and Schiller led Paul over. Schiller snapped up his arm. "Heil Hitler!"

Göring and Abetz returned the salute.

In German, Abetz introduced Schiller to Göring. Then Abetz addressed Paul in French. "Bonsoir, Monsieur Aubrey. I am honored that you are here."

"Not as honored as I am by your invitation."

Abetz addressed Göring in German. Paul made out his name and Aubrey Automobiles.

Göring looked like every cartoon drawn of him—round, sharp eyed, and dressed in an elaborate pale blue uniform weighted down with ribbons and medals.

As Abetz spoke, Göring's face brightened. Then he said something in German.

Abetz translated for Paul. "The Reichsmarschall remembers

your cars fondly, and he was pleased to see your trucks serving at his airfields."

At his airfields? Paul sensed opportunity, and he feigned bewilderment. "At your airfields, Herr Reichsmarschall? That cannot be. Under contract, my trucks are for civilian use only. As an American, I'm not allowed to produce military equipment—nor am I required to."

Before Abetz could translate, Schiller stepped closer and spoke to Göring, his voice emphatic and falsely light, his smile forced.

Paul didn't understand a word, but he understood what was happening. Months ago, Schiller might have been unaware that Paul's trucks were being converted for military use. But now he knew, and he was informing Göring of the lies Paul had been fed.

All three Germans looked at Paul with the same fake smile.

Göring spoke, and Abetz translated. "The Reichsmarschall apologizes. Of course, your trucks run on gazogène and could never be used by the military. He must have seen one of your civilian trucks making a delivery in a nearby town. As a man who appreciates fine automobiles, he recognized your logo."

Paul returned the man's smile. "*Danke*, Herr Reichsmarschall. I am honored that you remember my automobiles so fondly."

Small talk followed about the cold weather and the excellent company, all spoken with more joviality than warranted.

Before long, Paul and Schiller stepped aside. When they reached the center of the room, Paul sobered and looked Schiller hard in the eye. "Our contract is specific, Colonel. I'd hate to hear Germany was in breach of contract."

Schiller's smile flickered. "I assure you, it was a simple misunderstanding. The Reichsmarschall knows airplanes, not trucks. The military has no use for gazogène vehicles."

Paul took a pretend sip of champagne. "I'm sure it would be very difficult to convert from gazogène to gasoline."

Schiller hesitated a telling second. "It would."

"Good. I refuse to break the laws of my nation."

"We would never ask you to."

No, they would never ask. They did what they wanted. They stole and looted and destroyed.

But Paul would do everything in his power to fight back.

35

WEDNESDAY, DECEMBER 3, 1941

The majesty of the *grand escalier* in the Palais Garnier stole Lucie's breath, as it had every time she'd seen it.

Light from a profusion of wall sconces washed over the Belle Époque hall, filled with carvings and paintings and statues, all centered on a stairway that was beyond grand. White marble steps swept high, framed by red and green marble balustrades, then divided at the landing to rise to the right and left.

Lucie ascended along with dozens of men and women in evening dress. Her right hand held up the skirt of her floor-length gown, emerald chiffon layered over sapphire chiffon that created a shimmer of color with each step. Her left hand held her satin clutch with the precious ticket.

Above her on the landing stood Paul, and he stole whatever remaining breath she possessed. With one hand on the banister, he wore his black cutaway coat with elegant ease.

His gaze fell on her. His mouth softened, and his eyebrows lifted.

She allowed the slightest smile and climbed slowly to draw out the moment.

This morning he'd dropped by the store with the ticket and a plan. Foolhardy and impulsive, she'd leaped at the chance for an evening out with the man she loved—or the closest approximation to an evening out.

As she reached the landing, she ripped her gaze away as if she didn't notice him, as if his nearness didn't shred her heart. But to continue their resistance work—to continue to *live*—their relationship needed to remain hidden.

She brushed past him and climbed the stairs to the right. Then she turned left down a curved hall and found her box. Serge Lifar had been generous to the guests at the reception.

Red brocade covered half walls outlining the box, and Lucie stood at the balcony.

The Opera House's red velvet and gilt spread below her in the auditorium, capped by the opulent ceiling painting and famous chandelier. The grand smell of the theater filled her soul.

Most of her years in Paris had revolved around this building—from six years of training and ten years of practice to countless performances on the stage before her.

The Palais Garnier represented everything she'd loved, everything she'd given up.

Along with the sounds of the orchestra warming up, conversation fluttered around her, harsh German tones predominating. Men in Nazi uniforms occupied the boxes to each side.

Perhaps this evening was too foolhardy.

"Mademoiselle Girard?" Paul stood in the entrance to the box.

She paused as if trying to place him. "Why, Monsieur Aubrey. What a surprise to see you here." She extended her hand, encased in a long white glove.

"It appears we will be sharing a box, mademoiselle." He bowed and kissed her hand. "May I say how lovely you look. That dress reminds me of peacock feathers." He spoke like a polite acquaintance, not the love of her life.

"Thank you." She mimicked his tone for the sake of German ears. "A customer gave me this ticket."

"What a nice gift." Paul joined her at the balcony, but at a painfully polite distance.

"It was. Someone gave him the ticket, but he couldn't attend. He gave it to me, knowing I used to dance with the ballet."

Paul smiled and cocked his head. "This ballet?"

"Yes, for ten years."

"How fascinating." He gestured to the two red velvet chairs. "Please be seated."

Lucie settled into her seat and arranged her skirts. Paul sat beside her with the stiff smile of someone entering into a long evening with a mere acquaintance.

Her darling actor of an engineer, and she wanted to laugh and kiss him full on the lips. But German eyes were visible above the dividing wall. Watching.

So Lucie studied her program.

"Do you know any of the dancers?" Paul asked.

"Almost all of them, including my two former roommates."

"Former?"

She hadn't had the chance to tell him, and she pointed to Marie-Claude's and Véronique's names in the program. "They recently moved to an apartment closer to the Palais Garnier." Financed by Klaus, no doubt.

"You must enjoy having the place to yourself."

Lucie raised a flimsy smile. Actually it was empty and lonely.

The orchestra quieted, the house lights lowered, and the curtains drew back on the largest stage in Europe.

The first act of *Le Lac des cygnes* took place in the palace park, where Prince Siegfried's mother tried to convince him to marry. Tchaikovsky's magnificent music swelled inside Lucie and pulsed in her fingers and toes, which knew each step. Longed for each step.

For the second act, the curtains closed and opened again, revealing the famous lake and Odette, the most famous swan of all. Ballerinas in white tutus flooded the stage, including Marie-Claude and Véronique.

Something was off in Marie-Claude's dancing. Of the three friends, she'd always danced the most effortlessly. But tonight she exaggerated each step, as if fighting something. She dipped low, lifting her tutu and exposing elastic digging in under her derriere.

Lucie chewed her lip. Klaus's delicacies could cost Marie-Claude her career.

Paul rested his elbow on his armrest, and his shoulder pressed against hers. "Miss it?" he murmured.

Lucie nodded. Her vision blurred, and she blinked it away.

She didn't miss the bleeding toes, the rivalries, and the fear of getting cut. But she deeply missed the dancing, the camaraderie, the pageantry, and the joy of guiding younger dancers.

She'd given it up for her friends, for a bookstore she'd soon lose.

Then what? She and Paul were focused on getting safely to the US, but then what? His family lived in the Boston area where he'd have a job. Her family lived in New York where she had nothing. No education, no skills of any worth. At twenty-seven and over a year out of serious practice, she could never dance in an American ballet.

Paul slid his hand over her armrest and under the fan of skirts on the seat, and he tapped his fingers.

She burrowed under layers of chiffon until she found his hand. He gripped firmly, his thumb stroking the back of her glove.

A tear dribbled down her cheek. Almost three months had passed since their evening in the Tuileries. Since then, they'd sneaked three short kisses in the storage room while Josie practiced pliés.

Only under the concealment of full skirts and dim light could she enjoy the intimacy of entwined hands.

Lucie explored the breadth and length of his fingers, the ridges of tendons, each fold in his palm, and he returned the favor. Even though gloved, her hand had never felt so alive.

As the second act came to an end, Lucie folded her hands in her lap, and Paul withdrew to his side of the armrests.

During intermission, Lucie excused herself to the powder room, returning just before the curtains opened.

As the music rose and conversation lowered, Paul leaned closer, his voice low. "When it's over, follow me out at a distance. I arranged a carriage for you."

Lucie gave a tiny nod. How thoughtful of him.

When a grand ball opened in the palace on stage, Lucie slid her hand under the fluff of skirts. An invitation Paul accepted. If only they could share a true date, leisurely kisses, and open speech. But it couldn't be.

In the final act, tragedy unfolded. Siegfried unwittingly betrayed Odette, shattering her last chance to break the curse that kept her a swan by day. The two heartbroken lovers flung themselves into the lake.

Together in death. That was the happiest their ending could be, and Lucie's heart collapsed. Although she knew the story, now with her own love, her own danger, it felt raw and poignant.

As soon as the ballet concluded, Paul said goodbye and departed. But Lucie paused to absorb every detail of her beloved theater, perhaps for the last time.

Then Lucie made her way out of the box, down the grand escalier, through the glittering opulence of the grand foyer, and into the loggia. With each step, she left the audience behind as they discussed the performance and made sure they were seen.

At the cloakroom Lucie retrieved her opera cape and donned it.

Outside, fog obscured the buildings on the place de la Opéra, and Lucie raised her hood in the near-freezing air.

Carriages and automobiles and vélo-taxis cluttered the plaza. In a minute she spotted Paul standing beside a closed carriage with the driver.

As she neared, Paul strolled away to find his own carriage, giving her the merest nod from a distance. "Good night, my love," she whispered. He deserved a much better "good night" for such a lovely evening, and her chest ached.

"Bonsoir, mademoiselle." The driver bowed to her and helped her inside the coach.

A blanket lay on the seat, and she pulled it up to her chin, imagining Paul's arms around her instead.

The carriage rolled down the street, but with the blackout and the fog, Lucie saw nothing but darkness through the windows.

After the carriage turned a corner, it stopped. The door flew open, and a man hopped in.

Lucie gasped.

"Lucie, it's me."

"Paul! What are you doing here?"

He sat beside her, his form dark but familiar, and the carriage rolled away. "The driver's the son of one of my workers. He's on our side. I told him to take the longest and slowest route to your apartment, then he'll take me home."

"Oh, you're wonderful. I—"

He cut her off with a kiss and an embrace over layers of blanket, then he pulled away. "What?"

"The blanket." Lucie laughed, pried the blanket from under his legs, and drew it over both laps.

He was already kissing her cheek, her neck, dislodging her hood. In the darkness her mouth found his, and he pulled her close, almost lifting her from the seat.

Paul nuzzled her neck. "I've been going wild not being able to be with you."

"Me too."

259

"That dress. Lucie, you're so beautiful."

She caressed the back of his neck. "My hand will never be the same."

"Mine neither." He kissed her again, at first with fervency, then settling in for lingering enjoyment.

Now her lips would never be the same. "If only it could always be like this."

"It could be. It could if you married me."

Lucie pulled in a sharp breath. "Married?"

"Would you? Would you marry me? Please, Lucie." His voice rasped.

The kisses were talking. The kisses, the danger, the separation. "Paul, we can't. I love you, but we can't. And it's so soon."

He leaned his forehead against hers and sighed. "I know. And yet, I *know*. I know I want to spend the rest of my life with you. I'm the dark side of green, and you're the light. I need you. I want you. I love you."

Lucie's eyes slid shut, and she stroked the smooth hair at the nape of his neck. She also needed him, wanted him, and loved him. But would that be enough when they returned to the States and the danger waned and nothing forced them apart? Would he still be enamored by her, or would he realize she didn't fit in his world?

"Please," he said. "Please marry me now."

The poor man. He'd been lonely for so long. "I'd marry you tonight if we could. But we can't. The marriage license would be filed. Our relationship would be public."

He groaned, long and deep. "I hate this. Let's leave now. Tonight. I'm packed, Josie's packed, you're packed. Let's leave."

Her logical engineer wasn't thinking straight. "Darling, we don't have our rendezvous information. We have to wait for it. Yes, we have a plan in case we have to leave without it, but it's our last resort. It's too dangerous."

Paul shook his head, his nose brushing hers. "You're right.

Of course, you're right. Never again say you aren't smart, because you're the brains of this outfit."

Hardly, but she gave him a kiss. "Stay with the plan."

They had signals arranged, plans and backup plans, exchanged in notes through books, each note burned after reading. They were waiting for the signal that the resistance was ready to accept them into the escape line and the details on how to meet their contact in Orléans.

Paul worked his hand deep into her hair. "This might be the last time we can talk freely. Do you have any questions about the plans, about—"

This time she silenced him with a kiss. "I don't want to talk."

His smile rose under her kiss. "As I said, you're the brains of this outfit." He pulled her close and kissed her long and well.

36

SUNDAY, DECEMBER 7, 1941

After church, Josie ran upstairs to her bedroom to play.

Paul had always loved this house.

He set his Bible on a marble-topped table in the foyer and entered the dayroom. Rain pattered on the tall arched windows, and a fire crackled in the fireplace.

The wedding portraits hung above the mantel, where they had for over six years. Paul ran his finger along Simone's strong jawline, but all he felt was cool glass.

He'd hate to leave this photograph most of all. Madame Coudray had promised to store Simone's portrait in her living quarters when Paul left. The portrait wouldn't fit in his suitcase without folding, but he'd packed many smaller photographs.

He leaned back against the mantel, letting the fire warm his legs. He could practically see Simone in her favorite armchair, hear her laughter, and smell the perfume she wore to cover the smell of motor oil and gasoline fumes. When Paul left Paris, he'd lose this sense of her presence. All he'd have would be a few mementos and the daughter she'd given him.

He headed into his study. He'd lose the big desk he loved and hundreds of books—including those he'd rescued from Green Leaf Books. They would still fall into German hands.

Paul braced his hands on the desk. He'd lose the house, his belongings, and a substantial chunk of wealth. Although he'd transferred most of his funds home long ago, the capital stored in the factory and house would be lost forever.

The most important things remaining under his protection were Josie and Lucie. Lord willing, Paul would make a new life with them in the States.

The Aurabesque plans lay on his desk. This was his best work, and he'd take it home along with his tank designs. When the US went to war, they'd probably shut down passenger car manufacturing, same as in Europe, and his tank plans could help his father convert the factory in Massachusetts to wartime production.

But the Aurabesque . . .

He could almost hear Lucie—"If you can imagine it, you can work for it. And if you work for it, someday you might be able to achieve it."

Paul gathered up the plans. He chose to imagine a peaceful world where people could buy beautiful cars.

Back in the dayroom, Paul clicked on the radio. Nowadays he kept it on at all times in case of breaking news, but Radio-Paris played a Wagner opera.

Too bad he couldn't pick up a station from the States. He chuckled. Sunday morning wouldn't dawn on the East Coast for several hours. All he'd hear would be static.

Paul grabbed his Bible in the foyer and climbed the marble staircase.

If only he had the rendezvous information in Orléans. The urge to whisk Lucie and Josie out of the country grew each day.

Lafarge was causing more trouble. He claimed to have evidence linking Henri Silvestre to the resistance and threatened to turn him in. Paul had doubled his blackmail fees. Even if

Lafarge had fabricated the evidence, Silvestre could still be arrested, tortured, and shot. Also, the police might uncover Silvestre's actual resistance work.

In his bedroom Paul exchanged his suit jacket for a pullover sweater. Then he swung his suitcase onto the bed. He'd divided his necessities and Josie's among two suitcases and a small case Josie could carry. One suitcase went to work with him every day, and the others remained at home. Thank goodness Parisians often carried suitcases nowadays to cart groceries and goods.

Paul checked inside. Clothing and toiletries for him and Josie, a blanket, and a flashlight. In his overcoat pockets he kept vital papers, cash, and a pocketknife.

Every morning Madame Coudray—the only member of his staff privy to Paul's plans—returned Josie's favorite doll, stuffed cat, and blanket to her little suitcase.

"Hi, Daddy." Josie stood in the doorway, balancing on one leg.

"Hello, truffle." He swung her into the air.

Between giggles she said, "Truffle?"

"You're nothing but truffle." He blew a raspberry into her little neck.

She squealed with delight.

Paul plopped her onto the bed and checked through the suitcase.

When her giggles died, Josie rolled onto her belly. "What are you doing, Daddy?"

Paul scooted her Sunday dress down over her bottom. "Making sure we're packed to visit your grandparents." He couldn't tell her the real plans.

Josie rested her chin on her forearms. "I don't 'member them. Do they look like Mommy?"

"Sort of." Except Simone had known how to smile. Paul set his Bible in the suitcase and stuffed the Aurabesque plans into a manila envelope.

"Are you going to show them your car pictures?"

"Something like that."

"Oh! I need to show them my Feenee stories." Josie bounced off the bed and ran out of the room.

Paul groaned. He didn't have room. Closing the suitcase required effort, and every item was necessary. How could he explain to Josie?

He tucked the car plans next to the tank plans in the pocket inside the lid.

Josie ran back into the room, her curls bouncing. She grinned and held out crayon drawings scribbled on the back of his sketches for the Au-ful trucks. A pile as thick as his Aurabesque plans.

Paul squatted in front of her. "I'm sorry, but we don't have room."

Josie's grin dissolved. "But—but I want to show them."

On the top page, green-haired Feenee flew above the Eiffel Tower. When Josie learned they weren't returning to Paris and she'd lose all her Feenee stories, she'd be devastated.

Josie's brown eyes shimmered with tears.

Paul felt like a heel, but what choice did he have? Trade the Aurabesque for Feenee? Throw away a surefire hit of a car design in favor of doodles by a child not yet five years old? His plans represented untold hours of work and countless calculations.

Once again he could hear Lucie's voice in his head, but from a time when she didn't like Paul: *"Her gifts come from the Lord as surely as yours do. When you truly accept that . . ."*

Did he accept that or didn't he? And why did Lucie always have to be right?

Most important to remember, his little truffle was about to lose almost all she knew and loved.

"I think . . ." His voice cracked, and he swallowed hard and took the stack of stories. "I think Feenee would love to come on our trip."

Josie's grin returned, and she clapped her hands. "She would!"

Paul removed the Aurabesque plans from the manila envelope and worked his daughter's stories inside.

Tonight he'd feed the car designs to the fire so the Germans couldn't have them.

"Thank you, Daddy." Josie flung her arms around his legs.

Paul fondled her curly hair. No matter what, he'd done the right thing.

MONDAY, DECEMBER 8, 1941

The flames in the fireplace barely took the edge off the morning chill in Green Leaf Books. Lucie stoked the fire, then crossed her arms over her thick gray sweater.

She flicked on the tabletop radio she'd hauled down from her apartment so she could listen to the news when the store was quiet, which was most of the time recently. With all the bombings and reprisal killings, Parisians ventured out as little as possible.

Static crackled on the radio, and Lucie fiddled with the dial until Radio-Paris came in. The Germans controlled the station, but playing the BBC would mean a fine she couldn't afford. And every Parisian knew how to interpret the blatant propaganda.

As Lucie unlocked the cash register and counted the cash, the announcer intoned about the Red Army making a pathetic attempt to push the brave Germans from the gates of Moscow. That meant the Soviets had launched a major offensive.

Next, the announcer said Gen. Erwin Rommel had fallen back strategically in Libya. That meant the British had kicked the Germans and Italians out of Egypt.

Finally some good news.

At eight o'clock Lucie unlocked the front door. A thin layer of snow coated the street and sidewalks in the moonlight. So beautiful, and Lucie paused to absorb the sight.

"Early Sunday morning," the announcer said, "the empire of Japan made a daring attack on the American naval base at Pearl Harbor in the Territory of Hawaii."

Lucie whipped around and sucked in an icy breath. An attack?

"After the United States cruelly cut off their supplies of oil and vital materials, the Japanese took their vengeance. While American sailors slept, hundreds of Japanese planes ravaged Pearl Harbor. Battleship after battleship exploded, destroying the American fleet in the Pacific. A declaration of war is expected later today, but it is unknown whether the cowardly Americans will declare war on Germany as well."

Her mind whirling, Lucie ran to the radio as if she could extract more information from the box, but the announcer had gone on to another story.

Sunday morning? It was Monday. Why hadn't she heard yet?

Lucie grabbed an atlas, laid it on the counter, and flipped through. There was Hawaii, a tiny clump of dots in the middle of the Pacific Ocean. The time zone was Greenwich Mean Time minus ten hours, while Paris was on Berlin time—Greenwich plus two hours.

Math hurt her brain, so she counted. A twelve-hour difference. Early Sunday morning in Hawaii would have been evening in Paris, and it took hours for news to circle the globe.

"Paul." Lucie lunged for the phone. She knew his home and work phone numbers by heart, and she poked her finger in the dial.

But her finger froze. She was only supposed to call under two circumstances—if America and Germany declared war on each other or if she had to make an emergency escape due to her resistance work.

Japan's attack—as horrific as it was—didn't qualify.

Paul received the morning paper and owned a radio. Wanting to hear his voice was no reason to risk a call. What if the police or the Germans were listening in?

She settled the phone back in its cradle and gripped numb hands together. Once again her impulses had almost put them both in danger.

They had a plan, a smart plan, and Lucie just had to be smart enough to follow it.

The radio announcer had said war might be declared today. Washington, DC, was seven hours behind Paris. By the time Congress met, it would be afternoon in Paris.

Lucie might need to leave tonight. Thank goodness her ballet bag lay in the office, stuffed with necessities.

"You left the door open." Bernadette stepped inside and held up *Le Matin*. "Did you see the paper? America is in the war now."

"I heard on the radio." Lucie snatched the paper and read the article, which listed more details. And names of sunken ships. So many, many ships, and Lucie's throat filled with a sob. How many men? How many had died?

Bernadette unwound a scarf from her neck. "It may take a few months, but you will probably be interned."

"Yes." The word slipped past the clog in her throat. "I—I'm sorry. The store—"

"Don't worry about me." Bernadette's dark eyes softened. "I found a job at a bookstore on Montparnasse. This is my last day. I'm sorry for the short notice."

"Thank goodness." Tension poured out in a sigh. "I was concerned."

"Thank you." Her chin quivered, and she gazed around the store. "I hate to think . . ."

"Me too. Green Leaf Books has meant so much to me, but you've been here from the beginning." Lucie wrapped her arms around her belly. "All our hard work keeping the store open, but now I've lost Hal and Erma's dream."

"Lost it?" Bernadette drew back her chin. "They lost the store last June. But you—you kept it going, even with the Otto List and the British interned and the Americans leaving."

Lucie's lips clamped together. Only because of darling, generous Paul.

Bernadette tapped the desk in front of Lucie. "More importantly, by buying the store, you gave them the money to go home. If you hadn't, they might have been trapped here with all the antisemitic laws. They might have been arrested in one of those awful rafles."

Lucie shuddered. Only so-called foreign Jews, mostly from Poland, had been arrested—like Jerzy. But after the US and Germany went to war, American Jews in France would lose the protection of neutrality.

Bernadette plucked off her gloves and marched toward the office. "You and I will have one more good day together. No gloomy talk."

"All right." Lucie lifted a wobbly smile. "If there's anything you want in the store—books, photographs—please take them."

The assistant popped her head out of the office. "Anything?"

"I can only take one suitcase to the internment camp, and who knows what Madame Villeneuve will do with the contents of the store."

"Or the Germans." Bernadette scowled and surveyed the store.

Lucie smiled. Bernadette's little apartment would soon be full of books. "Tell you what. You live close, and the store is bound to be quiet today. Why don't you spend the day taking what you want?"

Bernadette pressed her hand to her chest, her eyes wide. "Are you—do you—?"

"Yes. If Hal and Erma return, you'll have something to give them."

"Yes. Yes. I'll take good care of it."

"I know you will." If time allowed, she'd reveal the hide-away behind the mural in the storage room so Bernadette could choose from the banned books as well.

Lucie's last tiny act of resistance.

37

THURSDAY, DECEMBER 11, 1941

Suitcase in hand, Paul headed from the Métro station under a leaden sky, returning from his appointment with Dr. Bentley Young for a "check on Paul's ulcer."

Paul finally had the rendezvous information. He and Lucie and Josie could leave at any time. Tonight after work, he'd visit Green Leaf Books to relay the information in case they weren't able to meet in Orléans. In case anything happened to him.

America had declared war on Japan—but not on Germany. But war with Germany was inevitable. On Monday, Paul had shut down the safe house, and the last RAF flyboys had left on Tuesday. Paul and his men had scrubbed the storage room of any sign of the British and filled it with crates.

The factory rose before him—the assembly building's stone façade and the tall steel lettering declaring Aubrey Automobiles—modern and sleek and only seven years old. It might not be his, but he'd done his best with it. For that alone, pride flowed in his chest.

Paul opened the glass door and entered the reception area, bright and welcoming, with a streamlined front desk.

The receptionist stood, her young face ashen. "Monsieur

Aubrey, you are wanted in the craneway. There has been an accident. A man is . . . dead." Her face warped.

A punch in Paul's gut. "Dead? Oh no." Accidents were common with heavy machinery, but no one had died at Aubrey Automobiles for almost two years. He raised a hand to the young lady to thank her, to tell her to sit, to stay calm.

Paul strode past the sales and administrative offices, jogged across the factory floor, and entered the craneway that ran along the back of the building.

In the craneway, motorized cranes on rails delivered parts and equipment to the tributary assembly lines.

Now the crane stood silent, and a couple dozen men huddled nearby, muttering.

"He was always careless."

"Silvestre told him to watch out. I heard him."

Paul stepped close. "Excuse me, men."

"Monsieur Aubrey." The men turned and parted.

Two feet stuck out from under the crane. A puddle of blood.

Paul's stomach coiled up, and he tore his gaze away. What a horrible way to die.

In front of the crane, Henri Silvestre sat on the rails, head in hands. "Non, non, non."

Jacques Moreau squatted beside him. "You did all you could."

"Moreau?" Paul called. "What happened?"

Moreau patted Silvestre's shoulder, stood, and motioned Paul away from the crowd. "A man tripped on the rails in front of the moving crane. I haven't called the police yet. I wanted to wait until you returned from lunch."

Paul grimaced at the thought of police in his factory again, but it was necessary whenever a man died. "Who was it?"

A long pause. Moreau rolled his thick lips between his teeth. "René Lafarge."

"Lafarge?"

"He wasn't watching where he was going. Silvestre warned him, but he didn't listen." Moreau's jaw edged forward and back, his eyes hard.

Something wasn't right. "It wasn't an accident, was it?"

One short shake of Moreau's head confirmed Paul's fears.

Paul groaned and pressed his fist to his mouth. For weeks, Lafarge had been denouncing Silvestre. Nothing had stuck, and Paul had told him numerous times to back off. Lafarge must have pushed Silvestre too hard, and now Silvestre had pushed back.

He scanned the scene of the accident. No, of the crime. The murder.

If evidence pointed to foul play . . .

If Silvestre caved under Gestapo interrogation . . .

The man was enmeshed in every aspect of resistance work in the factory.

Paul eyed Moreau. "Let's talk in my office. Give me a second." He approached the men around Silvestre, who looked for all the world like a despondent witness instead of a murderer.

"All right, men. Who's a witness?" Paul asked.

Four hands raised. "I didn't see anything," one of the workers said. "None of us did, but I heard Silvestre tell Lafarge to watch out."

Paul nodded. "You four stay here. I'll call the police. The rest of you, make sure the machinery in this section is shut down, then go home. I know how difficult it is for you to lose a colleague."

The men murmured and dispersed.

Paul and Moreau headed up to the office, while Paul's mind careened.

What was Silvestre thinking? Not only had he killed a man, but if the Gestapo broke him, he'd endanger dozens of lives in the factory and maybe even in the escape line.

And for what purpose? They had Lafarge under control. Paul

had given Moreau funds to keep paying him after Paul left. And after the Germans took over the factory, sabotage would cease and Lafarge would lose leverage.

Upstairs, Paul opened the office door.

"Good afternoon, Monsieur Aubrey," Miss Thibodeaux said.

"I'm afraid it isn't. Please call the police to report a fatal accident. Then phone the receptionist and have her call when the police arrive."

Wide-eyed, his secretary nodded. "Oui, monsieur."

Paul led Moreau into his office, set down his suitcase, and removed his hat and coat. "What happened?"

Moreau perched on the windowsill. "This morning Silvestre told me Lafarge found out Silvestre's daughter runs with a resistance group. He threatened to turn her in unless Silvestre gave him half his wages each week. Silvestre can't afford that, refused to ask you, told me he'd take care of it. If I'd known how he meant to take care of it . . ." Moreau hung his head.

Paul joined him by the window and huffed out a breath. "I would have paid him. You know it. Now he's endangered all of us."

"They'll rule it an accident. No one saw anything. Silvestre called out warnings as if Lafarge wasn't watching where he was going. Everyone knows Lafarge is careless and insolent. And there won't be any evidence."

Paul crossed his arms. "Unless Madame Lafarge knows about the blackmail."

Realization flickered through Moreau's black eyes. Fear.

"Here's the plan." It spun in Paul's mind, pieces flying together. "If they find out about the blackmail, they'll arrest me. So I'll leave town tonight. I have to leave soon anyway. Now, if they think it's murder and they still haven't learned about the blackmail, I want you to reveal it."

"What? No!"

Paul waved his hand to silence him. "Tell the police I forced Silvestre to kill Lafarge. I threatened him, his family—come up with a good story. It won't keep Silvestre out of prison, but it might save his life."

Moreau kept shaking his big head. "That is a bad idea."

"Likewise, when the Germans come, if they find evidence of sabotage, lay the blame on me. All of it. In the long run, it was my decision and my responsibility. I refuse to have you men pay for it."

Moreau's face screwed up. "What if—"

"I'll be long gone. In the meantime, pray hard that Lafarge never told his wife about the blackmail."

"I will."

"Good. Go back to the craneway. I'll meet the police at the door."

Moreau clamped his hand on Paul's shoulder, and his eyes glistened. "I will miss you . . . Paul."

From Moreau, the use of his first name didn't sound disrespectful, but affectionate.

Paul's throat clogged, and he clamped his own hand on his friend's shoulder. "And I will miss you . . . Jacques. It's been an honor working with you."

Moreau broke away and strode out the door.

Paul sent up a mess of a prayer and grabbed the phone. First, he called home to signal Madame Coudray to meet him at Gare d'Austerlitz with Josie and the luggage.

Madame Coudray came to the phone. "Oui, monsieur?"

"I would like my dinner precisely at 18:30. I apologize for my brusque manner, madame. I've had an appalling day."

A soft gasp. "Oui, monsieur. At 18:30."

Paul hung up, then rang Green Leaf Books. He wouldn't have time to visit the store and give Lucie the rendezvous information.

As the phone rang, Paul rehearsed the code. He'd ask if she

had a book about Joan of Arc. She'd say she did, and Paul would say he'd pick it up tonight. That would be the signal to leave tonight and meet him at the train station in Orléans.

But the phone kept ringing. Paul glanced at the clock—14:45. She should have returned from her lunch.

A knock on the door.

"Come in," Paul said, the ringing phone to his ear.

Miss Thibodeaux leaned in. "The police are waiting for you in the reception area."

"Thank you."

Still no answer from Lucie. Paul stifled a groan and hung up. He'd call later.

He straightened his tie and headed downstairs, but slowly.

The longer Paul kept the police at the factory, the better. The curfew had been moved back to twenty-one hours, and it would look suspicious if Paul left the factory before it closed at eighteen hours, especially after an accident.

The police would investigate at the craneway, question the witnesses, and call the coroner. When they were done, they'd notify Madame Lafarge. If she knew about the blackmail, they'd come for Paul. Even though his appointment with Bentley served as an alibi, he would be brought in for questioning.

Time was his enemy.

38

Chill penetrated Lucie's sweater, and she stamped her feet to keep warm.

Today she'd had only one customer and one phone call—and both had come at the same time, forcing her to neglect the phone.

Perhaps she could burn books for fuel, but how could she when she'd dedicated herself to keeping books out of the fire? At least Bernadette had sequestered several hundred volumes in her cramped apartment.

Lucie rubbed her gloved hands together. It was 16:30. She wouldn't close until nineteen hours, when she could escape her freezing bookstore to her freezing apartment.

The song on the radio ended, and the announcer came on, his voice frenzied. Those brash Americans had attacked too many German ships while escorting those treacherous British convoys. Hitler had no choice but to declare war on the United States.

Lucie's breath poured out in a strange mix of alarm and relief.

Today. They'd leave today.

Her bag, coat, and hat were in the office, ready to go, and

she forced her whirling mind to remember the checklist. First, call Paul in case he hadn't heard the news at work.

Lucie rushed to the counter and dialed Paul's office. His secretary answered.

"Bonjour," Lucie said. "I am calling from Green Leaf Books. Please tell Monsieur Aubrey that a copy of *The Last of the Mohicans* has come in."

"Thank you," the secretary said with a note of humor. "He's eager to read it. He told me to tell him immediately if you called."

Good. That meant he'd receive the message. Lucie thanked her and said goodbye.

If only they had the rendezvous information. They'd have to hide in a hotel in Orléans, and Paul would have to call his contact daily until they had the information. Not only were phone calls risky, but without false papers, they'd have to register in their own names.

Next on the checklist. Lucie swept the potted plant off the mantel, shoved the door open, and set the plant on the sidewalk. The signal to Renard and friends to shut down the letter box at Green Leaf Books.

Such a shame to set the plant outside in weather like this. She'd told Renard to change the signal, but he'd refused.

Lucie fluffed the plant's leaves. "I hope someone adopts you, you dear thing. You've served me well."

Back inside, Lucie grabbed the books behind the cash register so she could burn the remaining notes. Six messages to résistants that would never be delivered.

She set the books in front of the fireplace and stoked the embers. "Come on. You need to do your duty for your nation, same as the plant has."

Lucie pulled the note from the first book and poked it into the fireplace. Wispy flames curled around the edge, and she dropped it.

"Good afternoon, Miss Girard." Lt. Emil Wattenberg stood in the doorway, frowning at the sidewalk. "Why is your plant outside?"

Lucie's heart seized. Oh no! She hadn't locked the door. It was on her checklist. How could she have forgotten?

She sprang to her feet and onto stage. With the same luke-warm smile she always wore for him, she eased away from the fireplace and the books. "Haven't you heard potted plants need an occasional shock of cold to stimulate growth?" Almost as fantastical a story as a girl with wings and hair that changed color.

Wattenberg removed his peaked cap and gave her an amused smile. "It is so cold in here, you do not need to take it outside. Have you no heat?"

Lucie crossed the store into the center bay and straightened the nonfiction books. "Parisians receive no coal, as you know, and very little firewood."

"Hmm. I am good with fires." He strode into the store.

Lucie sucked in a breath. She couldn't have stopped him even if she had the words.

He squatted before the fireplace, the skirt of his gray army overcoat fanning around him. "The fire is not built well. If you . . . are you burning books?" His voice rose in dismay.

As if his own countrymen weren't responsible for burning millions of volumes. But this was no time to be plucky. "No, just scraps of paper. But don't worry about me. I'm used to the cold."

"Strange." He jabbed the poker into the fireplace. "The let-ters on this paper. No, not letters. What is the word?"

A sick feeling wormed in Lucie's stomach. Symbols. The word he wanted was symbols. But she had to sound innocent, distract him. "I make little drawings when I'm bored."

"This is a man's writing." He pulled out the scrap, only singed around the edges.

"Oh, that. It's a scrap I found in a book." She tried to inject amusement into her voice. "You wouldn't believe what people use as bookmarks."

Wattenberg glanced at the open book on the floor. The stack beside it.

No, no, no. But her stupid brain froze out all ideas, all inspiration.

The officer's long fingers reached for the top book. Riffled the pages. Plucked out a note.

It was over.

Lucie stood in the center bay with bookshelves blocking her routes to the front door and the back door, and an armed German officer in her way.

She was Odette, the swan, her path to freedom so close, now lost. Well then, like Odette, she would die gracefully, and a curious and sad freedom filled her heart.

Wattenberg stretched up to his imposing height, and he turned to her, the note raised. If only her fire had blazed as hot as his eyes did. "What is this?"

Lucie blinked. "A bookmark?"

Hobnailed boots clomped up to her, and gray eyes smoked. "It is a news article, written in pencil, but it is wrong. It says the Germans are losing in Russia and in Libya. Such lies could only come from the English, the BBC."

A transcribed broadcast meant for a resistance newspaper, but she put on an alarmed expression. "What a strange thing to use for a bookmark."

Wattenberg brandished the paper in her face. "It is from a terrorist, and you know it."

Righteous indignation came naturally. "I didn't put it there. And I certainly didn't write it."

He scrunched up his mouth and shook his head. "I thought you were a good woman. But you—you fooled me."

Lucie held her chin high and her voice steady, although her insides writhed. "I have done nothing wrong."

"I helped you. And this is how you pay me?" His eyes burned with the fire of a lover spurned, a man betrayed, even though she'd never once given him reason to hope.

"I must call the police." His mouth took a grim set, and he pulled his pistol from his holster.

It was her turn to have no reason to hope.

From a discreet distance, Paul watched as Maurice Boucheron gave a lengthy description of how the motorized crane worked. The policeman had taken few notes and kept glancing at his watch.

Paul had drummed up as many witnesses as he could to drag out the investigation and to show himself a concerned employer cooperative with the police. From what he could tell, the police saw Lafarge's death as a routine, if regrettable, industrial accident.

He sneaked a glance at his watch, not wanting to look impatient—17:15. He needed to leave the factory no later than eighteen hours to meet Madame Coudray at the station and catch the train to Orléans at nineteen hours. But every minute he kept the police away from Madame Lafarge gave him a minute's head start.

Somehow he had to call Lucie. Adding a stop at Green Leaf Books would take time he couldn't spare.

The policeman thanked Boucheron, joined his colleague a few feet away, and the two men came to Paul.

The senior of the policemen tucked a notepad in his jacket. "We are finished for now. We will let you know our findings."

"Thank you." Paul searched for signs of suspicion, but the

man's expression revealed nothing. "I hope my men were co-operative."

"Very. Thank you, monsieur." The policemen departed.

They passed Col. Gerhard Schiller, who frowned at their backs.

Paul stifled a groan. Not today of all days.

"Good afternoon." Schiller pointed with his thumb over his shoulder. "What happened?"

"A man fell in front of a moving crane and was killed. I planned to notify your office in the morning." Paul prayed Schiller wouldn't ask the man's name, which he might recognize from the investigation after Gilbert Foulon's arrest.

Schiller frowned at the crane. "What a shame. Workers ought to be more careful."

Paul murmured in agreement.

Schiller's frown deepened. "I have more bad news. America and Germany have declared war."

"Oh no." Did Lucie know? Had she tried to call him? Now he needed to call the store more than ever.

Schiller straightened his broad shoulders. "The German Military Command has ordered all American citizens to report to their local *Kommandantur* by December 17 at eighteen hours. All men under sixty years of age will be sent to internment camps."

Pain jabbed him in the gut. Just because a punch was expected didn't reduce its impact. "I understand." Six days. If Lafarge's blackmail remained concealed, Paul would have six days until the Germans came looking for him.

Sympathy puckered around Schiller's mouth. "On Saturday, you may take your daughter to her grandparents. Tomorrow we'll meet to discuss the transition at the factory."

Tomorrow? No. He absolutely had to leave tonight. Paul leveled his gaze at the officer. "I apologize, but I report for internment on the seventeenth. That means I will say goodbye to my little girl on the sixteenth. I have only four more full days with her, and I will not spare a single one."

Schiller's jaw edged forward. Would he order Paul to stay? If so, he could put out an alert at the train stations to prevent Paul from leaving.

Paul let pain and worry flood his face. "Please, Gerhard. She's only four years old. We might not see each other for years."

Schiller's jaw softened. "She can visit you."

"Her grandparents never thought much of their American son-in-law. I assure you, they will not bring her to visit. Please let us have these four days."

A long sigh flowed from Schiller. "Very well. As a fellow father, a fellow Harvard man, it's the least I can do. I'm sure all your affairs here are in perfect order."

"They are. I anticipated this day. And thank you for understanding."

"By the way, I requested to requisition your home for myself. If approved, I promise to protect your belongings and keep your staff employed."

"That's kind of you." But Schiller wouldn't be so kindly disposed if even a fraction of Paul's activity came to light.

Paul extended his hand. "If you'll excuse me, I'd like to inform my employees and make sure my office is ready for you."

Schiller shook Paul's hand. "I'm sorry we'll no longer be able to do business together."

The feeling wasn't mutual.

After Schiller departed, Paul headed for his office.

Moreau fell in step beside him. "What did the police say?"

"Nothing. They'll let us know. But Schiller has requisitioned the factory. America and Germany are at war."

Moreau mouthed a curse. All sabotage would now stop, all signs would be erased.

"I am to report for internment on the seventeenth," Paul said loud enough for others to hear. "Tomorrow I'll take my daughter to her grandparents. Colonel Schiller is in charge now. Please inform the men."

"I will."

Paul held out his hand to his friend. "Take care of yourself."

With a gruff nod, Moreau shook Paul's hand. Then he marched away, barking orders.

Paul climbed the steps to his office, where Miss Thibodeaux sat typing. "Any messages?"

"Oui, monsieur. The woman from the bookstore called. *The Last of the Mohicans* came in."

"Good. Thank you." A smile flicked up in relief. Lucie knew about the declaration of war and was on her way to Orléans. No need for Paul to stop by the bookstore.

In his office, Paul put on his coat and grabbed his suitcase and hat. He indulged in one last sweep of the room. He'd packed his personal photos, but he had to leave the paintings of the Aubrey car models, his work, and the factory he'd built.

Grief surged inside, but he tamped it down. All that mattered now was getting home safely with Lucie and Josie.

39

"How could you?" Lt. Emil Wattenberg's face reddened, and his eyes darkened with rage and hurt. "I helped you."

Lucie's fingers dug into the pleats in her brown wool skirt, as if digging for hope. Finding none. She would be arrested, turned over to the Germans, and tortured. Proclaiming innocence wouldn't save her, but it might save Renard and the others.

She steadied her voice. "I have done nothing wrong."

"I helped you." The gun shook in his hand. "I told you about the Otto List. I risked my career to tell you. I offered to pay your rent—rent for a *terroriste*!"

"I appreciate your help. I do." She implored him with her eyes.

With the gun trained on her, Wattenberg picked up the books by the fireplace, one by one, and shook them. Notes fluttered down like dead leaves

He scraped them up and thrust them in her face. "These—these are not bookmarks. They're messages. Terrorist messages."

If she'd been falsely accused, she would have been indignant, so she shooed the notes away. "How can I know what people put in books?"

"If you didn't know what they were, why were you burning them?" The truth of his words and the sharpness of his gaze sliced into her.

"I'm cold." She wrapped her arms around her stomach and shivered. That was no act.

"You are a liar. A terroriste and a liar." His face twisted with disgust.

She'd thought he was different, a man of culture, a man who cared for her. But his crush wasn't strong enough to override Nazi ideology.

"I will call the police." He backed behind the counter with the gun pointed at her. "If you run, I will shoot."

"I know." She shuddered as cold and fear united to undo her.

Wattenberg stuck the phone between his ear and his shoulder and dialed.

The shivering took hold, and Lucie let it.

Paul would arrive in Orléans tonight, but she would never join him, never say goodbye. A silent sob bubbled in her throat.

"The police, please," Wattenberg said in heavily accented French.

Queasiness rolled in Lucie's empty belly. Would she break under torture? What would she reveal?

Gripping her trembling arms, she eyed the door. If she ran, she'd never make it. But wouldn't it be better to die than to send others to their deaths?

"This is Lt. Emil Wattenberg with the Wehrmacht. I would like to report a terroriste."

Lucie's foot slid toward the door. But her impulses couldn't be trusted. She had to think, be disciplined, pray. *Lord, show me what to do.*

"Please transfer my call. I will wait." Wattenberg stared ahead, his jaw set.

The impulse to run grew. She was fast and agile and a small target. The back door led to the courtyard, to passageways to two streets. It stood about twenty feet away, next to the office.

Her breath stilled. The office. Her bag. Her coat.

Discipline, like molten iron, flowed into the cracks of her impulse and strengthened it.

"Excuse me, Lieutenant?" She hugged herself. "I am so cold. Prison will be even colder. May I please get my coat? It's in the office."

He eyed her, hard and cool. Then he nodded. "Unlike you terrorists, I am civilized. Get your coat."

"Thank you." She edged toward the office.

"Oui." He jerked his gaze to the phone. "I am at the bookstore Green Leaf Books. Terrorists pass messages inside the books. I have evidence, and the owner is in my custody."

Lucie stepped inside the office doorway, where Wattenberg could see her. She reached a trembling hand to the hooks on the wall and grasped her coat. Her distinctively green coat.

Holding her coat below the hook out of Wattenberg's sight, she punched her hands into the sleeves and whipped them inside out. Then she yanked on the coat with the black lining facing out.

Wattenberg kept talking, kept watching.

Six feet stretched between her and the short hallway to the back door. Her bag rested on the floor, but if she reached for it, she'd draw Wattenberg's attention and his fire.

"The store is on rue Casimir-Delavigne. Send officers right away." He glared at Lucie.

Standing with her left side behind the doorjamb, Lucie pretended to do up the buttons on her coat. She extended her left leg, poked her foot through the strap of her bag, and slowly curled her leg up behind her in *attitude derrière*. With her left hand, she slipped the strap off her ankle.

"The number? I do not know." Wattenberg frowned at Lucie as if realizing she'd never give him the address.

Heart pounding, Lucie wound the strap around her left arm several times. She only needed a moment's distraction.

"I'll read the number across the street." Wattenberg leaned over the counter and peered out the window.

Now! Lucie sprang out of the doorway, and in three leaps she reached the back door.

"Nein!" Wattenberg cried.

Lucie flung open the door to the stairwell, then the door to the courtyard, and she sprinted across the courtyard toward the porte cochère leading to rue de l'Odéon.

A door banged behind her. "Halt! Halt! Or I shoot!"

Lucie's wooden soles clomped on the stone pavement, and she fought for traction in the melting snow.

"Halt!"

She ran through the porte cochère. A shot exploded in her ears. Stone shattered beside her, pelted her.

She screamed, jumped in a *glissade* to the right, spun, sprinted, half running, half leaping.

Passersby ducked out of her way.

"Halt! I will shoot." Boots pounded behind her. "Stop that woman! She is a *terroriste.*"

Would he shoot among innocent civilians?

A startled elderly woman stood in the way, and Lucie darted around her. "Pardon, madame."

"Quinault!" the woman cried behind her. "Quinault."

Quinault? The printer? Two stores up, with a back door to the rue Monsieur le Prince. "Merci!"

"Out of my way!" Wattenberg yelled. "All of you—move!"

Lucie opened the door to Quinault's and ran the length of the store.

Monsieur Quinault stood up from his desk. "Mademoiselle Girard? What is the meaning of this?"

"Pardon, monsieur." She ran down the back hall and through the door, out onto the street.

A café stood on the corner, the outdoor tables abandoned in the cold. Lucie slipped through the door and strolled leisurely through cozy interconnecting rooms as if looking for a friend.

An empty room. Lucie ducked inside and fished in her bag for her black turban. She twisted up her hair and tugged the turban in place. Then she yanked off her coat and turned it right side out.

A commotion in the front of the café. Heated voices. Stomping feet.

Lucie kicked her bag under a table that hadn't been cleared, plopped into a chair with her back to the door, and raised a half-empty coffee cup.

"Did a woman run in here?" Wattenberg's voice drew near.

"Non. I saw no one running," a man said, probably a waiter.

"Black coat, light brown hair. She runs with her toes out to the side."

Lucie didn't look up, but what Parisienne would? To the German soldiers, the city was *Paris sans regard*, Paris without a glance, and Lucie would pretend no rock-monsters polluted this café.

"This is the last room, monsieur," the man said. "Why don't I show you the kitchen?"

Wattenberg's heavy footsteps came to a stop behind her, and Lucie took a sip of someone else's cold ersatz coffee, praying, willing her breath not to betray her.

"Yes." Boots stomped away. "Show me the kitchen."

Lucie's breath blew waves in the dark brew, and the cup tinkled in the saucer as she set it down with trembling hand.

The kitchen door slammed.

Lucie snagged her bag from under the table and sashayed out with a nonchalant expression, forcing her feet to walk in parallel.

She slipped outside and strode down to the boulevard Saint-Germain, her pace quick but not so quick as to call attention to the woman in a green coat and black turban.

The first place the police would search would be the Odéon Métro station. Lucie had to get there first.

She turned onto the boulevard. Two policemen hurried toward her, blue capes flapping behind them.

Lucie's step hitched, but an innocent woman didn't fear the police, so she kept moving.

"Green Leaf Books," one policeman said to the other. "Rue Casimir-Delavigne."

They were coming for her, but Lucie gave them a benign smile and walked on past.

The Métro, at last. She trotted down the stairs, bought a ticket, and found the platform for the number ten line, melting into the crowd.

Each minute passed as if slogging through mud, and Lucie clutched her bag to her stomach.

The number ten line led to Gare d'Austerlitz, the station for all southbound trains. Would the police realize she was trying to escape from Paris, not just within Paris? If so, they'd alert the train stations. And she had to show her papers to buy a ticket.

"Hurry, hurry," she muttered.

Finally the train pulled into the station. Staying in the middle of the crowd, Lucie stepped onto the train and found a seat. A copy of *Je suis partout* lay on the seat, full of hateful fascist lies.

Lucie grabbed it to toss it to the floor, but then raised the filth before her face, sitting tall as if she didn't care who saw her.

The doors closed, and the train pulled away.

Her eyes slipped shut in relief, but she was far from safe.

40

The crowds at Gare d'Austerlitz oppressed, impeding Paul, and police stood in pairs throughout the main hall, watching.

Paul gave the police wide berth and scanned the passengers near the ticket windows for the tall figure of Madame Coudray and the tiny figure of his daughter.

There they were. Tension poured out of him. The first hurdle cleared.

"Hello, candy cane." He hugged Josie to his side.

"I get to go on a train!" Joy danced in her big brown eyes.

Madame Coudray pressed a handkerchief to her eyes. "I—I was Simone's nanny. Now Josie's. I can't bear the thought—"

"We'll return Tuesday," Paul said in a pointed tone. A lie, as Madame Coudray knew, but he couldn't risk a teary scene that would draw attention. "Would you please stay with Josie while I buy our tickets?" And in case of Paul's arrest.

After she nodded, Paul approached an open ticket window. "I would like a round-trip ticket to Orléans, returning on December 16. My four-year-old daughter will accompany me to Orléans, but not on the return." Paul handed him his *carte d'identité*. At Josie's age, she didn't need an identity card or a ticket.

The agent inspected Paul's card, and a furrow split his brow. "You are American." An accusation, not a question.

"Oui."

The agent shoved the card back. "I have been ordered not to sell tickets to American men under sixty. You must report for internment."

Paul's gut clenched. He hadn't anticipated that, but he slid his card back. "I am to report for internment on the seventeenth. I am taking my daughter to stay with her grandparents in Orléans. I will return on the sixteenth."

"I'm sorry. You are not to leave."

No. He had to leave. With the gas tank on his 1935 Authority empty, he could only escape by train.

Paul pressed his lips tight together and riffled through his wallet. "I have permission from German commissioner Oberst Gerhard Schiller, a personal friend."

The man's thick gray eyebrows shot high, then drew together. "No, I—"

Paul slapped down Schiller's business card. "Call him to verify. He is at the Hôtel Majestic."

The agent stared at the card as if it were poisoned. "I . . ."

His hesitation was Paul's open gate. "Go ahead. I'm sure the colonel won't mind being interrupted during dinner."

A grimace crossed the man's face.

Now Paul gave a reassuring smile. "As long as I have a return ticket, oui?"

More grimacing.

"Please, sir? I am a widower. I want my little girl"—he gestured behind him to Josie's sweetness—"I want her to spend her childhood where she can play free, not in an internment camp."

The agent pulled out two tickets. "I am a grandfather."

"Merci, monsieur. I am indebted to you." At least women

weren't under the internment order, so Lucie wouldn't face the same problem.

Paul buried the ticket in the breast pocket of his suit jacket. The second hurdle cleared. The second of many.

The train rocked, but Lucie was in no danger of falling asleep. Either she'd beaten the police to the Gare d'Austerlitz or they didn't suspect she'd flee south. She was almost in Orléans. Almost safe.

Or was she?

The train slowed, and blocky black shapes whished by in the night.

Lucie willed her mind to still, her face to look bored. The less people noticed her, the better. Only Paul and his contact in Paris knew she was bound for Orléans, so no one would look for her in town. If they did, they'd look for a hatless woman in a black coat.

After the train came to a stop, Lucie pulled her bag from the overhead rack, exited the train, and headed down the platform toward the main hall.

Her throat tight, Lucie searched the passengers and the platform for the man she loved. "Please let him be here," she whispered.

But the passengers melted away into the night, and the train chuffed away.

Lucie stood on the platform alone.

Her heart and lungs pumped in an erratic rhythm, a wild, modern dance.

What if Paul hadn't received her message? What if he hadn't learned about the declaration of war until it was too late to catch the last train south?

No. One more train from Paris to Orléans would arrive in an hour, so she forced her breathing into smooth rhythms.

Lucie sat on a bench, raised the horrid newspaper as a shield, and reviewed the plan.

If Paul didn't arrive on the last train, Lucie would get a hotel room and meet him the next day in the train station.

But registering at a hotel in her own name carried risks. And what if Paul never came? She didn't know how to contact the resistance in town. Worse, if Paul didn't arrive, that meant something awful had happened to him.

But fretting had never once solved a problem.

With the fascist newspaper before her eyes, she imagined herself at the barre in the Palais Garnier, running through the Cecchetti syllabus.

The familiar music played in her head, and she mentally performed her *pliés*, *battements tendu*, *battements dégagé*, *ronds de jambe a terre*, each exercise in turn.

As she curtseyed in the final *grande révérance*, the tooting of a train horn replaced the music in her head.

Lucie folded the paper and stuffed it deep in her bag in case she needed a disguise again. Praying hard, she stood and scanned the train windows.

Before the train had completely stopped, a man in a gray coat appeared in a doorway, holding the hand of a little girl.

"Daddy, look! It's Miss Gee-jard."

Lucie's heart soared, and she ran to them. "Paul! Paul!"

The train stopped, and he and Josie hopped down to the platform. A suitcase thumped to the ground, and Paul threw one arm around Lucie and kissed her.

She melted with joy and relief and the release of kissing him freely.

"Thank God," he murmured against her lips. "Thank God."

Tiny nervous giggles rose beside them. Josie.

Lucie pulled back, but Paul didn't release her waist. She smiled at the child in her dark blue coat and bonnet. "Hello, Josie."

She bounced on her toes. "Are you going to my grandparents' house too?"

"I am." But to the other set of grandparents.

"Are you my new mommy now? You kissed Daddy."

Lucie suppressed a laugh and glanced at Paul.

"It's more complicated than that." His gaze shifted to Lucie, and he mouthed, "Someday."

"Someday," she mouthed back, her heart dancing with hope.

Paul picked up two suitcases bound with a luggage strap and gave Lucie a significant look. "Our reservations were made today."

"Thank goodness." That meant they had their contact. "Did you have any problems getting here?"

"A few . . . complications." He shot her a sidelong glance under the brim of his fedora. "I'll tell you later."

"I did too." She squeezed Paul's arm. "But we're here and we're together."

"I'll never let you from my side again."

Love for him welled inside, and she pressed a kiss to his shoulder.

Once outside, Paul hailed a carriage, gave an address to the driver, and helped Lucie and Josie inside.

Paul pulled his daughter onto his lap. "I have something to tell you. We're not going to your grandparents in France, but to your grandparents in America. Miss Girard is coming with us."

"To America?" Josie said.

"I'm from America too." Although Lucie had spent little time there.

"Our trip might seem strange to you, Josie." Paul bumped against Lucie in the dark carriage. "You must stay with either me or Miss Girard at all times. Never, ever let us out of sight. Do you understand?"

"Yes, Daddy." Uncertainty quivered in her tone.

"We may ask you to do something you don't understand, but

you must immediately do what we say. We might ask you to be quiet or to lie down or to run. If we tell you, do it."

"That sounds scary." Her voice broke.

Lucie found her little hand and held it. "It might be scary, but I know you can be brave like Feenee. Remember, God can make you brave if you ask."

Lucie leaned against Paul's shoulder. *Lord, make me brave too.*

41

ORLÉANS, FRANCE
THURSDAY, DECEMBER 11, 1941

The little hotel stood dark and silent. Paul shifted drowsy Josie on his shoulder and rapped on the door three times, paused, then four times.

Lucie's grip on his arm tightened. Meeting a resistance contact was dangerous. Paul had to follow procedures to ensure the legitimacy of the contact and to prove his legitimacy to the contact.

Footsteps padded to the door, and a woman in her forties opened the door a crack.

"Bonsoir, madame. The night is cold, and my family of three would like a warm room."

The woman glanced him up and down. "For how long?"

"Eleven nights."

"Eleven? Why not fourteen?"

The phrases flowed as planned. "I need no more than eleven."

The woman ushered them in. She led them up a narrow staircase for three flights, then down a crooked hallway, where she opened a door. "Wait in here."

"Merci." A tiny room with a bed barely big enough for Lucie and Josie and floor space barely big enough for Paul.

After he tucked Josie in, Paul sat beside Lucie on the edge of the bed and took her hand.

Before long, the door opened, and a man in his forties entered, nearly bald. He eyed the three of them. "Give me your cartes d'identité. I need the photos for your new cards. I also need your passports."

Paul hesitated, but they'd come too far to turn back. He pulled his card and his and Josie's passports out of the inner pocket of his coat.

The résistant reviewed the papers. "From now on, you are Frédéric and Colette Foucault. The child will remain Josephine. You will speak only French. The child must call the woman Maman."

"Josie will like that," Lucie said with a shy smile.

"What's happening?" Josie sat up in bed, hair bow askew. "Who's that?"

"He is our friend. Come sit with me," Lucie said in her flawless French. "Speak with me in French."

"Oui, mademoiselle."

Lucie hugged her. "Would you like to call me Maman?"

"Maman? May I?" Josie's eyes grew huge. "It's true. You kissed my father, and now you are my mother."

Lucie gave Paul a playful look. "Oui."

Paul grinned. In America he'd have to put a new spin on the meaning of "make an honest woman out of her."

The résistant tucked the cards into the passports. "I will give you cartes d'identité and German Ausweis passes to cross the demarcation line, both in the name of Foucault. I will add exit visas to your passports in your own names so you can leave the *zone non occupée*. You will hide your American passports on your persons until you reach the Spanish border."

"*D'accord,*" Paul said. "How will we obtain transit visas

for Spain and Portugal? Will we use our new identities or our American passports?"

The man gaped at him. "They said you were all fluent in French."

Paul frowned. "We are."

"You—your accent is horrible."

He did have an accent, but "horrible"?

The man ran his hand over his head. "The woman and child will pass for French, but you will never pass, monsieur. Never."

Paul's stomach twisted. "I won't speak. Lucie—Colette will do the talking."

"Non." He slashed his arm through the air. "The Germans will question you. You sound American, and they will not let an American man escape so he can fight against them."

Lucie's forehead creased, and her eyes rounded.

"We'll make it work," Paul said to comfort himself as much as to comfort her.

"No." The man knifed his hand down. "We must separate you."

"Separate?" Paul bolted to his feet. "We will not be separated."

"You have no choice. One sentence from you, and they'd know you are American, your papers false. You would endanger every man and woman in the escape line."

Paul clenched his fists. "I will not be sep—"

"No." A violent shake of his head. "We will send you with the British airmen."

Paul's breath heaved. His mind tumbled. "Then Lucie and Josie will come with me."

"Absolutely not. We do not take women and children. It is dangerous. You will cross the Pyrenees Mountains by foot in the winter. The child would not survive."

A tiny whimper rose from Josie.

Paul stared down at his daughter. So small.

Lucie held the girl tight. "It's all right, Josie." But her eyes spoke of despair.

"Monsieur?" Paul's voice cracked. "Please? If there's any way—"

"No. The woman and child can follow the original plan. They can travel freely. But you must follow the escape line."

Paul's fingernails jabbed into his palms. There was always another way, and he stared down the résistant with his steeliest glare.

But steel deflected steel. The résistant would never relent. Nor could he.

Paul's shoulders slumped. He wasn't in control. The resistance was. The only other choice would be to hide in occupied France. To risk internment for himself. Arrest for Lucie. Torture. Execution.

He sank onto the bed, rested his elbows on his knees, and dug his fingers into his scalp. "No . . . Lord, no."

"Paul?" Lucie's voice trembled. "I—I'm not her mother."

He snapped up his head.

Lucie's face buckled. "I—I don't know if I can do this."

"Daddy?" Josie's chin quivered. "What's happening?"

Paul stroked his daughter's curls, kissed her forehead, and then he gripped Lucie's face between his hands. "You can do this."

She shook her head. "No—"

"You have to. You're the only one who can get her home."

"But I—"

"I trust you. And you love her. I know you do."

"I do. But that isn't enough." Tears ran down her cheeks.

Paul swiped them away with his thumbs. How could she not see how capable she was? "I trust you. Now, listen carefully. My parents are Frank and Margaret Aubrey. They live at fifty-seven Cedar Street in Waltham."

Lucie repeated the information, her voice wiggling like jelly.

"Daddy?"

"Shh." He had to attend to Lucie first, so she could attend to Josie. "If you need money in Lisbon, cable my parents. They'll give you anything you need."

"I—I—"

He couldn't bear the terror in her eyes, so he smashed his lips to her forehead. "Take the first ship home. Don't wait for me."

"Paul—"

"Leave a message for me at the embassy, but don't wait."

"All—all right."

Paul drew back, nose to nose with her, his chest aching and writhing. "No matter what, do not get separated from her. No matter what."

Lucie's expression cleared and strengthened. "I won't. No matter what."

"I am sorry, monsieur." The résistant opened the door. "You and I will leave in the middle of the night."

Paul gave him a nod. He couldn't blame the man. He had many people to protect.

He pressed a quick kiss to Lucie's lips. Now for his daughter.

"Come here, sugarplum." He slid her over to his lap. "Do you know why I call you so many candy names?"

She shook her head against Paul's chest.

"It's because you're too sweet to fit into any one word, so I keep looking for new words. Never forget that. Never forget how much I love you. How proud I am of you."

"Daddy, I'm scared."

Paul was too. He buried his face in her curls, so much like Simone's. How could he send her away? Everything inside him recoiled, and he fought to find his voice. "Remem—remember how I told you this trip might be scary and we might tell you to do things you don't understand?"

"I don't like it." She grasped the lapel of Paul's jacket.

"Here's the first thing. This is your mother." He squeezed Lucie's knee. "She will take good care of you."

Lucie smashed her hand over her mouth and shut her eyes.

"I like that," Josie said.

"I do too." Paul wrapped both arms around his baby girl. "Listen carefully. Do whatever Maman says, same as you do for me or Madame Coudray. Better, in fact."

"I—I will."

Paul pulled in a breath through his swollen throat. "Maman will take you to America to your grandparents. I won't be coming with you."

"Daddy?" Josie's voice climbed.

"I'll come to you as fast as I can. But if I can't—"

"Paul, don't." Lucie's chest heaved.

He cut her off with a gaze. "But if I can't, my little bit of everything sweet—remember, always remember I love you."

Josie clutched at him and dissolved in blubbering tears.

Paul rocked her, his heart in pieces. All he wanted was to protect Josie and Lucie, but to do so, he had to leave them.

42

They had to look French, sound French, and act French.

Carrying her ballet bag over her shoulder, Lucie clutched Josie's hand and one of Paul's suitcases, packed with Lucie's and Josie's possessions. She walked down the cobblestone sidewalk in Vierzon past grayish-white buildings with slatted shutters.

That morning, the résistant from Orléans had guided them on the train to Vierzon. The demarcation line between occupied and unoccupied France followed the River Cher, which divided the town of Vierzon.

Colette Foucault. She was Madame Colette Foucault, and she recited her instructions to distract herself. After they entered the zone non occupée, she would take the train to Marseille. There she would obtain transit visas at the Spanish and Portuguese consulates.

"Maman?" Josie said in a tiny voice. "I miss Daddy."

"I miss him too." Lucie squeezed the child's hand as they passed a half-timbered house.

At least Josie's grief had turned the corner from inconsolable sobbing. The first night in Orléans, Josie had cried herself to sleep on the bed, sandwiched between Lucie and Paul. It hadn't seemed improper, the three of them lying entwined, Paul lavishing soft kisses on Josie's head and Lucie's damp cheeks, their tears mingling.

Sometime in the middle of the night, Paul had slipped away with the résistant. The next morning Josie had clung to Lucie.

Two blocks ahead, the road curved and a gate barred the street.

Lucie braced herself. All day yesterday, the résistant had drilled Lucie about the plan and Colette Foucault's story until they came automatically.

While they worked, Lucie had busied herself with needle and thread. She'd sewn a pocket in her slip for her US passport and a portion of the cash Paul had left them. She'd also sewn two of Josie's undershirts together at the hem to create a pouch for the child's papers, an envelope of Aubrey family photos, and more cash.

The hateful swastika flag flew over the sentry post, a hut next to a barricade painted with red and black and white stripes. People lined up to be interrogated by two armed German officials.

The men who might see through Lucie's story, recognize her as a résistante wanted by the police, and separate her from Josie.

Lucie tightened her grip on the little girl's hand. What would happen to Josie if Lucie were arrested? Would they take her to the US Embassy in Vichy or to Simone's parents in Orléans? Or . . . no, she refused to acknowledge anything else.

A sentry raised the bar crossing the road, and two Frenchmen walked their bicycles across. Then the bar came down.

A customs official in a gray uniform held out his hand to Lucie. "Carte d'identité? Ausweis?"

If Lucie looked tense, so did everyone else. She set down the suitcase and pulled the fake papers from her overcoat.

The résistant claimed his forger had never failed to fool the sentries, but Lucie had a child who could give her away.

A large and severe-looking man, the official scrutinized her papers. "Names?"

"Colette Foucault and my daughter, Josephine."

His gaze shifted to Josie, and he grunted.

Josie slid behind Lucie's legs.

"Reason for crossing?" the official asked.

"My father—he passed away. We are going to Marseille for the funeral."

"But you live in Paris." Bluish eyes narrowed at her.

"I came to Paris to study, and there I met my husband."

"Where is your husband?"

Lucie held her gaze firm. "He is a prisoner of war."

The official smirked. "In Marseille look for a man who will not surrender so easily." He handed her the papers.

Lucie lowered her gaze. She mustn't look defiant, but she also mustn't look overly relieved. "Merci, monsieur."

The official waved to his partner, who lifted the bar.

Every impulse told Lucie to run full speed, but she picked up her suitcase and led Josie under the gate as if truly on her way to her father's funeral.

They crossed a long, low bridge over the Cher, and Lucie passed people on bicycles or pushing carts. How difficult to live in a town with families and businesses divided.

At the far end of the bridge stood another sentry station, this one manned by French soldiers in blue overcoats, a sight Lucie hadn't seen in a year and a half. The Vichy government had been allowed to keep a small armistice army for defense.

"Papers?" A French soldier held out his hand with as brusque a manner as his German counterpart, but he gave the papers only a cursory look and let Lucie and Josie through.

The unoccupied zone, and Lucie's breath came more freely. However, even though no Nazi soldiers patrolled Pétain's French

State, the Vichy government pandered to the Germans and would gladly turn over a *terroriste*.

Lucie couldn't let down her guard. Not one bit.

CERBÈRE, FRENCH STATE
MONDAY, DECEMBER 29, 1941

As the train neared the Spanish border, Lucie read to Josie from a French storybook. Thank goodness Paul had packed it. Lucie had brought an English storybook from Green Leaf Books, but in public Colette Foucault only spoke French.

The train curved around green hills plunging down to the impossibly blue Mediterranean.

The past two weeks in Marseille had been trying, flipping between French Colette in town and American Lucille at the Spanish and Portuguese consulates, keeping papers and stories straight.

Back and forth Lucie had gone with weary Josie in tow, proving to the Portuguese that she had the means and ability to leave Portugal and proving to the Spanish that she had permission to enter Portugal. Flooded with refugees, both neutral nations refused to take more.

The train slowed. Above them, butter-colored homes clung to the hills.

The town of Cerbère on the Spanish border. Lucie's moment of truth.

Stamped in their American passports, Lucie and Josie had forged French exit visas and legitimate Spanish and Portuguese transit visas. To travel in France, she needed to be Colette Foucault. But to enter Spain, she needed to be Lucille Girard. So for one critical moment, she needed to present her true papers to French officials.

Surely Wattenberg and the police would think she'd hide in Paris, maybe the countryside. But what if they'd sent an alert to the border?

"Maman?" Josie sat on her knees with her nose pressed to the window. "Can we sing our song?"

"Only in our hotel room." Lucie had set the Aubrey address in Massachusetts to music so Josie could memorize it. Lucie had to make sure Josie got there, even if they were separated, even if Josie lost her passport.

Lucie's chest crumpled. She missed Paul so much, worried about him. Such a long and perilous route. How long would it take him to reach Lisbon?

The train pulled into the station. Lucie gathered the luggage and took Josie by the hand.

All the passengers filed off the train to go through French customs. Then they'd board another train, since French and Spanish trains ran on different gauge rails. The train would pass through a tunnel to Port Bou, where Spanish officials would examine their papers.

The Spanish officials didn't worry Lucie. Only the French officials.

"My hand hurts," Josie said with a whine.

Lucie glanced down at the tiny hand and relaxed her grip. "I'm sorry, sweetheart. Now stay close, remember?"

"I 'member." Indeed, she'd stuck to Lucie's side every moment. Which Lucie loved.

The line flowed into the station, loud with conversations in French and Spanish.

Voices rose from the front of the line, a woman wept, and whispers swept among the passengers. Someone didn't have correct papers.

Soon an elderly couple shuffled past Lucie, the husband's arm around his sobbing wife.

"Jews," a woman muttered with disgust rather than compassion.

Lucie gripped her papers. If only she could help. But what could an elderly couple do with passports for a twenty-seven-year-old woman and a four-year-old girl?

Josie pulled on Lucie's hand. "I'm hungry."

"Good. Soon you'll have your first Spanish food." To distract her, Lucie chattered in a cheery voice about what little she knew of Spanish cuisine.

At last a French customs official asked for their papers. Lucie offered both passports and a prayer. Paul had lost his wife and had been separated from his daughter. How could he bear it if Lucie lost Josie? And what would happen to this sweet child?

The official studied their passports with hooded eyes. "Your names?"

Lucie drew a deep breath and selected the proper identity. "Lucille Girard and my daughter, Josephine Aubrey."

Small dark eyes snapped up. "You have different surnames?"

Lucie had prepared for this, and she lowered her head. "I am . . . not married. She bears her father's name." Every word true.

The official snorted. "Shameful. Open your luggage."

Lucie lifted her suitcase and Josie's little case to the table and opened them.

"Any valuables? Cash?" Another official sifted through the suitcase.

"Non, monsieur." Lucie laid her ballet bag down. She'd depleted much of Paul's cash in Marseille, and she needed the reserve in her slip to tide them over in Lisbon until she could cable her parents for money. She'd ask Paul's parents only as a last resort.

Josie's little case held her doll, stuffed kitty, and blanket, but the official inspected them closely. Then he upended Lucie's bag, dumping out pocketbook, Bible, storybooks, and puppets.

Monsieur Meow tumbled to the floor.

"Monsieur Meow!" Josie ripped her hand from Lucie's, darted forward, and grabbed the puppet.

"Josie!" Lucie rushed to the child. "Don't ever leave me again. Do you hear?"

Tears filled Josie's brown eyes, and she hugged the puppet. "He fell. I can't lose him."

Lucie hugged the child tight. "And I can't lose you."

The customs official snorted. "The child obviously needs a father. Go back into France and marry him."

Lucie wanted to glare at the man, but more than that, she wanted to leave France. So she just stroked Josie's back. "Her father is no longer with us. Please let us go home to America, monsieur."

A harrumph. "Very well. Your papers are in order, mademoiselle." He twisted the final word with disdain.

"Merci." Without meeting the horrid man's gaze, Lucie shepherded Josie to the far side of the table, where she packed their luggage. And where she said adieu to France.

43

The year of 1941 was ending on an even lonelier note than it had begun.

Paul sat on his bed in his little room in a monastery somewhere—they wouldn't tell him where—in occupied France.

No one told him anything.

RAF men inhabited other rooms, but they weren't allowed to talk to each other. Occasionally a résistant visited Paul to review his new identity as farm laborer Jean Bonnet.

Paul scratched at his scruffy beard and tugged at the rough worker's clothing they'd given him. As to when he'd leave for Lisbon, all he heard was, "Wait."

The monks brought him food. He was warm and comfortable. But he hated waiting. Hated the lack of control. Hated the seclusion. Most of all, he hated not knowing if Josie and Lucie were safe.

He stood and paced the room, over and over, all day, days on end. He was Josie's father, her only living parent. He was supposed to protect her. And he couldn't.

Paul rapped his fists on his thighs and slumped against the

door, as caged as if in prison. Lucie would protect Josie with her life, but ultimately she had no control either.

"Lord, protect them. Please."

Paul took a few deep breaths. Mulling over misery never made it better.

Reading his Bible would distract him. He opened the satchel the resistance had given him to disguise his suitcase—which he refused to relinquish. If he were searched, his US passport in its belt under his shirt would give him away. What did it matter if he carried his few remaining possessions? The most precious were his tank designs and Josie's Feenee stories.

He should have sent the stories with Lucie, but he'd forgotten them in the turmoil of that last night. Paul groaned. "Isn't that typical of me?"

He pulled out the manila envelope, sat cross-legged on the stone floor, and worked out the papers. Color blossomed before him.

Green-haired Feenee soaring over an orange Eiffel Tower. Red-haired Feenee dancing with Monsieur Meow. Purple-haired Feenee poking a rock-monster with her horn.

Josie had printed random letters, her attempt to transcribe the stories in her head.

Paul's jaw felt tight and his nose stuffy. His little girl. So creative. How much harm had he done by dismissing her gifts for so long?

He sniffed and wiped his nose. Dampness marred his vision, and he worked out a handkerchief. Second time he'd cried in the past month, both times over Josie. Over leaving her. Over failing her.

Paul traced his finger over a crooked blue *J*. "Please, Lord. Give me another chance."

LISBON, PORTUGAL
TUESDAY, DECEMBER 30, 1941

Lisbon was an explosion of pinks and blues and yellows and greens. The Avenida da Liberdade stretched as broad and beautiful as any boulevard in Paris, only without Nazi soldiers.

"It's so loud." Josie clutched Lucie's hand as they left the train station, her eyes huge.

"It is." Lucie smiled. Cars careened down the street, honking at each other. Lucie hadn't seen traffic in a year and a half, beyond the range of Josie's memory.

They passed a café. The smells tantalized—meats and spices and yeasty bread—and no ration tickets needed. Lucie swallowed the water collecting in her mouth. "After we go to the American Legation, we'll celebrate with lunch."

Josie hung back and stared. "Are those people German?"

Lucie's chest tightened. "No, sweetheart. In Portugal you don't have to be German to buy food."

Beyond the café stood a newsstand, and Lucie gaped. The London *Daily Mail*. Paris's *Le Matin*. Germany's *Das Reich*. Side by side. Lucie scanned the headlines in the *New York Times*, the first news she'd read from a free press in ages.

But the news did nothing to raise her spirits. The Japanese were advancing in the Philippines and had taken Hong Kong. So many ships sunk in the Atlantic and Pacific. To reach America required crossing the Atlantic, and Lucie shuddered.

The next store said *confeitaria*. "Confectionary," Lucie whispered.

Josie pointed. "That store looks like Feenee's hair. What is it?"

"It—it's candy." Poor child couldn't remember candy stores. Lucie needed to go straight to the legation, but Paul would want his daughter to have candy. "You may have one piece now and one after lunch."

Josie hopped her way into the store.

One customer stood inside, a pregnant, dark-haired woman in a chic gray coat. The shopgirl called out a greeting to Lucie in Portuguese.

"Bom dia," Lucie replied, the greeting she'd heard in the train station.

Lucie lifted Josie to her hip and named the candies in the display case. She'd heard Paul call Josie many of the names. Her heart swelled with love for him, then wrenched with pain. He should be the one to watch Josie taste her first candy.

After the shopgirl finished helping the pregnant woman, she approached Lucie.

"Parlez-vous français?" Lucie asked. "Or do you speak English?"

Annoyance flicked on her face. *"Nao. Eu falo portugues."*

Surely Lucie could communicate a simple purchase. She pointed to sugar-coated jellies shaped like fruit slices and held up three fingers. "Three? *Trois?"*

"Sim." The lady dug a scoop into the bin.

"Non. Trois." Lucie made a pinching motion. Three pieces, not three scoops or pounds.

"Eu não entendo."

"Excusez-moi, madame," the pregnant lady said to Lucie. "I speak a little Portuguese. May I help?"

"Oui. Merci." Lucie gave her a grateful smile. "I would like three each of the fruit candies, these caramels, and those chocolates."

She smiled, an attractive woman with soft dark eyes, and she gave the order to the shopgirl, her words halting but effective.

The shopgirl bagged the candy.

"You are recently arrived in Lisbon?" The pregnant woman nodded to Lucie's suitcase.

"Yes, just now. You are from Paris too?" Lucie recognized the accent.

Sadness swam through those dark eyes. "Oui."

From what Lucie had heard, thousands of refugees swarmed Lisbon waiting for passage to a country that actually wanted them.

The shopgirl spoke.

"She told you the price," Lucie's helper said. "It's in escutos. Did you exchange money?"

"Yes, in the station." She pulled out her pocketbook, picked out coins as instructed, and exchanged them for the bag of candy. She smiled at the mother-to-be. "Thank you for helping a fellow Parisienne."

She tipped up a square chin. "I am no longer a Parisienne. I am soon to be an American."

"Oh? We're Americans. I'm glad you got a visa. I've heard how difficult it is."

"I am one of the lucky ones. My name was on Varian Fry's list."

"Varian Fry?"

"You have not heard of him? He is a hero." Her dark eyes shone. "He is an American reporter sent to Marseille with three thousand dollars and a list of two hundred authors and artists and intellectuals in danger from the Nazis. The Vichy government kicked him out of France recently, but not before he obtained American visas for hundreds of people."

"How wonderful." And a story that would never be reported in Parisian papers.

Crinkles formed around the woman's eyes. "Your daughter is patient."

Josie looked up at Lucie, bouncing on her toes.

Lucie chuckled. "I did promise you one." She squatted down, handed Josie an orange candy, and watched so she could report every expression to Paul.

Josie sniffed it, then nibbled. She recoiled a bit, as if in shock. Her eyes scrunched up, and she chewed. Slowly, wonder transformed her face. "It tastes like—flowers and—and sunshine."

"That's how sweet you are to your father. Sweeter, in fact."

"She's darling," the woman said. "Does she look like her father?"

"Very much."

The woman rubbed her rounded belly. "I hope my baby looks like its father too."

"When are you due?"

"February. I hope I will be in America. But it is hard to find passage." She gave Lucie a sympathetic smile. "You will see. I've been looking for a month."

"Does the American Legation help? I'm on my way there."

"Oh? I'm going that direction myself. May I walk with you?" The woman waved to the shopgirl. "*Obrigada.*"

"Obrigada." Lucie followed her new friend up the street. "I am Lucie Girard, and this is my daughter, Josie."

"A pleasure to meet you, Madame Girard. My name is Dominique Kahn."

Lucie had met many authors in her line of work, and it always thrilled her. "I am so pleased to meet you. I loved *La tempête tranquille.*"

"You read it?" Surprise dawned on Madame Kahn's face.

"I loved it." But the Nazis would hate the book with its Jewish heroine—and the author who wrote it. "You are friends with Saint-Yves, right? He talks about you."

"You know my Saint-Yves?" A broad smile erupted.

"I do. He's a dear. I owned a bookstore in Paris—Green Leaf Books."

Madame Kahn gasped. "I always wanted to visit, but my English—it is poor."

"You would have been more than welcome."

"I can see that." Madame Kahn's smile held uncommon warmth. "Tell me, do you have a place to stay?"

"I was going to ask at the legation."

"Here." She opened her purse, pulled out a notepad, and began writing. "This is where I'm staying. There's a vacancy. It's clean and safe."

"Thank you." Lucie took the piece of paper. "How can I ever repay you?"

Madame Kahn's smile tipped to one side. "How about some English lessons?"

"Gladly." In a few blocks, Lucie's new friend went her way, and soon Lucie and Josie arrived at the legation.

A line stretched around the building—refugees hoping for visas to America. Lucie's heart ached for them as it had for the refugees at the US Consulate in Marseille.

Bypassing the line felt rude, but Lucie didn't need a visa. She approached the guard at the door, showed her precious passport, and was admitted. A gentleman at the front desk pointed her to the department she needed.

In the office Lucie went to an available clerk. "Good day. My name is Lucille Girard. Do you have a message for me?"

"I'll check, ma'am."

Her heart beat in wild hope for a word from Paul, but the clerk returned empty-handed. "Nothing. I'm sorry."

"Thank you. May I leave a message for Mr. Paul Aubrey? He's an American citizen."

"Yes, ma'am." The clerk slid a piece of paper and an envelope to her.

In her note Lucie told Paul when they'd arrived, where they were staying, and her plans to find passage. Then she pressed a lipstick kiss to the paper and had Josie give her father a candy kiss.

After she slipped the note in the envelope, she gave it one last kiss. "Soon, my love," she whispered.

44

BAYONNE, FRANCE
THURSDAY, JANUARY 15, 1942

All the waiting and tedium had come to an end. Paul slumped in his seat, a laborer in cheap clothing, as the train pulled into Bayonne near the Spanish border on the Atlantic.

That morning a young woman with the code name of Denise had roused Paul and three RAF airmen and hustled them on to a southbound train.

The railway personnel had barely glanced at their papers and had given Denise knowing nods. The *cheminots* were among the first to resist the Germans.

Denise sat three rows ahead of Paul to his right, and the Englishmen sat behind him.

The train chuffed into a station with a peaked roof. After it stopped, Denise retrieved a suitcase from the overhead rack. Paul gathered his satchel and followed at a distance, not looking back to check on the airmen.

Paul followed Denise down the platform, through the station, and outside into cool, clear air. A wide road passed creamy buildings decorated with shutters and awnings in reds and greens.

Wary and tense, Paul scanned the passersby. A French policeman directed traffic and two German soldiers patrolled, but
none gave Paul a second glance.

At the base of a bridge over the Adour River, Denise entered
a building, the last they'd see of her.

Without pausing, Paul crossed the bridge and searched for
their contact, a young blonde woman in a tan coat and a red
hat. There she stood on the far side, next to bicycles propped
against the railing.

As the only escapee who spoke French, Paul would make
contact. Each exchange was dangerous, and résistants were
to be feared as much as soldiers and police. If they suspected
an infiltrator, they'd escort the man into the woods and shoot
him.

Paul had to be vigilant and precise. He blew out a breath
and approached the blonde. "Excuse me, mademoiselle. Are
those bicycles for sale?"

She met his eye in a cool manner. "That depends on how
many you would like."

That was the proper response. "I would like four."

"Show me your payment."

"Oui, mademoiselle." Paul fished a torn franc note out of
his pocket.

She lifted another torn franc note. The halves matched. She
pocketed them, mounted a bicycle, and pedaled away.

No time to waste. Paul straddled a bike and followed. Out
of the corner of his eye, he saw the three airmen dash over and
grab bicycles too.

Thank goodness he'd ridden a bicycle a few times over the
past year, because the girl set a fast pace, never looking back
to see if the men kept up.

Paul didn't know what lay ahead on the journey, but he knew
what lay at the end—freedom, home, and the girls he loved.

LISBON, PORTUGAL
FRIDAY, JANUARY 16, 1942

At the base of the gangplank, Lucie turned back to Lisbon, to Europe, to Paul.

For over two weeks, she'd waited for him, visiting the American Legation daily, leaving notes and Josie's drawings. But as soon as Dominique Kahn heard the Portuguese freighter *Espiritu Santo* was taking passengers to New York, Lucie and Dominique had booked passage.

Lucie's gut told her to stay, as if leaving meant giving up on Paul. But how much of her reluctance stemmed from fear of an ocean with German U-boats lurking beneath the surface? Although they weren't supposed to attack neutral Portuguese ships, accidents happened. And the Nazis were far from honorable.

However, Paul had told her to take the first ship home. And this was it. She had to take Josie to her grandparents, and she had to be disciplined enough to do so.

"Lucie?" Dominique said from higher on the gangplank. "It is time to leave."

Lucie hauled in a breath and led Josie up the ramp.

She had reason to look back, but Dominique didn't. During their time at the boardinghouse, the author's story had emerged.

When the Nazis invaded, Dominique and Fabien Kahn had fled to their summer home in Provence. As Jews, they were forbidden from returning to Paris—nor did they want to. But over time Fabien became determined to get information from Paris to de Gaulle's Free French in London. He'd sneaked back and forth across the demarcation line, smuggling news. He might even have passed messages through Green Leaf Books.

In September, he'd been caught. In late October, in reprisal for the resistance killing of a German officer, a group of hostages had been shot. Including Fabien Kahn.

At the top of the gangplank, a Portuguese sailor barked instructions and motioned the three dozen passengers inside.

Josie whimpered. "I don't like it here. It smells funny."

The stuffy passageway smelled of oil and sweat, and Lucie wrinkled her nose. Josie had rarely complained during the journey, despite the upheaval. With only ten more days to go, Lucie would do her best to keep up the child's spirits.

A sailor pointed down a staircase, more like a ladder.

"I'll go down first," Lucie said to Josie. "Let's sing our song."

"Okay." Josie peered down the ladder with a mixture of apprehension and adventure.

Lucie threaded the strap of her ballet bag through the handle of Josie's little case, put both over her shoulder, and took the suitcase in hand. Then she descended the ladder backward with Josie in front of her.

Josie's crystalline voice joined Lucie's in the tune they'd sung countless times, as they descended another ladder, walked down a passageway, and stepped through oval doors.

> I'm going to my grandparents' house
> To Frank and Margaret Aubrey's house.
> They live on a street called Cedar Street
> At fifty-seven Cedar Street.
> Waltham, Waltham, Waltham, Massachusetts.

A sailor pointed at two rooms, calling out orders.

"Men in there," Dominique translated. "Women and children in here."

They entered a cramped compartment filled with bunks stacked in threes. Lucie swung her suitcase on a top bunk. "Josie will sleep with me, so we can use this for our luggage."

"Thank you." Dominique lifted her suitcase up. "You are so good with Josie."

Lucie smiled down at the girl, who rolled around on the bottom bunk and giggled. "She's an easy child."

"I hope my child will be that easy." Dominique stretched her lower back.

"Even if not, you'll love your child just as fiercely."

"I will." She cupped her hand below that child. The only living legacy of a courageous man.

45

PYRENEES MOUNTAINS
SUNDAY, JANUARY 25, 1942

Paul's feet sank into the snow, wet and numb. After three nights hiking the Pyrenees Mountains on the border of France and Spain, he just wanted to lie down and sleep.

Wrapped in a Basque coat with a cap low over his ears and a scarf around his bearded face, Paul trudged up the steep wooded path with only half a moon to light his way.

He wasn't about to get shown up by the British airmen, nor by their guides, a Basque man two decades older than Paul and a tiny girl no older than sixteen.

He knew only code names, but the flyboys knew each other.

Nearing the top of a ridge, Paul adjusted the straps holding his satchel on his back.

The guides, Ander and Gigi, dropped to their stomachs and made patting motions.

Heart thudding, Paul fell to his knees and slid onto his stomach. He strained his ears, but he only heard the icy wind in the barren trees.

Then he heard faint voices behind him, and he shivered.

No one could be trusted this close to the border. German

soldiers and French police patrolled for RAF airmen and résistants. Spanish troops also patrolled to keep out refugees—and many Spaniards were fascists.

Paul lay still, straining to hear, his blood pulsing in his ears, snow burning his cheek.

In a few minutes, the voices faded. For a few minutes more, the party didn't stir.

Then Gigi swept her arm in an arc. Everyone crawled forward, elbows crunching in the snow, and the guides slithered over the ridge.

Paul did too. The ground fell away beneath him.

Down he slid, headfirst, stifling cries as he bumped down the steep slope. Ander and Gigi slid on their backs, feetfirst, as if they'd expected it.

A spindly bush—Paul grabbed it, and his legs swung past him, wrenching his shoulder.

A soft whistle from Ander. About twenty feet below, the slope ended in a ravine filled with dark brush.

Paul let go of his little tree, slid down about ten feet, and crawled the rest of the way.

Ander pointed to a lean-to deep in the brush, and Paul crawled over.

They'd sleep by day, taking turns on watch, then traipse ahead after the sun set. No talking, no questions, only silent obedience.

Paul sank to the cold ground and massaged his sore shoulder. His legs ached from hiking. His feet and hands and face ached from the cold. His stomach ached from hunger. And his heart ached from missing Lucie and Josie.

After Gigi passed out dried fish, Paul gnawed off a frozen chunk. As he chewed, it melted and released an unpleasant flavor. But he needed the nourishment, so he swallowed the fish and swallowed a joke about passing the beurre blanc sauce.

And he prayed.

The Lord had made the fish, and Paul gave thanks.

The Lord had created Ander and Gigi and given them courage to risk their lives to help four strangers, and Paul gave thanks.

And the Lord had created Lucie and Josie, the sweet faces that drove him forward, and Paul gave deep and heartfelt thanks.

ATLANTIC OCEAN
SUNDAY, JANUARY 25, 1942

Josie steepled her hands and squeezed her eyes shut. "God bless Daddy and Maman and Madame Kahn and Monsieur Meow and Feenee. Amen."

"Amen." Leaning over the middle bunk, Lucie tucked the blanket under Josie's chin.

Although they'd returned to their true identities, Josie still insisted on calling Lucie Maman.

On the frigid freighter, the passengers wore street clothes and coats to bed, plus the caps elderly Frau Abrams had knit for everyone. And life vests. They wore those day and night.

"Just think." Lucie tucked the puppets in bed beside Josie. "Tomorrow morning we'll be in New York City, and tomorrow night you'll sleep at your grandparents' house."

"At fifty-seven Cedar Street."

"First thing we'll do is give you a bath." Lucie poked her little belly, and she giggled.

The room stank of unwashed bodies and vomit. Lucie and Josie had been miserable with seasickness the first few days. Now they spun adventurous tales of Monsieur Meow and Feenee at sea.

Some of the women complained about the conditions, but most were happy to be on their way to America, and Lucie and Dominique led the charge to keep up morale.

A metallic *thunk*.

The ship lurched. Lucie lost her balance and grabbed the side of the bunk.

Women cried out in half a dozen languages.

"What was that?" Josie's eyebrows bunched together, and she gripped the blanket.

"I don't know." But chilly, slimy truth flooded her mind. That loud a noise could only be a collision or a torpedo.

Dominique rolled out of the bottom bunk. "I'll ask." Since she spoke the most Portuguese, she often served as intermediary.

"We're sinking!" Mrs. Jeffers cried out. As always, she gave Americans a bad name. "We're all going to die."

"Hush, Mrs. Jeffers," Lucie said in a soothing tone. "We need to stay calm."

Sweet Frau Abrams sat up in her bunk with a long white braid over her shoulder. She let out a strangled cry and said something in German or Yiddish, the only languages she spoke.

Lucie held on to the pole of her bunk. The ship listed at an unnerving angle, and she turned to Miss Shepard, a US correspondent who spoke German. "Can you speak to Frau Abrams?"

"Sure thing, toots." Miss Shepard checked her life vest, and she spoke to Frau Abrams in a stern tone.

Lucie frowned, but Frau Abrams closed her eyes, nodded, and took a deep breath.

"Will this help?" Josie reached into her coat pocket and handed Lucie a bright pink satin ball.

"One of Monsieur Meow's balls?" Lucie lifted a fragile smile.

"Uh-huh. You said you never know when it'll come in handy." Josie looked at Lucie with complete trust.

If Lucie had booked her on a doomed ship, she'd broken that trust.

But right now Josie needed Lucie to be strong, not to wallow in her failures. Lucie folded the ball back in Josie's hand. "That's right, sweetheart. Keep it in your pocket."

Lucie grabbed both pairs of shoes from the top bunk. "Let's put on your shoes."

"In bed? Why?"

Lucie worked a shoe onto Josie's foot. "Remember that lifeboat drill? We might need to do another one."

"That was scary." She poked out her lower lip, but she also poked out her other foot.

"It was, but we'll be brave." After Lucie buckled on the second shoe, she patted Josie's belly and felt the packet of passport and photos. "Let's sing our song."

Josie sang in a shaky voice while Lucie tied her dark blue bonnet over her knit cap and checked her life vest.

Lucie sat on the lower bunk and tied on her oxfords.

In the passageway, footsteps thumped and a sailor shouted.

Dominique stepped into the compartment, her face stark. "Abandon ship. Make sure you have your coat and life vest. Don't take any personal belongings."

Mrs. Jeffers let out a howl, and women cried.

"Maman?" Josie's voice broke, and she hugged Lucie's arm.

"It's all right, sweetie. We're going up to the deck and into a lifeboat." She grabbed Josie's beloved little blanket and tied it around her neck like a shawl.

"I'll be brave. I'll be brave." Josie's voice sounded high and tight, but her eyes held strength.

Lucie kissed her nose. "Yes, you will, my brave girl."

Josie burrowed under the blanket and pulled out the puppets.

Pain collapsed Lucie's chest. "I'm sorry, sweetheart, but we can't take any belongings."

"No!" Terror ripped across the child's face. "Monsieur Meow! Feenee! They'll die!"

Lucie chewed on her lip. Keeping Josie calm was more important than following every letter of the law. She stuffed Monsieur Meow in her coat pocket and stuffed Feenee down inside Josie's coat.

Ladies filed out of the compartment, and Dominique helped Frau Abrams with her life vest.

"Dominique?" Lucie called. "Do you have everything you need?"

"I do, thank you."

Mrs. Jeffers sat on her bunk, sobbing, trying to tie her shoes. Lucie grabbed Josie's hand and dashed to Mrs. Jeffers. "Please stay calm. I'll help with your shoes." After Lucie did so, she made sure Mrs. Jeffers had her passport, coat, hat, and life vest, and sent her on her way.

Dominique struggled to help Frau Abrams to her feet, and Lucie rushed to the elderly lady's other side and helped her up. Everyone else had left.

Lucie and Dominique edged Frau Abrams out the door, and Josie clung to Lucie's free hand. The foursome worked their way sideways along the tilting passageway.

At the ladder, Lucie sent Josie up first, then Dominique, then Frau Abrams, with Lucie behind her.

With each step, the elderly woman gained strength. They climbed the last ladder and headed out onto the deck near the stern.

A half-moon cast eerie light over the slanting deck, and fires blazed in hideous orange by the bridge. The front portion of the ship sagged to starboard as if the ship had been twisted by giant cruel hands. Sailors shined flashlights and beckoned with directions Lucie didn't understand.

Women dashed away from their lifeboat station on the starboard side and around the stern.

Lucie grabbed Miss Shepard's arm as she passed. "What's going on?"

"Our lifeboat—they let it down wrong and it shattered."

She jerked her head to port. "Come on! There might be room in another boat."

Dominique and Lucie exchanged an alarmed look and followed the other women.

A net flowed down toward a lifeboat, and women scrambled down. Mrs. Jeffers tossed a suitcase into the boat. The sailor at the helm shouted what had to be a curse and hurled the suitcase into the ocean.

Dominique faced Frau Abrams and pointed to the net. "Can you do this?"

The woman couldn't have understood the French words, but she nodded. With Dominique's and Lucie's help, she climbed over the side and worked her way down the net.

"Our turn." Lucie kissed Josie on the cheek, swung her over the side, and helped her grip with her hands. "Just like the playground. You can do it."

In the strange orange light of the fire, Josie's eyes glowed with fear and determination. "I'll be brave. I'll be brave."

Lucie and Dominique climbed down on either side of Josie, talking her down. Lucie latched her gaze on the rope and the child and the pregnant woman. Not on the sea. Not on the heaving dark sea below.

Soon the sailor in the lifeboat grabbed Josie and settled her in the lifeboat. Then he waved frantically at Lucie and Dominique and shouted.

Dominique's mouth drooped, and her eyes grew wide and bleak. "There—there's only room for one more. Only one, or the boat will sink."

"Oh no!" Lucie spotted a sailor leaning over the railing above. "Ask him. Is there another boat?"

Dominique shouted at the sailor. He gestured angrily at the sea and shouted back.

"This—this is the last one." Dominique's face shattered. "You must go, Lucie. You must be with your daughter."

"No . . ." Clinging to the net, Lucie stared at her friend, her heart writhing. She'd promised Paul she'd never be separated from Josie. But to abandon her friend to die? That would take every bit of discipline she had.

Dominique gave her a soft, sad smile. "Do not worry. Soon I will be with my Fabien."

Their baby would too.

No, that couldn't be the right decision.

Lucie clenched the rope. *Lord, show me what to do!*

Impulse swelled inside her, and Lucie worked Monsieur Meow from her pocket. "No, you will go."

"Lucie! No!"

Pain split her chest like a cleaver. She would die, but Dominique needed to live. She stuffed the puppet in Dominique's pocket. "If I die, if Paul dies, at least Josie will live. But if you die, your baby dies too. You must live. Go!"

"I cannot." Tears slithered down her cheeks.

The sailor in the lifeboat yelled, strident and angry.

"He . . ." Dominique glanced down. "He's going to leave."

"Go! I stand a chance in the water. You don't. Hurry!"

Dominique's face twisted. "I—I will never forget you."

Lucie scrambled up the net before she could change her mind.

"What have I done?" She was going to die. She'd broken her promise to Paul. And sweet Josie . . .

"Maman?" Josie cried in confusion. "Maman?"

Lucie climbed over the railing onto the ship. Below her, the lifeboat rowed away, and Dominique embraced Josie.

"I love you, Josie! Be brave!" A sob welled up, and Lucie clapped her hand over her mouth.

To her right, a horrid, shrieking, ripping sound.

The ship split in half.

The deck lurched. The stern tipped forward.

Lucie fell, clung to the railing, stifled her cries.

"Maman! Maman!" Josie screamed.

"Sing our song, Josie!" Lucie yelled, down on her knees. "Sing our song!"

"I'm going to my grandparents' house." Josie's voice warbled and broke.

Lucie crawled up the slanted deck. "That's it, sweetheart! Sing, Josie. Sing!"

"To Frank and Margaret Aubrey's . . ." Her little voice disappeared under the sounds of creaking metal and crackling fire.

46

**BASQUE COUNTRY, SPAIN
MONDAY, JANUARY 26, 1942**

At the tree line at the foot of the Pyrenees in Spain, Paul crouched with Ander, Gigi, and the RAF men. A three-story white farmhouse with a red tile roof stood on the far side of an orchard.

And a morning patrol passed on the road just beyond.

The Gestapo had agents in Spain and Portugal, and sometimes local authorities turned in escaping airmen and résistants as insurance against a Nazi invasion.

Wind rustled through the bare branches, and mist coated Paul's face.

Maybe tonight he'd have a full belly and a warm bed. How long had it been? The days blended together.

In a few minutes, Ander gestured for the group to follow him. Gigi remained behind. If they were compromised, at least she'd have a chance to escape. At the Basque guide's signal, the men ran between rows of bare fruit trees.

His senses high, his heart rate high, Paul ran quietly. This would be their last contact on this journey. But that didn't make it any less dangerous.

When they reached the farmhouse, Ander knocked on the back door.

A woman in a black dress with a black scarf around her head answered the door. She and Ander spoke in the Basque language, then she motioned everyone inside.

Paul stepped in—to a stable. A donkey brayed, and a sheep bleated. The smell of manure hit him, but considering how he had to smell, he couldn't complain.

The woman trotted upstairs, speaking briskly to Ander. The second floor appeared to be living quarters, but she led them up to the third floor. Baskets of apples, walnuts, and potatoes filled one half of the room, and hay the other.

"Lie down," Ander told the men. "No talking, no smoking, and do not eat anything unless offered. She will send her son to Bilbao to fetch the British consular officer."

"Thank you, sir," Paul said. "We appreciate all your help."

"Good luck." Ander tipped the men a salute and disappeared down the stairs.

The smell of apples and the fragrance of herbs drying overhead made Paul's mouth water, but he stretched out on the wooden floor with his satchel under his head. His companions lay down too.

One step closer to home, and a smile lifted his weary face. What would Lucie think to see him now, stinking and scruffy? He had a hunch she wouldn't mind.

Where were Lucie and Josie now? Six weeks had passed since he'd seen them, heard their voices, smelled their hair. Not much longer now. Not much longer.

Someone shook Paul's shoulder, and he woke with a start. The airman code-named Louis leaned over Paul and pressed one finger to his lips, his eyes wide.

Voices rose from below, a man and a woman. Footsteps clumped up the stairs.

Paul held his breath and eyed the opening to the stairway.

A black homburg appeared and a trim, mustached face. "Cheerio, chaps."

You couldn't get more British than that.

The airmen sprang over and shook hands with the consular officer in his tailored black overcoat.

Paul shook hands too. "I can't tell you how glad we are to see you."

Thin gray eyebrows sprang high. "You're—American?"

"Yes, sir. Guilty as charged."

The officer gaped at Paul, at the three airmen. "And you chaps—"

"We're British, sir," the man called Philippe said.

The diplomat held up one hand to the airmen. "I'll take you to the consulate in Bilbao for questioning, then send you to Gibraltar. But you—what are you doing here?" He glowered at Paul.

His stomach squirmed. "I came from Paris, sir. I'm going home to America."

"In the escape line? This is for men of the Royal Air Force."

Paul straightened his shoulders. "The resistance sent me because I worked with them and couldn't risk internment."

"That is none of my concern." He brushed a narrow hand in Paul's direction.

"Please, sir," Louis said. "He's one of us."

Paul gave Louis a grateful look, then addressed the officer. "You were planning on driving four men to Bilbao anyway. If you could take me to the American—"

"You don't have a consulate in Bilbao." He raised a pointed chin. "Your nearest consular office is in Madrid. And taking you would be a violation of protocol."

"How—how far is Madrid?"

The man's chin softened and shifted to one side. "About two hundred miles."

Two hundred miles? By foot? He didn't even speak Spanish. "Sir, please . . ."

Louis exchanged a look with his buddies and crossed his arms. "If he must walk, we shall walk with him."

"Quite right," Philippe said. "This chap ran a safe house in Paris. Dozens of our boys have been saved because of him. If you'd like us to return to Old Blighty and our bombers, you must take him too."

The diplomat blinked rapidly. "I—it's highly irregular."

"So is war," Philippe said.

Paul sent the official a look both firm and pleading.

The man pressed his lips in a line. "I'll take you to Madrid and not a mile farther."

"Thank you." Paul's breath flowed out in relief. Another step closer to the girls he loved.

ATLANTIC OCEAN
MONDAY, JANUARY 26, 1942

Black turned to gray turned to pink, and still Lucie lived. She huddled in a crevice on the ship's tilted hulk, along with two sailors and the captain. Shivers wracked her body, but she lived.

"Why haven't we sunk?" she asked the captain, who spoke French and Portuguese.

He pulled his coat collar tight around his bearded chin. "There are watertight compartments below."

The chopped-off stump of a ship bobbed in the waves. How long could it remain afloat? How long could they survive without food or water?

Lucie tugged her knit cap lower over her ears. It crackled with frost.

Josie's terrified cries still rang in her head. The girl had lost her mother, she'd been torn from her father, and she'd been abandoned by Lucie. Even if Lucie survived, Paul would never forgive her.

Once again Lucie had acted impulsively, and everyone paid.

An icy wind swept over her face, and she shook off the guilt. Her survival on the hulk had required agility Dominique didn't have so late in her pregnancy. If Lucie had taken that seat in the lifeboat, both mother and child would have died.

Lucie pursed chapped lips. Just because her decision was impulsive didn't make it wrong. She'd weighed lives and legacies, and she'd seen to Josie's safety.

Conviction rose inside her with the sun on the horizon.

She'd come to see discipline as good and impulsivity as bad. But discipline was only as good as the task it was applied to, and impulse was only as bad as the action it caused. What if the impulse was to kindness? Then discipline deserved to have its say and nothing more.

One of the sailors shouted.

Lucie snapped her gaze to him.

The sailor stood braced against the lopsided deck, and he pointed. On the gray waves a gray shape rose and fell. A ship? Or another U-boat?

The captain stood, tugged off his coat, and waved it over-head, shouting.

"What is it?" Lucie asked.

"A destroyer. An American destroyer."

Lucie cried out in joy. "We're saved!"

The captain kept waving his coat. "Not if they think we're a U-boat."

"Oh." Joy drained out. She forced her numb fingers to un-button her coat, and she shrugged it off. Keeping her backside firm against the deck for balance, she swept her coat overhead. "Over here! Over here!"

The ship drew nearer, and sailors bustled around on the destroyer's deck. "Stay where you are," a man said over a loudspeaker. "We will send a boat to you."

"They see us!" Lucie translated the instructions into French, broken by giddy laughter.

A motorboat lowered over the destroyer's side, then chugged over to the hulk.

The American sailors tossed up a line, and the Portuguese sailors secured it.

With great care, Lucie worked her way across the wreckage. A sailor helped her over the side and onto a rope ladder, and Lucie descended.

"I've got you, ma'am," a very American voice said, and strong hands gripped her waist.

"Thank you, sir. Thank you." Lucie collapsed on her bottom. "I'm so glad you saw us."

A handsome face stared down at her from under an officer's cap. "You're American."

"Yes, sir."

"Is this the *Espiritu Santo*? We received an SOS last night."

"Yes, sir." Lucie scooted over to make room for the other survivors.

"What was your point of departure, ma'am?" the officer asked. "Your destination?"

"Lisbon. We were supposed to arrive in New York this morning."

"How many aboard?"

"Thirty-five passengers. Captain?" She switched to French and addressed the man coming down the ladder. "How many crewmen?"

"Twenty-four."

Lucie translated.

The American officer glared out over the ocean. "Was it a U-boat?"

"Yes, sir. The captain saw the torpedo approach."

The officer's frown deepened with sympathy. "Just the four survivors, ma'am?"

A stone plummeted in Lucie's stomach. "Several lifeboats departed. Haven't you found them?"

"We haven't heard."

"Oh no." Lucie pressed her hand to her mouth, and sickness swam inside. "My—my daughter."

"Is she in a lifeboat?"

Lucie could only nod.

"I'm sure she'll be fine, ma'am. Several ships are in the area."

The American sailors called out to each other, and the engine revved.

"Sir?" Lucie tugged on the officer's sleeve. "When—when will we know?"

The officer gave her a quick, apologetic glance. "Ma'am, this is a warship. German U-boats are sinking ships up and down the coast, and our job is to sink U-boats. When our patrol is over in a few days, we'll return to Boston. I'll have to ask you to be patient."

Lucie covered her face with both hands, nodded, and prayed harder than ever for that tiny girl in that tiny boat on the great big sea.

47

In a pressed suit and a new fedora, Paul strolled down the Avenida da Liberdade, clean-shaven, well rested, his stomach full.

Even better, notes from Lucie stuffed his pocket.

His train had pulled in to Lisbon the previous evening. The city lights had almost blinded him after living so long under blackout.

Paul had been delayed in Madrid while American officials verified his identity and his loyalty. Thank goodness Col. Jim Duffy had already given Washington firm instructions to trust Paul and to dismiss all rumors about him being a Nazi collaborator.

First thing in the morning, Paul had visited the American Legation and retrieved Lucie's notes. They'd taken the first ship home as promised. By now Josie was charming his parents, and Lucie—well, he hoped she stayed in Waltham until he arrived. And forever.

His favorite note had a sticky kiss from Josie's first candy and a red lipstick kiss from Lucie. Both moved him, although in different ways.

Paul passed restaurants serving full menus as if a war weren't raging around the world. Yet it raged in Lisbon too. As the only major European port open to both the Allies and the Axis, Lisbon attracted agents from both sides who spied on each other.

He had almost a month to explore. Since the automobile industry was converting to military production, the legation had leaped to help Paul. He'd received a prized seat on a Pan American Clipper flying to New York. But not until February 27.

The next order of business was to cable home his arrival date. His feet wanted to skip like Josie's.

Down a side street, he spotted a post office. He stepped inside. "Bom dia," he said to a clerk. "Parlez-vous français?"

"Oui, monsieur."

"Good. I would like to send a telegram to the United States."

"Yes, sir. Your message?"

Paul had composed his message in his head. "May I have a piece of paper?"

"You do not have it? It must be typed."

"Typed?"

"Of course." He looked at Paul as if it were obvious. "In Lisbon, messages must be typed."

He'd never heard of such a thing. "Do you have a typewriter I can use?"

The clerk let out a long-suffering breath. "No, sir."

Where could Paul find a typewriter? But the rule wasn't the clerk's fault. "Thank you anyway."

Back outside, he filled his lungs with sea-scented air.

Although the thought of surprising Lucie brought up a smile, she shouldn't suffer an entire month.

Paul strode down the street. "Time to buy a typewriter."

WALTHAM, MASSACHUSETTS
FRIDAY, JANUARY 30, 1942

Her stomach roiling with worry and dread, Lucie trudged up Cedar Street. In a few minutes, she'd either have a joyful reunion with Josie or she'd have to tell the Aubreys their little granddaughter was lost at sea.

She shuddered in the icy air.

Along the street, large homes in a variety of styles stood apart from each other, surrounded by trees and lawns.

A young lady strolled past wearing a fashionable hat and coat, and she shot Lucie's knit cap a look of surprise and disdain.

Lucie ignored her. The clothes on her back were her only remaining worldly goods. At least the sailors on the destroyer had laundered them, even giving her dungarees to wear while they did so. They'd treated her like a princess. She had no use for women who looked down on others based on clothing.

There were far more important things in life.

Like a little girl who might or might not reach her fifth birthday.

Fifty-seven Cedar Street was the largest home in the neighborhood, adorned with gables and cupolas.

Lucie's wooden-soled Parisian shoes felt like lead as she climbed the steps, and she prayed Josie would be there.

Fingers shaking, she rang the bell.

A young woman in a gray dress and white apron answered the door.

"Good afternoon." Lucie offered a smile. "My name is Lucille Girard. Is Mrs. Aubrey home?"

"Yes, ma'am." The maid let her in, then entered a large sitting room to the left. "Excuse me, Mrs. Aubrey, but a Lucille Girard is here to see you."

"Lucille—Girard?" a woman said. "Yes! Yes! Please show her in."

Holding her breath, Lucie stepped forward.

A woman approached in a maroon shirtwaist dress, her gray-streaked dark hair rolled at the neck, her dark eyes wide. "Lucille Girard? Josie's—" Her voice cracked.

Lucie didn't dare release her dread. "Josie? She's here? She's—"

"She's here. She's fine." She grasped both Lucie's hands.

"Thank goodness." Lucie's voice and knees wobbled.

"She's so worried about you. Dora! Quick. Bring Josie down." Mrs. Aubrey guided Lucie toward a sofa. "Sit down. You look about to faint."

"Any word from Paul?" Lucie searched for signs of her beloved in his mother and saw a resemblance in her eyes and chin.

"Not a word. Please sit. I have so many questions."

Lucie's legs gave way, and she sank onto the sofa, still holding Paul's mother's hands. "When did Josie arrive?"

"On Tuesday. Three days ago. Your friend Mrs. Kahn brought her. She—she told me you sacrificed your seat in the lifeboat for her. That was so selfless." Her eyes reddened.

"She's a widow, expecting a baby."

Mrs. Aubrey gulped and pulled a handkerchief from her pocket. "Oh dear. Excuse me."

"How's Josie? Is she all right?" Lucie searched the doorway for her.

"As well as can be expected." She dabbed at her eyes. "She's been through so much, and she keeps asking for you. But may I ask . . . oh, how do I say this? Josie calls you mama. Are you . . . ?"

"Married to Paul? No, but we we're in love." She ached for him more than ever in this home where he'd grown up. "The resistance insisted on sending Paul in a separate escape line. It was safer if Josie and I were seen as mother and child."

"The resistance? There's so much Mr. Aubrey and I don't

understand. Josie can't tell us much." Mrs. Aubrey glanced at the door and raised a trembling smile. "Josie, darling, look who's here."

Josie stood in the doorway in a green plaid dress with a green bow atop shiny curls, staring at Lucie.

"Josie," Lucie murmured, and she pushed to standing.

"Maman?" Josie took a few tentative steps, then ran to her.

Lucie fell to her knees and pulled her into her arms. "Josie! Sweetheart!"

Josie sobbed, big heavy sobs, clinging to Lucie with arms and legs, her face burrowed in Lucie's neck.

Lucie rocked the child, her worries melting into tears. "It's all right, sweetie. I'm here."

A hand cupped Lucie's elbow, and Mrs. Aubrey helped her back onto the sofa. "Dora, please. More handkerchiefs. Lots of handkerchiefs."

Lucie settled onto the sofa as well as she could with little legs wrapped around her, and she rocked and murmured, her tears dampening Josie's curls.

Mrs. Aubrey sat beside them, wiping her eyes.

Josie's sobs quieted to sniffles, but she clung hard. "I was brave, Maman. I prayed, and I sang our song, and I made sure Monsieur Meow and Feenee weren't scared."

"Good girl. I'm proud of you."

"Your song—" Mrs. Aubrey's voice broke. "Your song brought our girl home."

"Oh, I'm so thankful."

Dora handed Lucie a handkerchief.

"Thank you." Lucie blotted her tears, then lifted Josie's head and wiped her face. "Let me look at you. My goodness, I think you grew another inch this week."

Josie nodded, her face slippery in Lucie's hands. "They have milk here. And candy, but it tastes different."

Mrs. Aubrey rubbed her granddaughter's back. "She hasn't

342

eaten much, poor thing. But you'll eat better now, won't you, my little lamb?"

"Uh-huh." Josie snuggled up to Lucie.

"Thank you, Dora." Mrs. Aubrey took another handkerchief from the maid. "Would you please make up a room for Miss Girard? Draw a bath?"

"A room?" Lucie said. "Oh, I—"

"I'm sorry." Mrs. Aubrey pressed a hand to her chest. "How presumptuous of me. I assumed you'd stay until Paul came home. Do you have plans?"

Lucie had thought little about what she'd do in America, but she didn't want to impose on Mrs. Aubrey's hospitality. "I—I should see my family in New York."

Mrs. Aubrey stroked Josie's curls and gave Lucie a kindly look. "Could you ask your parents to visit you here? We'd be honored to have you stay with us."

Her expression communicated plenty. Josie had been through an ordeal, and she needed Lucie. And Lucie was more than welcome. Besides, she craved this connection to Paul.

She pressed a kiss to Josie's forehead. "I'd like that very much."

48

LISBON
SATURDAY, JANUARY 31, 1942

In the American Legation, Paul smiled at the official at the type-writer. "Thanks again. A city this big, and I couldn't find a typewriter to buy."

"I'm here to help our citizens." He gave Paul a smarmy smile. "Especially those from my congressional district."

Ah, a future politician. Paul didn't mind, if he could get a telegram home. "My family is already home. They sailed on the fifteenth."

"Good." The man hit the carriage return. "It's hard to find passage. Most people have to take Portuguese freighters."

"That's what they did—the *Espiritu Santo*."

The man's round face drew long. "The—the *Espiritu Santo*?"

Paul's hands went cold. "Yes. Why?"

"It's been all over the Portuguese papers, but if you don't speak Portu—"

"What happened?" He clenched the counter.

"A—a U-boat sank it. Not the first time the Germans sank a neutral ship. The Portuguese are livid."

344

Paul tried to breathe, couldn't, his lungs burning. "Survivors? Any survivors?"

The man leaned away, mouth drooping. "I—lives were lost, but I can't remember how many. I'm sorry, sir. I'm sure your family is fine. I'm certain of it."

How could he lie like that?

Paul couldn't think, couldn't breathe, couldn't see. Josie . . . Lucie . . .

"Sir? Mr. Aubrey?"

His feet moved. The door. He had to leave. Had to find air.

"Sir! Your telegram." Footsteps pounded after him, and the official pressed a piece of paper into Paul's hand. He couldn't even nod in response. He kept walking, his step mechanical.

He had to find a post office, had to send the telegram, had to find out what happened, but first he needed to breathe.

Outside. Fresh air. But it didn't quench the flames in his lungs.

They couldn't be gone. Couldn't. Not after everything they'd been through. He'd lost Simone. How could he lose Josie? Lucie?

"Oh, God!" The prayer knifed through him, splitting his soul. The girls he loved—drowned? Lost at sea? "Lord, no."

Somehow his feet found his hotel, found his room. He'd send the telegram in a bit, after he collected himself. He shut the door and headed for the bed.

"Good morning, Mr. Aubrey."

Paul whirled around.

A man sat in a chair to the left of the door, a well-built middle-aged man in a gray suit. With a gun in his lap.

The Gestapo. They knew what he'd done, and they'd tracked him down.

Paul's grief churned in a foamy mess in his gut, and fury snaked in. The Germans! Wasn't it enough that they'd stolen his factory and home? Why'd they have to kill Lucie and Josie? He had nothing left—nothing but his life. And that was worthless.

He flung up his hands. "Get it over with. Shoot me."

The man let out a surprised chuckle. "Why would I? We want you alive."

So they could torture information out of him? Paul wouldn't allow it. He'd bolt for the door, take the bullet.

"Let me introduce myself," the man said in lightly accented English. "I am Helmut Eckert with the German Abwehr."

The Abwehr? Military intelligence. Not the Gestapo. The Abwehr didn't concern themselves with resistance activities.

Paul restrained his feet. Before making decisions that couldn't be undone, he needed more information. And he needed to collect himself immediately. He slowly lowered his hands. "I'd introduce myself, but you know who I am."

"Indeed. We have been looking for you. Col. Gerhard Schiller worried when you didn't report for internment. We planned to release you from the camp, but of course, you didn't know that. We were relieved to see your name on the manifest for the Clipper."

He had to use his real name to get the ticket. Apparently the Germans had an informant in the Pan American office. Paul's fingers dug into his thighs. "What do you want?"

Eckert smiled. "Please have a seat. No need to fear."

"You have a gun."

Half of his smile fell. "Only to be used if you are not who you have claimed to be."

Paul eased back to the armchair by the window. "Who have I claimed to be?"

"Schiller says you are a brilliant engineer, a cunning business-man, and a man smart enough to work with the winning side."

"A collaborator."

Eckert shrugged. "We prefer *zusammenarbeiten*—working together. It is the only logical course."

Paul lowered himself into the chair. He wasn't finished playing the role of collabo. "Working together has suited me."

"It has. And you are a well-informed man." He nodded to the newspapers on Paul's bed. "You know the Allies are losing. And the Americans? They can't even stand up to the Japanese. How can they stand against the might of Germany?"

Paul gripped the armrests. Herr Eckert didn't know how scrappy Americans were, or about the industrial power of the United States. "You still haven't told me what you want."

"Haven't I?" Amusement lit the man's wide-set eyes. "We want you in Germany, designing tanks."

"Tanks? In Germany?"

He sniffed. "You'll find Germany much more pleasant than France."

No, he wouldn't. "Tanks? I—I design automobiles, race cars."

"No need to be coy. Schiller lives in your house. One of your staff said you drew plans for a tank. You were secretive, but she saw. Of course, we are sad you never showed us. And needless to say, such plans must never go to America."

Paul's suitcase lay on the luggage rack to the right of the door. His breath came harder. Neither his plans nor his brain could fall into German hands. He could grab the suitcase and run. And he'd be dead. The Abwehr would find his plans, tucked behind Josie's Feenee stories.

His chest crushed. His little girl. What if she'd died?

But what if she lived? He couldn't give up. Not yet.

An appeal for sympathy couldn't hurt. "Sir, I'm a widower. I sent my daughter to America. I will not be separated from her."

Eckert shrugged broad shoulders. "Schiller said you were willing to be separated from her in the internment camp."

"No, I wasn't. That's why I left France."

Eckert ran a finger along the gun barrel. "We will not allow you to give those plans to the enemy."

Those plans. Behind the Feenee stories. Why did those colorful drawings flit in his mind, painting an idea? The idea danced like Lucie, in brilliant colors, in freedom. And he hated it.

Paul leaned his forearms on his knees. "You're an engineer, Herr Eckert?"

"No, I was a banker."

Good. "First, I have absolutely no interest in working for the US Army. Second, I know little about tank design. It took me years to draw up that plan, and it would take many more years to draw up a new one—whether for you or for the Americans. You don't need me—you only need my plans."

Eckert shook his head. "My orders are to bring you to Germany."

Paul gave him a stiff smile. "I will not be separated from my daughter. If you abduct me, I won't work. You'll have to shoot me. Why don't you let me go home to my little girl—in exchange for my tank designs."

"You have them here?" Eckert sat up straighter. "I must see."

The suitcase sat to the right of the door, Eckert to the left. The door opened outward. To survive would mean sacrificing a treasure.

Holding his hands up by his waist, Paul edged across the room. "They're in my suitcase."

Eckert leaned forward and folded his fingers around the gun. "Turn it so I can see what you're doing."

Paul pivoted the suitcase, opened it, and slid out a manila envelope. One glance inside revealed green crayon. With the envelope tucked under his arm, his heart thrumming in his ears, Paul latched the suitcase.

He had no gun. All he had was his determination to get home.

Eckert stood by the door, taller than Paul and heavier. And he pointed a gun. "Show me."

"Yes, sir." Paul stepped to Eckert's right, facing the door, close enough to show the designs but not close enough to threaten the man.

348

Paul slid the designs partway out of the envelope and chuckled. "I'm afraid my little girl colored on the back. Thank goodness, not on the front."

He flipped through, showing partial pages—lines and numbers a banker wouldn't understand—and not enough to reveal the designs were for the Au-ful truck. Not a tank. "It's all here. Specifications, configurations, years of work."

Paul worked it back into the envelope. "These plans are all you'll ever get from me, whether you take me to Germany, kill me, or let me go home. So I ask you, in light of my work for Schiller, for how willingly I give these plans to Germany, and out of consideration for a motherless four-year-old girl, to let me go."

Something moved in Eckert's hazel eyes, and he took the envelope.

Paul gritted his jaw and held his breath.

"I have my orders." Eckert gestured to the suitcase. "Pick up your luggage—slowly—and come with me."

Paul's chest and his hope deflated. He only had one more chance, and it was slim. He'd probably die. But he'd rather die than commit treason. And if Lucie and Josie still lived, he owed it to them to try.

He reached for his suitcase, angling his body sideways to the Abwehr agent. Feet planted wide, Paul wrapped his fingers around the handle. *Lord, help me. I want to live.*

With all his might, Paul swung the suitcase up into the man's gun arm.

Eckert cried out. A shot exploded, hitting the ceiling.

Paul lifted his knee and drove his foot into the man's belly like a piston.

Eckert fell, tumbled backward over the chair.

The gun clattered to the floor.

Paul flung open the door and ran down the hall.

"Aubrey! Come back! You will not get away from us!"

Us? What if the Abwehr had someone waiting out front? In the lobby?

The service stairs! Paul banged open the door and took the stairs two at a time, jarring his knees.

Four flights, and he burst out into an alley. No one there.

He ran close to the building, his chest heaving.

Alive. But for how long?

49

WALTHAM
WEDNESDAY, FEBRUARY 25, 1942

After almost a month in Waltham, the sight of cars and merchandise still surprised Lucie.

As she walked downtown with Mrs. Aubrey, colorful posters reminded her to buy war bonds. To date, only tires and rubber goods were rationed in the United States.

She passed the store where she'd bought new outfits and the shoe store where she'd purchased real leather shoes. The salesclerk had apologized for the meager selection, but to Lucie it was a cornucopia.

Mrs. Aubrey peered in the window of a drugstore. "I want to buy everything under the sun for Josie's birthday, but I mustn't spoil her."

"What do we have?" Lucie examined the parcels. "The darling yellow dress, four hair ribbons, and drawing paper and crayons."

"I'd like to buy a doll. All we have are her aunt's old dolls, and Josie isn't interested."

Lucie frowned. Josie wasn't interested in much except the

puppets, her blanket, and a battered stuffed rabbit that had been Paul's.

At least she was very fond of her grandparents and Dora, and she'd warmed to Lucie's parents and the Greenblatts when they'd visited. But the child grieved her father's absence.

So did Lucie. She hadn't seen him in almost three months. With each day that passed, his chances of survival diminished.

The sound of his voice had become a dim and elusive memory.

They passed a stationery store with a "Now hiring" sign in the window.

"Have you thought more about getting a job?" Mrs. Aubrey asked. "Not that you need to."

Lucie had been welcomed into the Aubrey home indefinitely—out of concern for Josie, out of respect for Paul, and out of genuine kindness. She gazed inside the store. "Maybe I could do something for the war effort."

"They always need volunteers with the ladies' clubs."

"I wouldn't fit in there."

Mrs. Aubrey chuckled. "They'd love you."

All Lucie's worries about Paul and the strain of the past year twisted into a cord, a familiar and strangling cord. "I'm not smart enough for that crowd. I have an eighth-grade education, and I'm eccentric. I have no idea what Paul sees in me or—" Her voice broke.

"Lucie?" Mrs. Aubrey stopped, eyebrows lifted to the brim of her elegant hat. "Whatever do you mean? You're intelligent and bighearted and creative. I understand why Paul loves you."

Lucie tugged her handkerchief from her coat pocket, pressed it to her face, and hauled in big breaths. She knew all that. She did. "I'm sorry. I don't know what came over me."

"I do." Mrs. Aubrey patted Lucie's arm. "You've been through a trial, and you're worried about Paul. It's natural to be emotional."

"I just . . ." Lucie sifted old insecurities away from concerns that had merit. She blew out a breath and lowered the handkerchief. "I love him deeply, but I don't fit in high society."

Mrs. Aubrey hooked her arm in Lucie's and continued down the street. "Neither do I."

"Of course you do." Lucie eyed her coiffed hair and tailored clothes. "You're so polished."

A sidelong gaze, and Mrs. Aubrey laughed. "I'm a farm girl who fell in love with a mechanic with crazy ideas about building automobiles. As for Paul—he's had the benefits of wealth, but his head's in the right place. He's a sensible man, and I like his taste in women. I liked Simone, and I like you. Besides, Paul could use eccentricity in his life." She winked.

Lucie laughed, a wet sort of laugh. "Thank you. Meeting you and Mr. Aubrey—well, I understand Paul even better now." And she loved him even more.

The next building—Waltham Dance Studio. The sign declared "Learn to Dance! Tap—Ballet—Ballroom."

All Lucie's talents and dreams and passions flowed together. "I—I wonder if they're hiring."

"That would be perfect. Let's ask."

Lucie adjusted her hat and entered a waiting room with a long window separating it from the studio. And the studio—oh, so large and bright with barres and mirrors all around.

To her right lay a counter and an office.

A dark-haired woman in her thirties approached the counter. She wore a long-sleeved black leotard and a black wraparound skirt. "Good afternoon. Are you interested in ballroom dance lessons?"

"Good afternoon. I'm Miss Lucille Girard." Lucie selected a business card from the display—Frances Thiel, owner. "Are you Mrs. Thiel?"

"I am." She pulled out a big, flat book. "Ballroom? Tap?"

"Are you hiring teachers?"

"Teachers?" Mrs. Thiel expelled a weary sigh. "I can't afford teachers until I find a new partner."

"A partner?"

Mrs. Thiel flung her hand dramatically toward the studio. "My partner and I opened in September. Do you know how much money we put into this place? Two floors of studios! We're nowhere near finished paying the bills. Then last week she quit so she can dance with the USO—and took her money with her."

"Oh dear. I'm sorry."

The woman gave Lucie a dismissive wave. "I danced on Broadway, so I've got tap and ballroom covered. Unless you can teach ballet and have a head for business and money to invest—sorry, miss."

Lucie's mind spun. "What sort of business help do you need?"

"Schedules. I make a mess of this." She slapped the big book on the counter. "And ads, mailers—I'm no good at that stuff."

Lucie could do that. "How about bookkeeping?"

"I hire a college girl. I have no head for numbers."

Mrs. Aubrey squeezed Lucie's arm. "It's perfect."

"It is." A smile bloomed on Lucie's lips. "I can do all that."

"Listen, Miss Girard, is it? Unless you know something about ballet—doesn't have to be much, but—"

"I danced with the Paris Opéra Ballet for ten years."

Mrs. Thiel's jaw flopped open.

"Yes." Mrs. Aubrey patted the counter. "*The* Paris Opéra Ballet."

"In . . . Paris? France?" Mrs. Thiel kept blinking at Lucie.

She nodded. "When the Nazis invaded, I quit the ballet to run my friends' bookstore in Paris. For a year and a half, I ran that store. I learned a lot about business. Thanks to Paul." Lucie sent his mother a fond smile. "I've ordered supplies, I've done mailings, and I've organized events. I could do schedules.

I even know enough about bookkeeping to make sure the college girl does her job."

Mrs. Thiel still hadn't closed her mouth. Still stared at Lucie.

"And she has money to invest," Mrs. Aubrey said.

No, she didn't.

Mrs. Aubrey gave Lucie a firm look that reminded her of the man she loved. "If Paul were here, he'd give it to you."

A protest rose in her chest, but she swallowed it. Indeed, he would. "Yes, I have the money."

"Miss Girard?" Mrs. Thiel closed her mouth and extended her hand. "Or shall I call you partner?"

Lucie grinned. "I like the sound of that."

LISBON
FRIDAY, FEBRUARY 27, 1942

Paul hunched low in the backseat of the cab as it approached Lisbon's seaplane base—Aeroporto Maritime de Cabo Ruivo.

Over the past month in hiding at the seedy hotel, the beard and clothes of Jean Bonnet had come to feel natural.

Would the Abwehr agents recognize him? They knew he had a ticket on today's Pan Am Clipper, and they couldn't afford to let him escape. And Paul couldn't afford to let them succeed.

The only thing Paul had left was his engineering brain, and he'd do his best to protect it.

A band tightened around his chest. Not knowing Lucie and Josie's fate had made the past month miserable. He didn't dare give in to despair, but he didn't dare hope too fervently.

He couldn't cable home, since the Gestapo monitored telegraph wires. He couldn't visit the American Legation, since the Abwehr would keep it under surveillance. So he'd hidden in his room, only leaving to buy food.

The cab entered a roundabout in front of the seaplane base.

A man stood about six feet from the front door with a suit-case by his feet, smoking a cigarette. Helmut Eckert.

Paul groaned and fingered the outline of the pocketknife in his jacket. He'd roughed up his suitcase. Maybe Eckert would think Paul had come to repair something.

About a hundred feet past Eckert, Paul tapped the cabdriver's shoulder and pointed to the curb. The man pulled over, and Paul paid him generously.

Paul opened his pocketknife, pulled his cap low, and stepped out of the cab. Eckert stood to Paul's left, between him and the door. On the far side of the door stood another man looking suspiciously casual. Paul had to pass one or the other.

With his suitcase in his left hand, he palmed the pocketknife in his right hand, the blade against his forearm.

Every nerve fired, on full alert.

Paul walked with a clumpy gait, his shoulders hunched. As he drew nearer, he struggled not to look directly at Eckert.

His legs itched to run, but he kept his pace.

A black car sat at the curb between the agents, with a driver and no passengers. Paul gritted his teeth. They planned to shove him in the car and abduct him.

Not on his life. And he meant that. He'd use the knife, he'd let them shoot him, but he would never get in that car.

His breath threatened to gallop, but he kept his gaze steady, his step sure.

He drew near to Eckert, and the man glanced past him. Did he notice? Did he see past the feeble disguise?

Paul gripped the knife hard, passed Eckert, lifted his suitcase hand, and opened the door.

The second Abwehr agent pushed from the wall and eyed him.

Paul strode hard into the terminal and pocketed his knife.

"Com licença, senhor." A young man, the doorman, hurried

alongside, speaking Portuguese rapidly and indignantly. Probably telling Paul the service entrance was to the side.

Paul kept walking, determined to get out of sight of the Abwehr agents. "I have a paid ticket and an American passport," he said in English.

"Sir, you must leave. You don't belong here."

"I have a paid ticket on today's flight." His posture straight and businesslike again, he passed a couple dozen elegant passengers, all gaping at him.

"Sir!" The doorman sounded exasperated.

A middle-aged man sat behind a desk labeled Pan American, and concern grew on his face.

"Excuse me, sir," Paul said. "Are you in charge?"

"I am." Concern turned to indignation. "May I ask what this is about?"

Paul pulled his passport and ticket from his pocket. "I'm Mr. Paul Aubrey with Aubrey Automobiles. I'm an American citizen with a paid ticket on today's flight. I apologize for my appearance, but I had to sneak past the two German Abwehr agents outside your door trying to abduct me—tipped off by an informant in your ticket office, I might add."

The man blanched, and he studied Paul's ticket, passport, and face. "I—I see, sir. All is in order. However, I'm afraid I can't allow you to board."

Paul glared at him. "I beg your pardon."

The man's upper lip curled. "We have a dress code, sir."

Holding a lid on his annoyance, Paul tipped his ratty cap. "Fifteen minutes in your restroom, and I'll meet your code."

"I'll be the judge of that," he said with a wrinkle of his nose.

"Thank you, sir." Paul crossed the waiting room. No sign of the Abwehr, only startled passengers.

In the restroom Paul checked the stall. Then he shaved off his beard, shed the worker's clothes, and stuffed them in the trash can. The cap, though, he put in his suitcase as a reminder.

Back in his gray flannel suit, he left the restroom.

The man from the desk stood by the door, and Paul gave him a bow. "Do I pass?"

"Ye—yes, sir. Yes, Mr. Aubrey, sir. I—I'll check you in my-self."

In a few minutes, men in crisp blue uniforms and white peaked caps ushered the passengers out the back door.

Paul inserted himself between two men close to his age and build, in case the Abwehr was watching, aiming.

A narrow pier extended onto the Tagus River, and the Clip-per floated at the dock, a large silver plane with pontoons below and wings above.

A steward helped the passengers inside, and Paul crossed the narrow gap between dock and aircraft.

He stood in an elegant dining lounge, each table set with tablecloths and flowers.

All at once his breath spilled out. Safely on board. The dis-guise worked.

"May I see your ticket, sir?" A steward smiled, held out his hand for the ticket, and read it. "Welcome aboard, Mr. Aubrey. You'll be in the compartment directly aft."

Paul followed him through a door into a compartment filled with plush chairs—more like couches, upholstered in medium blue.

"I'll take your suitcase, sir."

No. Paul clenched it harder, but he had to start thinking like a free man, soon to be living in a free nation, and he relinquished it and thanked the man.

Paul lowered himself into a luxurious seat by a rectangular window overlooking the Tagus. He'd never flown, but now he'd be in the air over twenty hours, with a stopover in Bermuda.

After the passengers were seated, the stewards told them what to expect in flight, and the engines came to life overhead, roaring and blustering.

The Clipper pulled forward, bobbing in the waves, picking up speed, sending out white wings of water on both sides.

Paul clenched the armrest and held his breath as the plane rose, escaping the water, escaping Europe, escaping the Nazis.

It took great work for Paul to relax, his muscles fighting the softening. For the next twenty hours he'd be pampered with all the food he desired, with exemplary service and luxury.

The journey would be a glorious adventure if it weren't for the weight on his heart. Soon that weight would either be removed or cemented permanently in place.

50

As Josie plunked out a discordant tune on the piano, Lucie sat on the floor of the second-story dance studio with business papers scattered around.

Lucie wore the stiff new pointe shoes her mother had brought her from New York, Josie wore slippers from the studio's storeroom, and they both wore skirted leotards Lucie had sewn from pale pink rayon.

She checked the preliminary class schedule. The girls enrolled under the previous teacher were coming tomorrow after school so Lucie could assess them and assign them to levels.

Six syllabi lay to her left, one for each level, listing the exercises she'd learned at the Paris Opéra Ballet School in the Cecchetti method.

She'd hired college girls to play the piano, she'd put ads in the papers, and she and Frannie Thiel were planning a dance recital to raise money for war bonds.

On Tuesday, the newspaper was interviewing her, excited about having a ballerina from Paris in town. The article would bring in even more business.

Lucie wouldn't mention her connection to the resistance, to protect Renard and the others in Paris as well as those who'd helped her escape—and might even now be aiding Paul.

The piano fell silent, and Josie spun on the stool. "May I play in the storeroom?"

Lucie smiled at the girl, glad to see her spirits rising. "As long as you pick up before we leave."

"Okay." Josie scampered into the storeroom, a wonderland of costumes from Frannie's time on Broadway.

Lucie brushed her hand over her paperwork. Paul's touch everywhere, and she could almost hear his voice. *"I know you can do it."*

"I miss you," she whispered to that voice, her heart straining as melancholy and hope battled.

Frank Aubrey had called a friend in the State Department. They were contacting the US Embassy in Vichy, and their people could find out if Paul had been interned, arrested, or . . . killed.

Melancholy surged, and Lucie shoved herself to standing. She needed to dance.

A phonograph stood by the piano, and Lucie opened the cabinet and flipped through the records. *Swan Lake*—the final, heartbreaking scene.

Lucie set the record on the turntable and lowered the needle.

Tchaikovsky's plaintive strains filled the studio, and Lucie danced as Odette.

She closed her eyes as she danced, as memories flowed. Sitting with Paul in the Palais Garnier, hands hidden and entwined. Stolen kisses. Tearful departures. Every joy tinged with the pain of separation and danger.

Eyes closed, Lucie became Odette, sharing Odette's pain, her sorrow, her despair. And in expressing them, she released them, released Paul into the Lord's hands, where he already was, whether dead or alive, captive or free.

The music soared to a crescendo. Lucie stepped onto pointe,

and an arabesque billowed up, the final pose before Odette would crumple, wings beating as she gave in to death.

Lucie reached the peak and held it, savored it, and the air shifted around her, different somehow, scented with hope.

A touch came under her front arm. "Arabesque," a man said. Husky. Beloved.

Lucie stumbled out of position. Her eyes sprang open. Saw. Didn't dare to believe. "Paul?"

"Lucie." His eyes shone, and he reached for her waist and drew her close. "Thank God. Thank God, you're alive."

She pressed shaky hands to his cheeks. Warm. Solid. Real. "You—you're alive."

Paul kissed her nose, her cheek, her mouth. "I heard your ship went down. I thought—"

She couldn't stop kissing him, over and over. "I thought you were—it's been so long."

He lifted her so high she had to stand on pointe. Anything to get closer, to look at him, touch him, kiss him.

Paul burrowed in her neck. "You saved her. You saved my little girl."

"Oh, Paul, I have to tell you." She settled down to her heels and pulled back. Her chest ached, but she had to be honest. "I promised never to be separated from her, but I put her in a lifeboat and—"

"Mom told me." He tugged her close again with a soft smile. "I went to the house first. She told me you sacrificed your seat to a pregnant widow. Then you—my plucky, generous, beautiful ballerina bookseller—you stayed alive on that sinking ship."

The admiration in Paul's eyes washed away all worries and doubts.

"I love you more than ever," he said, his voice rough. "I'll always be grateful for how you took care of my girl. Our girl."

Then he blinked and gazed around. "Where is she? Mom said you were both—"

"She's playing in the storeroom."

The record had stopped, the needle bouncing as the turntable spun.

Josie stood inside the storeroom door, still and staring, a too-big costume puddled about her feet.

Paul squeezed Lucie's waist, released her, and approached his daughter. "Hello, jelly bean."

A tiny gasping sob.

Paul ran to her, lifted her in his arms, and kissed her. "My little girl. My little girl."

Lucie's vision blurred, and she pressed her hand over her mouth.

"Daddy? It's you?"

"Yes, it's me. I'm home. I'm here."

Josie clung to his neck. "You're here."

Paul rocked her in a circle. "Tell me a story. Tell me about Feenee and her magical wings and her colorful hair and her horn."

Josie gave a wet little giggle. "Daddy?"

Paul pressed his nose to hers. "I was bored on my trip, but you know what I did? I read your stories. You kept me company, kept me happy. Because you're so creative and clever."

Josie hunched her shoulders and giggled.

Lucie's smile wobbled behind her hand, wet with tears. Only a year before, he hadn't known what to do with his creative daughter. Now he knew.

Paul's expression sobered. He beckoned Lucie over, then gazed at Josie. "You should also know Feenee saved my life."

"She did?" Her tiny nose wrinkled. "How?"

Lucie wrapped her hand around Paul's arm in his gray suit. "Yes, how?"

"By giving your Feenee stories to a rock-monster, Daddy was able to get away from that rock-monster."

Lucie's breath caught, and she hugged his arm tight.

Paul gave her a significant, I'll-tell-you-later look. They both had stories to exchange, but not in front of the child.

With a long sigh, Paul turned to Josie again. "I'm afraid that means I lost your stories. I'm so sorry."

Josie shrugged one shoulder. "I wrote those when I was four. Tomorrow I'll be five, and I'll write better stories."

"Just made your birthday, my little roll of Necco wafers." Paul bounced his daughter. "Would have been here on Saturday if big waves at Bermuda hadn't kept our plane from flying."

Josie squealed. "You flew in a plane?"

"Not as exciting as your birthday. Five years old. Look how big you are. What's Miss Girard been feeding—"

"*Not* Miss Gee-jard." Josie scowled at her father. "She's Maman."

Lucie pressed a kiss to Paul's shoulder. "She's following your orders."

Paul shifted Josie to his hip and circled his arm around Lucie's waist. "There's only one solution."

His grin had to be the most beautiful sight in the world, stirring up laughter and hope and joy and love. "What is it, Mr. Aubrey?"

He kissed her forehead. "Marry me right away so Josie can call you Maman without setting tongues wagging."

She gave him a teasing smile and snuggled close. "What if I don't want to?"

"I'll have to appeal to a higher authority." He jiggled his daughter. "What do you say, birthday cake? Should Daddy and Maman get married?"

"You already *are* married," she said with five years of wisdom. "You keep kissing each other."

"You heard her." Paul smacked a kiss on Lucie's lips. "Mrs. Aubrey."

Lucie overflowed with love for her two brown-eyed Aubreys. They were already a family in heart and soul.

51

"What do you think?" Paul stood with his father by the desk in Dad's office.

Dad rubbed his chin. "You risked your life for this."

Tank plans covered the desk—drawings and specifications gleaned from the original French plans, the German officer's analysis of tanks in combat, and Paul's knowledge of vehicle design. "Yes, I did." And he'd do it again.

"I don't know much about tanks, but this looks good." Dad crossed his arms over his stomach, pudgier than the last time Paul had seen him. "I'm not sure we have the capacity to build them here."

"We could expand, build another facility. But I don't even know if the Army will be interested."

"Our congressman's an old friend. He'll connect you with the right people."

Paul grinned. "After the wedding."

"Of course." Dad slapped him on the back in the unfamiliar American way. "Ready to see how the conversion's going?"

"I am." Paul returned the plans to the attaché case Dad had loaned him.

As they made their way out to the factory floor, Dad tugged down his suit vest. "It's a good day for you to be here with the ladies fussing over the wedding on Saturday."

"It is." As far as Paul was concerned, they only needed a preacher, a license, and rings—and that morning he and Lucie had started the process for each of those. Saturday couldn't come soon enough.

Paul passed through familiar halls filled with familiar smells, his step lighter than it had been in almost two years.

Last night he and Lucie had stayed up late talking. Not only had they shared their experiences since they'd been torn apart, but Paul finally told her—and only her—all of what he'd done the past year, from sending information to Duffy to sabotage to sheltering airmen.

For so long people thought the worst of him, but it all felt worthwhile to see the glow on Lucie's lovely face.

"Paul?"

"Hmm?"

Dad chuckled. "I asked you a question."

"I'm sorry. I'm—"

"In love. I know. Are you sure you don't want a honeymoon? You won't be much good to us."

Paul shook his head. "Josie needs us here. Besides, any place without Nazis is a honeymoon paradise."

Dad's forehead creased. "I'm sure it is."

Out on the factory floor, Paul inhaled the smells of oil and hot metal and energy.

"The conversion will be complete next week." Dad planted his hands on his hips. "We'll be able to produce two hundred utility trucks a day for the Army."

The irony of making trucks again made Paul laugh. But these would have gasoline engines, and they'd be for a good cause.

The silver standard had served him well, but he was glad to reembrace quality. "Well, Dad, let's set the gold standard for utility trucks."

"That's the plan." Dad flagged down a worker in his fifties. "Griffith, I'd like you to meet my son, Mr. Paul Aubrey. He'll take over as production manager. Paul, Griffith is the general foreman."

Paul extended his hand. "I'm pleased to meet you."

Griffith's nostril flicked up, but he shook Paul's hand. Paul didn't blame him. Throughout many industries, company founders were known for innovation and grit, most of them having worked for a living. But their sons were known as useless fops.

That was one of the reasons Paul had studied engineering and had started his own subsidiary in Paris. He gestured to the conveyor belt curving overhead. "So, Griffith, I'm eager to hear your opinion on the conversion. I'd like to meet with you and the other foremen, make sure the assembly line meets your needs."

Griffith blinked heavy-lidded eyes. "Uh, sure. That'd be good."

"Great. I'm looking forward to working with you."

Paul and his father continued down the line.

Dad shot him a glance. "I'm surprised to see you so friendly with labor. Last I heard, you were having big problems with your workers."

"I was. Let's just say I've come to see their worth, see the worth of all skills working together." He had the Lord to thank for that, and Lucie, and Jacques Moreau and the other men in Paris, now working under the Germans. Paul sent up a prayer for them.

His lungs expanded, the heaviness of oppression and secrecy and danger lifted, the prickling of social censure gone.

The last year had been the hardest of his life. But because of it, he'd be a better manufacturer, a better father, and a better man.

And because of it, he had Lucie to inspire him and chide him and love him.

Paul nodded and smiled to a group of mechanics. No, he wouldn't change a single thing.

SATURDAY, MARCH 7, 1942

The piece of wedding cake was too pretty to eat. But Josie, seated on Lucie's lap in a fluff of pink organza, had no such qualms.

"Enjoy it while you can, hon." Frannie Thiel winked as she sashayed by. "I've heard they're going to ration sugar. Can you believe it?"

Lucie smiled at her new friend's back. Yes, she could believe it.

She scooted Josie and adjusted the skirt of her ivory wedding suit. "Do you like the cake?"

"Mm-hmm." Josie swallowed, bits of white frosting on her mouth. "Why's Daddy so loud?"

Across the Aubreys' spacious salon—Lucie couldn't remember what they called the room—Paul stood with his younger sisters, laughing heartily.

Lucie wiped frosting off Josie's face. "He's loud because he's happy."

He was so happy, the man she loved. Her husband.

In Paris she'd fallen in love with a reserved man, guarded and slow to speak. Now he was friendly and open and talkative. She loved this part of him too. More importantly, she loved the man of integrity deep inside.

Paul said something that made his sisters laugh, then he turned away to speak to his parents, Lucie's parents, and the Greenblatts.

Lucie had tried to apologize to Hal and Erma for losing Green Leaf Books, but they wouldn't hear a word of it. They had a new bookstore in Manhattan and were using the proceeds to aid European Jews. They were simply happy to see Lucie come home.

Home. Lucie pressed a kiss to Josie's curls. Someday America might feel like home, but for now she found home with the people she loved.

"There's Johnny!" Josie pointed with her fork, flinging cake crumbs onto the white linen tablecloth.

"If you're done, you can go play."

"I'm done." Josie slipped off Lucie's lap. The past few days, the child had been thrilled to meet cousins and family friends. She especially liked two-year-old Johnny Lang, who listened to Josie's stories with worshipful fascination.

Josie ran to the tyke with his crown of chestnut-brown curls. The boy's parents, Peter and Evelyn Lang, skirted around the children and approached Lucie.

"We may have to hire your daughter as nanny." Evelyn grinned and lowered herself into a chair beside Lucie, her hand on her pregnant belly.

"She'd like that." Lucie hadn't chatted much with these friends of Paul's, but she felt an affinity with them since they'd lived in Nazi Germany before the war.

In his olive drab Army officer's uniform, Peter adjusted his glasses. "I'll warn you. My wife is here for business, not pleasure."

"Business?" Lucie asked.

"I want to write your story." Evelyn's brown eyes gleamed. "Yours and Paul's. I'm sure it'd be as big a hit as my first book."

Lucie cut into her wedding cake and gave the reporter a sly smile. "The Nazis banned your book, you know."

"Nothing makes me prouder. Now about your story—"

"It can't be told." Lucie gave her a compassionate smile.

"Too many people in France would be endangered, even if we altered details."

"After the war, darling." Peter rubbed his wife's back. "Cool those shapely heels of yours."

"Shapely? They're swollen up like melons."

Lucie smiled and swallowed the bite of cake. Evelyn's big belly and love of writing reminded her of Dominique Kahn. Dominique had sent regrets for the wedding for the best of reasons—she'd given birth to a healthy baby boy.

Warm hands settled on Lucie's shoulders. She gazed up to Paul's handsome face. "Hello, my husband."

He pressed an upside-down kiss to her lips. "I will never tire of hearing that, my wife."

And she'd never tire of hearing that.

"Now." Paul squeezed her shoulders. "Before Peter bores you talking about teaching German to soldiers and before Evelyn talks you into writing your story—"

"She already said no." Evelyn gave a little pout.

"I have a smart wife. And I would like to steal her away for a moment."

Peter patted his wife's stomach. "That's a dangerous road, my friend."

"Peter Lang!" Evelyn cried.

Lucie sputtered out a laugh. She doubted that was what Paul had in mind. At least not for another few hours.

She said goodbye to the Langs and took Paul's hand.

He led her out French doors and across the backyard. "Will you be warm enough?"

"Very much. It's almost . . . fifty degrees." She reminded herself to use Fahrenheit instead of Celsius.

"I thought my lóve kept you warm." He frowned in mock disappointment.

Lucie pressed up and kissed his jawline. "What's this about? Running low on kisses?"

"Always." He flashed a grin. "But I wanted to show you something."

"Oh?" She followed a pretty stone path over the lawn and toward the grove of trees at the back of the property.

"Come here." He led her under a winter-bare tree and pulled a branch down. "Look."

It wasn't bare after all. Leaves budded along the length, tiny spots of brilliant green unfolding to the world. "Oh, Paul, it's beautiful."

With his free hand, he encircled her waist. "Your favorite shade of green."

"It was." She gazed through the branches and into his eyes. "Now I love all shades of green."

"Even the weighty ones?" The weightiness of his character came through in everything he said and did.

"Especially those." With one finger, she traced the outline of his lips.

"And I . . ." He swallowed hard and kissed her finger. "I think light dancing on chlorophyll might be the most useful thing God ever created."

Her lips wiggled with a suppressed laugh. "You'll never be a poet, and I'm glad."

He leaned closer until the branch touched her cheek, his breath warm, his gaze even warmer. "Remember that day in Paris? With the leaves?"

She could barely nod, barely speak. "I'll never forget."

"All I wanted to do that day was to kiss you."

From what she now knew of his kisses, he might have changed her mind about him. But probably not. "And today? What do you want today?"

Paul eased the branch up and away, then took its place, brushing his lips over her cheek. "Oh, my love, a kiss is only the beginning of the life I want with you."

Lucie lifted her lips to him, her life to him. "Let's begin."

A double treat for you, my wonderful readers!

First, come read the opening chapter from my next book, scheduled for release in early 2023. The still-to-be-named novel is set in beautiful Copenhagen, Denmark, during World War II. There you'll meet Baron Henrik Ahlefeldt—Paul Aubrey and Peter Lang's friend from their Harvard days. You'll also meet Dr. Else Jensen, an American working at the renowned Institute of Theoretical Physics, now called the Niels Bohr Institute. And you'll see what happens on the fateful day of April 9, 1940, a day which propels Henrik and Else into secrecy and adventure and danger—and maybe even romance.

Second, brace yourselves for this teaser! I thoroughly enjoyed Kelli Stuart's well-researched and deeply moving debut novel, and now I can't wait to read her first book with Revell. Treasure hunts . . . the Russian Revolution . . . Fabergé eggs . . . family secrets! Are you intrigued? You should be. I've read the first few chapters of this story, and it's wonderful. Kelli knows how to do research, and more importantly, she knows how to tell a good tale. Enjoy! And place it high on your to-be-read list.

Sarah

★ ★ ★

Turn the Page to Read
Chapter One of Sarah Sundin's
Next Captivating Story!

COMING SOON

COPENHAGEN, DENMARK
TUESDAY, APRIL 9, 1940

The sun rose on the first day of another year in the wasted life of Baron Henrik Ahlefeldt.

Henrik stopped on the Bredgade outside his family's night-darkened home.

"Thirty. I'm thirty," he murmured to Svend Østergaard, the kind of friend willing to endure Henrik's crowd of dissolute aristocrats to celebrate his birthday, the kind of friend who understood what Henrik couldn't voice.

By thirty he'd planned to have Olympic gold, a seat in parliament, and a wife as brilliant and sweet as his own dear mother, God rest her soul.

"It isn't too late, Henning," Svend said. "I've never known anyone with so much—"

"Don't say it." Henrik raised one hand to block the hated word. "The only standard I've ever met is wasting my potential. And that standard I've surpassed most exceedingly."

Svend loosed a sigh into the dawn chill. "You think you're punishing your father, but you're only punishing yourself."

Henrik winced and restrained his fists. He'd known Svend since their first day at Latin school. As the only person in his life who spoke both honestly and kindly, Svend deserved to have his say.

A strange sound arose about a block over. A faint, rhythmic pounding. Like feet, lots of feet, marching in unison.

"What is—"

Pops rang out—sharp and cracking. Like fireworks. Or . . . gunfire?

Svend let out a strangled cry. "The Germans."

Henrik's eyes strained in the pale light. For months, Svend had ranted about how the Nazis would someday invade Norway to protect their shipping route for Swedish iron ore.

And tiny neutral Denmark stood in the way.

More shots rang out.

"Come on!" Henrik ran toward the sound, toward Frederiksgade, which ran to Amalienborg Palace, home of King Christian X.

Svend ran beside him. "Our army . . ."

Curses filled Henrik's head. Small and poorly equipped, the Danish Army didn't stand a chance against the German Wehrmacht.

He rounded the corner onto Frederiksgade. A block ahead, men in uniform filled Amalienborg Square. Not the scarlet coats of the Royal Life Guards. German uniforms.

"Stop!" Svend grabbed Henrik's arm. "We can't help."

Henrik shook off his friend and kept running. This was his country. His king.

"Henning! You're one man."

He skidded to a stop. One man. Unarmed. His heart and his shoulders slumped.

"I—I need to leave." Although Svend hadn't had a drop to drink all night, he looked ill.

With a sigh, Henrik gestured back the way they'd come. "Let's get you home."

Svend strode away. "No. They'll look for me there. I need to leave the country."

"The—country?" Henrik jogged to catch up.

"You read those articles I wrote."

Henrik hadn't, but the titles had warned of the evils of Nazi Germany.

Svend turned onto Bredgade. "That bag I asked you to keep? I need it."

"But—but Birgitte—the children."

"I'll call Birgitte from your house. She has instructions to stay with her sister. We knew this day would come. And right now I need you to row me to Sweden."

Henrik gaped at his friend. Svend had always made sense—until now. "Row?"

"It's about ten miles across the Sound. You can row that far."

"Yes, but—"

Svend spun to him and gripped Henrik's arm, his eyes sapphire daggers. "You rowed for Olympic gold. You row for your own pleasure. Now I'm asking you—begging you—to row to save my life."

Something stirred in Henrik's chest, something he hadn't felt for ages. The desire to do a good and noble deed. A stirring not to be ignored.

Dr. Elsebeth Jensen frowned at the cool morning sunshine as she walked to the Institute of Theoretical Physics. The light felt wrong, as if no longer both wave and particle, but neither.

Laila Berend chattered by her side, her black curls bouncing around her chin. Couldn't she feel it?

Laila nudged Else. "You're quiet. Didn't sleep well?"

Else shook her head. "Something is wrong. The light . . . the air is tense."

"No more reading physics journals before bed." Laila clucked her tongue. "They give you nightmares."

Else had to laugh. "Physics is my dream."

"And your great, grand love." Laila pressed a hand to her chest and heaved a dramatic sigh. "Until you, my Marie Curie, meets her Pierre."

"I should never have told you that." But Else gave her friend a fond smile.

On the sidewalk and spilling into the intersection, green papers littered the ground.

Else picked one up and read it over and over as the words bounced against walls of incomprehension.

"Oh no. Oh no." Laila's voice cracked, and her lips quivered. "If we don't surrender, they—the Nazis will bomb us."

"No . . ." She'd heard planes at dawn but assumed they were Danish, not German.

Else shoved the poisonous Nazi leaflet out of her hands, pulled her friend close to the building beside them, and scanned the sky, her thoughts whirring like the institute's cyclotron.

She'd seen newsreels showing the devastation in Warsaw after German bombing. Would Copenhagen be next? Beautiful, charming Copenhagen?

"Else," Laila breathed out, and her fingers dug into Else's hand. "It's too late."

Four rifle-toting soldiers sauntered through the intersection wearing German coal scuttle helmets and greenish-gray over-coats. No one opposed them.

Else's hands and arms formed a tangled knot with Laila's. Somehow, while they'd slept, the German Army had invaded. Why hadn't she heard shooting, bombs, artillery—anything? If only they'd turned on the radio, but Fru Riber didn't let her boarders disturb the morning peace.

All around, passersby walked and biked to work and school as if nothing had changed.

"Will you go home?" Laila's voice came out weak.

"I—I think we should go to work. Until—unless we hear otherwise."

"No. Will you go home to California?"

Else swung her head to her friend. "Cal—oh no. I worked too hard for an invitation to the institute. I'm not even a year into my postdoctoral work. And my grandparents." They cherished Else's visits, delighting in having a family member back in Denmark.

"Promise you'll consider it." Laila's dark eyes turned toward the German soldiers in the distance. "If I had a choice . . ."

Else shuddered. As a Jew, Laila had reason for concern. In Germany, the Nazis had slowly stripped away their rights and jobs. Else squeezed her friend's arm. "We'll dye your hair blonde, your eyes blue, stretch you two inches taller, and you can carry my American passport."

"Silly girl." Laila's pretty smile broke through. "Come on. Let's get to work."

They hurried down Blegdamsvej. When they reached the Institute of Theoretical Physics, Laila said goodbye and continued to the Mathematics Institute next door.

Else turned in to the complex of creamy buildings with red roofs and red-sashed windows.

What a thrill to be at the institute founded by and directed by Niels Bohr himself. Niels Bohr, whose model of the atom had revolutionized physics and chemistry, earning him the Nobel Prize. Niels Bohr, whose theory of complementarity had inspired Else's doctoral thesis.

Else opened the door and climbed the stairs. The same hushed, off-kilter tension filled the halls, and Else's heart lurched.

How many refugee physicists had Bohr brought to Copenhagen? Most were Jewish. Some had continued on to other nations, but some remained. Even Bohr was half-Jewish. Would the Germans take over the institute? Close it?

A door opened, and Georg von Hevesy stepped out, a balding physicist in his fifties, a refugee from Hungary.

Hevesy spotted Else. "Jensen! You're Danish, right? No, American."

Else smiled. "Both. I have dual nationality."

He studied her with dark, intelligent eyes. "Young, innocent. Christian, are you? Not a drop of Jewish blood?"

What curious questions. "I'm afraid not."

A smile lifted his mustache. "Come. I need your help." He marched back into his laboratory in his white lab coat.

Else followed. "Isn't Levi here?" Only a few years older than Else, Hilde Levi assisted Hevesy in his groundbreaking research in using radioactive indicators to trace chemical reactions in animals.

"She's Jewish too." Hevesy passed through his lab to a shelf of chemicals. "If the worst happens, I need someone to know my secret."

"Secret?" Else stopped short. Crates lined the lab, filled with rats, squeaking and skittering. The smell of fuming acid mingled with the smell of rat droppings.

Hevesy set two glass beakers on a lab bench, full of brilliant orange liquid. "Do you recognize this compound? Three to one ratio fuming hydrochloric acid and nitric acid. It dissolves gold and platinum."

"Aqua regia." Else leaned over and smiled in wonder. She'd never seen it used before. In the bottom of each beaker, bubbles covered corroding discs. "What—"

"Nobel medals belonging to Max von Laue and James Franck."

Else gasped. "Nobel medals?"

"They left them with Bohr for safekeeping. Laue is in Germany, speaking out against the Nazis. If they knew he'd smuggled gold out of the country, he'd be arrested. And Franck is Jewish. The Nazis would love to confiscate his medal."

Bubbles stripped gold atoms from the medals and whisked them into the orange solution. "You dissolved them."

"Someday we'll precipitate the gold out and cast new medals." Hevesy lifted one beaker to reveal the letter *F* on a piece of tape. "This one is Franck's, the other is Laue's. In the meantime, they'll sit on the shelf."

Where they'd look like ordinary jars of chemicals. "It's horrible and brilliant all at once."

Hevesy tapped his temple. "Sometimes a brain comes in handy. Bohr approved."

Else straightened up. A few months earlier, Bohr had donated his own Nobel medal to aid Finland in its Winter War against the Soviet Union.

The door swung open. "There you are, Hevesy." Sigurd Mortensen rushed in, looking past Else as always.

Else's hopes that the Dane would be her Pierre Curie had lasted less than a day.

"The place is in chaos. Bohr's burning papers about the refugees, you're dissolving—" Mortensen looked Else hard in the eye. "Never mind."

"I told her too," Hevesy said.

"Her?" Mortensen's nose scrunched up. "You told a woman?"

"I want two people to know."

Mortensen huffed and threw his arms wide. "Why not tell the whole world? Women can't hold their tongues."

Hevesy held up one hand. "Don't be rude. I trust her."

"Thank you. Please excuse me, gentlemen." Her head high, Else left the lab.

Couldn't hold her tongue? Why, she'd done an extraordinary job of holding her tongue.

Out in the hallway, she paused and prayed for her Jewish friends, for all the physicists, and even for her own research.

Fumes of aqua regia clung to her, as if determined to dissolve her dream of Nobel gold.

April 10, 1940

With each stroke of his oars on the way back from Sweden, Henrik mulled Svend's proposal.

He dipped his oars into the water, shoved with his legs, and leaned into the layback. Svend was crazy. He thought far too highly of Henrik.

He released, pulling the oars from the water and sliding forward to the crouched position. But what if Henrik did what Svend proposed? Could he?

A glance over his shoulder showed Copenhagen's lights in the night sky. At least the Germans hadn't blacked out the city yet.

Henrik rowed his double scull, built wider and sturdier by Thorvald Thorup for Henrik to row in the Øresund, the strait separating Denmark's island of Sjaelland from the southern tip of Sweden.

Every muscle in his body felt warm and twitchy from the long night's row. After seeing the German soldiers at Amalienborg, Henrik and Svend had fetched Svend's bag from the townhouse and driven north to Lyd-af-Lys, the Ahlefeldt seaside home in Vedbæk.

They'd lain low all day, flipping the radio dial between Denmark's State Radio and the BBC as they reported on the German invasion of both Norway and Denmark.

The State Radio described the surrender terms, accepted by the king before six in the morning. Denmark had allowed the Germans to occupy military facilities and control the press, while Germany kept Denmark's king and parliament in place and promised not to interfere in internal politics. They even allowed the Army and Navy to remain on duty.

The Danish government asked the citizens to behave themselves, obey the law, and treat the Germans correctly.

"Correctly." Henrik chuffed out a breath and yanked the oars. In the afternoon, he'd packed his own bag, determined to join Svend in Sweden. How could he live in an occupied shell of a nation?

A house full of priceless possessions, and Henrik had only taken cash, some clothing, a shaving kit, and photos of his mother and sisters, his American fraternity brothers, and the 1936 Danish Olympic rowing team. And his mother's Bible.

As they'd crossed the Øresund, Svend's idea had grown, and Henrik had decided to return to Copenhagen to think it over. If he went along with Svend's plan, he would stay in Denmark. If he didn't, he'd row to Sweden another night.

A lifetime of rowing infused his stroke, refined by coaching and diligence, and fueled by his love for the resistance of water, which allowed him to speed over the waves.

In neutral Sweden, Svend planned to visit the British legation and offer his services to the Allies. With his connections in the Danish government, military, and commerce, he could provide a great deal of intelligence. But to be most effective, his plan relied on Henrik.

Henrik and his scull, skimming across the Sound, carrying information, news—maybe even spies.

It was crazy. Dangerous. It'd disrupt his life. And yet . . .

His boat passed the tip of Nordhavn, leading into the harbor. Soon he'd pass the Trekroner Fort. It hadn't stopped German ships from invading the night before, but Henrik wasn't taking any chances. A dark knit cap covered his fair hair, and a black overcoat blotted out the bulk of his frame.

He slowed his pace to silence his strokes. When he neared the breakwater extending from the fort, he folded himself low and let the boat glide past.

In a few minutes, he sat up and scanned for patrol boats and obstacles.

Ahlefeldt Shipyard lay on the east side of the narrow harbor. Henrik would pull up to the private dock and nap until his shift started. If he slept through most of his shift again, his father would rant and rave. But Henrik had stopped living for Far's approval at the age of fourteen and he'd stopped caring about Far's opinion after Mor died.

He resumed rowing, slow and silent. Far would hate Svend's idea, and a smile cracked Henrik's chapped lips.

Then his smile drifted low. If word got out about an aristocrat rowing secrets to Sweden, it wouldn't take long for them to arrest Henrik, well-known man-about-town and Olympic rower.

As empty as his life was, he didn't want to lose it.

The boat glided toward the statue of Den Lille Havfrue.

Henrik planted his oars, and the boat stopped. Hans Christian Andersen's Little Mermaid sat on a rock with her bronze fins tucked beneath her, gazing wistfully to sea.

To gain what she wanted, she gave up her voice so she could have legs.

"What do I want?" Henrik asked as if the mermaid had the answer.

He already knew. He wanted to help someone other than himself for a change. Maybe even aid his country. But his voice would call attention to himself. His nobility stood in his way.

To have legs, he needed to sacrifice his voice.

To have mobility, he needed to sacrifice his nobility.

On the dark waters in the dark night before the wistful dark Havfrue, light flooded his mind. Baron Henrik Ahlefeldt had to disappear.

And in his place . . .

Henrik whispered his new identity. "The Havmand."

DO YOU LOVE HISTORICAL FICTION?

Read On to Get a Sneak Peek of
The Master Craftsman by Kelli Stuart

AVAILABLE APRIL 2022

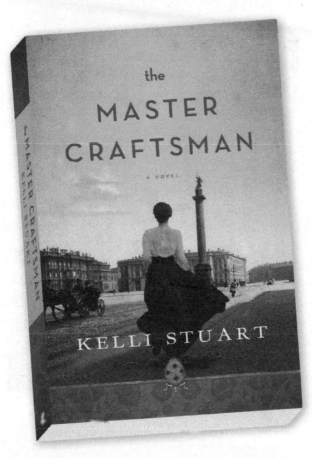

When Ava Laine's dying treasure-hunter father entrusts to her his mission to find a missing Faberge egg, she has no idea how high the stakes will be—or how her allegiances will be tested. Join the hunt in this lavish, dual-time narrative that plunges you into the 1917 Russian Revolution, the fall of the Romanovs, and long-buried Soviet secrets.

WE WANT TO HEAR FROM YOU ON THIS EXCERPT
from Kelli Stuart

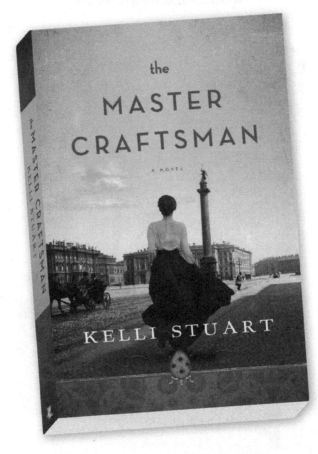

Visit bit.ly/2YlPHOU to fill out a quick survey
and be entered to win free books and fun book swag!

Revell
a division of Baker Publishing Group
www.RevellBooks.com

Available wherever books and ebooks are sold.

1917, St. Petersburg, Russia

He walked quickly down the narrow staircase, hand pressed against the cold wall to steady himself. On the last two steps, his foot slipped, and he went careening forward, catching himself just before falling. His hands trembled as he straightened and rushed into the next room. Glancing over his shoulder nervously, he ducked behind the counter and pulled back the rug upon which he'd spent countless hours standing. Beneath it, the wood panels showed only the slightest variation from the rest, expertly hidden, the attention to detail his most defining characteristic.

Slipping his fingertip beneath a slat of wood, he wiggled and pried until it released. The entire panel now sprung loose. He stared into the black space below and drew in a shaky breath. Lowering to his knees, he winced at the pain that nipped his joints and reached his arm down into the hole. It was cool inside, but dry. He had made sure that the climate of this hidden space was perfect. His fingers brushed the metal box, and he reached his hand around it, pulling it up, then quickly replacing the floor panel so that it would be hidden to the untrained eye.

Covering the floor with the rug, he pushed to his feet, wishing that his back and knees would better cooperate.

"Did you get it?"

He gasped and spun around, still clutching the metal box between his hands. He looked in her eyes for a long moment, a thousand needs and instructions swirling through his mind.

"It's here," he answered quietly.

389

Outside, a loud bang caused both of them to jump. She put her hand to her chest while he gripped the box even tighter.

"Not here," she whispered.

"No."

He nodded his head toward the room in the back, and the two ducked behind the curtain. They slid through the shadows until they reached the small desk next to the wall that faced the alley.

"Dust and shadows," she murmured as they tucked themselves beneath the window.

"I'm sorry?"

"It's nothing," she replied.

He set the box on the table and pulled a handkerchief from his pocket, mopping at his brow while she watched with tender eyes. Replacing the handkerchief, he slowly reached forward and unlocked the clasp on the box, opening the top and turning it toward the thin stream of light coming from the upper window. She drew in a long breath and let it out slowly.

"It's stunning," she whispered. She leaned forward, studying the detail, the intricacies, too in awe to touch it but rather wanting to just take it all in.

"It is my masterpiece," he said quietly. She nodded, standing back up.

"It is the finest you've created." She paused. "Why did you do it?" she asked quietly.

He held her gaze for a brief moment.

"I've felt it all unraveling for quite some time," he finally answered, eyes misting over. Another loud bang on the streets followed by angry shouts cut him short. He shook his head. "There isn't time to explain." He looked into her eyes with an imploring stare. "They cannot find it now. If they do, they will destroy it and they *will* kill me."

"I . . . I don't understand," she said. "Why? This looks so . . . ordinary."

"You haven't seen it all."

"The surprise?"

He nodded. At the sound of glass breaking, he leaned forward and, hands trembling, removed the treasure with the hands of a master. Beneath it was a bed of blood-red velvet. He tugged on a small string sticking out from beneath the fabric and pulled out the top to reveal a hidden compartment underneath. Two more objects lay nestled in the hollow space below. She leaned forward and gasped, her hand covering her mouth. Looking up, her eyes met his.

"Bloody Sunday," he muttered.

"I'm sorry?" She leaned forward.

His gaze glassed over as his mind wandered to that horrible morning when peaceful protestors were massacred on Nevsky Prospekt, St. Petersburg's main street.

"I was there." His words were a mist. He closed his eyes, trying in vain to chase away the images of the bodies and the sounds of the wailing. That was the moment when his allegiance had fissured. And this—he looked back down into the box that contained his secret—this had been his act of defiance.

"You have to take it," he said. His voice was stronger now, more sure and determined. He resettled the top shelf, covering the rebellion, then gently laid the treasure onto the velvet. Closing the lid, he clicked it shut, the sound echoing off the walls around them. "You must take it with you and go. And my dear girl . . ." He paused, searching her face. "You cannot tell a soul what you have until the time is right."

She was quiet for a long moment. "I will do this for you," she finally said.

The two held one another's gaze. Outside, angry shouts grew louder. They were getting closer.

"The Tsar has abdicated," she said quietly.

He nodded, then reached down and picked up the box that housed his masterpiece. He let the weight of it rest in his hands for the briefest of moments, like a father cradling his child for the last time.

"It's only a matter of time before it all disappears," he continued. "All of the pieces, all of the beauty."

He reached over and put the box in her hands. "But not this one." He looked at her tenderly. "You must guard it well. It could be the only one left."

The sound of shouting grew closer. She pulled the box to her chest and looked back at him, her eyes widening.

"What do I do with it?" she asked.

"Hide it until it's safe to give it back to the people." He shifted his stare back to the box. "It will be my legacy, but they aren't ready for that now. I trust that you will know when the time is right, and by that time I will be only a memory."

She shook her head, blinking back tears. "What will you do?" she asked, eyes shining. She reached out and grabbed his hand.

"Don't worry about me," he replied. "I'll be okay." He pulled her hand to his chest and gave it a quick squeeze before turning her toward the back door.

"You must leave now. Find a place to hide it until you can get out of the country." He looked around at the shop where he'd spent the last years bent over his own worktable, encouraging his employees and making his fortune.

"Not much longer now," he said quietly.

"Thank you for trusting me," she said, blinking back tears.

He nodded, leaning forward and placing a soft kiss on her cheek.

"Until we meet again, my dear girl," he said. "And Alma."

She looked up and met his steady gaze.

"Don't ever forget the things I told you."

He turned and walked quickly through the room, disappearing behind the curtain.

Alma heard him going back up the stairs to the flat he shared with his wife. His entire family was in danger now, angry rioters coming after anyone with a connection to the royal family.

She turned to the back door and flung it open, catching her breath as the icy wind smacked her in the face. Tucking the box beneath her coat and pulling it tight around her, she pushed out into the back alley. The metal burned against her chest, the weight of the secret heavy. She would do what he asked. She would escape, and she would hide his masterpiece.

She turned the corner and ducked her head, pressing into the wind and walking quickly past the front of the shop on 24 Bolshaya Morskaya. The Gothic Revival façade of the building that had once been a source of pride now screamed of excess and begged to be targeted by the Bolsheviks. Out of the corner of her eye, she could see the grey Finnish granite of the outside of the building, and she pushed past the display windows that had once gleamed invitingly but which now sat dark and despondent.

The noise of the crowd swelled in the distance, and she looked down at the ground, walking as quickly as she could without breaking into a panicked run. She didn't look up when she passed the door she'd walked by a thousand times before, and she didn't see the wisps of snow falling over the sign hanging just above her head. The sign that read K. Fabergé.

Dear Reader,

When we hear of Americans in Paris, we usually think of artists and writers on the city's artsy Left Bank. The genesis for this story came from reading about Sylvia Beach, whose famous English-language bookstore, Shakespeare and Company, served as a center for the American expatriate community in the 1920s. What intrigued me was how Miss Beach chose to remain in Paris as the Nazis bore down and how she kept her bookstore open until December 1941! That kind of plucky courage was just what I wanted in my novel's heroine.

Paul's story is inspired by the American Colony in Paris, the quietly respectable Right Bank business owners and professionals. About 2,000 to 5,000 Americans chose to remain in Paris during the occupation for a variety of reasons—business or artistic concerns, family ties, or simply a sense that Paris was their true home. US institutions continued to support the expatriates—the American Church, the American Hospital, the American Chamber of Commerce, and others. Some expatriates collaborated with the German occupiers—but many aided the resistance, including the staff at the American Hospital.

You may have noticed things "lacking" in this story. I don't mention Jewish people being forced to wear yellow stars because that law didn't go into effect in occupied France until June 7, 1942. Likewise, although I mention *the first two rafles (roundups) of Jews on May 14 and August 20–23, 1941, I don't refer to deportations or concentration camps. Before July 1942, Jews were held in camps in France. Not until after the grand rafle of over 13,000 Jews on July 16, 1942, did the Germans begin deporting them to Auschwitz.*

Also, where is the big, organized resistance we've all heard about? In June 1940, the French people were shocked and demoralized by the fall of France. Since the German soldiers generally behaved well in the early months of the occupation, resistance was confined to ignoring the Germans, pretending not to understand them, and giving them incorrect directions. It took time for the concept of resistance to take hold, for people to find others of like mind, and to figure out what to do and how to do it without getting killed. Of course, as the résistants grew bolder, the Germans grew less well behaved.

You may wonder why I never used the term Maquis to refer to résistants. That term was first used in early 1943. On February 16, 1943, France established the Service du Travail Obligatoire to conscript men to work in Germany, and many fled into the countryside and formed bands of Maquis fighters. By June 1944, the competing resistance groups had banded together to lend great aid to the Allied invasion of France on D-day.

All characters in the novel are fictional, but I did introduce or mention historical figures, including Serge Lifar, the famous ballet master and choreographer, Edmund Pendleton, organist and director of the American Church in Paris, Americans William Bullitt, Roscoe Hillenkoetter, Robert Murphy, and Varian Fry, German Ambassador Otto Abetz, German military commander Lt. Gen. Otto von Stülpnagel, ballerinas Yvette Chauviré, Solange

Schwarz, and Lycette Darsonval, movie stars Arletty and Danielle Darrieux, and actor Sacha Guitry.

All writers mentioned in this story are real except Evelyn Lang, Saint-Yves, and Dominique Kahn.

The story of France in World War II is complex and nuanced, with a spectrum of behavior from active resistance to passive resistance to quiet accommodation to active collaboration, with a variety of motivations based on survival, business and cultural interests, and ideology. I hope the characters in this novel shed some light—and compassion—on the difficult choices made by those living in indescribable conditions.

If you're on Pinterest, please visit my board for Until Leaves Fall in Paris *(www.pinterest.com/sarahsundin) to see pictures of Paris in World War II, fashions, and other inspiration for the story.*

Acknowledgments

This is my COVID book, written in the uncertainty and isolation we all experienced in 2020. Somehow it fit this story, with the "social distancing" Parisians practiced with each other during the occupation, not knowing whom to trust.

But no writer truly works in isolation, even if we work in solitude. My family puts up with all sorts of writerly quirkiness, and my "normal" friends in the nonwriting world hear odd monologues about characters and research. I love you and am thankful you love me back.

I'm also thankful for my writer friends who understand those quirks. I'm especially thankful to my critique partners, Marcy Weydemuller, Sherry Kyle, Lisa Bogart, and Judy Gann.

Although I decided to make Lucie a ballerina late in story development, long after her name chose her, her name is fitting. I was blessed to study ballet for ten years at Lucille McClure's School of Ballet in Whittier, California. I was delighted to learn the Paris Opéra Ballet School taught the Cecchetti method, which Miss McClure used. I never had the single-minded devotion—or the narrow hips—necessary to succeed in ballet, but I deeply appreciate Miss McClure's determination to give us each a solid foundation as if we were all destined for a ballet career. Much of the ballet advice spoken by Lucie will be recognized word for word by Miss McClure's students.

As always, I'm indebted to my incredible agent, Rachel Kent of Books and Such, and the phenomenal team at Revell—Vicki Crumpton, Kristin Kornoelje, Michele Misiak, Karen Steele, and countless others who make my little stories look good!

Thank you also to my wonderful readers! Your encouragement and support are an indescribable blessing. Please visit me at www.sarahsundin.com to leave a message, sign up for my email newsletter, and read about the history behind the story. I hope to hear from you.

Discussion Questions

1. The year of 1941 was critical in occupied France as those who opposed the Nazis began to work together—and as the Nazis cracked down on the résistants. What events or attitudes in the story did you already know about and which were new for you?

2. Knowing what we now know about the Nazi occupation of France, it's hard to understand why anyone would have stayed, especially Americans who could easily sail home. However, thousands of Americans did choose to stay, with about two thousand remaining in December 1941. What do you think of Paul's and Lucie's decisions to stay? Would you have?

3. Lucie is a true Left Bank artistic sort, Paul is a classic Right Bank businessman, and neither appreciates the other type at first. Which are you more like? Which do you gravitate toward in your friendships? Do you have a difficult time understanding those with different gifts?

4. Over the course of the story, both Paul and Lucie come to appreciate different gifts. How is this critical for Paul's relationship with Josie? How is it critical in

helping Lucie keep her bookstore open? What did you think of their conversation along the Seine in chapter 23 about different shades of green, about art and structure?

5. At the beginning of the story, Paul's relationship with Jacques Moreau and the workers at Aubrey Automobiles is tense and distrusting. How does that change during the story? And why? Are there people in your life you once disliked and grew to appreciate?

6. Lucie gives up her dream of dancing in the ballet to help her friends. What did you think of her decision? Have you ever lost or sacrificed a dream?

7. Paul is seen as a collaborator and loses friendships, respect, and more. How do you think it felt to be misunderstood and rejected? Would you have tolerated it as long as he did?

8. Both Lucie and Paul choose to aid the resistance. What dangers do they face because of this? What factors came into play as the French decided whether or not to resist? Would you have done so?

9. In the story I tried to show the range of actions during the occupation, from resistance to quiet accommodation to collaboration. Did the characters and events shed any light on those decisions? Which character do you think you would have been most like?

10. Lucie battles insecurities that arise at the worst moments—as insecurities always do. How do they hold her back? Have you ever battled insecurities? If so, what helped you overcome them?

11. Paul, as an active and successful man, likes to feel in control. The events of the story show him how little control he has. How does this change him? How does

the concept of stewardship help him accept it? Have you ever struggled with a desire to control?

12. Lucie is naturally impulsive, and Paul is naturally disciplined. How do they learn from each other? What did you think when Lucie realized, "Discipline was only as good as the task it was applied to, and impulse was only as bad as the action it caused"? How do you think that realization will continue to change her?

13. Lucie has always been able to trust her intuition and her ability to read people. How do you see her gift in play? How is it challenged in the story? What did you think when the marquise tells her, "Your eyes say one thing, and your heart says another. Ah, Miss Lucille, you're listening to the wrong voices. What does the Lord say?" Which voices do you tend to trust?

14. Leaves are a recurring motif in the story. What did you notice or enjoy?

Sarah Sundin is the bestselling author of *When Twilight Breaks*, as well as the Sunrise at Normandy, Waves of Freedom, Wings of the Nightingale, and Wings of Glory series. Her novel *The Land Beneath Us* was a finalist for the 2020 Christy Award, *The Sky Above Us* received the 2020 Carol Award, *The Sea Before Us* received the 2019 Reader's Choice Award from Faith, Hope, and Love, and *When Tides Turn* and *Through Waters Deep* were named to Booklist's "101 Best Romance Novels of the Last 10 Years."

During WW II, one of her grandfathers served as a pharmacist's mate (medic) in the US Navy, and her great-uncle flew with the US Eighth Air Force. Her other grandfather, a professor of German, helped train American soldiers in the German language through the US Army Specialized Training Program.

Sarah and her husband live in northern California and have three adult children. Their rescue Jindo dog makes sure she gets plenty of walks and fresh air. Sarah teaches Sunday school and women's Bible studies, and she enjoys speaking for church, community, and writers' groups. She also serves as co-director of the West Coast Christian Writers Conference. Visit www.sarahsundin.com for more information.

"Sundin's novels set the gold standard for historical war romance, and *When Twilight Breaks* is arguably her most brilliant and important work to date."

—*Booklist*, STARRED Review ★

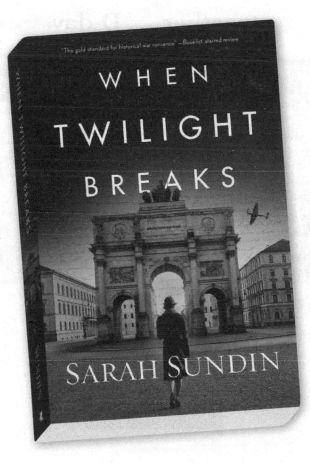

Two Americans meet in 1938 in the heart of Nazi Germany. Their efforts to expose oppression attract unwanted attention, pulling them deeper into danger as the world marches toward war.

One fateful night drove three brothers apart.
One fateful day thrusts them together . . . D-day.

War is coming.
Can love carry them through
the rough waters that lie ahead?

"Sarah Sundin seamlessly weaves together emotion, action, and sweet romance."

—*USA Today's Happy Ever After* blog

"A gripping tale of war, intrigue, and love."

—*RT Book Reviews* review of
A Memory Between Us

LET'S
TALK
ABOUT
BOOKS

- Share or mention the book on your social media platforms. Use the hashtag **#UntilLeavesFallinParis**.

- Write a book review on your blog or on a retailer site.

- Pick up a copy for friends, family, or anyone who you think would enjoy and be challenged by its message!

- Share this message on Twitter, Facebook, or Instagram: **I loved #UntilLeavesFallinParis by @SarahSundin @RevellBooks**

- Recommend this book for your church, workplace, book club, or small group.

- Follow Revell on social media and tell us what you like.

RevellBooks

RevellBooks

RevellBooks

RevellBooks